Water Striders

Other fiction by John Moehl

Phobos & Deimos: two moons, two worlds

Closer to God

Ann—a story of intolerance

The Agate Hunter

Waiting—almost there

Son of Paul

Water Striders

John Moehl

RESOURCE *Publications* · Eugene, Oregon

WATER STRIDERS

Resource Publications
An Imprint of Wipf and Stock Publishers
199 W. 8th Ave., Suite 3
Eugene, OR 97401

www.wipfandstock.com

PAPERBACK ISBN: 978-1-6667-3025-8
HARDCOVER ISBN: 978-1-6667-2150-8
EBOOK ISBN: 978-1-6667-2151-5

02/23/22

Contents

The Water Strider

WATER STRIDERS SEEM TO skip effortlessly across watery surfaces. Like hydrofoils, capable of surprisingly high speeds, "*. . . speed is essential for the strider's most important task: snatching prey off the water's surface . . . A water strider rapidly grabs a small insect with its front legs, then uses its mouthparts to pierce the prey's body and suck out its juices.*"

(Matthew L. Miller, April 10, 2017, https://blog.nature.org/ science/2017/04/10/7-cool-facts-water-striders-skippers-pond-skaters-weird-nature/).

Acknowledgments

T HIS WORK IS POSSIBLE only with the support of my wife of four-and-a-half decades. Side by side, we have wandered many avenues—learning much and learning how much we did not know. We have grown to expect the unexpected, yet never cease to be surprised by the hands we are dealt—appreciating how lucky we have been to have shared bits and pieces of these lives with so many. We have even taken time to watch the water striders.

Author's Note

THIS STORY IS A complete work of fiction. All the characters and events are imaginary. I am unaware of any existing or past companies with the names attributed to various firms and organizations in the text. Any connection to functioning or former firms, businesses, or groups is purely coincidental—all actions and events attributed to groups and enterprises in the following story are fictitious. Equally, all actions or events attributed to any public or private agencies come solely from the imagination and are not based on any facts. While these characters and actions may appear at real places—past and present—these are in no way intended to recount true happenings at these spots.

Water Ballet

Effortlessly gliding across mirrored surfaces,
dark shadows, both graceful and menacing;
elegant creatures using guile to fulfill their cravings,
not unlike those controlling their watery homes.

Good or bad, right or wrong—of no concern.
Like their overlords, creatures reacting automatically,
taking what they see as theirs,
indifferent to efforts to curb their appetites.

The end game, always the same,
power and self-satisfaction.
The field, always the same,
the troubled plains of our time.

Yet, the overlords, unlike the riverine ballerinas,
are deemed superior—more in control, more caring.
Alas, each, passing generation upon generation,
has shown a similar degree of nonchalance.

Ultimately, the river dancers and the river bosses
follow the same embedded actions.
Ultimately, they both do as they will—
they both feel they are the masters of their domains.

Prologue

T HERE HAVE ALWAYS BEEN, and always will be newcomers. Sometimes they come from nearby. Other times they come from far away. There are immigrants with different languages and cultures. There are people from the next county over who have different recipes for apple pie and different ways of planting a vegetable garden. Differences are a part of life.

Charlie Stancik and his family were both newcomers to this country and newcomers to the West where, along with a multitude of others, they played a part in reshaping both society and nature—possibly for the better.

Charlie was different. He shied away from the modest while comfortable life his parents had made for themselves and, they hoped, for their children.

Charlie was a boy who yearned to see more and to do more—even to have more. There was always a new experience waiting just around the next corner. He felt he was up to the challenge of meeting and mastering any new dilemma or opportunity. His perseverance and his ingenuity allowed him to successfully maneuver through a wide array of circumstances and activities. This path, successful though it may (just maybe) have been, was fraught with life-altering difficulties. If Charlie's life reflected the American dream, it was a mutation of that dream sought by so many.

Ultimately, Charlie's life, like the lives of those he encountered along the way, seemed to unerringly go full circle. He ended up not far from where he had begun his odyssey. As he looked back, he felt more than saw the exceptional wisdom of Helen Keller when she had said, "The best and most beautiful things in the world cannot be seen or even touched—they must be felt with the heart."

Book I
The Road to Antioch

"If we wonder often, the gift of knowledge will come."

—ARAPAHO PROVERB

Receding Waters

I N THE AIR, THERE was nearly complete silence, only broken by the screed of a mournful killdeer.

The tules along the marsh's edge rustled softly as the canoe slid past, the vessel made of these venerable plants similar to the papyrus *tankwas* canoes used on Lake Tana over 5,000 miles away. The canoe's occupants sought to harvest a patch of wocus—a staple of the *Maklaks*—the people whose name meant *"the people."* The canoe swayed gently as its residents bent over the rich green waters and harvested the lily's seeds that would be dried and pounded into flour.

In addition to the lily flour, the *Maklaks,* living in a watery land of plenty, feasted on abundant waterfowl (and their eggs), fishes, and deer—using the fields of tule reeds to construct their homes, weave their baskets, and make their footwear.

Plentiful but fragile.

The *Maklaks* had seen great flocks of ducks and geese fly low over the hills surrounding the basin, pushed down to arrow range by threatening snowstorms. They had seen great deer herds stretch from Medicine Lake to Badger Peak. They had seen great expanses of wocus, highlighted with yellow lily flowers, stretching as far as one could see across the marsh.

Those were the good times.

Then there were times when the baskets were empty of wocus, larders empty of meat, babies crying, people dying.

They understood the fluctuations of life like they understood the fluctuations of the waters. The ancients had written on the cliffs of what the outsiders now called Sheepy Ridge. When the waters were high, the ancestors carved petroglyphs with antler and bone more than fifty feet up the escarpment's face. When the waters were low, the carvings were made at a height barely above a man's head.

The waters rose and fell.

Life rose and fell.

Then the waters fell, not to rise again. In 1902, as part of the National Reclamation Act, the waters were dammed, drained, and diverted. By 1917 the dewatering was complete and the wetlands of the *Maklaks* had been converted into farmlands for the outsiders.

Even before the work was completed, in 1909 a group of sixty-six Bohemians from the Czech Colonization Club moved west to farm the reclaimed lands—lands in the shadow of the *Maklaks'* ancestors.

Dust, sagebrush, and herds of jackrabbits had replaced the marsh waters—the ducks and fishes gone or departing. It was a tough life for the newcomers (not to mention for the *Maklaks,* who were driven to drylands their forebears had never known).

The outlanders did not harvest wocus, cut tules, nor hunt for eggs. They built sawmills and farms. They raised cows, made cheese, planted potatoes. They survived.

By 1940, the erstwhile intruders now had roots—delicate and shallow, but roots, nonetheless. They had built a village. They had built a community. No one remembered the *Maklaks.* No one remembered the marsh. No one understood the petroglyphs.

As the war ended, the bygone neophyte Bohemians were now the landowners, the mill operators, the shop keepers, the restauranteurs. A new wave of post-war greenhorns arrived in the basin to a cool (at best) reception from those former members of the Czech Colonization Club.

ᛡ ᛡ ᛡ ᛦ ᛡ ᛡ ᛡ

The community seemed ensconced in its own sphere, trying to overcome the past in favor of a (unrealistically) bright and, in the view of some, (unnecessarily) chauvinistic future.

It was not just the shift of ecosystems that provided challenges.

Well before the arrival of the Bohemians, the area had been scared by the Modoc War that left a tart residue up to the present day. Moreover, as the ecology changed, so did the economy. Large cattle ranches had been the heart of the land for decades before the club members arrived but were later displaced by grain and potato farms.

Farming took over. With the Czech settlement, the installation of essential electric and water utilities, and the subsequent arrival of the Great Northern railroad, the community seemed launched on an arch of success.

Realizing dawn to dusk laboring needed to be offset with suitable leisure activities, a year after the arrival of the Bohemians, a community recreation hall was built. This was the venue for roller-skating, Saturday-night dances, boxing matches, and a surprising array of topnotch musicians (including, among others, Lawrence Welk, the Dorsey Brothers, and Phil Harris).

But this was not enough to keep all those from the first-generation, born in the community, *in* the community. Like the waters that had slowly, almost imperceptibly, drifted away, some of the youth, seemingly oppressed by a nouveau-Bohemia persona that was gaining ground in the settlement, drifted away.

Among those feeling the drag of the receding waters was Charlie Stancik.

Charlie adamantly maintained, as did several of his mates, that he was not Bohemian. Hell, his father had been born in Omaha. He had been born right here at their home, just three blocks from the cheese factory. He was not Czech—he was American. He didn't even speak Czech Cestina, albeit he understood a bit when Grandmother and Grandfather spoke slowly (which was not often).

Still, resolutely declaring you were not something did not necessarily mean you were not—at least in the eyes of others. First off, in the family, his grandparents were staunchly proud of their foreign heritage—maintaining just as steadfastly that they had only compulsorily come to this place because they had had to abandon their homeland—putting their future in God's hands, remaining Bohemians to their soul.

His parents, both native Cornhuskers, considered themselves Czech-Americans. They were proud of their ancestors, proud of their history, proud to be multicultural, proud to be the founders of a new enclave with old-world roots. They celebrated September 28th as "one of their national days." They hungrily consumed hotdogs just as voraciously as *vepro-knedlo-zelo* (a plate of roast pork, dumplings, and cabbage considered by some as the Czech national food). They were fully bimodal.

Then, whenever the family left their small and comfortable lake-bed community, going to the closest bigger town for special supplies or, occasionally, special events, the citified townsfolk clearly, openly, pointed to the out-of-towners as "THE Bohemians."

Charlie wanted to yell, "I'm American!"

But no one listened.

To people in his circle, it was a non-issue. To people outside, it was the issue—reason for shunning and isolation.

ʌ ʌ ʌ ʍ ʌ ʌ ʌ

Charlie was an American and Charlie was ambitious (as an American should be, he understood).

He did not yet have big ideas (he knew to his own misery that he had not experienced enough to be able to harvest momentous views—but he needed to do so).

Charlie did have big hopes. And Charlie was driven.

Poignantly, Charlie felt—more than felt—Charlie realized this energy (without knowing the full impact, his grandfather called it his "moxie") was corralled on the lakebed.

It was stifling.

The community's elders, his grandparents among them, seemed oblivious to what, to Charlie, were clearly the realities of the day—trade in the past for the future. To the contrary, the patriarchs ceaselessly referred to (kowtowed to, Charlie thought) their champion, their icon, Elisabeth, Princess Palatine of Bohemia (later abbess Elisabeth of the Lutheran convent at Herford, North Rhine-Westphalia). This was not just a link to the archaic past, this was, through the prism through which Charlie gazed, a 300-year-old time-enfeebled ligature to bygone nonsense.

His grandparents, and their peers, held Elisabeth up as a sort of patron saint (even if Protestant) for their new home—a guardian with ties to the ancient homeland. Elisabeth had overcome all manner of adversities, always pushing through, always focusing on the goal—faithful to her traditions, devoted to her faith. The founders urged their families and neighbors to follow the example of Elisabeth, to remember the *vlast* (the old country), to remember the objective, and to make this new community their new homeland.

To Charlie (as he liked to say), this was "bass-akwards." It was not about Bohemian culture nor about creating a new homeland—it was about moving up the ladder. This was not a Czech ladder; this was an American ladder. It was not old-world customs that would make the move possible, it was new world money.

Keeping one's focus on the goal meant making money—full stop.

Charlie was seemingly at odds with the core canons of his birthplace.

ᛰ ᛰᛰᚢ ᛰᛰ ᛰ

Charlie saw the only option as cutting ties with his home and family— releasing the bonds that impeded his upward movement. This, in his mind, was not a whack with an axe—severing the cords forever. This was a necessary but short-termed surgical operation with a tiny scalpel that would free his body from the excess connective tissue that pulled him down—that held him back.

He loved his family. He loved his home. He loved this land where he had been born. He would come back. But to survive—as his grandparents had survived when they first came to the lake bottom—he needed to leave. He was smothered by the old. He needed the new.

Therefore, the weekend after he graduated from high school, in the dark of night, having told no one, he jumped an east-bound Great Northern freight. After two weeks sleeping in parks, scrounging in garbage cans, and hiding from railroad police, he found himself in Chicago.

This was not sightseeing, not a study tour. This was not a rite of passage, not a pilgrimage to polish his soul or fine-tune his mind. From Charlie's vantage point, this was pragmatism. This was doing what needed to be done to achieve the aims he needed to achieve. In many ways, Charlie felt, this was maintaining through another generation the passions and aspirations for a better, more prosperous life that had first brought his family to the lakebed—a place he had now felt forced to leave.

ᛰ ᛰᛰᚢ ᛰᛰ ᛰ

Charlie had tried to prepare for his quest as well as he could from the confines of the lakebed. He had studied as much as he could in the school library—going so far as to look at which specific locale might best lead him to his aims—to his new life.

He had told himself that he would have to adapt to new places, adopt new ways, to be able to survive as his family had survived when they had come west to set up home on the lakebed. This was, of course, true. It was also much easier said than done.

Charlie had had no, absolutely no, concept of what a metropolis of over three million looked like—let alone what it was to try and live there.

And try as he might, Charlie found himself jobless and homeless—on the street. In Chicago, Charlie was indeed far from the lakebed.

Charlie was also alone, in a strange and unfamiliar place.

Charlie had now reached, it appeared, where he was going.

Still, Charlie repeatedly asked himself, "Where am I?"

His answer, at least in the immediate, was an overly romantic, "I am where I am, I am a vagabond." He rejected his mother's terms of "tramp" or "drifter." He knew (from Civics class) the police would consider him a "vagrant." A new word creeping into the vernacular was "homeless." But he wasn't homeless. His had a home on a lakebed. He had just decided to leave. No, he wasn't a bum. He was a wayfarer—a journeyer. But gadabout or derelict, he had to persevere.

He had initially targeted the Pilsen neighborhood as the best starting point—having read in the library that this neighborhood had been settled by many Czechs. However, his first visit quickly highlighted the fact that, at least now, the majority of folks in the area now seemed to be Latinx. While he felt he had no biases for, since he had no knowledge of, people of Latin American origin, he thought it prudent to look to a community that was culturally closer to home. He needed to cut the cord, but not totally.

He ultimately found himself in the Portage Park neighborhood. As he would later learn, this was an area that had more in common with home than was immediately obvious. In addition to being a center for Eastern European immigrants (over a third of the young people having parents who were born outside the United States), historically, this had been a spot of importance to native peoples—another wetland that had been dewatered for the development of outsider enterprises.

While there were some rather strange commonalities, at first glance Portage Park could not be more different from his birthplace. First, there were a lot of people. Then, these people lived close together in old houses—more than half, as he was told, having been built before 1940. It may have been what passed for a community here in the big city, but it was not the same community spirit to which he had grown accustomed while growing up.

There was no coo of the mourning dove nor whistle of the mountain quail. There was only the cacophony of the city and the wail of the crowd.

And, it was ever-boisterous, ever-moving.

These people moved in waves, ebbing and flowing to jobs outside the neighborhood while Charlie sat on a street corner with no idea what to do next.

His street corner was the corner of North Central and West Berteau Avenues, across from Portage Park—a place where he could find a secluded patch to sleep unless rousted by police. But sleeping in parks and scrounging for crumbs in garbage cans can only last so long.

It so happened; his corner was also next to Saint Mary Romanian Orthodox Church. It also so happened that the church operated, across the street from its chapel, a shelter for the homeless—this run by a monastic order of Orthodox nuns who divided their time between contemplation and prayer and caring for those in need.

One afternoon, while dozing on his corner, Charlie was approached by Father Marius from St. Mary's. The priest indicated the young man might be more comfortable in their hostel (as he called it) just up the street.

Father Marius then led a pliant Charlie to a nondescript building with big, double-wooden doors. Passing through the portals and moving down a dark and empty corridor, after going through another set of less-hefty doors, Charlie found himself in a large area more than twice the size of his high school's gym. About two-thirds of the area was occupied by row after row of white metal single beds, looking like something from war surplus—each with a coarse and equally military-looking grey blanket. The remaining third of the space was occupied by a potpourri of chairs, tables, and sofas—obviously, all having seen better days—where apparently residents could eat and socialize. Above all, in massive letters, written on the wall was the message to the lodgers: "HOW LONG SINCE YOU WROTE YOUR MOTHER?"

Charlie was sure he had not written his mother since he left home. Still, this fact had no relevance to his current predicament. Here, among the crew of St. Mary's, he felt no less lost than when on his street corner.

He wondered why he had followed this stranger and why he was now in this empty barn-like enclosure? He certainly was not looking for God. He was looking for the road to his future. This had little if anything to do with writing his mother.

Father Marius seemed to sense his ward's frustration. Then, in response to the good father's hailing, they were joined by a stout lady somewhat older than Charlie's mother. Father Marius introduced the woman as Sister Elena, the leader of this female monastic group who kindly looked after the spiritual and corporeal wellbeing of those partaking of the hospitality of the hostel.

Father Marius left Charlie in, as he put it, "Sister Elena's good hands." The Sister was in fact kind enough in a standoffish sort of way—reminding Charlie of the librarian at high school. A woman who apparently would help, but who answered a higher calling.

Sister Elena assigned Charlie a bed and told him he should be in the hall (as she called it) by five o'clock for a hot meal. Most of their charges, she added, were out and about during the day and only under the church's roof at night.

Here began a new chapter in Charlie's quest. He became an arrant adherent to the rhythms of St. Mary's hostel. This was not because this seemed the best thing to do, nor because he saw this as a wise move. Quite simply, it was because the big city had scared him, and he now found the hostel and its surroundings to be the only refuge where he could try and recalculate his way forward.

The city loomed over him. He could easily feel crushed. He felt he could easily be crushed.

He had to have a coping strategy.

His new schedule consisted of rising at six-thirty in the morning, after a night of tossing and turning as the night noises of the lodgers washed over him. Then, after a bowl of oatmeal and a cup of tea, he would exit the hall with the herd—most going to well-established destinations, he going to sit in Portage Park.

Some of his sitting was focused on observing the in's and out's of his new environment. But most was spent in introspection.

Going to the big city, as far as his family tales told, was nothing new for his forebears. His great-grandparents, as his mother had told the story, were from Sedlcany, a smallish village not too different from his birthplace (about fifty miles due south of Prague by road, called Seltschan by the Germans). The community, in Príbram District in Central Bohemia, was located on the Mastník River—an old settlement apparently dating back to 1057.

His great-grandparents, according to the family reports, were stay-at-home folks—totally involved in farming the land and raising a family.

By most accounts, they had never set foot in, never even considered setting foot in Prague.

But, as has been known to happen, their daughter, Charlie's grandmother, was cut from different cloth. She loved going to the city. She loved going to theater. She loved Shakespeare. Any chance she got, she would dash off to the Estates Theater, the *Stavovské divadlo*, to see a play—her favorite, Hamlet. In fact, she was renown in her family for quoting Shakespeare—sometimes at appropriate moments and sometimes not. According to Charlie's mother, grandmother's most cherished quotation was from Hamlet, "To thine own self be true." This was advice that Grandmother tried to follow herself and guidance she tried hard to impart on her family.

It was at the Estates Theater that Grandmother met Grandfather—another lover of the Bard. Charlie's mother had often said they all had Shakespeare to thank for being a family.

But Shakespeare aside, the fact of the matter was that his grandmother—by all accounts a real country bumpkin—had had the initiative and courage to go to the big city and ultimately to chart a path for herself that led to her family now living on a lake bottom in the Pacific Northwest.

Charlie had to find the gumption to follow in his grandmother's steps. Of course, his parents too had blazed new trails. Still, they had not done this alone. Grandmother had been alone. If she could do it, so could he.

As his thoughts migrated freely through his family tree, he realized that their pioneering spirits had been due to some sort of inner strength. It was not, as it had been for so many others, a question of religious zeal.

His family, seemingly for generations, had been practicing Catholics. Yet for them, the practicing part was generally at Easter and Christmas. They were all hardworking believers who believed that they had to first deal with the demands of today before worrying about the salvation of the soul.

To be clear, it was not to maintain a family tradition that Charlie found himself in a hostel at a Romanian church. This was simply the only door open at this time. He knew, he was confident, other doors would soon open.

/\ /\ /\ \/ /\ /\ /\

Charlie was unemployed and homeless, but he was not totally broke. Since his sixth birthday, his grandparents had modestly contributed to a bank account his parents had opened to celebrate the situation. Then, since he was twelve, he had done odd jobs, mowed lawns, raked leaves, washed windows, and otherwise earned a few dollars on weekends and during summer vacation, and joined these savings with his anniversary fund. When he had jumped that freight, he had $977 in his sock (his parents only discovering much later that their son's college account, as they thought of it, had a balance of one dollar).

This was not, however, money to live on. This was money to invest in his future. Until his way forward became clearer, the stash stayed in his sock.

Charlie had also jumped the train with a small, soiled khaki cardboard suitcase that had been his grandmother's (this added to the challenges of even getting onboard). It was small—what his mother would call "an overnight bag" (he referred to it as his "box"). But it was sturdy—the kind with reinforced metal corners, a tightly sealing metal frame that was held shut by a strong locking clasp, opened by an impressively large key.

His box held a cheap suit his parents had bought at Penney's one time when they'd gone into town—respectable clothes so their son could be somewhat presentable for those Easter and Christmas masses. Additionally, his grandmother's suitcase contained a light sweater knit by the lady herself, an extra pair of jeans, three sets of underwear, and three shirts (one dress to go with the suit complete with tie, one flannel, and one chambray). There was also a diary where he had been tracking his days—feeling he needed to get some benchmarks down on paper because the days themselves seemed to completely resemble one another. Finally, he'd put in a baseball cap, some toiletries in a case that had once held his grandfather's cigars, a flashlight, and a black-and-white photo of himself with his family when he had been confirmed.

In addition to his box, he had a calfskin wallet with his Social Security and baptismal cards along with his driver's license. This joined, in his jean's pockets, a big red handkerchief (three more in the box), a Swiss army knife, a key chain (with his box key), a military-style mini can opener, and a bright blue plastic clam-shell-like squeeze coin purse with his ration of daily pocket money (which he tried not to spend). Over all this, he wore a jean jacket, making him look like a nine-to-fiver ready to go to work at a construction site (much like, back home, one would go to the mill or the farm).

ᴀ ᴀ ᴀ ᴠ ᴀ ᴀ ᴀ

Each morning of Charlie's new routine, he would select his items for the day (often including his diary in the hopes this would somehow help him make those pending BIG life decisions), lock his box and push it under his bed (tactically placing a bit of toilet paper between it and the bedsprings to be able to see quickly if anyone had moved his sole possession) before going to the park after breakfast.

It soon became clear that sitting in the park would not resolve his dilemma. He knew he needed to be proactive—he just had no idea how to be proactive.

Deciding he needed to have that sense of community he had had at home, he began walking about, trying to engage local residents in discussions—to talk about anything, their homes, the burning issues of the day, or even the cost of hamburger.

While Charlie was not the sort of person who was just brimming over with loquaciousness, he was convivial enough. He had always been comfortable interacting with a wide variety of people. He was generally seen as outgoing and friendly.

Outgoing and friendly, however, were not adjectives that he would have chosen to describe the residents of his newly adopted neighborhood. While he approached many, few were willing to offer more than a very curt "uh-huh."

Nonetheless, he did begin to better see the topography. Indeed, many of the locals had their roots in Eastern Europe. Most had apparently been to high school, but not all that many had even started college. While nearly all worked outside Portage Park, it seemed they worked all over the city in a great mix of lower-level, white-collar jobs. No one seemed to know of (or care to think about) any job possibilities for a newcomer from who-knew-where.

While he was relatively unsuccessful in enjoining any useful conversations with people he snared on the sidewalk, he also cornered the barber, the grocer, the tobacco salesman, the florist, and on and on.

With a big smile and what he hoped was a kind word, he moved from shop to shop and store to store to try and gain a footing—to try and see if there were any help-wanted possibilities.

While the commercial folk were more open about the background of the neighborhood—more ready to chat with a complete stranger—they could really not shine a light on Charlie's way forward.

When he returned to St. Mary's, he forced himself to be positive and fell asleep planning his actions for the following day.

And, before bed, there was the evening meal. This was generally simple fare—mostly Romanian dishes, heavy on broth and light on food to sink your teeth into. Much like Bohemians, the recipes often employed garlic, cabbage, onions, and pork. There was *zama*, green bean soup, *sarmale*, cabbage rolls, and *tocanita*, pork stew with lots of paprika. In many ways, it reminded Charlie of home and he frequently went to his cot homesick.

While outside the hostel Charlie was outgoing and friendly, inside, among the scores of other down-and-outers, he was reserved and taciturn. He seemed to live in a somber cloud that few wished to enter. Basically, while living in a crowd, Charlie was alone.

His distressed status did not go unnoticed. While most just wrote him off as someone who would just disappear one day, freeing the bed for another lost soul, one of the hostel nuns took special interest—she seemed to sense a spirit in need, possibly even a kindred spirit.

Sister Mihaela was the first in her family to have been born in the US. In 1947, when King Michael had left the Romanian throne and the country, to be replaced by communism, her family had followed. They—the whole family, with grandparents, aunts, uncles, and cousins—had left the town of Urziceni where they had lived for generations in the shadow of the steeple of *Biserica Volna* (the Orthodox Church that watched over the townsfolk year after year). They fled to the coast, hired a boat at Constanta, and went down the Black Sea to Istanbul where they set up temporary residency—more like headquarters, given their numbers. Some relatives stayed in Turkey, others relocated to Italy, while Mihaela's parents had taken the bold step to move to the United States—ending up in Chicago near the end of the Truman Presidency.

Mihaela's parents had been devastated by what had happened in their beloved Urziceni, their beloved Romania. This desolation was not only about the drastic and dastardly changes to the country's political, economic, and social fabric, it was also about authoritarian atheists being at the helm. Their cherished church was under fire—possibly doomed. It was, therefore, logical to them that they encourage—strongly encourage—their one and only offspring to devote her life to this same church. They hoped, in some small way, they could contribute to the church's vitally even if people at home were trying to do the reverse.

Mihaela had followed her parents' wishes—even if somewhat be-grudgingly. It was not that she did not love the church—she did. It was not that she had plans to do something else—she didn't. It was mostly that she did not like her life being orchestrated by others. This might well be the best fit for her—but she truly wanted to make that decision for herself and not have it preordained by her parents.

Still in all, she had gone forward and was now a novice who would take her vows in the coming year. Pushed by her parents or pulled by her heart, for whatever reasons, she was now an established and happy (she thought) member of St. Mary's team.

She wanted to do good. She felt she was doing good. The needy who came to the hostel sought help. She helped (she hoped).

Sister Mihaela had great empathy. She understood distress, having grown up with distressed parents. She understood the caprices of life, having seen that her father had come here literally with nothing and had managed to find a good job and build a good life for his family. She understood duty. She was, after all, a devoted follower of the Orthodox God.

Sister Mihaela saw Charlie and she thought she could help. She was determined to do what she could to drive Charlie's clouds away.

It started simply enough. She would find him sitting alone in the common area after dinner. She'd sit down next to him and try to ignite some simple conversations:

"How was dinner?"

"How was your day?"

"What did you think of the snowfall?"

"What about that ball game?"

A stoic Charlie generally offered only monosyllabic responses, but Mihaela was intrepid. Finally, she managed to push a few of the clouds away—or, at least, make them less weighty.

Through perseverance, monosyllables evolved into short sentences and ultimately whole paragraphs. Charlie began looking forward to his pre-bedtime chats.

Charlie heard the nearly indistinguishable Eastern European gargle-ish vibrations in Mihaela's throat that so many of his back-home Bohemi-ans retained (as much as they tried to hide the slight oscillations of their larynx). He saw in her bright eyes an exceptional responsiveness—a rare compassion. He felt an aura of gentleness that was oddly juxtaposed with the real life and death sufferings of many of the lodgers.

Slowly, very slowly, his encounters with Sister Mihaela increased from just after dinner to include a period after breakfast when they would meet in the park. Once Mihaela had finished the morning scouring of the hostel (some of the least pleasant tasks falling to her as the novice), she'd go to the park to find Charlie sitting on a bench on the path to the pool, often concentrating on his diary or gawking at other park-goers.

They'd sit and prattle or walk about—frequently in random circles.

Charlie began laughingly calling Mihaela his Soviet Sister—but never when the two were back in the hostel. He began to feel comfortable with her as she with him. He even took her to one of his favorite places, Horner Park—about five miles east of the hostel along West Irving Road. The park was on the banks of the North Branch of the Chicago River. To Charlie this was more like a canal than a river—like one of the big drainage canals back home.

He would tell Mihaela how his home was on a lakebed, the whole area having been dewatered. To his surprise, Mihaela talked about how the government in Romania had wanted to do the same thing—trying to drain the Danube Delta to let farmers occupy the wetlands. Both young people had seen the impacts of receding waters.

The two would sit beside the slow-moving channel, watching the complex biosphere that lived there-in—the waters' creatures totally oblivious to the massive metropolis of Chicago that surrounded them— that fundamentally threatened them.

Their favorites were the water striders. These amazing bugs could glide across the glistening surfaces like skaters on ice. Whizzing about, seemingly weightless—with grace and agility—reminding Mihaela of stories her parents had told of ice skating on Irinescu Lake during hard winters back in Urziceni.

The water striders were her ice ballerinas.

But they were much more.

Charlie proudly—nearly arrogantly—was able to tell Mihaela all about these insects—after all, he'd learned about them in sophomore biology class.

"You'll be delighted to know," Charlie assured her, "that these nimble insects are also known as 'Jesus bugs,' obviously because they can walk on water. And you'll possibly be surprised to know that reportedly the males scare the female into making love. According to observers, after having sex, the female has to carry the male around on her back for up to several days—this tiring the poor girl out. From what they say, due to this tiresome aspect of lovemaking, the females are not very receptive to their male friends. So, what do the guys do? They scare the girls to jump into their arms—or more correctly, to jump under them and then copulate. The males will hit the water's surface with their feet, attracting fishes who ravenously feed on their species. The choice of being eaten or having sex seems a rather easy one, and ultimately the male gets his way—and his free ride."

Outwardly, Mihaela greeted the entomology lesson, as always, with aplomb. She smiled and assured Charlie that he was a wealth of knowledge—they'd both have to work harder to find him somewhere to apply all these, sometimes hidden, skills in gainful employment. However, privately, Mihaela was not sure what to make of the water strider story. She was secretly flustered, if not troubled. Was she the female Jesus bug and Charlie the male?

She had, as Charlie knew all too well, taken a vow of chastity. She was a nun, even though, strictly speaking, in the eyes of most Chicagoans, she did not wear a typical religious habit. Her head was always covered by her *apostolnik*—her black scarf that was an emblem of her piety—although she might usually be wearing some genre of a casual dark dress or dark skirt and sweater. She was, in fact, a novice and dressed accordingly.

Her clothing would become more symbolic and more canonical as she moved through her Orthodox life. Her clothing would become more strictly controlled after she took her vows and entered into the first phase of her sororal life, becoming a *Rassaphore* (a robe bearer). If she continued to progress, she would become a *Stavrophore* (a cross bearer). Then, if she were gifted enough, devout enough, she might reach the apex and become a *Schemanun*—the highest-level spirituality where she would wear a full habit including the *Analavos* (a woolen garment covering the back and chest in the form of a cross) and the *Kalymafki* (the headdress worn in addition to the veil).

She had a long road ahead of her—a difficult road.

Was Charlie trying to push her into a detour? Was he trying to proposition her? Was he trying to conjure up some imagined menacing predator that would push her under his loins?

Yet, Charlie made no overtures that indicated any impropriety. He was always correct. He was always polite. He was also frequently funny and sometimes insightful.

Charlie was, it turned out, her friend—perchance, her *cel mai bun prieten*, her best friend. She didn't know.

ᴧ ᴧᴧᴠᴧᴧ

Mihaela and Charlie had bonded.

She sensed this was not the right time (there might, she thought, never be a right time) to help Charlie with his self-evident lack of spirituality. She learned he had been raised in a close-knit family with rather loose childhood ties to the Catholic faith that seemed to have left few traces in his present life. She felt the religious ardor with which she approached her own life could possibly rekindle some flames in her friend's soul. But she knew at this moment he was too preoccupied with his seemingly distraught (his word, not hers) circumstances that he did not have the ability to be introspective about both the corporeal and spiritual portions of his being.

For his part, Charlie was as aware of the growing rapport that was developing with Mihaela—whether corporeal or spiritual was not, however, a distinction that entered his head. He just liked her. He thought she liked him.

But, of course, she was a nun—or a nun-to-be (Charlie was not too clear about this whole subject which he found rather mystifying). This obviously impacted on how their relationship would evolve, but this was a matter that was far from the forefront for someone who was homeless and jobless.

Charlie was simply very happy to have a friend; to have someone who knew the lay of the land and who cared, even if just a little (and he sensed it was more than a little), about how he was doing. The fact that she was, strictly speaking, a girlfriend, really didn't sink in. Charlie had not had any real serious girlfriends back home. There had been no one with whom, as had been typical for many in high school, he had gone steady. He had gone on dates. He had even gone all the way. Still, these had all been fleeting events—more a convergence of curiosity and opportunity than any meaningful union or liaison.

For Charlie, Mihaela was his screen and his filter (a heavy lift for the young novice—possibly one of which she was at least partially unaware). She, he felt, shielded him from the coarsest aspects of being alone in a throbbing megapolis while she filtered his inputs—his reality.

This is not to say that Charlie, with or without Mihaela's help, looked at his situation with rose-colored glasses. He did not. Indeed, if asked, he undoubtedly would have said he saw shadows everywhere—the future was dismal—he should have stayed on the lakebed. Mihaela could not erase the reality of his here-and-now. But she could help him cope. She could and did make suggestions and share information that seemed to make the impossible a little less impossible.

Part of Mihaela's handiwork on Charlie's behalf was to quietly enquire about any part-time jobs open in the neighborhood—somewhere where her new friend could try and gain some traction as he attempted to put down roots in the hard pavement of the city. After longer than she had hoped, her efforts were rewarded.

One night after dinner, she asked Charlie to join her briefly in the park. When they were seated on the bench Mihaela had chosen under the saffron streetlight, she excitedly jumped into her conversation.

"You know William who washes-up in the kitchen?"

"Not really."

"Ya know, the guy with the scruffy beard who wears the goofy knit cap."

"Oh, him."

"Yeah, he's got a cousin who works at that security company a few blocks west of the park."

"OK."

"Well, Bethany, that's the cousin, told William that they're looking for someone to be a part-time guard—a night guard at the Chevy dealership that's just on the other side of the park."

"Hmm."

"Apparently the guard there, or one of the guards, I don't know, anyway, one of the guys got sick and is in the hospital for a few months—guess it's pretty bad. Anyhow, they're looking for someone to take his place til he can get back on his feet."

"OK."

"OK? Don't ya see? This is a great chance. Even if the guy comes back, there may be another place for you to go. This could be a beginning . . ."

"Night guard?"

"OK, smarty pants—got somet'n better?"

"Well . . ."

"And I've spoken with Sister Elena. Since this is still real iffy, she says you can keep staying with us. So, whatever you get paid will be kinda a grubstake for get'n on ta somet'n better. Huh?"

Charlie shook his head.

Mihaela couldn't tell if he was happy or sad. "OK, I'll tell William to tell Bethany that you'll stop by the office tomorrow."

Charlie was sitting on a stool, wearing starched khaki pants and a matching khaki shirt with an emblem of Knight's Security on the left breast pocket. This was topped off by a navy-blue baseball cap and a two-inch-wide black leather belt that held his large flashlight. His clothes changed from tan to red to green as the neon light above his head flashed Harold Page Chevrolet—the marquis below proudly proclaiming, "Best deals on the lakeshore bar none!"

Charlie's attire, uniform if you will, was part of the deal—fortunately provided and laundered by the company. There was a room at the office like the locker room back at high school where the guards changed into their khakis. There was even a shower—a damn sight better than the ones at the hostel. This was a plus.

Charlie was looking for the pluses, because there were a number of minuses. The top two that really dominated all were the deadly duo of low pay and high monotony. While even senior guards received modest pay, a temporary guy was really paid a pittance. And the job was boring as hell!

Charlie would get to the office at about seven-thirty. After he'd changed, he'd wait for his other two partners—the Chevy dealership having a total of three guards. The trio would then walk over to Harold Page's for their eight-to-eight shift.

There was a senior guard, Lester, who was actually ensconced in a small cubbyhole off the showroom. He covered the inside of the main building as well as being responsible for oversight for his two junior team members. The back guard, Skip, who'd been doing this for years but somehow never moved up in the ranks, covered the outside-back—the body shop and used car lot. Charlie's domain was the outside-front—the garage and parts areas as well as the new car lot. Every hour the outside guards had to make the rounds with their watchclocks—inserting a key chained to each inspection point to validate their passing.

It was all well-organized. It seemed to all work. The thing was, the dealership was a small place in spite of the area covered by the car lots. It really didn't require three guards. Charlie could do his rounds in fifteen to twenty minutes. He then had nearly three-quarters of an hour, every hour, to wait at his post under the flashing neon lights. To say it was humdrum was to grossly underestimate Charlie's view of his job.

But it was a job, as Charlie repeatedly reminded himself—something he had not had a few weeks before. Something he needed even if he didn't like it.

It was also a job that had provided some unthought-of challenges that had been arranged thanks to the initiative of Mihaela. Charlie worked nights. The hostel was geared up to feed and shelter people at night—only at night. This was the way things were and certainly Sister Elena felt this was the way things should be.

The Sister was ready to rescind her offer for Charlie to remain once she realized he was part of a night crew. It was only Mihaela's quick thinking and good planning that kept Charlie from being back on the park bench.

Mihaela explained to Sister Elena how important it was to try and help Charlie. He was, after all, a good kid from a good Catholic family (not something, Mihaela quietly noted, that could be said about all, maybe even most of their guests). Furthermore, Mihaela suggested, there was a small storeroom off the main kitchen pantry that had apparently been used at one time to store propane for the kitchen's stoves and ovens. Since everything today ran on piped-in gas, this space was no longer used. It was, by God's grace (she hoped adding this was not overkill), just big enough for one of the hostel beds and a small table. Charlie could come in through the service doors after the first kitchen staff arrived since it was past nine in the morning before he'd get back to St. Mary's after getting out of his uniform and back into his jeans. He'd be in time for a late breakfast and could take his dinner just before leaving around seven o'clock in the evening to go back to work.

Sister Elena was, at best, unenthusiastic. Yet she felt her novice was trying to do the right thing and help someone in need. It was difficult to refuse out of principle.

So, Charlie began sleeping in the old propane room.

∧ ∧ ∧ ∨ ∧ ∧ ∧

Mihaela was uncertain why she felt so attached to Charlie—why she tried so hard to help him. Why? Was it right?

Sometimes she felt it was all about the receding waters. They can strand things. Were she and Charlie stranded together on a deserted island (an island in the city and not in the sea) by the fates? She wondered. Was it all about biology? Was this all just about the yearnings, maybe the needs, of a young boy and young girl? Wasn't this wrong? Was this all about charity? After all, her life, as it was, was relatively secure. Was she simply trying to help someone in need? Wasn't this the right thing to do? Was this all about faith? Shouldn't it all be about faith? She was among the faithful. Her job was to tend to God's flock. Charlie was part of God's flock. Were her feelings for Charlie a threat to her love of her God? Could Charlie derail her path to devotion? Was this all right or wrong?

ʌ ʌ ʌ ᴠ ʌ ʌ ʌ

Charlie was pragmatic. He didn't analyze the why's and the what-if's. He rapidly adapted to a new pattern of activities—to a new sleep cycle. Soon it was the mundane.

Guards worked six-day weeks. Charlie was off on Wednesdays. It didn't' make any sense to try to get back to a normal daytime cycle once he'd learned how to fall asleep in spite of all the kitchen clatter next door. Therefore, Charlie had to figure out what to do on a night away from the Chevy place.

The answer again came from Mihaela. She offered, as long as Charlie paid (novices didn't have much pocket money), to go to the movies on Wednesday night. She didn't ask Sister Elena and wasn't totally sure it was the sisterly thing to do, but it seemed to make sense.

She and Charlie would walk the ten blocks to the Portage Theater where they'd watch whatever was playing—hopefully double features. Then, after the movie, on the walk back, there was an all-night diner a few blocks off Warner Avenue where they'd stop for coffee and pie (by prearrangement, Charlie's treat). Finally, before going into St. Mary's, they'd sit on what they now considered to be their bench under the saffron light and talk about nothing and everything.

Wednesday bled into Thursday. Before he knew it, Charlie was back in his khakis watching the light change from red to green as it reflected off the shiny surfaces of the new Chevies looking for homes.

City Streets

WHILE FAR FROM THE dreams of a kid who was an offshoot of the Czech Colonization Club, life in Chicago began to have its own pulse. The city slowly became less threatening, if not less enigmatic. The days melded into months.

Charlie, equally slowly, began to move from living from minute to minute to actually looking at a longer horizon—often thinking in terms of things that were weeks, even months away. His job at the dealership continued as apparently the guy he was temporarily replacing was really sick. He began to see how he could use his time better. When not makings rounds, there had to be something to do beside stare out at a vacant Irving Park Road.

Again, Mihaela came to his aid. She introduced him to a used bookstore across the street from Wilbur Wright College on North Nagle Avenue. She then led him to a Salvation Army thrift store where he was able to buy a rather well-worn messenger bag without depleting his reserves. She finally topped all this off by giving him two sheets of paper with precise penmanship listing books she thought he should read—his "on-the-job literature assignment" as she called it.

Charlie had never been a big reader and had certainly never had much of an introduction to literature. But, as he had become accustomed, he unquestioningly followed his friend's advice and began using what he named his "stool time" to read works endorsed by his steward.

To read comfortably, he had had to move his stool away from the oscillating neon lights to a perch where he was bathed in the more subdued glow of the marquis. Following Mihaela's guidance, he had made two purchases at the Nagle Avenue bookstore (Mihaela, always looking for added value, suggesting he read some about the original proprietors of these lands, selecting two very different tales concerning the subject by well-known nineteenth-century writers). He started with James Fenimore Cooper's *Last of the Mohicans*. He followed this with Lydia Maria Child's *Hobomok, A Tale of Early Times*. He then returned the books to get two more for his messenger bag.

When he wasn't touring his zone and updating his watchclock, his nose was buried in a book. However, Lester didn't seem to mind. As had been clear early on, there were more than enough guarding eyes to look after the dealership.

In truth, even after feeling himself to be a well-seasoned night watchman, Charlie had to confess he had been confronted with very little in terms of action. There was the occasional drunk staggering about the lot. There was the odd cluster of kids, maybe trying to see what they could quickly rip-off. And, most often among these rarities, there was the random couple looking for a secluded place to sate their hormones.

After enough months on the job where it almost felt like a career (and enough books read where he almost began to feel literate), Isaac, the ill guard, returned to work.

Then, as Mihaela had hoped, with a sterling record, Charlie was moved to the night guard job at Lake City Service and Supply on Montrose—about ten blocks to the northwest of St. Mary's and six blocks north of the company's offices. Here there was no team nor any watchclock—he was it.

Being "it" had its pluses as he was his own supervisor. However, it meant that he had to be more judicious about how much time he devoted to his books—there were no fallbacks.

Another difference with the new assignment was that as the only night guard, the company attempted to let him have his night off on the weekend. Now his Saturday nights were his own.

This disrupted movie night with Mihaela but, quick as ever, she proposed they attend the Saturday meetings of the Vlachs League—a congregation of folks chiefly of Romanian ancestry. They met on the third Saturday of each month (this leaving other Saturdays for Mihaela and Charlie to go to the movies or find other suitable weekend entertainment).

Meetings were an all-evening affair; a cocktail followed by dinner (Romanian fare), followed by a guest speaker (Romanian subject matter).

Mihaela explained, while the league had a historical focus on Romania (recalling for Charlie's benefit that Chicago had received a wave of Romanians at the beginning of the twentieth century following the collapse of the Austro-Hungarian Empire), the group had been founded to assemble those called the "Wallachians"—people from the Danube Region including those from Romania, Albania, Bulgaria, and Yugoslavia. Then, given the diversity of the Chicago area, they had opened their doors to others from Eastern Europe. Now they had members from the Adriatic to the Black Sea and all the way to the Krkonose Mountain Range, reaching into Poland.

It was, as Mahaela never ceased to underscore, complicated. Nonetheless, Mihaela assured her friend that this jumbled mix was just a good group of people with whom to hang-out on a Saturday night.

Charlie was lukewarm, at best, about a formal night out with his ancestral brethren (or their neighbors). But if this was the price of having the rest of his Saturdays to share privately with Mihaela, then so be it.

As her Vlachs League chaperone, Charlie was welcomed if not immediately appreciated. There were no thoughts of impropriety—no worries about a young novice and a young outsider. After all, none of the league members could even imagine any more serious and honor-bound relationship than one with someone who was wed to the cloth—transgressions were not a consideration.

The first evening, Mihaela had shepherded him around, introducing him to everyone, perhaps embellishing ever so slightly his story, as though introducing one's mother-in-law to one's golf club. By the third reunion, Charlie was freely floating about the group as though he had been a member for decades. It all seemed to mesh.

Still, league or no league, their relationship remained as muddled as ever to each of them. But they enjoyed each other's company and tried to leave the self-examination to other nights of the week when they were alone and possibly more objective.

The adopted coping strategy was definitely enjoying the here and now. Perhaps tomorrow will take care of itself.

Six months and a dozen books later, as City Services became the new routine, his accommodation was turned upside-down by Sister Elena. The good sister had long felt Charlie had overstayed his welcome—sucking up resources better used on the truly destitute. After all, he now had a job and, like other folks with jobs, should fend for himself while the hostel held its hand out to those truly in need.

Mihaela had been able to blunt her elder's decision for some time, but ultimately, she could no longer fend off the inevitable; Charlie had to move out.

To no one's surprise, Mihaela had a plan. Her path had crossed several times with Sister Yulia of the St. Volodymyr Ukrainian Orthodox Cathedral. This parish was (of course) located in the neighborhood called Ukrainian Village, to the southeast of St. Mary's, closer to the city center. Mihaela reached out to her sister and in a markedly short time Yulia informed her that a parishioner had a small studio apartment on West Haddon Avenue, just a few blocks from the Cathedral, whose previous tenant had recently passed. The landlord would be most happy to have a solid and reliable Christian renter. Moreover, given the contact through the church, the proprietor would offer Yulia's friend a special reduced rent (a St. Volodymyr discount, Sister Yulia called it) if he could pay three months in advance.

It seemed just right. Mihaela wasn't too sure of the "Christian criterion," but felt Charlie, as an employed person with good manners, could meet the owner's expectations. His Romanian roots would likely help push him through the door if an added push was needed.

Charlie, for his part, was, once again, fully appreciative of Mihaela's efforts. However, he was far from keen about moving to a neighborhood where he knew no one and nothing. It had taken him weeks, painful weeks, to feel at ease around Portage Park. In this massive and intimidating megalopolis, he wasn't sure if he had the gumption (there it was again, this father's favorite word) to start over.

Mihaela understood. She talked to Father Marius. If memory served her (and it always did), she had heard the Father talk about his cousin who worked at the Chicago Transit Authority.

Indeed, Father Marius proudly confirmed (possibly thinking of *Proverbs 29:23*) his cousin Alexandru worked in the head offices of the CTA. Sister Mihaela then explained the situation with regard to Charlie, someone who Father Marius proudly considered as, "His good catch." After fruitful exchanges, Mihaela was able to go back to Charlie with a full strategy.

"It's coming together," she began, hoping she was positive enough to raise his dampened spirits.

"Sure."

"Really." She smiled, "I've got the whole deal here for you to consider. Think it's pretty good."

"OK."

"Well, here it is." Another smile. "This room on Haddon is honestly
a good deal. I know it's nearly a dozen miles from here and that this is a
huge city. But this distance honestly isn't all that much. Father Marius has
helped me, and we've been able to get you a special pass on the CTA—it'll
cost next to nothing and it's good for a year. You can honestly go anywhere. You can go from Haddon to here at St. Mary's or to your office
or even to City Services in about an hour, taking the Number 85 and
the Number 70 buses. It'll make your day a little longer, but you'll be
free to come and go as you please and have your own room. Finally, and
this is honestly exceptional, Stefan from the hostel kitchen, you know,
the old bald guy. He honestly likes you. He says you've always been kind
to him. So, he's agreed to make two box meals a day—paper bag meals,
honestly—and you can come by here on your way to and from work to
get your eats. How about all that?"

Charlie felt there were a few too many "honestly's," but he was *honestly* dazzled by the arrangements made by Mihaela. Other than going
back to the park bench, it didn't appear he had too many options. And
she'd done a terrific job. He smiled honestly at his friend, offering a more
cordial, "OK!"

Yet another new routine was soon established.

⩗ ⩗ ⩗ ⩗ ⩗ ⩗ ⩗

Charlie's studio was sparsely furnished but functional. The neighbors
and many of the tenants in the apartment complexes that occupied the
block seemed to be middle aged and older, of Eastern European origin.
He should fit in since demographically, it wasn't all that different from
home on the lakebed.

Charlie felt he should fit in but wasn't sure at all that he did. It wasn't
the lakebed. More than having Eastern European lineage, these folks
were now first and foremost Chicagoans—something he very obviously
was not. As best he could, nonetheless, he attempted to break the ice.
While he did not effervescently try to embrace his neighbors, he did always make an effort to smile and offer a "good day."

The responses this solicited were reminiscent of his first interactions
when he had valiantly attempted to engage local residents of Portage

Park—dismal failures. While people back home were probably considered by newcomers as somewhat aloof, they'd never let a "good day" from anyone go by without a smile, a nod, and a "same to ya."

Here, the reaction was a scowl—or nothing at all. He was not able to penetrate the walls. He was an outsider to the outsiders.

This pushed him even more into Mihaela's sphere even though the distance was now greater.

He would see her when he got off the bus near St. Mary's to collect his paper-bag meal she'd so thoughtfully arranged. He'd see her in the morning when he'd repeat his steps for a second paper bag to take back to Haddon Avenue.

Back in his studio, having spoken with no one en route, he'd spend some time updating his diary. He'd developed a backlog during his move, and he struggled to add a few sentences at the very least for each passing day. Somehow his scratches on the pages seemed to validate the day—seemed to contribute to the stack of things that made it all worthwhile.

Once he'd drained his thoughts onto the pages and eaten his now soggy paper-bag repast (supper for him, breakfast by definition), he'd jump into bed for some much-needed sleep until his despised alarm angrily sounded at five o'clock in the evening when he'd wash up, put on his civvies (as he now thought of his non-uniform clothes), and catch the Number 85 bus to start another day at night.

∧∧∧∨∧∧

During those occasional moments of calm, at St. Mary's or elsewhere, Mihaela and Charlie would sit side by side on a park bench, a pew, or just about anywhere and intentionally make small talk. They would discuss the book Charlie was reading or the books he'd read. They'd discuss the new lodger in the hostel who wore pink socks. They'd discuss how the hostel showers still didn't drain very fast. They'd discuss how there seemed to be a lot of vacant apartments on some streets and not on others. There was a lot they'd discuss. But there was also a lot they didn't discuss. They didn't talk about the upcoming time when Mihaela was scheduled to take her vows (a date that always seemed to be just over the horizon, making Charlie wonder if she might be thinking of forestalling the pivotal event). In fact, they didn't talk about family, about religion, or about the future.

It was, therefore, a break with the normal when Mihaela recalled something for Charlie, "Remember what's written on the hostel wall?"

"Sure."

"And."

"And?"

"And, what about it? How long since you wrote to your mother?"

"Oh. Well, quite a while."

Mihaela knew that the subject made Charlie uncomfortable. Yet, she hoped they were now close enough that she could bring up sensitive subjects she felt were important. "Be honest, have you written at all?"

"Not really."

"Not really?"

"Not at all."

"And?"

"Well, I left."

"Of course. But don't you think she'd like to know you are OK?"

"She might try and find me or try to get me to come back or something."

"Maybe. But don't you owe her some sort of word?"

"Probably."

"And?"

"I'll think about it."

"Think about it?"

"Yeah. When I do write, and I will, I want to be able to tell folks at home that I'm OK. I want to tell them I've a job and a life."

"You do. You've been working for a long time now. You have an apartment—you even have an address where they can write to you."

"Yeah."

"So, what are you waiting for? They've gone through hell not knowing what happened to their child. You should tell them."

"Yeah."

"It's really late, but at least now you're stable, you're employed, you're healthy. Let them know. This would make them happy."

"Yeah."

"And?"

"I will."

"When?"

"Soon."

"How soon?"

"Real soon"

"Like tonight at work?"

"No, not at work, but soon."

"Charlie . . ."

"I will."

Mihaela knew her friend well enough to know that when the conversation started spinning in circles, it was best to change topics. She'd raised the issue. They both knew it was important. And, as important as it was, they both knew it was terribly difficult because he had waited far too long. The fresh memories of the past had cooled. The separation had solidified on a poor footing. In any case, it would be hard to reset the clock and undo the pain and suffering. But what had to be done had to be done.

At least, Mihaela reminded herself, as she had emphasized to her friend, he did have a job and some stability. He was better off than so many others.

⋀ ⋀ ⋀ ⋁ ⋀ ⋀ ⋀

Job or not, guard duties had never been a shining light in Charlie's world. They had been a choice for someone with no choices. They had, hopefully, been (or would be) a means to an end—although Charlie was still completely unsure of what end.

Still, even though the shine (if there ever had been one) had rubbed off, work and all that went with it had allowed Charlie to mentally transition. He was no longer, in the dark of unfamiliar nights, overwhelmed by feelings of doubt. He was no longer wishing he'd stayed the course on the lakebed and would now be charting his path with his parents by his side. He no longer waxed nostalgically for the scent of fresh sage and the whirring of mallard wings as they took to the ever-blue skies. He no longer thought of the hum of the crickets on a still night. He now accepted sirens, crying babies, and loud, angry voices as the night sounds of his new life.

He was a resident of Haddon Avenue in both body and mind.

The monotony of the night watch, however, could no longer be fully offset by Charlie's bag of books. With no negative impact on his efficacy, Charlie was sure, he was still able to find time to read while safeguarding City Services. And he continued to enjoy the books Mihaela kept vetting for him. But, sooner or later, as the heavy night crept forward ever so slowly, he found himself enclosed, nearly smothered, by a leaden cloak of his own making. The emptiness of the night seemed ultimately to seep into his core, emptying his soul.

He did accept his condition. He knew he was where he was because of choices he himself had readily made. He knew, or valiantly tried to convince himself that he knew, that this was just the first step down the road that would lead him to his destiny—a destiny that could not be found on the lakebed. Yet, his thoughts could only go so far to offset the solitude he felt as the reinforced concrete ceilings of City Services seemed to weigh on his head, pressing through to his spine. At its peak, the pressure seemed to immobilize him—make him feel like he was moving through spaces filled with Jell-O.

As the pressure built, so did the anxiety.

The uncertainties returned.

The question kept reappearing, "What the hell am I doing here?"

ᛗ ᛗ ᛗ ᛦ ᛗ ᛗ ᛗ

To no one's surprise, Mihaela seemed to know exactly where she was and what she was doing. She was doing God's work and, by extension, her work. Equally importantly, she was being herself.

She knew all too well that her earliest decision to join God's sisterhood had been more to make her parents (whom she adored) happy than an outcome based on religious fervor or deep-seated piousness. Her parents had felt more than just lucky. They had seen their comrades who had also fled the homeland slip and slide as they tried to gain traction in a new world. Many had failed. Many had found only misery and an early death. Yet, with God's Grace, they had managed not only to get traction, but to succeed—to have been able to live their dreams.

They felt the best way to express their gratitude, to tangibly show how blessed they were, was to offer their daughter to God's service.

Although Mihaela had not resisted her parent's desires, truly happy to do their bidding (as she saw it), at first, she was spiritually uncommitted. She accepted her future out of filial love and family loyalty—not out of keen devotion.

Nonetheless, if all paths lead to one's destiny, she had found hers. She exulted in her place in life.

As a novice, she had a full slate of novitiate responsibilities, dominated by hours in prayer to review her contract with God. Still, even when the work at the hostel was added on, Mihaela managed to find time to move about the neighborhood, visiting the infirm, the ill, the stricken, and the morose.

She helped many. She was loved by all. She demonstrated more than espoused an exceptional faith. And, although her own modesty would preclude her admission, she was viewed by those inside and outside her reverent community as a young woman who was exceptionally smart, energetic, and empathetic.

Mihaela was not flattered by accolades. She did not do what she did for self-aggrandizement. She knew she was where she was meant to be, doing what she was meant to be doing, and that was more than enough.

Now, doing what was to be done meant trying to help those who found shelter in St. Mary's hostel—trying to help Charlie. Trying to help Charlie when he entered into the depths of uncertainty and frustration that bordered on clinical depression.

In many ways, Charlie was her avatar of human need and the opportunities for salvation—both spiritually and matter-of-factly.

ᛉᛉᛉᛉ

Charlie knew, and Mihaela reminded him often, that he needed to focus on the positive and sideline the negative.

Quite to his surprise, one of the unexpected bright spots was the monthly meeting of the Vlachs League. Despite spending most Saturdays together, these regular collective get-togethers were a chance for the two of them to change the pace and interact with a much larger and divergent group. While, when Mihaela had first suggested attending the regular gatherings of folks with Romanian and similar heritage, Charlie had imagined a bunch of delusional old men with long white beards, sitting in rocking chairs, and talking about how great things had been in the old country; things turned out to be very different.

Indeed, the centerpiece of the league was the common bond of Romanian or related roots. But the discussions were much more about tomorrow than yesterday. These were, in fact, in the majority, congregations of middle-aged and younger Eastern Europeans who basically were strategizing on how to grab their piece of the American dream—an object that often slipped away due to bigotry and anti-immigrant policies that disadvantaged many, including many Romanians and their kin and cousins from across Eastern Europe.

It was, in truth, Charlie deduced, this fundamental search for equity if not equality that attracted Mihaela to the group. It was not the commonness of culture nor history; it was addressing the perceived normalcy of prejudice that accompanied each one of them in one way or another. Mihaela had chosen the pathway of religious servitude to honor her God and her faith—but also to fight for justice and tolerance. She was, Charlie now understood, a devout civil libertarian as well as a devout Orthodox Catholic.

It was probably in this role as justice advocate more than as proselytizer that Mihaela was, as Charlie now learned, one of the most popular members of the league. The same humanity, the same caring, and the same exceptional planning skills she had shown in unselfishly helping Charlie had been, for some time, known to the group. She was an inspiration. More practically, she was a damn good tactician. Since her niche with the church was seen as stable and guaranteed (even believed to be blessed by some), she was viewed as an objective and astute advisor to many as they contrived how to do better, get more, and beat a system that all too frequently seemed stacked against them. Sister Mihaela was, for many, the savant of the Vlachs League.

The League assembled all manner of folk as could be expected when drawing from such a large and diverse pool as that of metro Chicago. Yet, in spite of size of bank account, residential neighborhood, social status, or educational level, all appeared to be on equal footing in the Vlachs League.

This equilibrium certainly seemed to be a major attraction for Mihaela. In truth, some maintained that the environment of impartiality was at least in part due to the good sister's gentle influence on the leadership (others whispering that the behind-the-scenes pressure Mihaela could and did apply was often anything but sweet-tempered).

The leadership of the league was undeniably more in line with Charlie's initial stereotype. They were, in effect, the tribal elders, all born in the homeland. They were more comfortable speaking in their mother tongues and still looked at life through the now cloudy lenses of their youth. However, the leadership was more ceremonial than functional. After all, the public facing image of the league was as a Romanian enclave where the old ways and the old values could endure. To fulfill this perception, they held public celebrations of Orthodox holidays as well as Unification Day on January 24th, Romanian Independence Day on May 10th, and Great Union Day on December 1st. During the festivities, the elders would don an assortment of traditional clothes representing the seven regions of the country; *itari* or *cioareci* trousers with any of a variety of shirts (*camasa*) covered by a sheepskin vest (*pieptar*) and, in colder weather, this topped off with a peasant overcoat (*suman*).

The public performances were intended not only as a recognition of Romanian culture (and by inference, Eastern European cultures in general), but also as vehicles to attempt to accelerate the integration of these folk into wider Chicago society. Embedded in this second aim was the transcending work by Sister Mihaela and others to facilitate the economic integration of league members into the community for the mutual benefit of all—to give all a slice of the national pie.

These more utilitarian objectives of the league, the activities that most attracted and benefited from Sister Mihaela's acumen, were coordinated by a second tier of league officers who were much less visible, but often more influential than the elders. These principals, both men and women, represented a small subset of the group who had, through good luck and hard work, managed to somehow break out of the lassitudes that seemed to have adversely affected others of their ethnicity. These lieutenants of the league were striving diligently to find tactics and methods whereby all who wished to could escape the prevalent economic hebetude and the all-too-common bigotry (dampening such slurs flung at them by an often unreceptive populace such as "Onionhead," "Gypsy," "Taran," "Cabbagehead," or even "Mudak," or "Cossak").

Most Saturday meetings, following the meal and allocution, Mihaela would sit with those engaged in this (considered by some as "reactionary") subgroup of lieutenants. They would review job and education opportunities, look into ways to counter any anti-Romanian (equated to anti-Eastern European) sentiments, and generally discuss how to help people do better tomorrow than they were doing today. Charlie kind of felt like a mouse in her pocket. He was there, seated with the others (he called them "the eggheads"), but apparently unseen. The discussions flowed around him as a current around a boulder in a stream—and, in fact, he felt about as implicated as an inert boulder. Yet, he still enjoyed being there. He enjoyed watching Mihaela as she energized her partners. He enjoyed the commitment of all. And he enjoyed (maybe vicariously) seeing—almost feeling—that many of the outsider afflictions he had suffered and was suffering were common among many.

As the evening progressed and the ardor waned slightly, there was always a break when beer would appear, and the discussion would shift

from the weighty issues of economic survival to the more mundane topics of the weather and baseball. During these respites, Charlie was embraced, even if perfunctorily, as though he had been an active participant
throughout. And, through these respites, Charlie began to get to know,
in addition to Mihaela, the real trailblazers of the Vlachs League. Know
them, but not truly know them.

Mostly, this vanguard was composed of serious (Charlie thought
a better adjective would be grim) middle-aged men and women who,
from their comportment and mannerisms, were already doing well and
wanted to extend a helping hand to their confreres. These stern folks were
polite to Charlie, but, he felt, kept him at arm's length (he was always
Mihaela's guest).

The exception to this generally cool and measured reception was
Julian Badescu (Mahaela told Charlie his given name was Iuliu, but he
had tried to Americanize it to Julian). Julian was younger than most, not
too much older than Charlie. He had, as he later told Charlie, inherited
a goodly sum from his uncle, and started a small, specialized printing
company. Things had gone well, and he now had a dozen employees and
a thriving business in East Garfield Park. Thanks to his uncle and the
blessings of karma (as he called it), he was, exceptionally, able to sit at
the table with the really big actors as these heavyweights tried to help the
group move upward and onward.

Julian liked to chat with Charlie over a beer. Julian was inquisi-
tive—more than most. Julian had never been outside the Chicago metro
area. He was curious about Charlie's hometown, about living out west,
and about trying to get by when one really had nothing (something he
himself had been spared). Julian and Charlie, with Mihaela's approval,
became friends.

Perhaps it was an exaggeration to say that Julian and Charlie were
real friends. After all, it was more than age that separated them. Julian was a successful businessman and Charlie was, as he saw himself,
a hobo. This was a gap probably too large to fill with a few beers on a
Saturday night.

Nevertheless, Julian showed every sign of sincerity when he con-
versed with Charlie after both had witnessed the tough business of trying to give others a leg up. These casual repartees with Julian were not
in-depth conversations nor even serious exchanges. They were just the
type of prattle people have while drinking beer. And they were chats that
were only monthly events. Although Charlie still saw Mihaela as often as

possible, his interactions with Julian were limited to league meetings—
not exactly a close friendship.

In spite of the evident fragility of the relationship, Charlie valued his
link to Julian. He was all too aware that a drifter such as himself (they'd
call him a "tumbleweed" at home) was, to make a little inside joke, way
out of his league when he tried to bond with stalwarts of the league. Still,
this reality notwithstanding, Charlie was glad to say he knew someone
other than Mihaela.

As the months passed and meetings joined one to another, Julian
appeared to reinforce his regard for this professedly aimless outsider from
a far-off lakebed. As the evening events wore on, he and Charlie would sip
bears, Mihaela and others from the league's avant-garde elite still laying
plans for ways and means to achieve their august aims. The imbibing pair
would converse about nothing in particular, Julian visibly taking pains not
to make Charlie feel uncomfortable given the transitory nature of his circumstances. It looked, Charlie observed, like Julian was somewhat overwhelmed by the solemnity of the whole help-your-brother campaign and
simply wanted to relax in a low-energy space. Charlie offered such a space.

Charlie and Julian poked about each other's histories while the
diehard league adherents tried, under Mahaela's watchful eye, to right
social injustice.

Then, as members slowly trickled from the venue, Mihaela would
join the boys for a last beer at a nearby pub before Charlie and his sister
accomplice headed back to Haddon Avenue and Portage Park; Julian
would go in the opposite direction.

Saturday nights at the league often ended late (or early the next
morning).

∧ ∧ ∧ ∨ ∧ ∧ ∧

Once again, a new iteration of an old routine settled into normalcy. Charlie cycled through the days, weeks, and months. Some days, especially
those hot and muggy middays of summer, Charlie was unable to get his
hoped-for sleep. Accepting the inevitable, he would leave his bed and get
ready for work several hours ahead of schedule. Then, he would break his
typical pattern and skip the 85 bus. He would take the Blue Line of the
Chicago "L" and connect to the 49 bus to go to Grant Park—downtown
and on the shores of Lake Michigan.

As he was whisked through the city streets by the CTA's best, he marveled at his surroundings. The wide-open spaces of the lakebed were replaced by the jumble of steel, concrete, and asphalt on the shores of another lake that made up one of the country's major metropoles. He continued to be awed by his surroundings.

Charlie would meander through the central business district, called "the Loop," feeling like a round peg in a square hole. He would wonder how long it would take to feel at home among the throngs and byways. He would wonder how long he would remain an outsider—both to them and to himself. Then he would sit and watch the lake throb—realizing that the waters that had once covered his birthplace had once throbbed in the very same way.

Charlie would wander randomly about the city's core until it was time to retrace his steps and take the Blue Line northwesterly to connect to the 80 bus and get to the office in time to change into his uniform and make it to City Services for the changing of the guard.

Charlie was punctual. He was reliable.

And, reliably, the hours would relentlessly follow their course.

Then they didn't.

One afternoon he was awakened by a hysterical Sister Yulia.

Before he had fully opened the door, his eyes still fuzzy with sleep, she rushed in, wailing, "Sister Mihaela has been killed!"

Paying the Price

THERE WAS A HOLE—A gaping hole.

His guide, his shepherd, his friend—Mihaela was gone!

She had been visiting a bereaved parishioner who lived on Hutchinson Street, just around the corner from St. Mary's. Reportedly, there was a drug dealer at the same place and the same time. A drive-by shooting (a term Charlie had never heard before he came to Chicago) targeting the dealer had gone badly. Mihaela had been hit by a ricochet—dying before the ambulance could get her to the ER, even though it was less than ten minutes away.

There was a hole.

Charlie had tried to find out more from St. Mary's. He had tried to see Father Marius or Sister Elena to enquire. The church's always-open doors were closed. He could learn no more than the crumbs he had already sifted from the wind: his dear friend was gone.

Mechanically, he went to work—no longer stopping for his meal bags at St. Mary's. When not at City Services or in bed, he would wander purposelessly about city streets, unsure where he was—uncaring and unseeing.

Saturdays were dreaded. There were no more pizza parlors nor coffee shops. There were no more league meetings.

Charlie was, therefore, bewildered when, one Saturday afternoon, Julian appeared at his stoop to accompany him to a meeting. It was totally unforeseen but hard to refuse.

When Julian and Charlie got to the meeting, all appearances were
that all was as it always had been. People, typically, were reservedly cool
but even overly polite to Charlie. However, after the evening's presenta-
tion, there was no gathering of the, as a few had begun calling it, "Empow-
erment Subgroup." Mihaela had been the driver and without her catalytic
presence things had faded into nothingness. So, Charlie and Julian did
not follow their custom of having a few beers at the venue. Instead, they
left early and went to one of the local pubs where they used to have an
after-meeting drink with Mihaela.

As the beer arrived (Julian was running a tab), the young entrepre-
neur raised his glass, "To Mihaela."

Charlie raised his beer, feeling as though it weighed ten pounds,
emptying the glass in a few painful gulps.

Julian tried to gain a foothold, "Her death is terrible—a terrible, terrible thing. She was so special."

Charlie said nothing.

"Mihaela," Julian continued, "will be greatly missed by us all. But I
know you and she had a special bond."

Charlie said nothing.

"Charlie," Julian tried to be sympathetic but somehow steady like a
big brother, "this is really tough, I know."

Charlie said nothing.

"But," Julian barely waited for his mate to intervene, "when horrible
things like this happen, sometimes the best thing to do is to try and make
a major change in your life so you are forced to focus on the present and
not the past."

Charlie indicated to the barman he needed a refill (his third).

"It is a shame," Julian modulated his speech, "that I bring this up
now. I have been thinking about it for some time and the horrific events
regarding Mihaela have made me jump forward and ask the question
now, even if it is the worst of times."

Charlie had nearly drained his glass.

"Let me get straight to it. How about coming to work for me?"

There it was, out in the open, out on the bar like a bowl of nuts to
be picked through. But Charlie was not moved. He stared into his glass.

"Let me just explain a bit and then you can think about it and let me
know later. I know you've got a lot on your mind. I also know you're a
sharp guy and a hard worker. I've told you my printing business is doing
well and now I'm expanding again. I'm putting on another shift. I was

thinking, 'Who does well in the depths of night? Why my friend Charlie who works well at night.' So, there it is if you want it. I'd want you to work with the day shift for a month or so to get know the ropes, then, if all went well, you could take over the night crew. Think about it."

ᛘ ᛘ ᛘ ᛦ ᛘ ᛘ

Charlie had got shit-faced.

He wasn't completely sure how he ended up back in his bed and he sure was sure that he had one helluva hangover when he headed out for work Sunday evening. Still, he remembered Julian's offer. He began mulling it over as he stared at the same old musty corners of City Services through another week of nights.

Ultimately, unable to seek sound advice from the wise Mihaela, he concluded, "What have I got to lose?"

He called Julian and accepted the offer. He gave notice to Knight's Security—having to work another thirty days before he could leave with no loss of pay.

During the transition period, Julian was more than helpful in finding alternative accommodation for Charlie. The Haddon studio had been Mihaela's creation, it was too painful to stay. Moreover, it was now better to find another place from where it was easier to get to and from his new job.

Julian's printing works, Mid-West Calligraphs, were on West Walnut, off North Kilpatrick Avenue—logistically close to State Highway 50 for moving products in and out. However, this was an area of light industry, healthcare centers, elements of the city's film trade, and rents that exceeded Charlie's still modest income.

Julian put out word that he needed a good, affordable apartment. His network was large and efficient. He soon had Charlie hooked up with a landlord of a nice furnished apartment on Norwood Street in Melrose Park. Using the 313 bus and the Green Line subway, which ran close to the print shop, Charlie could, once again, get to work in about an hour— still using the pass Mihaela had procured (this a painful memory like a nail driven into his troubled brain).

As Charlie prepared to move—not that he really had anything to move—Julian advised him that he was moving into what had traditionally been an Italian neighborhood. This, of course, had little meaning today. It was just a mix of folks like all over the city. Nevertheless, there were always nuances. Charlie had spent nearly all his time in Eastern

European enclaves. This was a little different amalgamation and, Julian advised, Charlie just needed to take it a step at a time. I'd all be fine.

ᴧ ᴧ ᴧ ᴡ ᴧ ᴧ ᴧ

It all was fine—at least as fine as could be expected.

Charlie got set up in his new apartment without any glitches. Julian even offered to pay for the installation and service of the telephone since they might need to call him during his off hours—the office's busiest period.

His introduction into the business of printing was equally uneventful. There were a lot of moving parts, but Charlie demonstrated a strong capacity for multitasking (Julian comforted in his choice for night supervisor).

Soon Charlie was installed in his new position, working from seven o'clock in the evening until four in the morning (the relatively late starting time due to a two-hour break between the day and night shifts when the machines were maintained, and the premises cleaned by a special third crew called "the sweepers").

Charlie would get back to Melrose Park just as the bakeries were taking their first trays of fresh bread and pastries out of the ovens. At a small early-opening café, he'd get a great cup of *caffè Americano*, two *cornettos*, a glass of fresh orange juice, some Fontina cheese, and prosciutto.

It was an excellent way to wrap-up his working day.

It was, more importantly, excellent to have a job and to be able to pay the bill for such delicious fare.

So far, so good.

Charlie liked the work and enjoyed the challenges (it was miles above being a night guard, although his book bag was now unused, and he did very little recreational reading—he hadn't visited Nagle Avenue since Mihaela's death).

Unlike being a guard, there was a lot of variety. Each printing job was unique, but the process was more or less standard. Big banners or small bookmarks all followed the same conduits as they were transformed from blank to printed pages.

The specifications and layout of each job were done by the front office—members of the day crew. The night crew had to carry on with the day's jobs—switching over to the next one in the queue as necessary. Charlie's team of six included someone who kept the paper warehouse in order, receiving the odd night delivery, and assuring that the hungry presses had their fodder. On the other end of the chain, the shipping room had a pair of night workers who packaged and boxed the newly printed products as well as carried on with the shipping of all outgoing orders. In the middle of all this was a trio of typographers who proofread script, operated the machines, and ensured general quality control as the rollers of the machines processed ream upon ream of paper.

Charlie's job was simply to keep it all running smoothly.

It was easy until it wasn't.

There were breakdowns, paper jams, absent employees, and squabbles. There was always something. Still, Charlie enjoyed it.

He, as the supervisor, had a small office on an overhead walkway that overlooked the printing area. When he was not walking about the shop (using his old guard skills, he thought with a smile), he was taking a sample of the current job up to his office to peruse. This was not a pastime; this was part of the job. While proofreading had been done and redone, he still looked over the items knowing it was really too late to make any editorial changes. Moreover, somewhat to his surprise, a good number of the items were not in English. An assortment of fliers, handbills, brochures, and other low-density products seemed to be in a whole variety of languages and prints—from, he imagined, Mandarin and Arabic to French and German. His linguistic tools were very limited, and he could only suppose the actual dialects being processed. But he could see they were many and varied.

Fortunately, his scrutiny was irrespective of the language being fixed to the page. He was looking for signs of any mechanical problems—misalignments, ink blobs, off-colors, torn pages, crumpled or folded sheets. At the first signs of any irregularities, he would have to have the presses halted to see if they could rectify the problem. If the concerns exceeded their in-house technical abilities, someone from the sweepers was always on-call and would promptly show up to try and make any required adjustments or repairs. If the dilemma exceeded the sweeper's technical skills, there were professional repair services available 24/7. So far, Charlie had not had to put in a call to the calvary.

Professionally, print shop night shift supervisor seemed a good move for the young man form the lakebed.

ᛗᛗᛗᚢᛗᛗ

Personally, Charlie still mourned Mihaela. She had been his anchor. She had been his touchstone. She had been his soulmate. She had been his protector and guide. She had been his friend. Now, when no longer there, she seemed to have been so much more.

Just the reverse of the Jesus bugs' rituals, life had shocked him. Life had scared him. Life had threatened to consume him. And, he had jumped into the arms of Mihaela who had been more than willing to help him confront his threats—real and imagined.

This was now all in the past.

Still, Charlie couldn't really cope with the loss.

While he had never lost a close family member to death (premature or otherwise), he was, after all (and due to his own choices, he reminded himself), two thousand miles from home. He had effectively lost his entire family (and up to this very moment, in spite of what Mihaela would have wanted, had not written to his mother). Yet, up until now, he had felt no remorse. He had felt no pain. He had felt no regret. He had felt no hopelessness nor heartbreak.

Then, with Mihaela's passing, he felt it all: remorse, pain, regret, hopelessness, and heartbreak. He felt it all and he felt it all magnified a hundred times. It weighed on his body. It weighed on his soul.

When he awoke each day to meet his workday at night, he felt no joy. He only felt disconsolateness.

Nevertheless, he was grounded enough to know that he should also feel lucky.

He had a new and better job (indirectly due to Mihaela). This was a job packed with new demands and new responsibilities. This was a big thing. It was, gratefully, big enough to force him to push all his anguish for Mihaela's passing into a small, locked room in a special part of his brain. He could not let the grief consume him. He had new and serious things to do.

As he wrote in his diary before going off to work, as he gazed absently upon the now dogeared and frayed black-and-white confirmation photo, he was somewhat bewildered at how far he had come—how much his life had changed—it seemed nearly a dream. Then the wail of a siren and the screech of brakes brought him to the here and now, reminding him of where he was and how far he still had to go.

ⴷ ⴷ ⴷ ⴷ ⴷ ⴷ

One evening, as Charlie was getting ready to go to his bus stop, the phone rang. It was Julian. After some very kind words about his job performance, Charlie's boss asked if he could please come to work a little early the next day. Before going to the shop, he'd like Charlie to come to his place about four in the afternoon. With a chuckle, Julian said he was, "Inviting Charlie to tea."

As arranged, the next afternoon Charlie followed Julian's directions, walking about four blocks east of the print shop to West Maypole Avenue, around the corner from Tilton Park to an old Chicago greystone—in a line of equally aging brownstones.

From the outside, the home was a bit bedraggled. It was clean enough and seemed well-kept, but it gave the impression of an old sweater that should only be worn at home in winter. It wasn't seedy but it was a little frumpy.

Unlike the exterior, when Julian ushered his guest in through the entrance hall, it was instantly obvious that the inside was elegant with polished hardwood floors and bright brass hardware set off with oriental carpets and fine antique furniture.

Julian noticed his visitor's reaction, "You're right."

Charlie started.

"There's quite a difference between the outside and the inside. That old adage, 'don't judge a book by its cover.' But here it's the reverse. I want the book to be judged by its cover. It's by design. I want the cover to be a little tattered and shabby."

Charlie looked confused (as Julian intended).

"Here, if you noticed, I'm not in the best of neighborhoods. It's OK—there're a lot worse, I promise you. But these old greystones, built with Bedford limestone back at the turn of the century, they're really special. You take what you can get, and I took this one."

Charlie smiled.

"Still," Julian continued somberly, "you don't want to invite problems. If you've got a nicely appointed home, and I think I do, you really don't want to advertise it to the whole world. That wouldn't be wise."

Another smile.

"So, you keep the outside a little dingy so folks will think you're just like the rest, scraping by and nothing inside worth going after."

"Makes sense to me," Charlie finally chimed in, thinking of his overnight bag that held all his possessions—just as dingy on the outside as inside and definitely with nothing inside worth going after.

"Well." Julian stiffened nearly unnoticeably, seeing his guest's thoughts seem to shift, "enough nonsense. Please come through, there's someone I'd like you to meet."

Host and guest continued down the hallway past the living and dining rooms to a small solarium at the back of the house. As they entered, Julian interjected, "This is really cozy during our infernal Chicago winters."

"I'm sure," Charlie politely replied as he took in the tight space with four wicker chairs adorned with flowery cushions that reflected in the room's glassed walls, a middle-aged man seated in one, remarkable for his ivory hair and rosy (almost parboiled, Charlie thought) complexion.

"Charlie." Julian stiffened even more visibly, assuming an air of punctiliousness, "I'd like to introduce you to Robin—the reason I've invited you here this afternoon."

The white-haired red-faced man stood, showed only the slightest trace of a smile, and offered his hand with a very firm, nearly vice-like grip, "Happy to meet you, lad."

Charlie didn't think he'd ever been called lad before, but returned the grip pound-for-pound, replying simply, "Thank you, sir."

Formalities accomplished, Julian pulled attention back to his role was host, declaring he'd be right back with some refreshments.

In his absence, Robin marveled at the glazing of the solarium windows. Charlie enjoyed the sunshine.

Julian returned with three tumblers of iced tea and some small open-faced sandwiches (obviously having prepared in advance for the get-together), announcing with a grin, "I hope you'll all accept some light nonalcoholic tidbits? Charlie's still gotta get to work so we don't want to delay too much nor to give him too much to partake so he'll get sleepy—after all, he's a supervisor and he's got the whole night ahead of him."

Julian took the silence as consent and continued, "Charlie, I—we—wanted you to come by to meet Robin. He's a key stakeholder in Mid-West Calligraphs. He's also a very diversified businessman with interests in a lot of areas. He's asked me to keep an eye out for young energetic talent. There may be greater opportunities for some beyond the print shop."

Robin put his glass on a silver and crystal coaster on the polished mahogany coffee table, delicately wiped his mouth with a linen napkin also provided by Julian, seemed to stretch his face muscles as though he had just risen from bed, and declared, "We're always looking for good people."

Seamlessly, Julian picked up, "I've told Robin about our chats at the league. Robin has Romanian roots too, so this is of interest to him on multiple levels."

Robin sipped his tea. Charlie nibbled a sandwich.

"I've explained," Julian continued, "that you were really in a dead-end position at Knight's Security—a position that did not make good use of your capabilities and dedication."

Robin nibbled on a sandwich. Charlie sipped tea.

"I've also affirmed," Julian went on, "that my decision to offer you a position at Mid-West Calligraphs was a good one—you've already proven yourself to be an admirable and hardworking employee."

It was Charlie's turn to put down his tea and smile with a nod of his head.

"However," Julian carried forward, "I've told Robin that I think you're still underutilized—excuse my maybe brash assessment from an employer's perch—as the supervisor of the night shift. You're doing well, but you could do better."

Another smile and nod from Charlie.

"So, in short," Julian seemed to be wrapping up, "I wanted Robin to meet you. After this introduction, if there's something of interest to you both, I'll be happy to be an intermediary and we can see if you, Charlie, can continue to move up to grander things."

It was Julian's turn to take a big gulp of tea as Robin again daintily wiped his mouth and summarized, "We live in a fast-changing world. I try to keep a list of savvy people who might like to work with us. Now, thanks to Julian, I've got your name on the list. As long as you're OK with it, if anything comes up, we'll reach out to you."

For the first time, Charlie spoke, "That'd be great. I am so indebted to Julian for helping me get this new job—a job I really like. But I am eager to do and see new things. If something comes up, please do let me know."

That was it. Julian confirmed his role as liaison, reminding Charlie that it was about time to think about the night shift. One final fierce handshake and Charlie was heading back to West Walnut and a night listening, not to the buzz of cicadas, but to the strumming of printing presses.

ᛗ ᛗ ᛗ ᚥ ᛗ ᛗ ᛗ

Back with the presses, the job began to feel familiar if not ever boring. Charlie settled well into his supervisory role—working smoothly with his team. One of the biggest challenges regarded his personal and not his professional time. He now had weekends off—two full days. This was a lot of time off. There was no Mihaela, no league, not even Portage Park.

By a process of elimination, actually when looking for a good used bookstore to get back to his reading as he knew Mihaela would have wanted him to do, he found a good partial remedy for his long weekends—River Grove. This neighborhood, bisected by the Des Plaines River, was home to both Jerome Huppert Woods and Triton College. The woods offered secluded trails through woodland and thicket extending along the riverbank. The college, in addition to having a good used bookstore nearby, was home to Cernan Earth and Space Center—a planetarium that opened completely new realms to someone who thought of stars as nothing more than tiny points of light in the night sky he saw going to and from work. To make it all even better, these spots were only half an hour away on the number 318 bus (Charlie continuing to use his apparently never expiring CTA pass thanks to Mihaela's typical yet uncommon insight).

Much like the first time, as Charlie was getting ready to visit the woods, the phone rang, and it was a call from Julian. His employer apologized for disrupting his employee's well-earned weekend respite—however, he wanted to invite his night supervisor for a drink the next Saturday. Julian enticed Charlie, saying it would be his treat and he'd make reservations at Billy Sunday's—a high-end downtown bar named after a famous baseball player turned evangelist.

Charlie could not say no.

At the appointed place and time, Charlie found Julian seated at a corner table in a packed bar—the patrons and the din somehow shunning Julian's sheltered corner. When the drinks and some special hors d'oeuvres arrived, Julian scootched himself back into the plush leather cushion and began, "I've just heard from Robin."

"Great," Charlie mumbled around a mouthful of crab cake.

"Well." Julian eyed Charlie, "let me start first with some background. I'm sure as you've noted, this may be one of those 'in for a penny, in for a pound' situations. Our own history notwithstanding, free lunches are hard to come by. And, as you've already learned the hard way, I know as you undoubtedly do, there's always a price to pay, one way or another. But, before I get ahead of myself, let me tell you a story."

Julian concentrated. "According to the rumor mill, to which I cannot attest, Robin has an interesting history. First, I should lay all my cards on the table; my assets, my shop, my position—these all did not come from an uncle as widely believed. Much like in your case, I was spotted as a potential candidate—for me, it was while I was still in school—really just a kid. Somehow or other I was called to Robin's attention, and he sought me out. Though I knew little of him personally, Robin offered me many things I could not have easily achieved otherwise. Robin brought me into his flock. What I now have is due to this alliance and this alliance alone.

"Through this relationship, I've heard some about the man's story—my benefactor's story . . ." Julian went on to tell Charlie about Robin from the beginning. Robin, his full name Robin McCandless, and his younger brother were born in Romania during the height of the Soviet Union. He was christened Razvan and his brother, nearly two years his junior, was named Horatiu. Their family was poor—really poor. When he was eight, his parents, to their great stupefaction, had twins. There were now simply too many mouths to feed. His parents were devout Orthodox Christians. They beseeched their priest to help, to find a way whereby they could all survive. If they went on as they were, surely some members of the family would perish. They could not feed and clothe the entire household, including an ailing grandmother. Somehow, with no authority from the church nor the state, the priest reached out to his confrere in Hungary who in turn contacted a confrere in Austria. The upshot of all this networking was that two families were identified, one in the US and one in the UK, who were looking to adopt a child and were willing to adopt a boy from Romania. It was a terrible decision for his parents, and probably for their priest, but ultimately, at the age of ten Robin was adopted by a family here in Chicago while his younger brother, then almost eight, was adopted by a family in London. The boys' lives changed completely. Among other adjustments, they were now Anglophones. He was now Robin, and his brother was Horace. By most accounts, it seems as though Robin got the best of the deal. His adopted parents were better off and able to provide for their new little boy in ways that Horace's new family could not. Robin lived in a lovely home. He attended good schools. He started work with backing from his family—reportedly starting his own investment firm before he was picked up by a larger now megacorp called Delpro. He had been lucky. However, by the time he was thirty, he began to notice that his hair was turning white and that his skin was becoming even paler. The doctor's best guess was that there had been some latent albinism in his family tree, and this accounted for his light complexion—often verging on rose-colored—and the white hair. Some years later, he was able to hook back up with his brother—now going by the moniker Sir Horace Barthley (but that's another story)—from whom he had been more or less completely separated through time and space. Reportedly, to his total astonishment, his brother was his mirror image: alabaster hair and coral skin. Those genes were strong. They were also, it turned out, brothers in more than genes and complexion. They seemed, in spite of the long separation, to see life in the same way. Perhaps it was their Romanian roots. They both knew they had to fight their way to the top—the consequences be damned. They were brothers to the core. Blood and history combined with their Patzinak heritage held them tightly together.

Robin, it appeared, due to his more affluent childhood and youth, had been able to follow Romanian events more closely than his sibling. He learned that their birth family's fortunes had reversed. Their real parents had cut their ties to the church and jumped headlong into local politics. Their true father had even become a high-ranking member in the local communist party. The family was doing fine. In fact, due to their birth father's connections, the brothers were able to link up with a powerful Ukrainian group, part of an interconnected global conglomerate. Horace joined the group directly, taking up duties that focused mostly on Africa and Asia. Robin also plugged into the group, but through Delpro—his original conduit and now a growing and diversifying US-based firm.

Julian took a breath and a long swig of his drink then continued. Robin had been employed at a relatively young age by Delpro. In fact, his career and Delpro were one. Delpro was known by nearly everyone who mattered as simply Delpro. But it was quite a different company that started 175 miles southwest of here in Delaven, Illinois. Roy Franklin was its founder. His family had run the Midwest Grain and Rail Coop in Delaven for years. Roy volunteered for World War II. When he returned home after the war, his father was old and in poor health. Roy took over the coop. But he found time had passed them by. They could no longer do enough business for Roy to be able to support his parents while starting a family of his own. He needed to reshape his family's company and he needed money to do so. Still feeling, perhaps, some of the spontaneity of war, he reached out to Louis "Little New York" Campaga of the Chicago Outfit—the mob. With their backing, and, of course, under their control, Roy was able to transform the old family run coop into Delaven Professional Industries—Delpro. But Roy learned, like in that old Hawaiian song about the Princess Pupule, when those in power give you the sweet fruit, they often hang on to the root. Roy had Delpro but Roy and

Delpro were in the hands of the outfit. Yet, with the outfit's sponsorship, Delpro, nearly over night, was transformed into a major enterprise doing all sorts of business—much of which remained buried in the company's locked files. Apparently, they were involved in construction, transportation, pharmaceuticals, and even farming—with rumors of more nefarious activities. Soon it was all too much for Roy to handle alone and he brought a young investment manager, a young Robin McCandless, on as a General Manager. After a few years, Roy died, and Robin took over the company. He moved the offices to Lake Forest, north of Chicago. He then began making other changes. With his recent Ukrainian connections, he was able to negotiate with the outfit, now under a variety of lamentable pressures, to assume a lower profile, and for the eastern European group to basically buy Delpro from its Italian patrons. Since then, the already shady and veiled Delpro has mushroomed into even more puzzling and cloaked activities—these making Robin very wealthy and very powerful.

"It's quite a story," Julian concluded, "I can't vouch for all the historical details, but I can assure you that Robin is both rich and powerful. I can also assure you, whether by design or by happenstance, Delpro is this nebulous and formidable enterprise that is at the same time nowhere and everywhere.

"The company is still formally run by Robin from Lake Forest. However, they have a big US corporate headquarters out west in Menlo Park. They've also become transnational with offices all over the place. Yet, in spite of this surge around the globe, according to folks I know who claim to know stuff, the overall direction for all Delpro does or even thinks about doing does not rest solely with Robin.

"People tell me that Robin is very influential. He is definitely the public face of the multifaceted, multinational conglomerate. Still, major decisions are in the hands of some sort of board or committee. No one seems to know. Some say it's all tied into the Ukrainian mobsters who were associated with Robin's father. No one knows.

"It can be scary. It certainly is intimidating. But it is also good business."

Throughout the taletelling, Charlie had managed to consume two very potent, very expensive cocktails as well as the majority of the accompanying delicacies. This had, however, only magnified for Charlie the story being woven by Julian. He was, at once, impressed and daunted. Uncertain of the right thing to say, he could only mutter, "That's amazing" (choosing this as opposed to the oft heard and over-used retort 'awesome!').

"Well, Charlie," Julian resumed his serious tone, "as you clearly know, we have more than an employee-employer relationship. We knew each other through the league and through Mihaela well before you started working at Mid-West Calligraphs. So, both out of a professional responsibility and out of friendship, I wanted you to hear this account from me personally so that you would know at least what I know about the people with whom you may be joining hands.

"This is very serious business.

"It can be very rewarding business. But you needed to know. I truly cannot advise you. I am on the inside already. I have opted to taste the sweet fruit and, while I do not regret my decision, I know that it has irrevocably impacted on my life in many ways—some of which I am probably still totally unaware.

"Robin has asked us to come to his home in Lake Forest in two weeks. I wanted to fill in as many blanks as I could, so you'll have time to think about the whole situation before we're sitting in front of him, and the pressure is mounting."

On cue, Charlie added all that was needed to allow the conversation to dwindle off to less weighty topics, "I really want to thank you for your frankness and for taking the time to update me on things that are critical for me in order to really see the lay of the land. I confess, I now have more questions than I did when I first sat down. But you've really helped. My mother used to say, 'put on your thinking cap.' That's exactly what I'll do. Thank you."

ʌ ʌ ʌ ∀ ʌ ʌ

Charlie had a lot to consider—he trusted his thinking cap was working. He recalled what he hoped was not a premonition. In Horner Park with Mihaela, he remembered watching the water striders. He remembered telling his friend about how the males used tricks to get the females to jump into their arms—how the female feared being gobbled up by some fish more than mating with a male that may not have been her first choice. He remembered recalling that this would be, at the very least, coercion if it happened to people—maybe rape. Yet, for the water strider it worked. Fear made them jump. It worked for people, too. In Julian's tale, fear of starvation had made Robin's parents give him up for adoption. In his own case, what would fear of failure make him do? What would be the price to pay?

Lakeshore Forests and More

O N THE DESIGNATED DAY, Julian and Charlie, in Julian's late-model BMW, drove to meet Robin. Julian suggested they take the scenic route and they followed Sheridan Road north out of the city, along the lakeshore. The lake, the skyscrapers, the sky—it was all inspiring—Charlie realized at moments like these why he had left the lakebed.

As they moved slowly through the congested route, Julian explained that the road was named after Civil War general Philip H. Sheridan. In 1887, he had supported a project by the Commercial Club of Chicago to build a military base near the city. After the Haymarket Massacre of the year before, this and other disruptions all intertwined with unwelcome efforts by labor to organize for higher wages and better benefits, the city fathers felt a resident army camp would provide the necessary leverage to discipline the undisciplined. The club donated 600 acres, thirty miles north of town, to the army and the army built a fort. This base became an important benchmark in World War II when half-a-million GIs passed through its doors.

Reaching the fort, they continued another ten miles northward, coming to Lake Forest. Robin actually lived in Lake Bluff, a small appendage of Lake Forest. After they went by the diminutive Lake Bluff police station, they turned east toward the lakefront on Crab Tree Lane. Meandering through a shuttered community of oversized homes behind high fences, they came to a walled entry with no posted address nor mailbox. There was only a nine-foot, red-brick wall with a single opening concealed behind a pair ornate twelve-foot steel gates. To the right of the portcullis was a small box on a swivel arm. Charlie was able to pull the box to his window like a speaker in a drive-in movie, speaking softly into the device.

The gates magically opened, and they slowly drove down a cobbled, quarter-mile drive hedged with populars. They came to a stop on a small rise overlooking the lake where there was a breathtaking stone home that would best be described as a palace. Charlie could only think of reading *Wuthering Heights* in high school. The edifice in front of which Julian now parked reminded him of the Lintons' home, Thrushcross Grange.

The doorbell was met by a liveried servant who silently ushered them through a home as impressive inside as out. They followed the stilted chamberlain down an ornate hallway to the rear of the manor where they found their host seated under a parasol, kitty-corner to a polished marble-topped table and near an impressively large swimming pool.

The steward vanished as, without standing, Robin motioned to his guests to take seats at his table. No sooner had they sat down than a tawny-complected maid appeared with a tray of tea and biscuits.

It was only when the maidservant had left and each had served his own cup of tea that Robin spoke, "Glad you made it."

Charlie noted there was no "thank you for coming" nor "welcome to my humble home."

Julian seemed to notice nothing irregular, replying, "We're happy to be here."

"Well," emotionless, Robin continued, "I know you've both got a lot going on back in the city, so I'll keep this short."

There was obviously no expectation for his visitors to intervene.

"Charlie, Julian has spoken well of you." The rose hue of his cheeks seeming to glow in the reflections from the pool, as Robin continued, "Julian may have told you that he and I are sort of partners.

"So, I know his operation well and know it's doing good business. It's growing. It might be just the place for you, lad."

There was the lad again.

"But, before your roots seep too deep into the ink of the printing business, with Juliann's blessing, I wanted to ask you if you are interested in trying something else?"

It was a question, and Charlie knew a reply was required. He attempted diplomacy, "I am most appreciative of Julian for his kind words and to you, sir, for the enquiry. I am always open to new opportunities.

I do like my work at Mid-West Calligraphs, but would be honored to consider other options that might be appropriate for my skills and . . ."

Cutting cleanly through the hyperbole, Julian rather sharply interjected, "So the answer is 'yes?'"

"Yes," Charlie confirmed.

"OK," a nearly dispassionate Robin concluded, taking a small card out of the pocket of his white embroidered *barong*, the shirt looking as dapper as if it had just been pressed and was not being worn in the humid poolside heat. "Here are the contacts for my representative, Samuel, in Waukegan. See him and work out the details."

It was over. In just minutes, potentially Charlie's life had changed. Teacups were drained, biscuits untouched, and sooner than expected Julian and Charlie were returning to the city.

As the powerful car purred along the interstate, Julian seemed to concentrate on the nearly empty road as Charlie's thoughts ricocheted through his mind.

Robin had a beautiful home—swimming pool and all. A beautiful home complete with luxurious furnishing, beautiful art, and a skilled household staff.

Robin had influence and money (as though the two were different).

It was so different from the lakebed.

It was all good.

Charlie wanted a slice of the pie.

ᎶᎶᎶᏝᎶᎶᎶ

Charlie was back in his apartment on Norwood Street. It had been eighteen hours since Julian had dropped him off after their barebones meeting with Robin McCandless. It was Sunday and he had gone out early for his *caffè Americano*, *cornettos*, orange juice, Fontina, and prosciutto—bringing it all back to his place to enjoy while he mulled over the events of the day before as he updated his diary.

First off, Robin was far from an open-hearted, cheerful person. Charlie's first impressions, in which he put great stock, were not all that sterling. The snowy-haired man appeared to reflect a strange mixture of churlishness and arrogance. He certainly made no visible efforts to be warm and friendly. Yet, to the extent these attributes (be they true or not) did not affect his business acumen nor his engagement with his staff, they were trivial. His wealth was self-evident. His clout was equally unmistakable. As Julian had said, he was "both rich and powerful."

Charlie thought it was like getting married. If he were to get married, if he had married Mihaela (he imagined, with a pang of anguish), he would be marrying his fiancée—he wouldn't be marrying her parents. Everyone knew in-laws were a pain in the ass, but you still married the person you loved.

As with marriage, there were risks to offset the benefits. And, though still pretty much a locked box, Robin likely, as all with power and influence, engaged in questionable activities—possibly improper or even illicit activities. What of the risks? What of the risks to get his own slice of the pie?

After all, he was not contemplating marrying Robin McCandless. But in many ways, he could end up marrying a position overseen in one way or another by Robin McCandless.

It was a big decision.

It was a difficult decision—made more so by the fact he honestly liked his present work at Mid-West Calligraphs. He was basically happy with where he was and what he was doing. Why change?

It seemed, also as often with marriage (so he'd been told), all the critical analyses aside, even with all the scrupulous weighing the pros and cons and the attempts at careful objective decision-making, in the end, it was a decision of the heart (or the gut).

What did Charlie's heart (or gut) say?

One hidden element was that, somehow, he wasn't exactly sure how, Robin McCandless was already interlaced in his life since he was a partner—probably the principal partner—with Julian.

Could he really say no to Samuel in Waukegan and still stay at Mid-West? Should he have stayed at Knight's Security? Hell, perhaps McCandless owned that too. Christ, the guy was Romanian. He probably even had inroads into St. Mary's. Was this dancing with the Devil?

⚐ ⚐ ⚐ ⚐ ⚐ ⚐ ⚐

Not for the first time in recent months, Charlie was frustrated. What to do?

Ultimately, he retrieved the card Robin McCandless had given him and called Samuel on his direct line discretely embossed on the bottom in fine print.

Once again, he thought, "What have I got to lose?"

Samuel, polite and cheerful on the phone, gave Charlie the address of Spot On Enterprises on Genesee Street in Waukegan, suggesting he stop by the office. Then, when he learned Charlie relied on public transport, he unexpectedly offered to meet him somewhere convenient in Chicago when Charlie was off work over the weekend.

A few blocks north of Charlie's apartment, on North Avenue, also called Route 64, there was an Italian family restaurant with ample space to accommodate large local groups coming to get a good taste of the old country. While crowded on weekends, it had lots of nooks and crannies, providing a good venue to meet Samuel.

As Charlie was waiting at a table tucked neatly away in the back of the restaurant, wondering yet again why he was doing what he was doing, a man in his mid-fifties approached. He was short and stocky with an olive complexion, a very bushy mustache, overseen by a full head of dark wavy hair. Eying the table's sole occupant, the swarthy would-be diner began, in a remarkably soft voice, "Excuse me, are you Charlie?"

"Yes," the young man from the lakebed replied, "I'm your man" (regretting it almost as soon as he had said it).

Taking his seat, the older man extended his hand, smiling broadly, "Well, you may or may not be my 'man,' but I'm happy to meet you and thankful to experience a new eating establishment in the city."

Recovering some needed decorum, Charlie was quick to reply, "It is I, sir, who am thankful that you were able to come to my hone ground—it certainly makes it much easier for me."

"Not 'Sir' please. Just Sam."

"I saw," Charlie said, digging deeper to try and get the conversation rolling, "from your card that your surname is Loila—a new one on me."

"Ahhh. I'm Basque. Liola literally means 'muddy place.' My given name is Samso. But this is sometimes too much. Samuel is fine. Sam is easier."

Charlie was happy to see the Basque gentleman's simple cordiality—quite a contrast with his unnamed overlord. Samuel was not what Charlie had expected, although he had not been sure what to expect. Charlie did not anticipate McCandless' agents (he imagined Samuel was in some way the boss's agent) would display the same type of *beau monde* snobbishness exhibited by Robin. He rather imagined the master's minions were probably cast in the mold of Julian—young, ambitious, eastern European, hungry, and readily snared into the morass represented by Delpro. It was indeed interesting that the meeting and greeting of the two diners had taken place in the complete absence of references to Robin McCandless or Delpro. Still, Charlie could almost feel their presence and hoped Sam was not leading him to a muddy place where he would be sucked in and then find himself unable to clean the goop off his shoes.

But hell, Charlie reminded himself, this was just a look-see.

There were a few more pleasantries, then Sam, acknowledging that he knew his way around Mediterranean cuisine, offered to do the ordering as an apron-swathed waiter appeared with several large menus and a wine list.

From antipasto through to coffee accented with Sambuca, Sam did an admirable job including the wine selection. It turned out to be an excellent meal. Moreover, it was accompanied by some intriguing, if admittedly imprecise, details about the possibility of coming to work for Sam in Waukegan.

Spot On Enterprises, as far as Charlie could discern, wasn't very spot-on. According to the founder, "We do a little bit of everything."

"I'm sure you know," Charlie said, feeling obliged to specify, "that I'm not what you'd call specialized or even very experienced. I've just moved to the Chicago area not too long ago."

"Sure," Sam quickly countered, "I know some of your background." Still, no direct referenced to the catalyst that had brought them here.

"Well," Charlie said, trying to paint the best picture, "as a newcomer, I'm still looking for my niche. I like working at Mid-West Calligraphs. But I'm happy to explore new options. Do you know Julian from the print shop?"

"We've met, but I haven't spoken to him for a while."

"Well, I've a lot to thank him for. He's put a lot of trust in me."

"I'm sure it is well-founded."

"I try to do my best."

"That's clear and that's why I'm here, of course."

"It's just that I want to be careful. My mother always said, 'look before you leap'—I grew up in a pretty rural area and it was sometimes hard to tell if you were leaping or falling."

"Hopefully, I'm not asking you to leap and definitely not to fall."

"That's good."

"Like I said, my company does a lot of things. We're located on the fringe of one of our nation's biggest metropolises and on the shores of one of her biggest lakes. There's always something going on."

"Yeah."

"So, ya see, I'm always on the lookout for young guys like yourself who are flexible. I'm really not looking for specialists or guys with what I see as too much experience. The company is very diversified, and I need a staff that can quickly change gears."

"OK."

"As it turns out, I was just getting ready to put an ad in the paper. I've recently had a guy retire and I'm looking for a replacement. Have a look at this." Sam withdrew a small slip of paper from his shirt pocket.

"Thanks."

"If that's of interest to you, give me a call."

"OK, thanks."

There was then some meaningless chitchat before Sam excused himself saying he had to get back for a family affair in Waukegan.

There was a warm handshake and sincere thank-you's to Sam from Charlie for coming into the city, for the excellent meal (for which he did indeed pick up the tab), and for the job notice.

When Sam had left, Charlie unfolded the paper as he drained the last of his Sambuca. It was a short, typed text apparently destined for the local want-ad column:

> Spot On Enterprises, Genesee Street, Waukegan, is seeking an Operations Assistant. The successful candidate must have an outgoing personality, hold a high school diploma, and have at least two years' experience with increasingly responsible assignments. The position is open for immediate recruitment. Salary and benefits package commensurate with experience. Interested parties should contact 847-756-3398. Spot On is an equal opportunity employer.

⋀ ⋀ ⋀ ⋁ ⋀ ⋀

Charlie would have asked Mihaela—that would have helped.

He even thought of calling his parents—after all, he'd promised Mihaela he'd write and still hadn't. But that wouldn't work—especially not now. Too much to explain—too much unexplainable.

Julian was a good guy. And Julian was his boss. Julian was also Mc-Candless' guy. That wouldn't work.

There was really no counsel to seek. It was up to him. He dug deep, writing what he hoped was a thorough analysis of the situation in his diary. His mother would have advised prayer. He decided to sleep on it. In the end, there really was no choice.

He had unceremoniously left the lakebed to chase his dream. As OK as it was, his dream was not the print shop night shift.

There were real (and, he knew, serious) questions about the appropriateness of getting closer to the core of the McCandless organization. Still, there were no other doors on which to knock—paths to follow.

It was a "yes or no" decision.

The answer was "yes."

⋀ ⋀ ⋀ ⋁ ⋀ ⋀ ⋀

Charlie called Sam's private number and, after the formalities, stated, "I'd like to apply for the Operations Assistant job."

"Fine," Sam said. Charlie could almost see Sam's warm smile across the line as he continued, "I'll start the process here and you do what you need to do. Please get back to me in a week."

It was done. With no fuss and an ample dose of propriety, it was done.

Charlie discussed with Julian who obviously knew the whole story. Julian reiterated his satisfaction that Charlie was moving onward and upward (assuring him this was upward), asking him to keep supervising the night shift for two weeks while he found a replacement.

Charlie called Sam as planned. It was as cordial and straightforward as before. All was arranged. Sam's secretary, Wonlyn, had found a furnished apartment at a good price on the corner of Clayton and Country Streets, just five blocks north of Spot On's office. Whenever he could clear up all his affairs in the city and get to Waukegan, everything was prepared.

It was almost too easy.

Charlie gave notice to his landlord.

On the appointed day, he bid his Mid-West Calligraphs' colleagues and Julian goodbye (imagining, with all the common connections, he'd see his now former boss again) and packed his things—now occupying a cardboard box as well as the small, soiled khaki cardboard suitcase (still being home to his diary and rumpled confirmation photo).

He splurged and rented a car for his exit from Chicago and his entry to Waukegan.

Another chapter had begun.

ᐱᐱᐱᐯᐱᐱᐱ

Spot On's address turned out to be a small office on the sixth floor of the Waukegan Building occupied solely by Wonlyn and Sam. While the building, having survived decades of service, seemed to reflect better times gone by, the office itself was frugal but clean and possessed all the things Charlie thought an office should possess. There were a few chairs that passed as a waiting area in front of Wonlyn's large oak desk. Sam's office was to the left—good sized, with a view to the south, overlooking a small park. There was what appeared to be a meeting room on the right and, squeezed into the corner, a space with a photocopier and what Charlie guessed was a restroom. All in all, not too different from what he expected.

After an amicable introduction to the middle-aged, red-haired Wonlyn, Sam ushered Charlie into his office.

"Welcome." His new boss succinctly outlined the next steps before sending his newest employee back to the capable hands of his assistant-cum-secretary-cum-receptionist, "First things first. Wonlyn will show you the apartment we've found—hopefully it will be OK. She'll then show you around town so you can get your bearings. Then tomorrow morning we'll dig into your work."

It all happed just as Sam had outlined.

That evening Charlie was arranging his few possessions after, being most favorably impressed by Wonlyn's choice for accommodation; signing a lease immediately. The major sticking point for Charlie was the one-year period for the lease. Under his current circumstances, a year seemed like a long time to make a commitment. Nonetheless, he accepted this as part of the process.

The apartment itself had the feel and character of his room on Haddon Avenue—and this was fine. Moreover, across Country Street, next to the county courthouse parking lot, was a small restaurant with take-out. And, even more interesting, across Clayton Street was the city's public library.

Seeing the library, Charlie dug into his suitcase, finding the crumpled pages Mihaela had scribbled for him as she tried to highlight books he should read. Some of the titles were now crossed-off, but there were still a goodly number untouched—now was an opportunity.

Thinking of Mihaela brought all too familiar pangs to Charlie as he carefully folded the wrinkled pages and replaced them in his suitcase. He recalled his grandmother, with her strong ties to the old country, saying,

"The past is for our God, the future is for our family." To which, grandfather would always reply, "Ahh, yes *Milácek*, yet the past still smells like a bouquet of roses to your aging but still beautiful nose." Then they would all laugh.

For Charlie, the past was not for his God, as he was unsure if he had "his God," and the past was certainly not a bouquet of roses. Nonetheless, the past—whether the past from the lakebed or the past from Portage Park—was the past. The past was his family to whom, in spite of his promise to Mihaela, he had still not written or even called. The past was many things. Still, it was gone—done with.

His focus was tomorrow. His focus was starting a new job. His focus was finding his way.

ᛗ ᛗ ᛗ ᛝ ᛗ ᛗ ᛗ

"We're really well situated," Sam said, continuing his briefing to Charlie, "we're in the shadow of one of the greatest cities in the world and on the shores of one of the greatest water systems in North America.

"So, we try to use our blessing wisely. This means we do a variety of things where we feel we have an advantage. We've our fingers in several pies, but for the moment, as concerns your work, I want to focus on your job.

"If you were to go down Genesee Street a few blocks, you'd come to the Waukegan River. If you went upriver to the other side of Powell Park, you'd find a workshop and storeroom on Mill Court. This is one of our operations and this is your new job site.

"Now, before we get into the details of the job, as I said yesterday, let's deal with first things first. Mill Court isn't too far from the corner of Country and Clayton Street—nothing's that far away in Waukegan—but it's still not all that close. And, let me tell you, you don't want to have to rely on public transport here—this isn't Chicago. So, like we've done for other folks, we'll help you get your own car so there's no problem with getting to work whenever you're needed. This sound OK?"

Charlie was impressed and tried to show it with a big smile and a nod.

"Now I said 'help.' This isn't a company car. It's your car. But we'll advance you the money to get a good used car—nothing too fancy and nothing new. If, at the end of a year, everything's fine, we'll just write it off. Otherwise, we'll have to ask you to repay the loan—without interest of course. Are we on the same page?"

Another nod.

"Then, to the job. The Mill Court place is headed-up by Hank. I don't want to say he's your supervisor. I know you were just a supervisor, and I don't want you to think you're going backwards and now having your own supervisor. Think of Hank as a liaison with me, or maybe a coordinator. Mostly you'll be supervising yourself or working on a team synchronized by Hank. It's real flexible.

"Anyway, let's take care of the first stuff first. See Wonlyn and she'll give you a list of places where we usually advise our staff to buy their cars. You can then go and look around and see what you like. As soon as you're ready, Wonlyn will arrange for the licensing and payment. Sound good?"

Sooner than expected, Charlie was out of the Waukegan Building and shopping for a car—his very first car.

After reviewing more choices than he thought possible, he settled on a relatively late model Subaru Leone. It was a four-wheel-drive, pale-yellow station wagon in good shape (he hoped). It was something that would have been great for the sage savannah that surrounded the lakebed back home. He figured it would be pretty good on the shores of Lake Michigan too, since (as he had been told) the winter snow required special oomph to navigate.

As had been the case so far, when he informed Wonlyn, it was only a matter of hours before the wagon was parked on Country Street near his apartment.

He was unaccustomed to having things go so smoothly. It was good.

ᴧ ᴧ ᴧ ᴠ ᴧ ᴧ

Hank smiled.

Hank, a sinewy and tawny man who easily could have been in his sixties, seemed to nearly always be smiling. He didn't seem to be smiling at anything in particular, he just seemed to like to smile. Charlie figured he was one of, as his grandmother used to call them, the "happy folk," people who look on the bright side.

As far as Charlie's first impressions could tell, Hank was an OK guy.

When Charlie had reported for duty, Hank had welcomed him with a firm handshake and an even wider smile, "*Bien venue* to our shed!"

Hank went on to explain to the somewhat bewildered Charlie, with only the slightest of an accent, that he was French Canadian, born in Trois-Rivières, about midway between Montreal and Quebec City.

"It is," he continued, "no accident that a *Québécois* is here with you in this *hangar*—this workshop. Most of our work here for Sam and Spot On deals with Canada. The company does a lot of business next door and, when the head office has got the deals set, we're the folks who make them happen.

"As you can see, we're a pretty busy place." Hank expansively gestured to the rest of the work area. The utilitarian and unvarnished covered space extended over several thousand square feet, disappearing into the gloom of the unlit rear of the combination warehouse-workshop. There were cartons and pallets nearly touching the twelve-foot-high rafters. Among these stacks, it looked like a team of five or six people moved about like rangers in a forest. Along the left side, there was an enclosed office and next to it a lunchroom and toilet facilities. It was much larger than he had imagined from Sam's description.

Hank then let out a shrill whistle and the rangers left their arboreal stacks of *matériel* and descended on their leader to greet the newcomer.

There was a series of "hi's and hey's," no formal introductions, no putting names to faces. Then it was back to the pyramid of stuff that was under their roof.

Hank led Charlie into the small office where there was an equally small Formica-covered desk accompanied by a lopsided wooden office chair that the older gentleman occupied with a rather sudden plunk.

"I'm sure Sam told you we do a bunch of things. We're what my dear grandmother, God rest her soul, would call a *bricoleur*—a jack-of-all-trades. Sam lines things up and we run with them. It's that simple," Hank said, still smiling.

"While we change like the seasons, at any point we have a number of teams. Right now, I want you to work with Tim. But before I call him in to go over the specifics, do you have any questions?"

Charlie had none and soon he was sitting in front of Hank's cock-eyed chair, next to a blond-headed, athletic-looking man of about his age, listening to their leader describe their assignment.

As Hank outlined the job for Charlie, his new employee strangely thought of Paul Revere and the famous signals of one if by land and two if by water. For Charlie, it was two. As somewhat of a surprise, he discovered his job was on the water. He had a quick flashback to the water striders. He was to be a water strider.

Apparently, Spot On had a number of boats for different purposes in the Waukegan marina. One of these, Hank announced with a grin, was a twenty-five-foot Bowrider with a 180-horse inboard (Hank's grin getting even wider at the mention of the powerful engine). This was, in Hank's words, "One helluva boat."

As he explained, the company used this vessel for fast trips for either passengers or small amounts of cargo. Their task was the latter—delivering and receiving relatively small packages that were part of business agreements with Canadian partners.

Their destination, Hank elaborated, was Blind River, Ontario. The company had a small guest house on Rowley's Bay in Liberty Grove, Wisconsin. They would overnight there before crossing from Lake Michigan into Lake Huron and then over to Ontario. They'd then spend a night near Blind River before retracing their steps. All told, it would be a three-night trip—long but easily doable. It would also be a trip they would repeat every fortnight (Hank had to remind his disciples this meant every two weeks). After each trip they would service and clean the boat. Their water work would, therefore, account for about half their time. For the remainder of the month, they would work in the shop. They would prepare cartons into which they would pack a number of smaller boxes—these smaller items given to them by another team. They'd seal, address, and mail the cartons. Pretty easy going, Hank assured them, between trips on the water.

In line with recent trends, everything went to plan.

Tim, it turned out, was a good guy. Not the brightest star in the sky, but someone who was practical and, more importantly, someone who had worked for Spot On for five years and knew his way around.

Charlie and Tim got to know each other as they got the boat (named the *Velvet* for some unknown reason) ready for Charlie's first run—Tim apparently had made the trip many times before though this pertinent point had escaped Hank's overview of their work.

Tim was four years Charlie's senior, born and raised in Pleasant Ridge, Indiana, not far from Rensselaer and about fifty miles south of the southern tip of Lake Michigan. Although, in Charlie's view, a local boy, Tim's story was very similar to his own: moving from disinterested high school student to seeker of dreams. His pilgrimage had taken him just a little over one hundred miles, following the shore of Lake Michigan to the doorstep of Spot On.

Tim admitted to Charlie that he really didn't know all that was going on—Spot On was, in his words, "playing lots of games at the same time." But he didn't ask questions. He didn't explore. He was happy he'd found a job that had got him out of the rut he felt he was digging for himself back home. His work paid much better than anything he'd imagined (Charlie wondering about Tim's imagination) and it allowed him to follow what he had found to be his real passion: baseball. He was a member of a local softball team and never missed a Cubs' game. To top it all off, he had a steady girlfriend who worked at Louie's Restaurant and who, he added in great confidence (and with a sparkle in his eye), was dynamite in bed.

While Charlie sensed he and Tim had a little different take on life, he was glad to have someone with whom to talk and someone who had done it all before. Tim proudly showed Charlie how to get the boat ready for an extended trip. They then spent a day on the water, skipping about (like a giant water strider Charlie thought) as Tim let his workmate, as he put it, "get the feel of the boat."

Charlie told Tim it was a hoot.

When both the boat and the crew were ready, a pickup showed up (from who-knew-where, Charlie noted), the driver (who Tim didn't know) helping load a dozen medium-sized boxes into the boat's cabin. Then they were off to Rowley's Bay. After an uneventful but rather uncomfortable night in a rustic cottage (Sam had actually called it a chalet, but Charlie saw it more as a shack), they quickly continued to Blind River.

Blind River was a small community sitting roughly ninety miles east of Sault Sainte Marie, a major border crossing between Michigan and Ontario. It was located on North Channel, separated from the main body of Lake Huron by Manitoulin Island—the largest freshwater island in the world.

They crossed the channel and motored into Dorothy Inlet, tying up at the marina. After the *Velvet* was tied off to the stout wooden dock, asking Charlie to wait in the boat, Tim went ashore, returning only minutes later, motioning to the shadows, and saying, "They'll take care of everything."

Two husky and nondescript men of indeterminate age appeared from the darkness, silently stacking the boxes from the cabin on the dock. With a lighter craft, Tim quickly cast off, slowly leaving the harbor and heading north, exiting the lake proper, passing under the bridge of the

Trans-Canada Highway into another channel that, if they had continued would have taken them to Lake Duborne. However, they tied up under a bridge on Highway 557, locked the cabin, and walked a short distance to the Sunset B&B. Here, to Charlie's slight surprise, Spot On seemingly had two upstairs rooms permanently leased.

After a good meal and too much good beer (for which they only had to sign), Charlie and his mate hesitantly made their way up the creaky staircase to two very comfortable beds from where early the next morning, after a full English breakfast, they rejoined the *Velvet* for the two-day return leg to Waukegan.

When Charlie threw his little overnight duffle into the Bowrider's hold, he noticed the boxes that had been off-loaded onto the dock at the marina had miraculously been replaced by roughly the same volume of tightly sealed packages.

He prodded Tim about how the boxes got into the cabin, which, as far as Charlie knew, had been locked when they were not aboard.

Tim assured his shipmate that this was always the way things were. After all, as Hank had repeatedly said, they were in the business of delivering and receiving. This was the receiving part.

The two of them were simply the transporters—the boat crew. As far as Tim knew (and he admitted it wasn't a whole lot), it was the guys from Blind River who loaded the stuff at night while the crew slept. And, he added, to make their life easier, they didn't even have to unload the cargo or even contact customs on their return—the guys from Waukegan took care of everything. All we have to do, Tim concluded almost triumphantly, is turn in the keys—they even give us an extra day off to make up for the rigors of the travel—not bad.

As the *Velvet* knifed back into the heart of Lake Michigan, all thoughts vanished except an awe at the magnificence of this great inland sea.

᛭ ᛭ ᛭ ᚥ ᛭ ᛭ ᛭

Just as with all his previous endeavors since leaving the lakebed, soon there was a new but steady rhythm. The bi-monthly trips north were more or less the same. The number and shape of the consignments varied. The drop-off points sometimes changed, but the room at the pub was always the same as was the Rowley's Bay shack cum chalet.

The non-boat-related work was tedious, quickly becoming boring. But the ever-changing surface of the lake made each water trip unique and broke the monotony that otherwise could have become septic.

From a personal perspective, Charlie and Tim would go out for beers maybe twice a month. They weren't really good friends, but they got along and did enjoy each other in limited doses (almost as much as they enjoyed beer in less-limited doses).

With the exception of Hank, Charlie did not have any other relationships with his coworkers. In fact, the band that moved about the workplace on Mill Court seemed to mutate constantly. Faces that had become familiar were suddenly no longer there while new faces appeared— sometimes for months, sometimes for days. There were no names for the faces and no roles for the actors—it was just a panoply of images.

With few leisure or social activities, Charlie resorted to his pattern established on Norwood Street. He would go across the street to the library at least once a week to look for another candidate from Mihaela's reading list. Then, in his off time, in place of exploring Jerome Huppert Woods, he would, new reading material in hand, make the short drive to the Illinois Beach State Park, squeezed between the North Dunes Nature Preserve and the Illinois Beach Nature Preserve. All in all, this area provided acres and acres of land over which to roam and lakeshore along which to wade. The open spaces, similar yet dissimilar from the lakebed, seemed to calm his spirit and rejuvenate his vitality while the books briefly transported him to higher planes from which he could see a distant horizon where he hoped to find his aspirations (whatever they might be—he was still not totally clear on this point).

One evening, Charlie was leaving the library, content to have borrowed a copy of *A Hazard of New Fortunes* by William Dean Howells. Mihaela had emphatically recommended this novel as only she could— stressing its themes of social justice were critical for her protégé (Charlie remembered her exact choice of words) from the far west to grasp. He was thumbing through the pages as he exited the building rather than paying attention to his route. This distraction resulted in his running head-on into another of the library's patrons attempting to enter the edifice.

After the thump of their bodies colliding, Charlie looked up to find himself staring into the face of a strikingly handsome woman of about his age. As he gathered his wits, he realized the woman had dropped a book she was possibly returning. When Charlie bent down to retrieve the book, the lady was in the process of doing the same and they again collided, this time knocking noggins. Charlie's casualty was the first to recover the tome and the two straightened up in unison, laughing.

As Charlie regained both his balance and his civility, he realized the burden was on his shoulders to right the wrong (if not a wrong, a stupidity).

"I'm so sorry," he said, trying to smile sheepishly, "I was wrapped up in my book. I'm so sorry."

"It's OK." His victim shrugged and then flashed a dazzling smile, "the risks of going to the library—we live in a dangerous world, you know."

"Yes," he said, half chuckling, "many risks, but an oaf scurrying from the building shouldn't be one of them. Let me buy you a cup of coffee or something to apologize."

"I really have to return my book, it's due today."

"No problem, please, let me take it, there's a return drop box just inside the door."

Without really waiting for his sufferer's response, Charlie grabbed the book, bolted through the door, and was back at the scene of the accident before the object of his attention completely realized what had just happened.

"Now," Charlie said, feigning nonchalance, as though nothing had happened, "please, there's a restaurant that makes a descent cup of coffee as well as being not-too-bad a bar just across the street and, at the very least, I can offer you a drink to try and sooth your near concussion."

"You seem to be most persistent," his possibly-wounded co-patron of the library announced with a barely concealed giggle, as the pair descended the steps of the atheneum, crossed Clayton and then Country Street, and entered the small bistro where Charlie often bought brown-bag-encased meals to take home.

They took a window booth and happily, when the waitress arrived, Charlie's guest ordered a beer. Charlie asked for the same and, as his companion looked out at the intermittent traffic on Clayton, he took a long look at the woman he had immediately judged as being strikingly handsome. He realized she was black. This was no shock. It was simply something that he had initially not noticed. He had only noticed nearly knocking down a woman. Now he saw he had nearly toppled a young black woman, a strikingly handsome, young, black woman. She didn't have a pale complexion that was blurred by the twilight. She had a beautiful—flawless he thought—ebony complexion that glowed in the reflections of Clayton Street.

Unabashedly, he found her gorgeous.

She shifted in her seat, noticing his stare, "Is everything alright?"

"Yes, yes, of course. Excuse me," he said, feeling more timid than he felt he should, "I should have introduced myself. My name is Charlie Stancik. Sorry to have smacked your head."

She smiled that dazzling smile again, raised her glass and simply said, "Cheers!"

When they had each taken a welcome gulp, she added, "My name is Jo McCormick—pleased to meet you, Charlie Stancik."

"I hope I'm not keeping you from important things."

"Nope," she said, again with that smile, "I'm basically home."

Charlie was visibly puzzled. "Home?"

"Yeah." She pointed across the street. "I've an apartment there."

"Wow! Me too."

"Small world."

"Very."

"So," she said, trying to bring some order to disorder, "what brings you to the not-so-active Waukegan?"

"I work at Spot On, ever heard of it?"

"Not really, but there's a lot of things here-about that I don't know much about."

"Well, they do a lot of different things. I work on logistics for their business in Canada."

"That's great. Been here long?"

"Not really. I was working in Chicago, and they asked me for an interview and before I knew it, I was here.

"How about you, been here long?"

"Well, I was kind of born here—in Chicago at least. I work at Midwest Bank just a block down on Madison Street."

"Sure, I've actually got my checking account there."

"Great. You're my customer."

"Yep."

"But it doesn't feel like you're originally from Chicago?"

"No. I was born out west and came here because I didn't want to work in a sawmill or on a potato farm."

"Makes sense."

"How about you—your family been on the shores of Lake Michigan long?"

"Well, I don't want to bore you, but my forebears were slaves in Virginia—on the McCormick Plantation. My surname comes from that root—like a label on a package. You may have heard of the International Harvester Company—especially if you know much about farming—the white McCormicks—not my McCormicks—are part of that. Cyrus Mc-Cormick and a slave named Jo Anderson did a lot of the work on the harvesting machinery they invented. When the machines were ready for manufacturing, part of the white McCormick family moved to Chicago to oversee the factories making the farm machines. They brought with them some of their slaves to do the work, among them my great grand-parents. So, my given name is from the slave who aided the master, and my family name is a reminder of the master's plantation. All pretty funny when you think about it."

Yet, there was no dazzling smile.

Charlie, realizing they were drifting close to somber subjects, tried to redirect. "So, as I've found out myself, this rather bland burg is quite a change from big city Chicago. How do you like it here?"

"Oh, it's fine," she said, giving just a glint of a smile, "it's my assignment, so to speak."

"Assignment?"

"Well, not really, I guess. I'd studied business and finance at Harry S. Truman College. When I finished, I entered a career development program at Midwest Bank. This is basically an apprenticeship that takes me through various parts of the bank's overall program with the intent that at the end I will be part of mid-management with a shot at senior management if the gods smile. I've really just started and am assigned to the loan department here in Waukegan. Who knows where I'll be tomorrow?"

"That's swell."

"Don't know about swell, but it's fine by me. I'm the first in my family to go to college, even if only a community college. I feel fortunate."

"I'm sure, as long as you avoid doofuses hurling themselves from the library, you'll do great."

This seemed to settle the dust. Their histories, spiced with herbs from their private gardens, were on the table. As underscored by Jo, they didn't know about tomorrow, and today, in spite of potential nonlethal cranial bruises, seemed to be OK.

After another beer, they agreed it was serendipity and, since they were neighbors, they should have dinner together in a week.

The dinner was a success.

⋀ ⋀ ⋀ ⋁ ⋀ ⋀ ⋀

There were more dinners. There were joint trips to the library. There were days spent on hikes in the lakeside nature preserves. There were days spent on trips to the city. And, inevitably, there were nights spent in (what turned out, to Charlie's supreme surprise) the heights of passion.

Jo and Charlie began sharing their lives—transforming their relationship more into "we" than "me."

This changed everything.

Work and striding across the water on Spot On's behalf continued, much within the established tempo of the day. But this was no longer center stage. For the first time, Charlie had a significant other and this consumed him.

Mihaela had been a very close friend. She had been someone with whom Charlie fantasized sharing his life completely. Yet, as they both had come to accept, she had steadfastly given her life to God in spite of how much she had grown to love Charlie. Fate had decreed parallel paths for them; Mihaela's ending in her terrible and premature parting.

Now, Charlie felt (and hoped), his path with Jo was much more intertwined—interwoven—much like the two lovers became in the fervor of their couplings.

Their relationship seemed to gain strength and deepen as the days passed.

Life far away from the lakebed seemed to be on track.

⋀ ⋀ ⋀ ⋁ ⋀ ⋀ ⋀

Not only, for the first time in his life, did Charlie have a serious job and a serious girlfriend, Charlie now had some money in his pocket. The pay for his job as a security guard, as many security jobs irrespective of their importance, Charlie thought, had been pretty feeble. Once he'd had to leave St. Mary's and move to Haddon Avenue, he'd been able to save little in spite of his frugal lifestyle.

Mid-West Calligraphs and Julian had been more generous but life in Melrose Park had also been more expensive. Although Charlie had been able to open a saving's account, his savings had still really only been a trifle.

Now, Charlie happily found, Spot On paid its operations assistants well. Salary had not really been one of the determinants when deciding to move to Waukegan. In fact, he had barely noticed the compensation and benefits offered. The want ad had said, "Salary and benefits package commensurate with experience." With his very limited experience, Charlie had not been sure what constituted "commensurate," but there was a salary. That was about all Charlie had cared to tease out when he had been deciding whether or not to take the job.

He realized he should have asked more questions and was grateful that he had been lucky enough to incautiously fall into a job with both good pay and good benefits—no thanks to his negotiating skills. With all the perks, he was banking a good sum at the end of each month. His initial $977 grubstake had grown many times over.

He was even now the full owner of a not-too-old Subaru Leone. His first year had passed unmarred. He was in good standing with Spot On. As promised, Sam had written off the initial loan.

Charlie felt as though he was moving into Middle America with all the necessary signs of membership. He was even accumulating personal effects that greatly exceeded the capacity of his small, soiled khaki cardboard suitcase, which he relegated to a back corner of the closet (with his diary and confirmation photo still inside)—a closet that no longer held the cheap suit his parents had bought at Penney's (which he had long since donated to Goodwill), but, in its place, held a collection of suitably stylish yet casual clothes appropriate for an Operations Assistant at Spot On.

Life far away from the lakebed seemed to be on track.

In fact, his days of late seemed to be doing so well that Charlie actually dug his neglected diary out of that well-worn dismissed suitcase and, after a long hiatus filled with doubt and uncertainty, wrote for the first time in a long time. He penned penetrating sentences reflecting a fresh optimism and passion. His dubious decision to flee the lakebed appeared to be bearing fruit—he hoped it would be savory and not spoil quickly.

Seeing the Forest for the Trees

C HARLIE RARELY SAW SAM.
Hank remained the fulcrum for Charlie's routine—the young assistant's tasks toggling between lake trips and shop work.

Then, unexpectedly, he was asked to stop by and meet Sam at the Waukegan Building.

Wonlyn greeted the still somewhat novice employee with a warm smile, motioning him directly into Sam's office.

"Thanks for coming so promptly," Sam said, smiling in turn, and directing Charlie to a chair in front of his desk, while he extended his hand for a vigorous shake. "You've been busy, and I haven't wanted to interrupt your work, but I felt we could do with a chat."

"It's good to see you," Charlie assured his boss, unsure whether or not he should be apprehensive.

"First off, I'm happy to tell you that everything is fine. Hank speaks well of you as do our Canadian partners. You reportedly handle your undertakings in the shop with ease and seem to work well with Tim as the two of you meet all the challenges the Lake has to offer."

"I'm glad everyone feels that way—I like my job," Charlie posited as, he felt, a rather inadequate rejoinder—questioning whether or not he should be addressing Sam as "sir."

"Well, I'm sure there're good days and bad—but you seem to manage them all in good form. So good, in fact, that we've been wondering if you'd like a change?"

Reflecting a bit about the reference to "we," Charlie almost instinctively answered, "Always looking for new things."

"Excellent. Now, as an operations assistant, as I've said, you've shown you're up to the job. However, we think in the near future we'll be having an opening for a company representative. This is a big step, and I don't want to push you."

"I'm willing to try anything," Charlie replied, still feeling his responses were lame, but unable to come up with the more glittering statements he felt the moment warranted—and still ruminating about the "we."

"Sure. However, we want to go slowly. Like I say, this is a big jump."

"Fine."

"So, what we're suggesting is that you represent us on a trip to Costa Rica. This actually might turn out to be more than one trip if things go well. Does that sound interesting?"

"Yes," Charlie said, this time with spontaneous effervescence, yet still hooked on the "we."

"Great. Let me provide a little background, then Wonlyn will help you with the details."

"Awesome."

"That first day we discussed, I told you Spot On was involved in a lot of things. I think you've now seen this firsthand in the shop and on your travels. We have a variety of products that pass through our shop and, as you've witnessed, we deliver to our partners a large assortment of items.

"What may not be evident from your experiences thus far is that we're truly involved in businesses worldwide. Some of the stuff you're helping transship through our shop or delivering to the Canucks comes from representatives far away in China, India, Iran, Russia, or anywhere. We really have alliances all across the globe.

"I say this, not to intimidate you, but to help you realize that you are an important part of a big group and that you may have the possibilities of becoming an even more important part.

"But I'd be remiss if I didn't highlight the fact that the more you move out into our global affairs, while your benefits increase proportionally, so does the responsibility. We are very careful about to whom we offer posts like those of being a company representative.

"We don't want to make mistakes or regret sloppy decisions. We really don't.

"Anyway, enough about the big picture. Getting to the specifics, here's what you need to know about the Costa Rica job; it relates to starting a dialogue with some local businessmen about us importing fish which would initially go to our processing plant about halfway between Austin and Forth Worth, Texas. We would move this product, if we can come to an arrangement, into a stream that supplies grocery stores and restaurants in the South and the Southeast. But the first step is just getting the folks to sit around the table and consider what we're offering.

"So, that's the panorama. Wonlyn will give you the files on the Texas facility, our targets in Costa Rica, as well as some details about the fish piece of our operations. She'll help you with your travel arrangements, too. Then, when all's set, you and I'll have another chat before you get on the plane. Sound OK?"

"Just fine," Charlie almost breathlessly acknowledged, being really taken aback as to how diversified Spot On appeared to be and how he now might be making a major move closer to the good life he sought.

$$\text{\large ʌ ʌ ʌ \lor ʌ ʌ ʌ}$$

After he had finished, spending another hour with Wonlyn making all the preparations, he carried the promised files to the car parked on Washing Street, just north the office. He realized, for the first time in his life, he needed a briefcase. This honestly amazed him. A briefcase for his work. Unbelievable.

Nonetheless, with this realization, he drove to a stationery and business supply store on Glen Flora to get kitted-up for his upcoming assignment in Costa Rica.

Evening was approaching when he got back into his Subaru with a band new, shiny black fiberglass *Samsonite* briefcase—they called it an attaché case. As it was too late to go back to the shop, Charlie decided to go to the corner takeout and get a bucket of spicy Louisiana fried chicken for their evening meal—the "their" being Jo and himself.

He and Jo had agreed some time back that it made no sense for them to occupy two apartments in the same building. It was daft. There- fore, since Jo was much better established, having more in her life than a cardboard suitcase and a cardboard box (although his personal stuff had considerably augmented over recent months), Charlie moved into her place and, much to his companion's joy, agreed to pay the rent if she paid the utilities.

Nonetheless, before her delight at their living arrangements took root, Charlie had to satisfy her concerns that he was not simply being transactional—that this was not the nascent businessman speaking but the honest lover who was most motivated by strengthening their relationship. Once reassured, their cohabitation blossomed as did their rapport and they could get to the serious business of satisfying their pleasures.

However, when Charlie told Jo about his Cost Rica assignment, the satisfaction, even the contentedness, was replaced by a dose of uneasiness. Jo was immediately cynical (maybe part of being a banker). What possible qualifications did Charlie have? He who spoke not one word of Spanish (she assured him "taco" did not qualify), who knew nothing about the fishing industry (catching trout in Spring Creek at home also did not qualify), who had never been on an airplane—what in the world was his boss doing sending him to Costa Rica?

Charlie had no answers. He could only relate to his significant other that this was, as far as Sam had told him, all part of some upward trajectory that was being arranged for him given his good record with the company. His specific qualifications indeed seemed lacking. But, as part of a bigger effort to move him up in the company, maybe it all made sense. He hoped so.

Jo could only accept the situation with the caveat that she was and would likely remain suspicious.

"When things seem too good to be true, they generally are," She reminded him. But she was unprepared for his reply.

"You're not."

"What?"

"You're too good and you're true." He smiled as he grabbed her about the waist, and they scurried off to the bedroom—thoughts of Costa Rica now gone from the present.

ʎ ʎ ʎ ∀ ʎ ʎ ʎ

A week or so later, Wonlyn called informing Charlie that all was ready, and that Sam wished to have the final briefing before Charlie set off on his big adventure (Wonlyn realizing how groundbreaking this was for the young man from the west).

As always, Sam was cordial and open. "Well Charlie, looks like everything is prepared for your trip."

"That's what Wonlyn's told me."

"I don't need to tell you again how important we feel this assignment is—we're all counting on you."

"I know," Charlie said, feeling he really should have ended with a "sir."

"So, I won't go over tilled soil. You get the picture."

"Sure do."

"Then, let me go over some of the details that were in one of your folders—like your attaché case though—good choice."

Charlie smiled, hopefully not embarrassingly.

"You know this is all about us getting good quantities of fish from Cost Rica to supply our customers here in the US. Demand is growing fast, and we need new sources."

Another smile from Charlie.

"We've been in discussion with the FNP—the *Federación National de Pesca*—the national fisheries association. They're the ones who have made most of the arrangements on the ground for your trip. They've organized the meeting in Quepos, about midway down the Pacific Coast side of the country. This location is, as I understand it, mostly for political reasons. There are actors from that area whose support we need, so they felt this was politically the best place for the first discussions.

"However, as you've read in the files, our idea is to build a packaging, and possibly processing, facility on the Gulf of Nicoya, south of El Roble, on the Rio Barranca—eighty miles north of Quepos but only about fifty miles west of the capital San José from where we can easily air freight some product even if other items go by sea. Local fish would be packed and, in some instances, processed for shipment to our Texas plant where they'd be prepared for various US retailers.

"This El Roble unit would ship products from the entire Pacific Coast." A somber Sam further elaborated, "And, we need the buy-in from the FNP. And they need the endorsement of the local fishing communities and other local organizations. We can take care of the high-level processes and approvals from here—we do it all the time. But to be able to move the local authorities, we need someone on the ground. That someone is you. You will be our voice—you will be our face. It's a lot. I assure you."

Charlie felt a smile was too much at this point, so he solemnly nodded.

"We understand this," Sam continued, this time the smile back on his face, "and we don't want to do too much too fast. Given the importance we attach to this venture, we want to go slowly but surely.

"The key at this time is for you to be seen and accepted as our representative. Again, we're not concerned about the upper echelons or about the association—we know how to handle them. Right now, we need to effectively reach out to the essential local personalities—both pro and con. If there are any con—and we hope not—we need to bring these folks on board. That's your main job.

"We've already set the stage for you.

"In the files you've seen the papers we've prepared—basically handouts in both English and Spanish—highlighting the advantages fishers would have selling to us. This is the drum you need to beat.

"We've already budgeted at least one more trip to Quepos to make sure all the bridges we need are built there and then some trips to El Roble to help build the foundation for our venture once you've forged the base—and we're confident you'll mold that critical base.

"This is really a quick trip—you should be back in three days. So, I don't want to spend more time in the briefing than you do on the beach. When you're back and can debrief me, we'll plan best how to move ahead. I know you'll do great."

After a little wrap-up chitchat, Charlie left the Waukegan Building feeling like he was getting ready to step on the Niña to begin a voyage to a yet-to-be-known new world. Still, as he walked to his car, he could hear Jo's suspicions whispered in his ears.

⋀ ⋀ ⋀ ⋁ ⋀ ⋀ ⋀

Jo's concerns aside, the day arrived for Charlie to get on his first airplane and to take his first international trip (at this point, he was more worried about falling from the sky than about being qualified to negotiate international fisheries agreements). He told himself, "Everybody's gotta start somewhere."

Spot On had generously booked first class, so this made the day all that more special.

From O'Hare he flew to Minneapolis where he took Delta's flight to San José. After clearing immigration and customs, he boarded a local Skyway flight to his Quepos.

Although he couldn't explain it, and in spite of the fact that, en route, his stomach had frequently jumped up into his throat, the planes managed to stay in the air and even land without shattering to bits. Somehow, amazingly, air travel worked.

With a sigh, he realized he had reached his destination.

Wonlyn had booked him at the Hotel Mares Azures, two miles south of town on highway 618 toward Parque National Manuel Antonio. This was also to be the venue for the meeting. She had reserved a small meeting room for the next day including arranging for coffee and lunch—Wonlyn had done everything.

Charlie had little to do other than connect the dots—all had been organized to the smallest detail. He was meeting with members of the FNP for dinner when they would review the specific actions for the next day.

As laid out in the agenda in the meeting's document package (prepared by Wonlyn), FNP would open the meeting and introduce the participants. There were fishers and processors. There were fish farmers from Lake Arenal. There were folks from several environmental NGOs—ecotourism, as Charlie was witnessing firsthand, was a really big thing in Costa Rica and any activity like fisheries had to at least cosmetically contact those who saw themselves as Nature's stewards. There were community groups including missionaries. All in all, it was a very diverse assemblage.

After the introductions and a few words by Charlie, already crafted by Wonlyn and in his folder (of course), the meeting would be chaired by FNP. The handouts would be handed out (Charlie noting from the example being discussed and with little surprise, the small logo of Mid-West Calligraphs in the lower righthand corner), coffee would be served, pleasantries would be exchanged, followed by a gourmet lunch. Then, on full stomachs and after ample servings of wine for those partaking, the group would be asked to make any comments before endorsing the strategy outlined in the handouts, and to schedule a follow-up meeting in two months.

It all went to plan. And, thought Charlie, as he tried to appear attentive to the exchanges in Spanish, why shouldn't it. It had all been meticulously planned. He was, as had been foreshadowed, simply the corporeal representation of the cloaked powers pulling the strings—his strings too, as he was learning, being delicately maneuvered. The puppet masters had it well in hand. And, from what he'd seen in the papers distributed on behalf of Spot On, why shouldn't they. They were prepared to offer twenty percent higher prices for fish delivered to their new El Roble facility as long as they met company criterion: at least one-and-a-half pounds individual whole weight and being certified fresh. What was there to complain about? The fish were already being caught or raised. This was just another sales option for those involved at the bottom of the supply chain. It seemed to make perfect sense; sell for the highest prices.

ᐱᐱᐱᐁᐱᐱᐱ

During lunch, Charlie found himself straddled by a little-over-middle-aged couple—a couple from America (Charlie thought of them as fellow Americans yet later the FNP Treasurer reminded them all that they all were Americans from the Americas). Obviously, whomever, probably Wonlyn, when making the seating plan, had known that Charlie would best be able to communicate with native English speakers.

There were opening mechanical greetings with his lunchmates, the couple thanking Charlie, nearly unwillingly, for traveling all this way to meet with them. They introduced themselves as April and Mark—Charlie would later learn, April and Mark Volman—Baptist missionaries from up the Rio Naranjo in Londres, a small community about ten miles to the east. They had, in their own words, "Been here forever."

Mark seemed to endure the discomfort of the lunch with an ascetic stoicism only possible with deep and abiding faith. April initially attempted to mirror her husband's malaise, but slowly melded into the forced camaraderie of the moment as her wine consumption increased under the disapproving eye of her spouse. By the time coffee was served with *bananes flambée* and vanilla ice cream, she was primed to try some conversation with the young outsider.

"You know," she said, smiling and showing uneven and none-too-bright teeth, "when you serve the bananas and the ice cream like this, it's called *Bananes Foster.*"

"I didn't know that," Charlie said, trying his utmost to be sociable.

"Ahh, you see, you can come to far-off Quepos and learn new things." She appeared to almost taunt him.

"I'm sure. I'm sure the two of you could really teach me a great deal about this area. As a first-timer, I really know so little," Charlie parried.

"Indeed," she said, seeming wistful, "we've been here a while."

Then, bit by bit, she recounted the short version of their story—her husband looking to be in another world.

Mark had grown up in El Dorado Springs, Missouri. April was from Myrtle, in Oregon County, right on the Arkansas border. They had met at a Greyhound bus station. After a short courtship, they had married, and Mark had been ordained in the denomination of a pious community in Springfield through the American Baptist Conclave. Soon after ordination, they had decided their calling was to bring God's Word to those most in need. The fledgling missionaries had been assigned to the small parish in Londres. And there they had stayed. They had had four children—all boys. As their home congregation in Springfield assumed no direct responsibilities for the education of their missionaries' children, once their boys finished local primary school, Mark and April had sent their offspring back to Missouri to various extended family members who oversaw their continued education where they could speak English and learn how to become real Americans. All four were now married with children. Luke was an insurance salesman in Sumner. John had a hardware store in Warrenburg. Mat was a schoolteacher in Farmington. And, praise God, Paul, whose stateside home had been in Gravois Mills, was now, with his lovely wife Lynn, a Baptist missionary in Africa—in Ghana. With God's blessing, it even looked like their son, Peter, would follow in their footsteps, too.

"We are so proud. Paul wrote to us when Peter was born, saying how thankful and blessed he felt that he had been able to, 'grow up in the Garden of Eden with parents who were, by the Grace of God, clairvoyant and virtuous.' We have all truly been blessed. We only hope we are able to share these God-given blessing with our parishioners in Londres."

It was part biography, part sermon, and Charlie was not really sure how to classify this latest load of information amongst the onslaught of new data rapidly overloading his brain. He wasn't totally sure why the Volmans were there. He guessed there must be some fishermen and probably some artisanal processors in their village, but they were definitely not big actors on the scene. Still, they certainly were not there for the free lunch and Mark unquestionably was not there for the ambiance—he remained immersed in his own world while April, evidently fatigued by her allocution and possibly out from under her spouse's deprecating glare as he appeared totally disenfranchised, concentrated on her now refilled wine glass.

After the meeting had validated all the proposals, strategies, and plans, Charlie noticed the couple from Missouri had already left—possibly, Charlie thought, seeking the refuge of their refuge.

For his part, Charlie retired to the hotel bar with the FNP members to do the postmortem. There had been no major stumbles. As an initial step, there was, at the very least, muted support for Spot On's proposition. Charlie scratched the highlights on a legal pad from his still shiny attaché case as a precursor to the debriefing notes he'd have to prepare for Sam. He and the FNP agreed that the next meeting would be held at the same place and, if there was still no organized opposition, they'd move up to El Roble for the third gathering.

It was all straightforward.

∧∧∧∨∧∧

Charlie got back to Waukegan still incredulous that planes could fly.

He debriefed a very satisfied Sam who said they'd do future planning at a later date and then spontaneously gave Charlie a week off to celebrate his good work.

Charlie and Jo managed to find ways to spend the unexpected and gratefully received free time, rarely leaving the apartment—Jo (miffed at still having to go to work and not able to fully spend this unanticipated respite wrapped in her lover's arms) obviously relieved that Charlie had not been whisked away into the forest or held hostage as a rich American.

After a week thinking not at all of Spot On, but trying to be spot on in terms of his attentiveness to Jo, Charlie was back briefing Sam.

Hearing the whole story, although he'd already had corroborating reports directly from Costa Rica and doubtless knew the ending before the story was even told, Sam was upbeat.

"You did well. Looks like we're on schedule. You'll need to think about getting back there in about seven weeks for the next get-together. Right now, though, I'd say you should work with Wonlyn and prepare the minutes of this meeting—things as you see them. Nothing too elaborate, just the main points we want to stress. You need to add a list of all who attended. I'll go over it all and then Wonlyn will have it translated into Spanish. We'll print it bilingually and then you will need to send this final version of the report and a thank-you note to each participant. That'll keep you busy for a while."

"Fine," Charlie said, smiling at his boss, "but one minor point. I'm no Gore Vidal nor James Michener (Charlie choosing authors not from his Mihaela's List, as he thought of it, but from the shelf of new releases at the library). It's been sometime since I left school and had to think about writing much of anything. It's not that this is a problem. I'm happy and ready to do it. It's just that I don't think that the shop is the right place to write—and you don't seem to have an extra office here."

"Good point. I'll need to look into it," Sam reacted with apparently total understanding.

"If it's OK," Charlie continued, feeling he had an opening, "while you're looking for the best place for me to work, may I suggest that I start by working at the library. It's just across the street from my apartment, as you probably know, and it'll be quiet and comes already with a dictionary."

"Another good point," Sam said, not feeling manipulated, "go ahead and work there until I have other arrangements. We really don't want our staff working full-time in public spaces like that—not good for the image, you know. But for the immediate, it's fine. I'll call you when I've made some arrangements. Better still," Sam said, reaching into a drawer in his desk, extending his hand to Charlie, "take this—it's something new—at least new to me—it's a 'pager.' So, they say, it rings or vibrates or something to let you know I'm trying to reach you and then you can call into the office to get an update. This'll be just the ticket. Go ahead and get started at the library and I'll, 'page you,' as they say, to let you know when I've managed to make more suitable arrangements."

This all seemed fine to Charlie.

He could sleep in with Jo, whom he constantly reminded kept bankers' hours. They would have an extra hour or so in bed in the morning to better prepare for the day. Then, for the day, he'd be just across the street in the library and could meet Jo for lunch as well as be home to get a start on an early dinner.

This was not to say Charlie did not have work to do nor that he wasn't serious about the tasks at hand. Every evening, he arranged things in his attaché case so that, as soon as Jo left for the bank, he'd shower and get to the library with several yellow legal pads—some full of notes, others with drafts of letters to go over with Wonlyn.

This was a major shift. Heretofore, he'd been doing much more physical work (or at least non-mental work, as being a night guard wasn't really all that physical). Now it was entirely mental work—something he thought he'd left at home when he'd left the lakebed. And now all those useless high school classes were beginning to take on a different form— were beginning to have some real value.

In addition to exercising his mind, he was exercising the relationship he was building with Jo—and she was building with him. More time together doing all sorts of things meant more highs and lows shared as a couple—more patience, more tolerance, more love.

Working close to home had its advantages.

ᛟᛟᛟᛉᛟᛟᛟ

It was about two weeks before Sam paged him. Charlie called in and made an appointment to see his boss as soon as possible.

Sam thought he had good news—Charlie was not so sure.

As Charlie had undoubtedly surmised, Sam reminded him once his young hireling was comfortably seated in his sixth-floor office, Spot On was one of a large family of companies that were linked to Robin McCandless (Charlie remarked, this was the first time he recalled the powerful man from Crab Tree Lane being emphatically mentioned—most often, he was an inscrutable omnipresence but rarely referred to by name). Indeed, Sam unnecessarily pointed out, it was through Robin McCandless that he and Charlie had first met. Well, Mr. McCandless (Charlie noting that for some reason it now was Mr. and not Robin) was involved in a number of firms in the vicinity of Waukegan (Charlie a bit uncomfortable at the curious pains Sam was taking to provide background—maybe this unusually rambling soliloquy from the generally straight-talking manager did not bode well?). One of the family activities involved a rather small and select legal office in the community of Downey that focused on commercial law as it related to imports and exports. In fact, this office was less than five miles away, to the South, in the direction of the city.

As these guys were lawyers, Sam further explained (Charlie somewhat more assured—possibly this was all just prating legalese), they had a cluster of small meeting rooms where they could engage their clients. It had been arranged (no question as to the arranger) that Charlie could use one of these spaces for the time being. It'd take another week for them to organize for Charlie's security badge, as access to the building was controlled by a private security company (something Charlie knew all about, Sam added with a wink). So, week after next, Charlie should be ready to go straight to Downey and the law offices of Saphir and Spader where he'd collect his security pass and any other needed items at the door (Charlie settled back—hopefully all's well that ends well).

Another new twist to his story. Sometimes Charlie wondered what type of tapestry he was weaving for himself. There seemed few common threads.

ᛟᛟᛟᛉᛟᛟᛟ

Jo's misgivings continued. Her feelings for Charlie were deepening and expanding. She was loath to try and classify or cubbyhole these emotions. For her, they were new and bittersweet. She hoped she was investing in a relationship and a person who would be a stark contrast to most of her previous interactions where she had, more times than not, come away feeling at the very lease used, and often abused as well as racially slurred.

Charlie did seem different.

Maybe it was, as he often made reference, due to his early unpolished and disengaged life on the lakebed. Maybe he had acquired some sort of untarnished character that had not, or not yet, been sullied by the realities of struggling to survive among the throngs of the Midwest.

Things had not been easy for the Chicago McCormicks. But, Jo reconciled, things had never been easy for the black McCormicks—unlike their white namesakes. She had second cousins in the south and their daily life was often a battle of trying to lift the weight of centuries of mistreatment and neglect.

Many of the same negatives could be applied to Chicago. Yet, she guessed it was better. She knew it could always be worse.

In the end, it could all get a lot worse. Things were not all that bad.

Jo liked her work and seemed to be on an upward trajectory. Growing up poor had imprinted on her psyche that she'd always be far away from "big money." Now she worked in a bank. Her family was doing fine, too.

Her mother, Cecily, still lived in the family home in Chicago. The home where she and her husband had raised five children through the, she guessed, normal pains and joys of having a family.

Jo's father had died ten years ago, taken by a massive heart attack just as he was starting to think about retiring from his backbreaking city maintenance job. This added to the sorrow of having lost their firstborn— a brilliant daughter who had died of measles at the age of five.

The rest of Jo's siblings were scattered to the winds. One brother was in the military and another was a policeman in New York City. While both brothers were single, her older sister was married and a schoolteacher in Oakland.

Charlie seemed to take sincere interest in Jo's family and its story. While he rarely spoke of his own, he thoughtfully often asked his inamorata about her mother, brothers, and sister. They had gone three times to visit Cecily and the now aging lady who was still the dignified head of the family seemed to take no notice of Charlie's race or origins. She quite simply seemed to like him and immediately accept him as part of her growing family unit—her older daughter having just had twins.

Things could be worse.

Charlie was attentive and loving. While, like she, he enjoyed (possibly just a wee bit too much) a glass or three of beer, he had few bad habits. He was considerate. He was hard working. And, if he wasn't out of town, he was home every night.

Jo's worries were not about Charlie the person—they were about Charlie, the employee of Spot On. After all, who calls their company Spot On?

These trips to Canada and Costa Rica just didn't smell right. And, from what Charlie said, there was more travel in store. Growing up (unlike Charlie, she assured herself), she'd been exposed to enough of the wrong people (as her mother called them) to get a feel for things—to recognize that when the hair on the back of her neck stood up, it wasn't for nothing.

When she thought of Spot On and the shadowy Robin McCandless, of whom Charlie occasionally spoke in very ambiguous terms, her hairs became electric.

So, with doubts about tomorrow, she could only live in today.

Charlie acknowledged Jo's concerns. If he were honest with himself, he could not disregard them as totally unfounded. From various vantage points, there did appear to be a mismatch between his skills and experience and the jobs he was being offered—just as there was between his earning's record and his current compensation.

For Charlie, it was a choice: don't turn over too many stones too fast. Like on the lakebed, you might find a scorpion and it might sting you.

Pots of gold were found by looking to the horizon.

To Charlie, his horizon looked pretty damn good—good job, good money, great girl. What more was there?

Step over, don't turn over, the stones. Hence, Charlie took a big step and, as scheduled, showed up at Saphir and Spader. There were no surprises.

He obtained all he needed to be able to work in one of the small meeting rooms—nicely appointed spaces that were more comfortable and definitely calmer than working in the library (although, he lamented, no longer just across the street from his apartment).

There was soon a new cycle of activity where he would stop by to update work with Wonlyn twice week before going to Downey and scribble and re-scribble pages of notes, letters, and minutes while also making arrangements, with Wonlyn's close guidance, for his next trip south.

Before he knew it, but thankfully when he was at least prepared, the trip south came up on his calendar.

This time it felt like almost immediately after kissing Jo goodbye, he was back in the Hotel Mares Azures—this time no wonder about how planes flew. Truly, he was now a seasoned traveler.

Following discussions with Sam, one of his priorities of this trip was to meet with the Volmans. Sam felt strongly that community buy-in was critical to garner the needed political support in view of the competitive landscape that was Costa Rican fisheries. He was banking on the Volmans to be the catalyst for this support.

While the country was over three-quarters Catholic, there was an important and influential Evangelical segment of the population—a politically significant segment. Sam's hopes were that the Volmans themselves, or as an entry point, could bring key members of this group onboard. Through logic or flattery, Charlie needed to get the Volmans' backing.

To get some quality time with the possibly sullen couple (Charlie's first impressions), Charlie had written the missionaries, courteously asking if he could visit them before the second meeting kicked off.

Wonlyn had arranged for a rental car for this assignment.

Then, as confirmed, Charlie drove to Londres for lunch with the couple, meeting them at the rectory next door to their modest tin-roofed Baptist church.

The greetings were, at least on the part of the hosts, staid—more like unavoidably meeting the tax collector than welcoming a fellow countryman. It was effectively as though they had never met.

After a tepid shaking of hands and being ushered into a sparsely furnished living room, Charlie felt he needed to try and warm things up.

"So happy to see you again, I hope you're both well," he said.

"We're fine," Mark rejoined without a smile.

"I was so happy to have met you on my first trip," Charlie said, gallantly trying to maneuver, "when I told my colleagues in Illinois that I had meet an American couple who knew so much about Costa Rica, they encouraged me to reach out to you and benefit as much as possible from your wisdom."

The riposte seemed to have missed its mark. The pastor seemed to have already transcended into some ethereal zone above the living room—disconnected. April managed a weak smile and intoned, "We are glad to see you again. But I confess we're not too clear about why you came all this way to see us?"

The quick trip to Londres didn't feel like "all that way," but regardless, Charlie deemed, as in his first encounter with the couple, he would have to engage the wife and hope she would in some way impact on her spouse.

He tried to prod the conversation.

"Well Mrs. Volman, as you so eloquently explained to me the other time over lunch, you are pillars of the community here and we feel that our proposal for exporting Costa Rican fish would start a project that would create jobs and bring money into communities. We'd really like your support and I personally wanted to meet you before tomorrow's meeting to see if you had any questions."

"Oh, lunch," April said, seeming almost shocked, "indeed, you've come for lunch. Marie has it all ready to go, I think. Let me go check."

She scurried to the kitchen while her husband appeared to be counting the revolutions of the ceiling fan that silently rotated above them mixing hotter upper air with the already sultry, ground-level breeze.

With stunning speed, it was over. Charlie was driving back to the Mares Azures. April had served Marie's chicken and rice with fruit salad for dessert after an incredibly lengthy and twisted blessing by Mark. There had been little conversation—no meaningful exchanges. Once the fruit was finished, with no coffee in spite of the country's production of excellent Arabica (the country reportedly having a law prohibiting the production of anything but the highest quality coffee beans), Mark announced he had to work on his sermon while April was needed to assist Marie with some visits to sick parishioners. It was over.

ᴧ ᴧ ᴧ ᴠ ᴧ ᴧ ᴧ

Back at the Hotel Mares Azures, Charlie had a rendezvous for dinner with Manuel, no relation to the national park's namesake. This Manuel was the president of the FNP. They strategized and prepared the final agenda for the next day's meeting.

Over coffee, as the serious matters had been addressed, Charlie let curiosity into the conversation.

"How does a predominantly Catholic country feel about Baptist missionaries?" Charlie asked.

"Well," Manuel offered, with a wry smile, "we generally don't like them. We've a long history of what we might consider as foreign intervention—from the secular to the spiritual. We've also a long history with the Catholic Church and Her agents who have always come and continue to come in large numbers from outside our borders.

"These fathers, brothers, and sisters, however, tend to be here first and foremost to render services. They have schools and hospitals—they even have garages and carpentry shops. They, unlike or perhaps because of their predecessors, the original gruesome Catholic conquistador interlopers, seem, if one can generalize, to want to show God's way through good acts and kind deeds—not so much through easy words, sharp reprimands, and long sermons.

"To the contrary, the Protestants, the Baptists—mostly from our Big Uncle from the North, loudly proselytize—they harangue. Paternalistic and condescending, they treat us as though we know nothing. We have no culture. We have no thoughts. We have no salvation. We can only achieve a good life—a life of their God—when we follow the ways they adamantly prescribe. This may sound rough, but from my seat as a resident spectator, it is true.

"Yet, having said all this—more than I normally would—I will add that the Volmans are different. They're more like Catholics—though I could never tell them that.

"They seem to really want to help—to really make a difference. They have been very helpful to local fishermen. They have established trust and are important to our work."

In light of Manuel's insight, Charlie hoped he had laid the needed foundation with the missionaries from Londres. He had certainly left their home with a large dose of uncertainty as to how they saw him and his assignment. He didn't know if he had been able to set the hook (never having been much of a fisherman himself).

The next day, it seemed Charlie had done his job well. The meeting was a success. Plans were moving ahead quickly.

ᛗ ᛗ ᛗ ᚢ ᛗ ᛗ ᛗ

With equal rapidity, it seemed, Charlie was back on his plane heading to O'Hare. The meeting had gone well. There were no serious opposing opinions. A third session of the main parties in two months, this time in El Roble where the site of the proposed new trans-shipment facility would be visited, was endorsed by all. During the meeting's open discussion period, Mark, to Charlie's dismay, had stood up and said it looked like the new project was a good idea that might even be good for the village fisheries of Londres—not much, but more than expected.

The centerpiece of the gathering had been, unbeknownst to Charlie, but as arranged by the FNP, the inputs from a senior officer from the Department of Environment and Energy, one of the chief agencies responsible for Costa Rican fisheries. This august personage, as he was introduced, assured those assembled of the government's support for the proposed export of fishery products for processing or repackaging in Texas. The high-level civil servant was most enthusiastic about the new possibilities, although he failed to mention the healthy sum Spot On had contributed to his current account—a fact that Charlie only learned some time after his return.

Nevertheless, Charlie did return to accolades from Sam and, after a respite, more paperwork to take care of in the small cubbyhole at Saphir and Spader. There were more minutes and letters to draft, and a third trip to plan. The wheels appeared to be turning and they appeared to be turning more easily with each revolution—today's work less challenging than yesterday's.

⚔ ⚔ ⚔ ⚔ ⚔ ⚔

Jo's worries no longer included her concerns about Charlie's know-how as a traveler or even an outsider working in Spanish-speaking areas—he'd shown he was apt and enjoyed the travel. Still, the overarching matter of his position with Spot On continued to gnaw at her subconscious. These trepidations were, however, pushed back as she enjoyed Charlie's presence during another post-trip week-long home vacation offered by Sam—a vacation when she had to pry herself from the bliss and ardor of the bedroom to make it to the bank each day.

Still, her cyclical disquiet continued as Charlie made more visits to Cost Rica. Each time he returned, Sam blessed them with a week to themselves while Charlie gushed about all the stupendous things he'd seen and done. Jo began to see it as the new pattern of their common life, overlying her work at the bank like a gossamer curtain.

Her restlessness ebbed and flowed as Charlie flew back and forth to Central America. When the arrangements for the fish export channels firmed, Sam had Charlie, now a known presence in Costa Rica, look into other areas of investment. More travel and more responsibility translated into raises and she was hard-pressed to complain about their lifestyle and her ability to invest more of her earnings as Charlie's growing income was more than enough for their combined needs.

Jo was just on the verge of concluding that her overactive imagination was simply that, and there was no justification for her uneasiness, when Charlie was invited (more convoked, she thought) to meet with Robin McCandless. The hair on the back of her neck was fully upright.

When Charlie had returned from his most recent trip south, after debriefing Sam, his boss informed him that Mr. McCandless had been following all his work in Costa Rica and would like to meet with him to thank him for his efforts. Mr. McCandless hoped (Charlie knew it was a little more than hope) that Charlie would be able to have a drink with him at Crab Tree Lane on Saturday afternoon.

At the appointed time, as the first time when Charlie had visited, the doorbell was answered by a liveried servant who silently ushered him to the patio, encircling the large swimming pool, where his host was seated comfortably under a parasol, wearing a candy-striped seersucker shirt above neatly pressed khakis, and highly polished penny loafers. Charlie thought he looked for all the world like the international businessmen he saw congregating around the hotel swimming pools in Costa Rica—but this one was different. As he approached Robin McCandless, Charlie could almost feel the power radiating from the smiling older man who was getting to his feet to warmly greet his young agent.

"*Buenas tardes mi joven amigo, bienvenido a mi humilde hogar y a las orillas de mi pequeña piscina. Por favor tome asiento,*" his host offered.

Charlie was no linguist, not by any stretch of the imagination, but by now he had been in Costa Rica often enough to recognize language that flowed—Robin's flowed.

"Thank you, sir. It is so kind of you to see me this afternoon," Charlie nearly feebly replied.

"So first," the owner of the palace interjected, "let me get you something cool—it's hot, but, of course, not as insufferable as in many of those slipshod places you've recently visited."

Robin raised his hand ever so slightly and from some secreted bower another liveried employee appeared, acknowledging his master's sign and disappearing only to return in minutes with a chilled aluminum tumbler topped with a sprig of mint.

"Please try our house mint juleps—they're really special." Robin practically beamed.

As Charlie sipped the frosted drink, enjoying the sweetened burn of the bourbon, his commander continued, "Well lad, you've done a smack-up job down there in Costa Rica—my guys in Texas are gearing up for all those fish that'll be coming their way.

"We're really happy with your work."

Charlie smiled around the edge of his tumbler.

"We're happy enough, in fact, to think about maybe offering you something new. How does that sound?"

"Sir," Charlie said, mustering his thoughts already being tickled by the healthy dose of spirits, "that sounds fine."

"Fine indeed," Robin said, forging forward, "I realize you already appreciate very well that Spot On is quite diversified—you've been on assignments from Canada to Central America. But let me tell you, lad, Spot On is only one tiny cog of a great wheel that is turning across the globe. My principals and I are very active—we are everywhere, and we do everything."

Robin let this sink in.

Charlie nodded around his sprig of mint.

"This is not the time nor the place, lad, to go into all the details—why it'd take the whole rest of the weekend for me to just sketch the most general outline.

"Suffice to say that with all these things going on, there's ample opportunity for people who're willing to work hard, who have imagination, and who can follow orders."

Charlie smiled.

"Are you such a person, lad?"

"Oh yes, sir!" Charlie could almost taste his piece of the pie.

"Fine." Robin's pink jowls seemed to glow as the sun followed its trajectory, reflecting off the pool. "So, here's what I propose. You'll stay with Sam for another three months to wrap up all your projects and give him time to find a replacement. Then I'd like to offer you some work at one of Spot On's sister businesses, J. P. Thorne. Is this OK?"

Before Charlie could reply, at an unnoticeable signal from Robin, another mint julep appeared—Charlie having quickly drained the first goblet, the palliative's fingers tickling his brain with increasing speed. Exchanging the tumblers, Charlie could only interrupt the nearly numbing sensation enough to mumble, "Wonderful."

"Fine, lad. Now I want to be upfront with you. Just like now with Sam, you don't need to know everything—things are very complicated, like I've said. And, by their nature, entangled things require special means to untangle them. We do the job. We are real handymen—as I like to think of us. We're very good at what we do. We fix things. We're involved in a multitude of highly diversified and scattered activities— far more than those simply involving Thorne. Still, Thorne's portfolio is truly complex. The company reaches out to a wide variety of people in a wide variety of places. A number of these activities might be considered by some as distasteful—a critic might even call some improper. This, of course, all depends on how you see things. This does not involve you. You need to know that, if you take this position, you agree to do as asked— understanding that we're always doing things as we see best. Others may disagree. Others may try to worry or even threaten you. You need to ignore all but your direct Thorne colleagues. They're the handymen. This is important. Do you see any problems?"

Charlie offered a syrupy, "Nope."

"Now," his host said, his mane of ivory hair slipping over his forehead, "here's what you also do need to know—much more pleasant material, I assure you. Thorne is in Libertyville—so you're still in Illinois and still in the same neighborhood. However, I think you'll want to leave your apartment in Waukegan—it's just no longer suitable—you've outgrown it. So, to help out, we'll assist you in finding and financing a home closer to work. We'll also help you scale up so you can get rid of that old Subaru. Seem reasonable?"

Charlie was shocked. He could only provide a gurgly, "Awsome."

"Well, lad, you can discuss all this with that lady of yours and you'll have plenty of time to study the lay of the land since you'll stay with Sam for a while longer."

Charlie had no idea how Robin knew about Jo. But at the moment he was overcome by mint juleps and career changes.

⚜ ⚜ ⚜ ⚜ ⚜ ⚜

Charlie returned to the corner of Country and Clayton Street to find Jo had been busy preparing for his homecoming from the dubious *Chez Mc-Candless* (as she thought of it in a rather unflattering way)—any outward signs of her fretting, at least for the moment, replaced by an elegantly set table with candles and wine. After a delicious meal of *coq au vin* accompanied by Caesar salad and topped off by tiramisù, a hot shower *à deux* to wash away any crumbs, some rambunctious bedroom gymnastics to help the digestion, and cognac and coffee, Charlie told Jo all about his meeting with Robin.

Charlie was not fully aware of Jo's concerns—he was certainly unaware of the depth of these worries. Nonetheless, he instinctively knew that the subjects of work in general, and Robin McCandless in particular, were delicate and, at least to some degree, stressful. He understood intuitively that his relationship with Jo would have been simpler if he had been a teacher at North Elementary School up on Franklin Street. As Robin (or should he think of him as Mr. McCandless?) had said repeatedly—things were complicated.

For her part, Jo, although by her nature open and forthright (to a fault), had not shared with Charlie the full level of her anxiety. After all, she herself teetered back and forth as to how serious this issue really was when unwrapped of all the emotions and puzzlement in which the topic was entangled. Her reactions were based mostly on suspicion in her gut. This, in and of itself, made her uncomfortable. She wanted, however, to react based on analyses of her brain.

She had forced herself to evaluate her relationship with Charlie cerebrally and not reflexively. She had methodically assessed their differences in ethnicity, geography, education, and personality. She had weighted their compatibility, both in the bedroom and elsewhere in and out of the apartment. She had carefully reviewed their time together. And, from her brain (and her heart) she had concluded they were good together. She had concluded she loved him, and he loved her.

Yet, she could still not reconcile the distress in her gut when she thought about her better half's choice of a career and the associates and associations that were buried there-in. Things were out of sync.

Now, as Charlie recounted in detail his exchanges with Robin—the new the job, the new house, the new car—the hair on her neck was upright.

On the surface, it was wonderful news, moving up in many ways. But it was out of sync. What was the real agenda? She couldn't know.

Charlie was a good guy. He was a hard worker. He communicated well. He was likable. All traits that had drawn him to her, after all. So, why shouldn't others appreciate and even encourage these same traits?

Her brain reminded her this was the upwardly mobile career of a young man who had been investing years of his life in getting to the top. This was simply the next step.

Her gut knotted. The shadows were too dense. There was too much obscurity. Charlie's boss of bosses had said things were complicated— that things might even be improper. Where was this leading?

∧∧∧∨∧∧

Priming the pump of conspiracies was, however, not getting Jo nor Charlie anywhere. Charade, villainy, or good fortune, Jo realized there was truly no choice. Charlie would go ahead—he had to go ahead. He could go alone, or she could go with him. But go he would.

And, the ever-pragmatic Jo concluded, this new path to explore was a new path for Charlie. She would keep working at the bank. She would follow her career while still being there for Charlie if and when he needed her—her own ambitions much more modest and, she hoped, levelheaded than Charlie's.

She would stay grounded. She would keep a handhold on realism— following her brain (while listening to her heart). Nevertheless, things were changing, and she often felt she was losing her grip.

Still, there was the bank and the bank seemed resolute—a solid cornerstone for her (possibly, for both of them). However, now, instead of walking to work, she would drive the ten miles or so from Libertyville— this facilitated by Charlie giving her his Subaru as he had already co-signed with Thorne for a new, bright-red BMW.

Slowly, almost in spite of her attempts at objectivity, the unsettled feelings from Jo's gut were pushed further to the background. It appeared as though the good times had really arrived (for better or worse). After viewing a number of homes in the Libertyville area highlighted by Thorne's staff, they chose a beautiful three-bedroom split-level on a large, forested lot on Forest Knoll Road in Knollwood, less than five miles east of Thorne's offices—the mortgage covered by Thorne.

For Jo, it was nearly a dream come true, a big, magnificent home in the suburbs. What more could she want?

Good Life

I T MAY OR MAY not have been a dream come true, but it was a time filled with lots to do. There was a new house to transform into a home. They had no furniture. But, to their welcome surprise, Thorne had an account at a local furniture store where they could purchase items at a special reduced price—amazingly, a price that seemed to be a fraction of the normal retail ticket.

These same special-price arrangements popped up for all their house-related matters—carpeting, curtains, appliances. Everything was marvelously available at below bargain-basement prices.

Then, with no clear explanation, but to her great joy, Jo was promoted, jumping several steps, named branch manager at the Mundelein Midwest branch on Seymore Avenue—just five miles from Thorne's offices on Lakeshore Drive, on the shores of St. Mary's Lake.

This was all great. Yet, in those dark hours after midnight, after hugging Charlie as he fell into a sound sleep, Jo would stare into the nothingness over their bed, pondering if they were blessed or cursed. All this special treatment certainly did not happen randomly. The gods had not just decided to smile upon them. There was a hand on the tiller, and it was not their own. She felt they had entered uncertain, if not dangerous ground.

ΛΛΛVΛΛ

Charlie seemed untouched by their apparent serendipity. Things were, as he saw it, rolling out as planned.

His final months with Sam and Wonlyn and Spot On had been uneventful. He had made one last trip to Costa Rica. He had logged his reports and settled all accounts. It was straightforward. Sam had obviously been apprised. He was helpful and grateful for Charlie's good work on behalf of Spot On.

The morning the door at Spot On closed, the door at J. P. Thorne opened.

That first morning, Charlie was met at reception by Wilson Watkins.

"Mr. Charles Stancik?" the bespectacled slender man a few years older than Charlie enquired as Thorne's newest employee crossed the threshold into what was to be his new job—the new center of his life.

"Charlie, please."

"Fine. Charlie. I'm Wilson—Wilson Watkins. I'm here to introduce you to J. P. Thorne LLC. Please follow me."

It was all very formal, very practiced as Wilson led Charlie into an ornately appointed, glassed-in conference room just off the reception.

As Charlie took his seat, his still shiny attaché case at his side, a middle-aged rather stern lady entered behind Wilson.

"This is Martha, she's the receptionist but also one of the key people in the office, stay on her good side," Wilson informed Charlie with a toothy smile.

As Charlie stood and greeted the gray-haired and almost overweight lady, she took his hand in a firm grip, and asked, "Would you like tea or coffee?"

"Please to meet you. Coffee please. Black."

After the coffee had arrived, accompanied by a plate of mini pastries, and when Martha had retreated behind the marble screen of her niche, Wilson slid a folder across the highly polished oak table, "You've probably seen these already (Charlie hadn't). They're all the documents relating to your position here—salary, benefits, NDA—nondisclosure agreement."

"Thank you," Charlie tried to reply with confidence, really unsure what to say since this was all new to him—all news to him.

"Please look them over and sign them as soon as possible."

"Sure."

"While I'll be your focal point, at least for the time being, these all need to go to Robert Howell at HR or his secretary, Helena—they're down the corridor to the right as you come in the building."

"Fine."

"In addition to Robert, our comptroller and head of accounts is Diana McNeal, and our CEO is Danut Lazarescu—we call him 'Dan.'"

Charlie thought he recognized Romanian roots in the boss, given his previous contacts with Vlachs League, yet this seemed irrelevant.

"Now," Wilson said, then paused for a breath, "with all the boilerplate out of the way, you may be asking about the company. I'm not sure how much you know about Thorne."

"I'd really enjoy hearing more," Charlie tried to calmly reply although he knew basically nothing about his new employer other than the tiny introduction offered by Robin McCandless at poolside.

"Excellent. Well, J. P. Thorne—John Paul Thorne—started this company well over a hundred years ago, after immigrating from his family's farm outside Dorset in southwest England. John Paul's older brother, Richard, reportedly was a manager at Bridgewater Textiles in Lancashire. Building on Robert's position and influence, the brothers set up an American import business—Bridgewater's textiles first coming into J. P. Thorne and then sold to retailers in both the US and Canada. People say they did really good business—the Thornes becoming twentieth century millionaires. John Paul's family ran the company until after the Second World War—through time shifting from English textiles to products coming from across Asia. Then, after the war, the Thornes sold to a group called Consolidated Imports. These folks kept the company going, basically untouched, for a number of years before selling to another one of those big amorphous companies, Delpro."

"Quite a history," Charlie offered.

"Indeed. But today we're far away from English textiles. Thorne is now—I guess the best way to describe it—a catalyst. In the current global environment, we've tried to maintain the trade links to Europe and Asia as well as build new alliances. We link suppliers with processors. We link raw materials with manufacturers. We link supply with demand."

"That's quite a job."

"Yes. Of course, we're just one of lots and lots of companies that do the same things. We have our lists of partners, and we try to make sure those that need things get them.

"Now, you might ask, 'how do I fit in?'"

"Yes, indeed."

"Right now, we'll start with following up on some of the work with which you've already been involved when you were at Spot On. We'll also, if you're OK with it, begin a program of on-the-job training or "sharpening" as Dan calls it. Here you'll work mostly with other in-house colleagues, but sometimes you'll benefit from other special skills upon which we rely, but which are not in-house."

"Sounds great."

"Let me show you to your office."

With that, the briefing was over, and Charlie learned that he was, for the first time his life, to have a real office—a space unto himself with his name on the door.

Then, at home from the name-on-the-door office and the bank, with two cars parked in the over-sized garage, Jo and Charlie began to adapt to the life of a regular suburban couple. As they set up home, they set about getting to know their neighbors and their neighborhood—becoming part of the wider Knollwood community.

Charlie could practically feel his piece of the pie growing.

They even felt secure enough—or maybe, just the opposite—to think about themselves for once in the medium-term rather than just in the short-term. Should they formally marry? Should they plan on children? What was over the horizon that was now building before their eyes?

※ ※ ※ ▽ ※ ※ ※

In the end, security, as in stability, was still determined to be an objective yet to be fully achieved. Ultimately, they were both in new jobs—jobs about which they were not fully clear exactly why they had them. Charlie had (again) followed the current. He had chosen Thorne (or been chosen for Thorne) not knowing what Thorne did (what could go wrong following Robin's advice?). Jo, as well, was not really sure why she was where she was. She had been promoted to be manager in Mundelein—from all appearances, extemporaneously.

When they looked at the broader strokes, the landscape in front of their horizon didn't feel all that secure. Were they living on other's whims?

They tried to unravel their situation—the good, the bad, and the unknown.

Chasing loose threads bothered Jo more than Charlie.

Nevertheless, they concluded formally cementing a relationship that they both agreed was steadfast and loving was deemed to be important, yet a task that could be postponed—the formalities in no way distracting from the strong, and growing stronger, bonds that joined them. It was the same for children. Now was not the time.

This rationalization of getting their feet firmly on the ground, and understanding the contours of this ground, continued for more than five years. It wasn't that the ground was slippery. They just didn't seem to be able to get a grip on the best road to lead them to that looming horizon.

While there was some perplexity about how they had come to be where they were, this did not dominate their lives. They had too much going on. It was not just establishing a new home and getting established in a new community. Jo had an entirely new job description. She was up to it. She did well. But it took additional effort.

Charlie, as vaguely foretold by Wilson, found himself in near perpetual motion. There was more to do for the fish work in Costa Rica as well as exploring other activities with which he had been involved in the country. He was then asked to look more widely at Central America and see if there were lessons or opportunities to glean from the work in Coast Rica. He even made the occasional trip south with any of various assignments all revolving about securing either markets for US exports or identifying importers to provide products Thorne deemed of interest in the US.

Interspersed with all this—frequently dominating all this—was the "sharpening." It was really on-the-job training. It was in actuality like going back to school. Charlie had long—all too often, he felt, very long—one-on-one sessions with Thorne specialists. Those in accounting drove bookkeeping and auditing skills into him until he found himself dreaming about going over other people's accounts. The company lawyers (there were quite a number) went over and over import and export legislation and regulation. People from logistics dove deeply into packaging and shipping, helping him realize how haphazardly he had handled all those consignments on which he had worked in the Spot On shop. He went outside for short sessions with architects and civil engineers. Robert Howell, who oversaw his "sharpening," told Charlie he needed to know the basics about planning and developing various types of sites and buildings since at times he might be involved in scoping new facilities like those he had helped promote in Costa Rica. He was even asked to take a First-Aid course. Robert said, "You never know."

Jo and Charlie were very busy.

Still, they always found time for each other.

They had built a sauna at their home, and this turned out to be not only a place to relax but also a space that could quickly be ignited by both external and internal heat flamed by their still fierce passion.

The days and the weeks blew by. Soon it felt normal. They were Knollwood residents. Jo was the bank manager. Charlie was a vested employee of J. P. Thorne—a company that was still largely an enigma, but a company that he at least understood did many things in many places—some of these things and some of these places known to him. Even so, the pay was excellent, he was on his second BMW, and life far away from the lakebed seemed good.

⋀ ⋀ ⋀ ⋁ ⋀ ⋀ ⋀

Not long after celebrating their fifth anniversary in their home on Forest Knoll Road, Charlie received a call at work from none other than Robin McCandless. He was again invited—summoned—to Crab Tree Lane—again on Saturday afternoon.

It was a rerun of the previous visit, this time Robin McCandless, drinking a daiquiri, was wearing a powder blue Gucci golf shirt over cornflower yellow worsted gabardine slacks and highly polished black oxfords. Once Charlie had been served his identical beverage, the boss of his boss began.

"Thanks again for coming on short notice. I appreciate it."

There was really nothing to do but smile and say, "Any time."

"I understand you've been keeping busy at Thorne. Everyone says you're doing a grand job."

"They're very kind." Charlie gave another smile.

"Well lad, by now you've seen a lot—a lot more than when you were cooped up at Spot On. I trust you're getting a better feel for the business?"

Charlie wasn't really sure how to reply. He certainly didn't have a feel for the business—he wasn't really sure he even knew what THE BUSINESS was. But he knew he couldn't say this, and he knew he did know more—or at least had seen more—than when he had been here last time. So, he tried to walk a narrow line.

"I'm impressed, sir, with all I've seen—Thorne is definitely doing a lot. I feel fortunate to be involved."

"Let's not be too politically correct," Robin said with a sharp edge on his voice, "what do you really know?"

When in doubt, tell the truth (at least, that's what his mother used to say), "Sir, I do honestly feel fortunate—but I also honesty feel over-whelmed. Thorne does so much I really can't encapsulate it all."

"More bla-bla-bla," Robin said, almost cutting him off, a spark of irritation fleeting across his pale eyes, "What do you know?"

"Not a whole lot," Charlie admitted in retreat.

"Exactly. Lad, that's where I want you to be. You don't know a whole lot. Now do you want to know more?"

"Certainly, sir."

"Well lad, that's good to know. It's good that you think about want-ing to know more. But to know more, you have to do more."

Charlie looked quizzically at his overlord.

"It's not enough to want." The older man's rose complexion nearly glowed under his mop of snowy hair as his head bobbed up and down; he was getting more and more agitated by the conversation. "You have to do. This isn't to say you're not doing—you are. But the more you want to know, the higher up you want to move—or the higher we want you to move—the more you have to do. And it's not just doing—it's doing with heart. It's excelling!"

Charlie had a flashback of his father giving him a pep talk when he was disgusted with school, with life—when he was first beginning to feel the pressure in his soul to do something different—be somewhere different. His father had been trying to encourage his son—entreating him to "stay the course"—his farther pleading almost woefully with his disaffected son to "stay the course."

Robin McCandless had no apparent reason to want Charlie to stay the course. He certainly was not in any way nor fashion pleading—quite to the contrary. Why should he?

Charlie was ordinary. He was just everyday flotsam off the street. He was but one of thousands—millions—of young folk seeking their dreams, prepared or not to embark on the odyssey, able or not to attain the desires for which they so hungered.

Robin McCandless had no reason to care.

Strangely, McCandless seemed to be reading Charlie's thoughts. "You see, lad, I care. I need good people. I need people upon whom I can rely. I need carefully selected people who can help push us forward—keep us being successful—keep us in the game.

"That's why, in fact, I asked you here today. I am watching. And what I see is promising. It's like preparing a great soup, a *bouillabaisse*, that is only beginning to simmer—the real taste only coming after it has cooked ever so slowly, gently cooled, and is tasted the next day when all the delicate flavors can fully express themselves—each distinct, but each a part of a whole. Not to be trite, but you're in the soup—and I mean that in a good way."

Charlie had a hard time jumping from dream chaser to soup. He could only sheepishly smile and nod.

"So," Robin continued, his voice now several decibels higher than when he had started, "I, too, want you to know more. I've already told you we, the corporate 'we,' are very active—we are everywhere, and we do everything. Like Spot On, Thorne, too, is only one tiny cog of a great wheel that is turning across the globe.

"And, though we're everywhere, doing everything, we're often un-seen—unrecognized—unknown. That's it lad, you are striving to know the unknown because so many know so little of what we do and so few know enough to see even the tiniest slice. If you continue to move up, you must continue to know.

"But I've also told you that to the outsider—and there are many, many outsiders—a number of the things we do might be considered as distasteful or improper. To be honest, there are outsiders who would say much of what we do is offensive or even illegal. I must say that, while we're unnoticed and unseen by most, some whom we encounter don't like us—some may hate us. But this is all just part of doing business on a global scale. You can never make everyone happy. You can never follow everyone's rules or plans. It's like that tired cliché, to make the omelet, you know lad, you have to break the eggs."

Omelets and soup—Charlie wondered how far down the menu he would be dragged. Fortunately, one of Robin's no-see-um servants brought a fresh daiquiri swimming in rum. As the alcohol swept through his capillaries, he managed a smile to his host and now his orator.

"Yet, lad, this again is not the time to go into all the details—all the fine points. I really just wanted to check up with you. To see how you're doing. After all, I was the one who suggested you move to Thorne and if you or that lovely girl of yours are unhappy, it's on me."

Draining the stemmed glass in a gulp, sensing the end was near, Charlie did his best, "Oh no sir. There's no problem. There's no issues. Everything is fine. We're so grateful for all that you've helped us do—the home, the car, the job. Why even Jo has managed to get a promotion out of all this transition from Waukegan. It's been wonderful for us."

"I'm so glad to hear that. I'm happy things are working out for you both. You've promising futures in front of you. I just want to make sure you're aware of the situation. There are more doors to open—but we do it one door at a time.

"If you do find you're having problems—any problems—do let me know. I really want to see you do all you can do—know all you should know. You're on a good path. Keep it up."

Charlie realized that was the closing hymn. They chatted casually for a few moments to let the daiquiris and the serious conversation settle. Then Robin made a pretext that he had to make an important overseas phone call and one of the liveried attendants showed him back to his BMW.

ᛉ ᛉ ᛉ ᚥ ᛉ ᛉ ᛉ

Charlie stopped for some Thai takeout on his way home. Over the spicy curry, Jo asked, "How'd it go at the master's palace?"

Around mouthfuls of the redolent sauce that heightened a whole different family of nerves than his recent daiquiris, Charlie filled his partner in on the discussions that so fundamentally affected their lives.

"Seems like each time I visit with the great man I have more questions when I leave than when I arrived—expect this is his plan."

"Huh?"

"It seems, at least in part, to be a game for him. He seems to want to see what he has to do—how much suspense or anticipation or expectation or power or riches, I don't know what—but how much bait he has to use on his hook to catch his prey."

"Weird."

"At the very least. Still, I suspect he's always working on at least two different levels at once, if not many more. He almost certainly is always looking for new blood to infuse into his massive organization—if there is a massive organization—I honestly don't know—like I say, there's more I don't know than I do.

"But maybe I'm beginning to see some things—I don't know. He doesn't trust. He doesn't take things on face value. He even appears to have a hard time accepting what he himself sees—not to mention what his own minions tell him.

"So, while he's trying to make his own assessments—his own judgements—he is busy playing cat and mouse. He intentionally let slip small

bits and pieces about his—or their, I don't know—operations, always trying to gauge your reaction, your interest, your understanding.

"He knows he's the one who has launched our careers. He knows
we know. He knows we owe him. He knows we know nothing is free.
Therefore, he can amuse himself with our discomfort at being in his debt
if things go no farther. But, if he deems us truly worthy, he can throw
some more gifts under the tree and watch us snap them up—now adding
to our debt. In so doing, he moves us up the ladder to do things that are
to his own advantage—don't know if they'd be to ours or not?"

"It's complicated."

"Yeah. When I distill it all down, it looks like he was preparing me
for an offer for another move to another of his companies or organizations folded into another promotion. I just don't know. He kept on about
how much I knew about his expansive operation. It was a mess. He said I
needed to know, but I knew I did not know, so I had to know how much
I didn't know . . ."

"That's twisted."

"Yeah. It was all about needing to know more but to know more
I had to do more and to do more I had to become more active, I guess,
in the use of or engagement with the vast interconnected operations he
continues to flaunt as some sort of global monster business."

"Well, I sure don't understand. It's far from clear. The guy seems
deranged."

"Clear it is not—you got that right. But I don't think he's got a screw
loose—like I say, it's a game to him. He has nothing to lose. If we totally
washout, we're gone and he's no worse off—we are—or I am—I don't
know his role in your position—your promotion. I reckon he's got a finger in there, too. But alternatively, if we don't disappear from his stage, if
it turns out the status quo is our final resting place in the grander scheme
of things, then here, as well, there's no harm and no foul. We're OK. We're
in his debt, and we're tiny pieces on his big chess board to be played as
he wishes. Then, behind door number three, if we meet the mark and he
decides to give us another boost, we've climbed another rung and I guess,
in addition to doing better ourselves, he's doing better, too."

"Like I say, twisted."

"Yep."

Later that evening, after he and Jo had almost lasciviously celebrated
the weekend, after his passionate inamorato had fallen into a sound sleep
bathed in afterglow, Charlie went to the kitchen, got a beer, and then

reclined in his favorite chaise lounge on the patio. The night sky was clear—the stars seemed close enough to touch. He remembered many summer nights on the lakebed when he felt he could stretch out his hand and tickle the edge of the universe. Now his visions had to be much more nearsighted—his fantasies more grounded.

As he had tried to explain to Jo and Robin—Mr. McCandless—he knew very little. While he had attempted to portray this shortfall as simply a normal aspect of his situation, he had to admit to himself it was anything but normal.

At Spot On he'd been a messenger, an intermediary, and a handyman. Though the total landscape was not his to see, he had been able to compartmentalize each assignment—each assignment appearing to have a beginning and an end—a reason and a plan.

Now at Thorne, while he'd hoped things would become more coherent—the overall panorama more visible—so far, things were, if possible, evermore obscure. While much of his time was, like it or not, focused on "sharpening," those activities that he undertook appeared less as discrete packages and more as snippets from a stream of ongoing processes.

He would be asked to review a dossier on cotton farming in Bangladesh or a tea estate in Kenya. He would be given a folder of export regulations of Malaysia or labor laws in Ecuador to summarize and pass up the in-house conveyer. He would be sent to Indonesia or Angola as a courier or to Italy or Argentina as some sort of agent or formal representative.

He was a vagabond.

On the surface, it was exciting. It was great. As a bumpkin from the lakebed, he could visit wonderful places he had never known existed and then he could return to his wonderful partner and their wonderful home. What more could anyone want?

But it all had the feel of fantasy and illusion.

There was no visible cause and effect. There was no beginning nor end. There were no results nor conclusions to examine. There was no final product to touch. There was only one mirage following another.

Charlie had always separated his work and private life. He had really done all he could to keep his work colleagues at arm's length from his social life (meager as it was beyond his close bonds to Jo). Julian had been somewhat of an exception since the two had first met via the Vlachs League—had been drinking buddies before they became employee and employer.

Wilson at Thorne was verging on entering into the friendship category. While the two were not drinking buddies, they did share cups of coffee in the breakroom and did have not infrequent chats about anything from the weather to politics. Anything from the weather to politics, but little about Thorne and absolutely nothing about the wider landscape.

Would the bigger picture ever come into focus?

The spiraling galaxies seemed to promise answers came to those with patience (maybe it was the beer). Or were these not the labyrinthine galleries of space but the swirling waters of a flushing toilet carrying him away with the rest of the offal. It was time to go to bed.

The need (or desire) to get the view from thirty-thousand feet still front of mind, Charlie decided to break with norms. Late one morning they were alone in the modern and well-fitted breakroom after the usual ten o'clock rush had come and gone. It seemed like the right time.

"Say, Wilson," Charlie said tentatively, "ever since you so kindly welcomed me here those years ago, I've done so much, seen so much—it's amazing."

"I'm happy to see everything has worked out"

"Yeah. Remember that first day you said Thorne is one of lots and lots of companies. While I've been here, I've seen threads and crumbs of those many companies—we tend to be one of the many moving parts in a big complex machine."

"You could say that."

"Well, I've been trying to see the broader panorama—to see where we—where I fit in. Sometimes I think I'm a fixer, but I don't really know what I'm fixing. Does that make sense?"

"Yeah, sure."

From Wilson's basically monosyllabic replies, it was apparent that his colleague, whether or not he knew anything, was reluctant to come forward with any revelations other than the vague platitudes with which he had been greeted on day one. Charlie figured it was worth one last stab.

"Yeah. Know this is probably sensitive to some—maybe most—but it's difficult. I feel like someone who's never seen an elephant and is looking at a toenail with a magnifying glass trying to imagine what type of animal has such a toenail? I would never be able to envision the trunk by only seeing the toenail. Here it's the same. I try to do my best, but I feel I'm only seeing the toenail. I have no idea of on what sort of beast I am working. It's difficult. I don't feel I'm able to contribute optimally because I can only contribute to a tiny slice. Maybe I'm just overreacting?"

"No," Wilson managed to say with a slightly wilted smile, and looked like he wanted to help his colleague, even if not his friend, "you're just going through what we all go through. We're all seeing our own small toenails—it's a jigsaw puzzle where only one piece has any imagery, all the other pieces are blank—snow white. We're trying to imagine the tableau by looking at our one infinitesimal piece. It's frustrating. Still, it is what it is."

"You get it?"

"Of course."

"How can we see more pieces with images and less snow?"

"It's simple: we can't."

"Really?"

"Yeah. As we're so good at feeble metaphors, let me try to close this out by suggesting you think of yourself, ourselves, as eaglets. Now there's a noble image. We're stuck in the aerie; we still can't fly. Our parents go and rip things apart and come back to the nest to drop small morsels of who knows what into our mouths. Likewise, our masters drop morsels down our gullets, and we gobble them up—never knowing where they come from—often not even knowing what they are."

Unable to find answers, unable to have a practical alternative strategy for moving forward, unwilling to strike out on a new course, Charlie acceded to his current reality and reverted to what had become his latest routine. Unless there was travel, and there often was, he effectively had an eight-to-five job. Jo worked nine to six. They'd have lunch together every day he was in town. By the time she got home, he'd a good start on dinner—to his own surprise, proving himself to be an able hand in the kitchen. Then, after dinner, they'd find any of a number of ways to enjoy each other's company. Things could be a lot worse.

Charlie's outward re-embracing of the status quo did not truly calm his inner incertitude. And, regardless of any cosmetic front, his everything's-OK proclamation did nothing to appease Jo's continued and growing apprehension.

She had not vigorously reacted to Charlie's last encounter with Robin McCandless. How could she? First and foremost, as was painfully evident, neither of them knew much. Second, and equally regrettable, they were, as Charlie had emphasized, in McCandless' debt. And, finally, to her own chagrin, if she scraped all the dramatic conspiracies and scandalous mystery off the subject of an overview of their lives, she knew she was grateful to be where she was—far away from inner-city Chicago and the burdens carried through the years by the McCormick clan. She liked where she was. No, she loved where she was. All expectations had been exceeded—partner, home, job. Life was good. If she could just put the incessant gnawing inside her to rest, life would be great.

⩘ ⩘ ⩘ ⩗ ⩘ ⩘ ⩘

Seasons passed. Midwest Bank and Thorne LLC counted their profits. Their employees, including Jo and Charlie, counted their paychecks.

Having just returned from a Thorne assignment to Peru exploring options for fertilizer sales, Charlie was again invited to the McCandless Estate for a Saturday afternoon aperitif.

Everything unrolled as in previous visits, his patron's ensemble and drink of choice having changed, but all else was a mirror image.

Charlie received his beverage, a Moscow mule, as he was informed by his host—which was quite tasty, though he did not comment on the spicy flavor nor the possibly ironic choice of drink (he saw himself often as a mule and always curious about any Russian roots in their activities). Once settled, Robin McCandless pushed back a shock of snowy hair and welcomed him.

"Thanks again, lad, for popping around."

Charlie found "popping around" a strange synonym for being summoned, but said nothing, and offered a humble smile.

"I won't keep you long as I know you enjoy your weekends with that wonderful lady with whom you keep house. I really only wanted to take the temperature."

Charlie smiled warmly.

"I continue to hear good things about you from my guys over at Thorne. They think you're an up-and-comer. What'd you think?"

"I'm happy to do my part."

"More bla-bla-bla, my little brother'd call it 'bullshit,' but I try to be more polished. But I'm not looking for hokum, I get fed enough of that from others—I'm looking for raw introspection. I've told you about knowing and doing. I need doers. I need them now and I'll always need them. People who get the job done regardless of the cost, regardless of the circumstances, even regardless of the personal sacrifice or risk. I'm an old man, maybe (he added with a half-smile), I don't know. But I sure do know that I'm a man who's been around the block a time or two. I've been in this for a long time and plan on being in it for a long time to come."

McCandless seemed to get winded as he got wound up—his complexion beaming. He took a long drag on his drink, the effervescent ginger beer seeming to rejuvenate his countenance if not his neurons.

For his part, Charlie sensed his best maneuver was to follow the patron's lead and take a great swig of his tasty and nearly completed drink. Then, as before, the liveried help appeared magically with new beverages—refills for both the master and the guest.

"I know, lad," the lord of the manor continued, refreshed, "you're doing and learning every day. Thorne's got you on a wild schedule and their doing all they can to fast-track your exposure to many aspects of their, and by default, my work."

"It has been busy," Charlie said, almost more to himself than his host.

"OK, lad, since I'm not hearing much in any direction from you, I'm going to make some assumptions. But first, please excuse my crudeness, but my dear brother, of whom I just spoke, has a much-loved phrase—'assumptions are the mothers of all fuckups.' I don't like coarse talk or vulgarity. But more than my dislike for this rudeness, I really, really dislike, to use my brother's word, fuckups.

"So, lad, while I'm making some assumptions, these are made with the understanding that they will not lead to my dissatisfaction—to my asperity. You follow me?"

"Of course, sir." Charlie felt—sensed—reticence was probably the best tactic. He felt Robin—Mr. McCandless—was still deciding how best to bait his hook.

"And you, of course, (almost spitting out these syllables) want to get ahead, to have a good life with good things . . . good things that come with good pay . . . good pay that comes with good work. Is that the way it is, lad?"

"Indeed, sir."

"Fine." More than a shock of the alabaster hair fell across his host's forehead. "We're on the same page, lad. I just wanted to be sure—like I said, take the temperature.

"So, lad, here's what I want you to do. Go back to Thorne, I understand from Dan that you'll finish most of your current tasks in about nine months. When you've got everything tidy in Dan's shop, take some time off, as long as you need, to have some relaxation with that lovely girl of yours. Then, when you're all reinvigorated and full of *savior faire* from all the fine-tuning Dan's done, I'll have a special assignment for you. Does that sound OK?"

"Sounds excellent, sir."

The encounter had reached its end.

In what seemed a split second, Robin had returned to the bowels of his palace and Charlie was driving home.

ᛗ ᛗ ᛗ ᛦ ᛗ ᛗ ᛗ

Visits to Chez McCandless were now nearly becoming milestones in their new pattern of life. The powerful pink man, as Jo often called him with just a hint of exasperation, seemed to always be probing, making veiled promises, and changing bait to see if the response varied with the lure.

Nonetheless, her practically stoic reaction to Robin's (she always referred to him as Robin if not the pink man) job-related pitch was a stark contrast to her enthusiasm about the potential of having an extended vacation with Charlie. This was wonderful.

While Charlie wrapped up his "sharpening" and made a few required trips (these fortunately not extended assignments, but short sojourns in Latin America), Jo got approval for a vacation and began exploring the where's, when's, and how's.

Jo was able to rather quickly zoom-in on the where. She'd often heard tales of the indescribable beauty of the Canadian Rockies. A city kid growing up with buildings looming over her head, she longed to see the majesty of nature—hoping its splendor would take her breath away. It was easy, seeing pictures of the nearly ten-thousand-foot peak of Cascade Mountain commanding the Bow River Valley below, to choose Banff and Lake Louise as the site for their long-awaited, very special getaway.

Jo saw this opportunity as very special not only because it gave them both an opportunity to get away from jobs that were demanding and life-styles that could be fatiguing, but it was also the first time since she and Charlie had been together that they would have a chance to totally relax and review objectively their situation—where they were and where they were going—not to mention, how they were going to get there. It was a chance for critical and loving discussions. All those not-now questions could be addressed—questions like children and marriage that could, at the very least, be possible releases from their current bondage (or however she could best describe their present situation which she felt tied them in unseen threads) and should be put on the table for frank examination—no pressure from either side, of course.

Jo saw Banff and Lake Louise as the perfect place to unwind, settle back, and look at their lives while they were overwhelmed by Mother Nature's grandeur.

Charlie was all in.

Jo hadn't gone into any detail about her overall plans, hopes, and aspirations for the vacation. But Charlie didn't need to be pushed. The pictures Jo had selected to illustrate the stunning landscape were more than enough to convince Charlie this was a must-do.

As to the when, Charlie had nearly an instantaneous answer: Jo's birthday. August 16th was not all that far away—just long enough for them to be able to make all the necessary arrangements. Jo and Charlie could celebrate Jo's birth in the Canadian Rockies. What could be better?

For the how, Wilson unexpectedly added some special spice to their idea. While they had been considering taking commercial airlines to Banff, Wilson suggested an alternative. He had friend who had a six-seater, twin-engine King Air C90 hangared at Campbell Airport about fifteen miles from their home. Wilson could, he assured his coworker, arrange for family rates for the four-and-a-half-hour flight into the Rockies. They could really go in style befitting such an upwardly mobile power couple.

It was settled.

There was a high level of excitement. It was like, as a child, waiting for that birthday that never seemed to come. It was hard to wait.

The practicalities still had to be dealt with, but they were effectively on their way.

On the anxiously awaited day of their flight, Wilson kindly took them to the small airport. Their plane was sitting on the tarmac, serviced and ready to go, among a handful of other small planes coming and going from or to who knew where. It was really quite a busy place.

When their bags had been loaded onboard, they bid Wilson a fond goodbye and the pilot, Lewis, accompanied them across the concrete apron in front of the hangar. Lewis was mid-sentence, marveling at what a wonderful day it was to fly, when there was a loud crack and Jo crumpled to the ground.

Tearful Ascent

CHARLIE HAD NO IDEA what had happened.

Jo was lying, unmoving on the concrete.

The noise had sounded like a gunshot. Who would shoot Jo?

Lewis ran to the hangar and called an ambulance.

With amazing speed, the EMTs were there, and Jo was whisked off to the hospital.

Five hours later, a surgeon approached Charlie in the waiting room. Jo was in a coma. Her vitals were stable. But it was too soon to know the full outcome.

Through a combination of the medical deduction and a reconstruction at the airport done by the police, it was concluded that Jo had been the victim of a one-in-a-million accident—a terrible, terrible accident.

A Cessna 310R had been powering up for takeoff next to the King Air. A nut had vibrated off a bolt on the cowling. The nut had hit the revving propeller and shot across the tarmac, striking Jo in the head. She had lost consciousness immediately and, as of present, not regained her senses.

The police informed Charlie, much to his angst, approximately ten people a year were killed or injured by propeller-related accidents.

∧∧∧∨∧∧∧

Jo was strong. Her body recovered. Yet, her head had received a horrific blow. Her brain was concussed. She remained in a coma. After a month, she was discharged from the hospital and transferred to the Lake Center in Waukegan where she was put on life support under long-term care.

Charlie was, at least in his eyes, not as strong. At first, he totally fell apart. He was inconsolable. He was wracked with misery—agony for both Jo and himself. He was furious. Life wasn't fair. He was swept by guilt; he had been the author of many of the arrangements. He was crushed. He was on the verge of collapse.

Charlie could no longer stay in their home. He put all the furniture and most of the other belongings Jo had so carefully selected into storage. He moved himself and his meager belongings—nearly back to only one suitcase—into an apartment in Abbott Park, just off Highway 43.

The house was in their names, but the mortgage had been under-written by Thorne, so Charlie discussed with Dan who assured his dread-fully bereaved employee there were no problems. Charlie put the house on the market.

Charlie then dove into work, making tasks when there were none—complicating assignments that were generally simple. Anything and everything to keep occupied. When he was not able to wrap himself up into some knots at Thorne, he tried to lose himself in the outdoors as he had when mourning Mihaela. Then he had meandered endlessly through Jerome Huppert Woods. Now, on the same river, the Des Plaines, he wandered aimlessly through Independence Grove Forest Reserve on an oxbow lake next to the river.

People said it would get better with time. It didn't.

People said the great hole he felt in his chest would slowly fill in. It didn't.

People said there'd be a light out of the darkness. There wasn't.

People said, with time, he would be able to think of her without crying. He couldn't.

People said he would get over it. He couldn't.

The anguish continued.

Then, this time, atypically, in the middle of the week and for lunch, he was called to Crab Tree Lane.

Not only were the day and time different, Robin McCandless was different. When Charlie was shepherded to a dining table set poolside, his host was seated at the table wearing a simple grey button-down over black slacks and black oxfords, a contrast to his usual colorful choices in clothing. Also, in the place of an exotic aperitif, the manor's lord was drinking a simple red wine, undoubtedly of rare vintage.

Standing as Charlie approached, with the appearance of true sincerity, Robin offered his hand. "So, so sorry lad about the terrible events that have befallen you. Such a terrible thing. Something no one could imagine. Something no one could ever have thought of. Truly horrible."

Charlie's throat tightened and he could say little other than, "Thank you."

"How are you managing?"

An almost whispered "OK" was all the guest could produce.

"Well," Let's have a bite of lunch," the convener proposed.

As had been demonstrated many times before, the manor's staff was minutely attuned to the lord's wishes and, as soon as the two men were seated, Charlie had a full wine glass and a plate of salmon salad on the placemat in front of his seat.

Charlie picked at his food while Robin carried on, breaking only for occasional sips of wine.

"I know, lad, this isn't the best time, but I had advised you I'd have you back to go over more details. For a number of reasons, this is that time. My apologies, but I cannot postpone this discussion."

Charlie muttered something unintelligible around a morsel of fresh salmon.

"As I've already intimated, I want you to come in from the field. All these places—Spot On, Thorne, and so many others—they're simply satellites. The heart, the core, the nucleus is Delpro. I want you in Delpro. Are you OK with this?"

Another mutter, obviously of assent—Charlie silently thought back to that perhaps fateful day when Julian had first told him about Robin McCandless and Delpro, the two intertwined from the beginning.

"Wonderful. I told you last time I had a special assignment for you. I do. These are not the happy circumstances under which I had hoped we'd embark on this assignment, but we need to move. Time is always against us.

"So, here's what I want. I'll quickly brief you as to the overview of what's needed. I do need to emphasize that time is a critical factor here. Then you'll go to Fredericks, Higgins, and Woods. These guys are my lawyers—one of my law firms. You've already encountered Saphir and Spader. Well, these other guys are real close. They're in Lake Bluff, catty-corner between the police station and Artesian Park—real easy to find.

They'll take care of all the practical arrangements. Then you'll come back here for a quick chat before heading off. OK?"

Charlie nodded—no smile.

"Now this is a bit different from a lot of the things you've done so far. Here I need you to go first to Geneva. I need you to be my representative to meet with González Philip Albardi, the Director General of the Ecumenical Humanitarian Trust—EHT. We're not really very engaged with EHT. They're one of those help-the-poor groups. Not something in which we get overly involved. But we are heavily invested in the International Center for Democratic Ideals—ICDI. These are people who have, even if rather covertly, a genuine business eye. And we're all about business. While ICDI is a very big actor in EHT activities, this is all totally hush-hush. ICDI is like a silent partner—in many ways, real silent. There's a little bit of the interaction in the public record—only a little bit. The key parts of the relationship are undisclosed—or they're supposed to be. No one knows the full level of the interconnectivity. At least, no one should know. We don't want anyone to know. González knows, of course. But that's it. This is important. I'd say it's critical.

"Now one of our friends has informed us that a high-level advisor to González, some American named Paula Patterson, has begun researching all of EHT's links and history. I don't know, some sort of PR campaign, spin to donors, I don't know. But this damn woman's good at what she does and she's way too damn close to uncovering details about EHT's ties to ICDI. Anyway, while that's a big problem, that's not your problem, at least not today. I want you to get González's view of the situation. Then, posing as a journalist from this woman's home state or somewhere out West, I want you to talk to her to see if you can get any details about how deeply she has dug and what she thinks she's found. You can couch all this as part of a series of interviews you're writing about folks from her state working overseas. It's not a real tough assignment, but it's real important.

"When you leave Geneva, I want you to pass through Granada and stop by the Delpro offices there. Our head-of-office has some important documents for me and it's always best to hand-carry these if the opportunity arises. That's it. Pretty straight-forward. Pretty easy. But, to repeat, very important. Pass by the lawyers' place on your way out. Get them started on getting your bookings and all made."

As Charlie got up to go, most of his food and drink still untouched on the table, his host bid him farewell. "Lad, this is important!"

The transatlantic flight on Swissair was a totally new experience, dwarfing the short hauls to Latin America and a step above his relatively few long-haul trips. Happily, the McCandless lawyer crew (or one of them) had booked Charlie first class and the trip—long as it was—was filled with excellent food and drink accompanied by an amazing selection of movies. Yet, he could only wish he could be sharing this luxury with Jo.

He had gone to the Lake Center before going to O'Hare. He had sat by Jo's side and told her all about his latest discussions with Robin (yes, the pink man) and his upcoming travel. The room was filled with the hum and the swish of machines, but Jo didn't seem to be there at all. There was a little pool of tears under his chair when he finally left to try and get on with his life.

Arriving in Geneva, he took the shuttle to the Novotel Centre Ville Genève where he had reservations. This was an easy walk to EHT offices which were squeezed between downtown and the lake, directly on Quai de Mont-Blanc.

The next day Charlie was received formally in the eloquently simple offices of the DG on the first floor of the large modern high-rise in which EHT occupied three full floors. Over aromatic espresso, González solemnly recapped what McCandless had already said: EHT was wonderful, they did tremendous things helping those the most in need, and they had a relationship with ICDI. This relationship, as the DG was quick to emphasize, was not public facing. According to González, the EHT-ICDI bond was historic, innovative, and synergistic. However, there were some aspects that might be hard to explain to the common man-on-the-street—it was complicated. So, simply to avoid confusion and not raise any unnecessary concerns, it had long been decided to keep this liaison in the background—far in the background.

González hoped Charlie understood—as he most surely did—there was nothing to hide here. There was nothing untoward. There was no misconduct. Certainly, there was nothing illegal; or even really objectionable. It was just doing things the way they had to be done. It was pragmatic. And, it was just respecting people's privacy, ensuring the main parties, as they wished, were able to maintain their anonymity. It was normal—very normal. Yet, it was indeed complicated.

The DG really had nothing more to add—there were no new revelations. He had been and was still concerned about the work of his

American employee—one Paula Patterson. Nonetheless, so far there had been no major problems. He only felt these could possibly—only slightly possible, he reckoned—happen. He wanted to make sure all the chief actors like Delpro were aware. He was just doing due diligence. There was no reason to loudly sound any alarms. It was a precaution—that's all it was.

Of course, he concluded, as Charlie certainly already knew, Delpro was not really a primary factor in EHT operations. They honestly had nothing to do with each other. After all, Delpro was big business and EHT was humanitarian assistance. Still, to be safe, they (Charlie was again unsure who "they" were) wanted to be proactive and make sure Delpro was informed. That was all. He was just doing due diligence. He was sure everything was OK—things really had to be OK. It was just complicated.

Charlie thanked the DG for his time and for the detailed information. He was then accompanied to a small meeting room, nearly the mirror image of the small room where he had worked on his reports for Sam at Saphir and Spader.

Awaiting him, again with cups of fragrant espresso, was a middle-aged-ish woman who really could have been anyone anywhere. She had no outstanding features nor did her clothing reveal very much about its wearer. She was attractive, well dressed, and not kitschy—that was about as far as Charlie's first impressions could go.

As Charlie entered, she stood up, held out her hand, and with a firm shake said, "Hi, I'm Paula Patterson. I understand you want to see me."

"Hi," he said in reply, "I'm Charlie. I'm a stringer for the Denver Gazette, pleased to meet you."

By prearrangements, Charlie had been advised not to use his surname unless really pushed and, unsure of her actual western roots, claim his home base as a major Rocky Mountain city.

"I appreciate," Charlie continued, "you taking time out of your undoubtedly hectic schedule to meet briefly with me."

"No problem—I can use the break."

So far, so good.

"I'm writing a piece, actually kind of a series, about Americans—especially Americans from the west—who live and work overseas. Our readers truly know so little about what it is like anywhere else, we thought it was past time to let them know about how some of their sisters or cousins are doing in, as they see it, far-off places."

"A little oddball maybe, but I can see the point."

"Thanks, I'd just like you to tell me about your work and then I'll boil it down into a short article that I'll share with you before I send it to the Gazette. Does that sound OK?"

"Fine."

"Great. So, let's have at it."

Paula very rapidly gave a rundown of how she, as a cultural anthropologist, had ended up in Geneva with EHT. She quickly touched on her work at Three Mile Island, with Peace Corps, working with refugees in Guinea and with disadvantaged people in Namibia, before accepting a position at EHT from where she had grown and been promoted to become a close colleague of the DG. She then easily recited her current work—the most important part for Charlie.

Under González's leadership, as charitable contributions became more and more competitive, it had become necessary to clearly show that EHT was at the cutting edge—impactful and efficient. This had become her assignment. She was, therefore, working on an in-depth analysis of EHT's past, present, and future—looking at sustainability. Over the last twenty-five years, had EHT succeeded?

She worked with a team of outside experts who were assessing the specific works of EHT over the two-and-a-half-decade period. The study was scheduled to be completed next year. Early results were already illuminating. Overall, the consensus seemed to be a validation the EHT approach.

Nevertheless, as the preliminary findings looked positive, she noticed that many of her in-house colleagues impulsively lost interest in what she considered to still be an active case and a potentially watershed analysis. She wanted to make sure everyone was fully engaged and informed. She decided, accordingly, to look more deeply—to assess the issue of sustainability as thoroughly as possible. She dug through boxes of archived files. She contacted outside colleagues. She admitted what she found was at first perplexing. Then it became disturbing. Much of the on-the-ground funding for EHTs projects came from the International Center for Democratic Ideals. ICDI's professed mandate was to promote democratization. It was unclear how these aims dovetailed with those of EHT. She needed to dig even deeper. She had just presented an interim report to the DG asking for more resources to more fully illuminate the EHT-ICDI links. González, however, had not agreed. He saw this as a tangent to the main objective of evaluating EHT. He wanted to close the case—or as he put it, promptly make the pitch to the donors. He simply (or pragmatically, as he said) wanted to use the present positive though preliminary evaluation results for launching new efforts for increasing funding for essential work in the field.

"This all made some sort of sense to me," Paula said, completing her story, "but I don't see how the two pathways are mutually exclusive, frankly. I lobbied to quickly kick off the drive for new and expanded funding while still undertaking a deeper dive into the organization's institutional linkages and on-the-ground long-term impacts. After all, our partnerships are all about our lasting successes or failures. Still, the boss has spoken, and we'll go forward as he wishes. You can tell your readers that working overseas is just like working in the US, it's all about doing what your boss wants you to do. I truly don't know if I'll be able to add a bit more of my personal touch on what has become my pet project before this all wraps up. I'll see. Again, just like back home, we all only do what we can do."

Thanking Paula for her time and the careful briefing on her activities, Charlie returned to the hotel not to kill two birds with one stone, but to use one stone to serve two birds. He drafted a three-paragraph article of what Robin McCandless would have called "bla-bla-bla". This was the pretend journalistic piece for the Denver Gazette. It was all fluff and only superficially floated over Paula's work at EHT, focusing on how she, a girl from the West, had slowly worked her way to the shores of Lake Geneva (her trajectory somehow touching a nerve when he thought of his own). Surprising himself at his own journalistic abilities, humble though they may be (possibly the "sharpening" had actually done something), he put this platitudinous composition in an envelope to drop off the next day at EHT on his way to the airport. He added, by prearrangement, the telephone number of the offices of Fredericks, Higgins, and Woods with a brief explanation that he had contracted with a Chicago area secretarial service by the same name since, as a stringer, he did not have any home office support. Paula could leave any messages about the article with the secretary at the enclosed number.

Using the mock article as the starting point for the second bird, Charlie then prepared several pages of detailed notes on his yellow legal pad (also from Fredericks, Higgins, and Woods). These were his debriefing notes for Robin (Mr. McCandless, he still wasn't sure). His conclusions were that there was no immediate problem, but that the issue should be monitored. The DG, in spite of an appearance of nonchalance, was likely concerned about what Paula could still uncover—and there appeared to be quite some material to uncover if things went pear-shaped. For her part, Paula was intelligent and hard working—through years of experience she had acquired a keen understanding of what made sense and what didn't. She wanted to know more about the ties between EHT and ICDI. If they weren't very lucky, there could be some revelations that both EHT and ICDI would likely regret.

The next day Charlie, now feeling very much the seasoned traveler, took the three-hour Iberian flight to Granada. The staff at Fredericks, Higgins, and Woods had booked him at the Alhambra Palace Hotel. He took the hotel limousine and was nearly in shock from the time he entered the plush leather seats of the Mercedes-Maybach S650 Pullman until he took his shoes off on the equally plush Savonnerie carpet in his extremely luxurious suite—it was almost embarrassingly extravagant compared to his ordinary lifestyle. Nonetheless, he enjoyed this chance to, as his mother used to say, "See how the other half lived."

He wished Jo could see it.

Then it was off to the Delpro offices.

The Granada Delpro office was located on the top floor of a six-story building with a 1940's vintage stone façade, in an old and rather shabby part of the city. The empty and dimly-lit reception area was adorned with dirty Moorish tiles on the floor and unkept mahogany siding on the walls—all speaking of better times gone by. There was an old steel and bronze lift with a metal accordion door and open, screened sides. When the contraption screeched to a stop on sixth floor, he found himself in a surprisingly well-lit corridor with doors at each end. Delpro was simply stenciled on one frosted glass window.

Passing through the door, Charlie found himself in a contemporary office space. To his right was a marble-topped counter, serving as a parapet for a modish glass-topped desk at which sat an equally modish and youngish, well-groomed blonde woman who greeted him with an unmistakable Brooklyn accent.

Charlie asked to see Mr. Smith, saying casually he was coming from Mr. McCandless. With what seemed to be amazing rapidity, a rather rotund late-middle-aged gentleman with an impeccably tailored suit appeared at the marble-topped counter.

Before escorting Charlie down the hallway to an office with good quality but functional furniture and a remarkable view of this piece of the city, the gentleman extended a firm and toughened hand, introducing himself as Horace Smith. As Charlie entered the office with the panoramic view, he found himself wondering about the name Horace. He had spent his entire life up until recently never encountering anyone named Horace. Then Julian had told him about Robin McCandless' younger brother, Sir Horace Barthley. Now he was entering into an office in Spain of Mr. Horace Smith. Strange.

Strange or not, Mr. Horace Smith had communications of suitable importance for his, and it seemed everyone's, overlord, Robin McCandless, that they were to be hand-carried from the home of The Alhambra to the shores of Lake Michigan.

Over a cup of coffee equally savory as that in Geneva, Horace Smith handed the young emissary two large manila envelopes sealed with wax.

"Here you are, son. Take good care of these."

"Thanks," Charlie said between sips, "anything else to go or anything I should tell Mr. McCandless?"

"Often, the least said the best," the corpulent office manager replied, "just tell him I send my warmest regards."

With that, the cup was drained, and Charlie was back in the squealing lift to retrace his steps to the hotel.

Then, within less than twenty-four hours, Charlie witnessed that dizziness and almost out-of-body experience that befalls international travelers as he was almost robotically herded from hotel to airport, through security and immigration, to the first-class lounge, to his seat in the plane, through US Immigration and Customs at O'Hare, and to a taxi back to his apartment in Abbott Park.

Without Jo there, he could not think, *God, it's good to be home.* But he could think, *What the hell, it's good to be back after a satisfactory assignment.* He hoped things were truly satisfactory. The next day he would meet Robin McCandless and then he would know.

⋀⋀⋀⋁⋀⋀⋀

Charlie was again slated to have lunch with Robin McCandless so, before going to the mansion, he stopped at the Lake Center.

In some bizarre way, he was always glad to see Jo in her private room. It was, of course, not at all that he was in any way happy to see her in this purported vegetative state. It was terrible beyond words. But at least she was peaceful. At least he could hope—could pray—that she would come out of this horrible state (whatever it really was) and come back to him as the Jo he so loved.

It almost hadn't been so.

It wasn't enough that he had had to contend with the terrible accident.

First, her health insurance company began threatening to stop coverage; saying long-term care was not part of the coverage. Then, Jo's family wanted her moved closer to them, to a facility in Chicago. Finally, he was pressured by some—especially the doctors—to unplug the machines. They assured him that she was already braindead and putting an end to it all would be the best thing to do for all concerned.

Charlie had fought all these battles.

It had seemed he was losing—at least with the insurance companies and possibly with Jo's family. The doctors really couldn't do anything without her family's consent, and they were completely flummoxed. However, his own position, if anyone cared, was clear. He was not about to suggest anyone give approval for any irrevocable action since he was sure this was not permanent—that it too would pass.

Then the gods blinked.

Robert Howell from Thorne contacted Charlie. He wanted to let him know that there was a supplemental insurance plan that may not have shown up when they were making the initial arrangements for Jo's treatment. This would cover one hundred percent of long-term care including a private room and even a private nurse if necessary. And the plan, a recent optional add-on for Thorne employees, would cover all household members, even if not legally part of the family. He and Jo would not need to be married to be covered.

Charlie was more than grateful. Although he sensed Robin McCandless' fingerprints all over this supposedly heretofore untapped policy, it was what was needed. Jo's care was assured. Jo's family, acknowledging they could not provide the same level of support, begrudgingly agreed for her to stay at the Lake Center where they visited at least once a month.

Thus, as Charlie went through the center's swinging glass doors before going on to meet with Robin McCandless, he was well aware that he had much for which to be thankful—and probably much for which he had to thank Robin McCandless.

As had become his routine, he sat by Jo's bed and told her about Geneva, González, Paula, Granada, Horace, and flying first class on Swiss Air and Iberian. He shared with her his thoughts and feelings. He reminded her that she had been the first one of them to shine a light on how complex and confusing all things Delpro and all things related to the powerful pink man were—how the unknowns always seemed to outweigh the knowns. He felt he should, nonetheless, also remind her that they had a lot for which to be thankful, including this very room where the two were currently together—probably all this due in one way or another to that very same pink man.

Charlie then silently surveyed the room, took a deep breath, and with a lump in his throat and tears on his cheeks, gave Jo a kiss on her forehead and went back to his BMW for the run over to the pink man's palace.

True to form, Robin met Charlie poolside, more dapperly dressed than the last time and seated at a table resplendent with literally dozens of plates.

"Welcome back, lad. I greet you with a smorgasbord to accompany our discussions and to celebrate your well-done assignment."

After shaking hands, handing over the package from Mr. Smith (including his handwritten notes on legal pad sheets), and taking the proffered seat, Charlie tried to acknowledge his recent work with simplicity.

"Thank you, it's good to be back. Everything went well because everything was well organized, and everyone cooperated fully. It was a snap."

"Sadly, probably not totally a snap. You had to draw people out, ask the right questions, and take meticulous mental notes. You did well."

"Thank you."

"Have you figured it out," Robin offered what seemed to be a non sequitur.

"Figured out?"

"Yes." He gave a conspiratorial half smile, "Delpro?"

"Probably not."

"I don't imagine so. It's complicated."

"Way back when—way back when I first met you, Julian had given me a brief history. But that's about as far as I've ever gone—just skating on the surface."

"Julian knows parts of the story. I'm sure he tried to educate you about our origins, about Roy Franklin and all?"

"I did get the five-minute summary."

"That's a good start. Of course, things always change, and they've changed a lot since Roy's days."

"Sure."

"Once we started testing our wings, we set up, what we naively and boorishly called a global headquarters on the West Coast.

"I have always been here, right in the center of the country. Our headquarters were sort of a feint to attract all the attention away from the true leadership. Still, there were also practical matters. We were rapidly expanding and developing offices in other countries. We needed a good way to coordinate and communicate. A global hub made sense.

"Yet, as we grew both geographically and in terms of the type of work we did, a hub in the US seemed to be a liability and an unreasonably high cost in order to assemble all the high-caliber high-priced staff we needed to do what had to be done. A few years ago, for tax purposes as well as to lower our profile, we moved offshore—to the Cayman Islands.

"Right now, Delpro, *sensu stricto*, has no US offices. In this country, in fact, we have only limited work that we openly label as 'Delpro.' We, along with some close colleagues, may continue to speak of 'Delpro' as though it was synonymous with all that we do. In some ways this still may be true. In a meaningful way, one cannot unwind Delpro from all we do.

"My role has changed little over these years. Delpro has, however, grown a lot on the world stage. And we've changed the way we see ourselves and, hopefully, the way others see us. Our public image and structure have metamorphosed into something a little less extravagant than a gaudy high-rise in Menlo Park, California.

"We may continue to think, and even speak of 'Delpro' as the umbrella covering all we do—and this isn't really wrong—to many, Delpro is everything. However, to the outside we need to present the image we hope we have created. To the outside, Delpro is the overseas part of our work. So far, we've not coined a title to encompass all we do domestically.

"This two-pronged organization—these two baskets of activities—really have little impact on what I do. Therefore, they have equally modest effect on what you do. Nonetheless, you need to be aware of this bimodal structure and shine a light on it when need-be.

"Well, enough of the high-altitude snapshots. As I've insinuated, this work you've just completed was, I think, the first of many such assignments. I do want you at Delpro—the quintessential one-size-fits-all Delpro—although one size may not fit all, it certainly covers all. I want you closer to the center of things—even if this means focusing principally on offshore events. I've arranged with Fredericks, Higgins, and Woods. They've a spare office they'll set up for you. You'll be able to use their secretaries and library. You should have everything you need—otherwise let me know.

"They need about a week to get everything shuffled about in their office, so take some time off and then come by here in a week—at nine a.m.—and we'll get a list of assignments that you can work on in your new office. But I warn you, there'll be a lot of travel so don't get too comfortable in that overstuffed desk chair you'll probably have."

With that, to Charlie's surprise, there was no more shop talk. There was no debriefing. No discussion of EHT nor ICDI. No queries about González nor his American colleague perhaps turned nemesis. Nothing.

They focused on the weather, the pollution in Lake Michigan, and the price of corn. As Robin guided the meandering conversation through a mishmash of topics, they equally meandered across the table sampling tidbits from the wide assortment of meats, fruits, and vegetables—all accompanied by a very good *Liebfraumilch*.

As he was leaving the patio, Robin called after him, "Don't worry, lad, we'll talk about it all after I've read your notes."

ᛉ ᛉ ᛉ ᛦ ᛉ ᛉ ᛉ

He was unsure if Robin McCandless was aware (probably), but a week off was not a welcome event for Charlie. He wanted just the opposite—cram two weeks of work into five days. But it was what it was.

He made daily visits to the Lake Center and Grove Forest. He washed and waxed his car. He vacuumed and washed the floors of his apartment. He even went out to try going to a bar but got lost without Jo.

Most of the time, he felt like he was simply spinning his wheels.

Then there was a call from Fredericks, Higgins, and Woods; his office was ready. The next day he went back to the pretentious palace of Robin McCandless.

The now well-known pattern repeated itself (with a few variations: no spirits, coffee; no sit-down meal, pastries) and soon Charlie was sipping a cup of coffee that rivaled that of Geneva or Granada, listening to his keeper.

"Lad," Robin said, picking up as if on cue, "I'll not bore you with a rerun of all we've already discussed. I hear my folks down the street have your office ready. You're here, so I assume you're ready. It's time to move."

It was not a question and Charlie continued concentrating on the wisps of vapor that slowly lifted off the surface of his coffee cup.

"We need to start with a follow-up to the material you carried from Mr. Smith," Robin went on. Charlie was unsure exactly to whom 'we' referred, but he continued listening hoping it would become clearer.

"Then I want to add some related concerns into which you can look. No testing the water for you. You have to dive in—into the deep end. The people at Fredericks, Higgins, and Woods will provide you with all the detailed material—past and present. You'll dig out all you need to know. I'll just tell you what I need to know.

"As you did in Geneva, we need you to examine what we're doing—especially in places where there are others who are snooping around or otherwise trying to meddle. We don't want, we won't tolerate meddlers. We're doing too much too fast to get sidetracked by busybodies—any busybodies. I don't give a good god damn from where they come, they have no business getting into our business. I hope this is clear!

"Granada is a critical link in a chain we've carefully forged. A chain that connects lots of businesses and makes us all lots of money. I need not say more. Study and let me know how you'll keep this chain strong.

"This same chain loops down to southern Africa. You'll have all those documents, too. I need you to look these over very carefully and include them in your review. You bring new eyes and probably new ways of looking at things. I, we, want you to honestly look at what we're doing and let us know how we can keep doing it. We can't afford to have people like that Paula what's-her-name prying into our affairs.

"I've dropped you into a very important job. You! You who literally fell into my lap with no experience. You who apparently are running from you don't know what to where you don't know.

"I am not trying to berate you. I am not trying to be rude or even unappreciative. You have done good work for us and we've been watching very closely. Still, you need to know, I'm taking a big risk here. You're still basically an unknown—especially to my colleagues who are always looking over my shoulder. You must understand that there's a lot at stake and there's no going back. Failure is not tolerated. It evaporates. I hope this is clear!"

It was clear to Charlie that it was unclear. Nothing was clear. But he had never seen his master so energized—so bound and determined. And, it was clear, as the patron had stated, that he was as an unknown just as the justifications for most of his actions were unknown. While he frequently felt himself inexperienced and even exposed, others must have more often than not seen this as a much more precarious weakness—an identifiable risk that may not be worth taking. Although it was not clear, it was apparent that it was a very serious matter, both to his chief (now nearly incandescent carmine as the natural hues of his features darkened with his enthusiasm) and the overlords in general. He had to say something. Remembering Mr. Smith's words about the least said, he tried the minimalistic approach.

"I know it's important. I know it's a lot. So, I'd best get my butt over to the office and start."

This seemed to satisfy his host. An appointment was made for an update in a week. A tiny bit of small talk accompanied the draining of the coffee cups, and Charlie was soon parking in front of the offices of Fredericks, Higgins, and Woods. The next chapter had begun. His slice of pie was now considerably more consequential.

ᛉ ᛉ ᛉ ᛃ ᛉ ᛉ ᛉ

Charlie's new office had no real pizazz. It was functional and the right size but lacked personality. To Charlie, it was a perfect fit with the people who worked at Fredericks, Higgins, and Woods: business-like and staid, verging on glum. Everyone was polite—polite as though they were greeting a doltish dowager aunt.

His guard jobs, his part in the nightshift at the printery, his time at Spot On, and even his stays at Saphir and Spader as well as J. P. Thorne had all had a certain ambiance—a certain, though often not too profound, camaraderie among staff. Apparently, with similar thoughts as Mr. Smith's, the powers that be at Fredericks, Higgins, and Woods felt less was more in regard to personal interactions. The place was downright dull.

Still, Charlie's major worry was not his working environment—it was the work itself. As promised by Robin (Mr. McCandless, he was never sure), his office was also fully stocked with reams and reams of papers—reports, letters, contracts, memos, anything and everything. As he began to peruse these pages, he realized he was not going to be able to immediately absorb the totality of their content. It was going to take a lot of work. He had to learn a lot on the fly to be able to digest the necessary background in order to do what was expected. It wasn't going to be easy.

It wasn't just the terminology, the geography, nor the methodology—it was everything. It was all foreign. It was all baffling. It was frequently indecipherable. While Charlie needed more than just help at grasping the legalese, the team at Fredericks, Higgins, and Woods felt this squatter (as they apparently thought of him), this interloper forced upon them by their master, was imposing more than simply on their space—he was imposing on their time, on their billable hours. And this was totally unacceptable. He brought nothing but question after question after question. This intruder was clearly out of his depth but safeguarded by Robin McCandless' blessing. While they could try and tarnish this meddler's apparent shine in the eyes of the patriarch, this would take some contriving and some time. In the immediate, they needed a buffer.

The partners decided, out of their own pockets and for their own preservation (couldn't have such nonsense cutting into billable hours, after all), to provide the uninvited guest with one of their very junior legal aids. Thus, Sue Ann was assigned to Charlie for the foreseeable future.

Sue Ann Hoffman was a local girl. She had been born and raised nearly fifty miles east of Fredericks, Higgins, and Woods' offices in the town of Harvard. As many in a community that considered itself as the "Milk Capital of the World," Sue Ann had grown up on a dairy farm; her older brother still minded the cows. She had gone on to follow a path in legal studies at the College of Lake County, finding herself at Fredericks, Higgins, and Woods fresh out of school.

The partners had no real feelings about nor assessment of Sue Ann. For them it was just simple process—last on, first off. They physically moved her to a desk right outside Charlie's office. They told her to help as much as she could for as long as she was needed. And they bid her good luck.

The partners might have been surprised if they had taken the time to know Sue Ann better.

Sue Ann was really smart. Classmates and teachers alike had called her resolute—at times, stubborn. She still had somewhat of a cute-country-girl demeanor—now more cultivated than a true remnant of her childhood. She dressed to blend in. She worked on being polite but unremarkable. She completely believed that actions spoke more loudly than words; and she was determined to sparkle through her actions. She understood people well. She read situations well. She had an excellent vocabulary. She was a good writer and a rapid reader. In short, she was, though completely by accident, the perfect match for Charlie.

For Charlie, Sue Ann was initially just another part of the Fredericks, Higgins, and Woods' scenery. He was struggling to get grounded. She was pleasant. She was helpful. She was not overbearing. She was a welcome addition to his daily struggle. But he honestly had no appreciation of who she was nor of how she could help. At first, she was just another fixture in this strange melancholy office where he had been thrown. He wasn't even sure if the melancholy was totally due to the office or to his state of mind.

⋀ ⋀ ⋀ ⋁ ⋀ ⋀ ⋀

Sue Ann knew knowledge was power. She realized immediately that assigning her to assist a seemingly ill-equipped and unwelcome outsider because of orders from above would open doors to her that she could never have hoped to open if she were still sitting in her old seat as the newest untried legal aid in the office. To her, this was a chance of a lifetime (if the partners only knew).

In addition to her other attributes, Sue Ann was a very well-organized person. She was a problem-solver. She also, in the politest of ways, was more than willing to move out of her slot and imperceptibly become an important piece on the chessboard.

As Charlie struggled to gain any footing, Sue Ann, now a formal member of the team, gently guided the guy who was ostensibly her immediate boss. She suggested to an anxious Charlie that perhaps the best thing to do was to start at the beginning.

While Robin McCandless had targeted some special topics when he set his apostle loose in the archives, the compliant partners of Fredericks, Higgins, and Woods had effectively blazed the trail for Charlie to have access to any and all Delpro papers—possibly even active files (this latter still untested).

With this broad canvas upon which to work, Sue Ann offered that the most effective way for Charlie to enter the subject—to get to where Robin McCandless ultimately wanted him to go—was to retrace his steps as he had started any work in any way related to Delpro.

This appealed to Charlie's pragmatism. It allowed him to initially deal with more of the known than the unknown. However, in spite of its apparent logic, he was unsure of the outcome. As he shared with Sue Ann, many of the activities with which he had been involved under the watchful eyes of Sam or Dan—and definitely under the scrutiny of Robin—had been wrapped in secrecy. Undoubtedly by design, he had never seen nor been privy to more than a thin slice of the wider operation. There were so many secrets. How could they ever pierce the solid wall of darkness?

Unwaveringly, Sue Ann recalled for Charlie a quote from Samuel Johnson, the eighteenth-century writer, she had unavoidably studied in college: "*To keep your secret is wisdom; but to expect others to keep it is folly.*"

Scratching the Surface

S UE ANN WAS TALENTED. Sue Ann worked tirelessly.
To get started, she prepared a notebook for Charlie to fill out including tables that outlined all his Delpro-related (in any way, she stressed) assignments. When he had filled in the dates, the locations, and the main objectives as he had understood them, using the tables as her principal references, Sue Ann dove into the archives. She developed an individual folder for what she saw as each separate project. She photocopied prime documents such as budgets or activity summaries. She then developed an annotated bibliography for each project so she could easily go back to the files to get supplemental information as needed.

While she began to build the foundation, she proposed Charlie go back over all his own material from his days at Spot On, Saphir and Spader, along with J. P. Thorne to refresh his memory about all these "projects"—as she now called them.

As Sue Ann filled files and deciphered chronicles overflowing with legalese, Charlie, after rereading his recent biography through safeguarded notes and journals, would take the opportunity of down time to visit Jo. He would sit by her bed, introduce her to Sue Ann, ask if she knew anything about Samuel Johnson, tell her of last night's thunderstorm. He would share his deepest worries that he wasn't up to the job. After all, a kid from the lakebed with a high school diploma—how far could one hope to go? Did she, he asked, think he was already over his head? He would be very open about his almost always hidden concerns that he really didn't understand what everything he was doing was all about. Maybe Sue Ann would help. Did Jo think so?

Generally, Charlie went to the Lake Center to keep her company and keep her up to date as he remained confident that she would, as a Phoenix, rise from her bed one day. Generally, Charlie went to the Lake Center to try and retain his sanity.

⋀ ⋀⋀⋁⋀⋀

Sue Ann had to use a liberal dose of imagination in her work. This came naturally. She would interpolate from what she found—trying diligently to be as objective as possible. Yet, objective or not, it was hard not to be shaken by the potential implications of what possibly had happened and equally possibly still was happening. It was hard not to be stunned by the conceivable sheer scope of many of the activities in which Charlie had shared to varying degrees.

As she broke through the surface layers, Sue Ann probed deeper and deeper.

She worked chronologically. Her fist plunge was into the voyages of the *Velvet*. Here the initial view was outwardly clear, surreptitious movement of contraband between the US and Canada. It seemed obvious the *Velvet's* crew dropped off and picked up relatively small volumes of cargo that were intentionally kept undisclosed—contraband.

Given the relatively small size of the cargo—the *Velvet* indeed only a twenty-foot craft—it appeared logical that the cargo consisted of high-value products. Here size didn't matter. Sue Ann was looking for pricy articles moving across the northern border.

Using the firm's law library as well as Fredericks, Higgins, and Woods' good name (possibly embellishing her own role in the organization), Sue Ann was able to take a wider look at activities that corresponded with the trips of the *Velvet*. She was able to look for quality and not quantity. She was able to look at various commercial inventories, bank records, consumer sales, or any other indicators that had noticeably changed around the time the *Velvet* dropped off its cargos—those in Canada and those in the US.

It was a big task that she narrowed by assuming the reactions to the *Velvet's* passing would happen in a relatively small if complex geographic area that included the margins of Lake Michigan in Illinois and Ontario—near the points of origin and departure of the *Velvet's* voyages.

It was a tough job, but slowly enough pieces began to fall into place to allow Sue Ann to get at least the grossest outlines of a set of actions that were in all probability part of a much larger picture. One of the law firm's partners' longtime contacts, who somehow understood Sue Ann to be a partner herself, sketched for her the pathway of money being laundered from the US into Canada. With this vignette, she zoomed in on southern Ontario and was able to find the beginnings of a trail that showed considerable movement after each of the *Velvet's* landings.

Employing similar tactics, she was able to deduce that the items being injected into markets around Chicago at the times of the *Velvet's* voyages were likely pharmaceuticals. This made sense as there was a well-established black-market trade in medications coming from Canada where these vital products sold for significantly lower prices. One of the critical matters, however, was whether or not the remedies coming from the north were pirated or not. Markets everywhere were flooded with fake treatments. These were at best ineffective, at worst, harmful.

Sue Ann then attempted to trace the origins of the drugs—looking for any manufacturer who had noticeable sales at times corresponding to visits by the *Velvet*. Painstakingly, she was able to tentatively identify one company that kept appearing in her searches: Natural Products, Ltd. This verdict was then confirmed as she discovered that Natural Products Ltd. imported a variety of base materials to make their medicaments from companies that were part of the wider Delpro family scattered around the world. Reversing course, she was then able to uncover the path of significant sums also coming into Natural Products' coffers at the times of the *Velvet's* landings.

At least some of the dots connected. It appeared the *Velvet* brought back prescription medications—whether fraudulent or not was unclear. On the outward-bound leg, nearly certainly the craft carried large sums of cash for these medications along with additional amounts to be directed to still-to-be-identified actions. The vessel may also have carried hard-to-find pharmaceutical ingredients. Furthermore, Sue Ann's digging revealed that special labels and packaging were often used to try and fight against illegal imports. It was equally likely, as her sources recounted, that the *Velvet* carried wrapping, branding, and marketing materials on the northward journey for use by Natural Products such that the finished Canadian products could be easily disguised as being made in America when set out on pharmacy shelves in the greater Chicago area.

The pieces were falling into place—or at least a lot of them for but one project. Spot On was an intermediary (possibly one of many) to transfer significant sums coming from the Delpro hub in the Caymans and going to Delpro operations worldwide. Completing the circle, pharmaceuticals were brought back that were in all likelihood sold for high profits, assisting Delpro not only with the direct sales of these drugs but also with the earnings from the continued manufacturing of the drugs that used Delpro inputs. It was a twofer.

Yes, it was largely hypothetical. Yes, it was not part of Charlie's immediate task as defined by the great Robin McCandless. But it did set the stage for future research that would follow the same template. It also considerably enhanced Sue Ann's basket of knowledge (facts and near-facts) that she knew would serve her well in the future.

⋀ ⋀ ⋀ ⋁ ⋀ ⋀

In the present situation, Sue Ann's and Charlie's priorities seemed to align. This alignment was, of course, heavily influenced by Sue Ann's (not so impartial nor flexible) views as to the best way forward and her ability to convince Charlie, her ostensible immediate supervisor, that she should be in the lead as they moved together in this chosen direction.

While Charlie was focusing on getting a wider understanding of the various operations with which he had been involved to be able to better interpret the issues that had been flagged by Robin McCandless, Sue Ann was motivated by enlarging her hamper of information to the maximum possible—seeing this as a springboard to bigger and greater things. As long as their aims overlapped and she could persuade Charlie that she should take the first cut at the subjects to prepare briefings for him (all that legalese to decode), there was a joint effort where she was subtly in the driver's seat.

So far, so good.

Guided by her work following the *Velvet* and thinking of the old adage about the best is yet to come, Sue Ann shifted her attention to the information provided by Charlie about his trips to Costa Rica.

Similar to the northern case, here things were multidimensional.

As before, at the onset, there were more questions than answers. For example, Sue Ann pondered, why was Delpro insistent on linking-in community development groups like the missionaries? At least on the surface, their project was this really about establishing a more profitable export market for local fishers—pretty straight forward. Where did the pertinacious proselytizers (as Charlie had described them) fit? For a starting point, she decided to probe this evangelistic angle. The public information about the fish exports was easily accessible. But why the missionaries?

Charlie's only reference was the Volmans. Sam had stressed the importance of working with them, but as far as Sue Ann could tell, beyond Charlie visiting their mission and their attendance at a few preliminary meetings, their role was insignificant. There was something more.

The first something was rather readily apparent as Sue Ann dug deeper. Delpro always wished to portray itself as charitably minded and donated considerable sums to the church and church annual reports indicated a fair portion of these gifts filtered down to the Volman's mission budget.

Sue Ann then discovered that the Volman's mission was one of the charter members of the Costa Rican Missionary Society. This alliance regrouped Christian proselytizers from across the country—reportedly both for solidarity and tactical benefits. In the society's quarterly newsletter, Sue Ann found articles from the Volmans, supporting the new fish export endeavors and proposing that the society organize training sessions for community youth to give them basic skills that would help them apply for potential new better-paying jobs at the upcoming fishery facilities. As part of this process, there was a census of potential trainees. In the society's publicly available archives, Sue Ann was even able to find a master list of unemployed youth in communities served by society members. It was unclear how many of those registered would actually be able to find a good job in fish processing. Yet, by a fluke, Sue Ann found the name of one of the hopeful job seekers in a later version of the same newsletter. He was now missing; his family was asking churchgoers to provide any information as to his whereabouts.

Sue Ann then enlarged her scope and looked at any records of missing people where these people were also on the society's list. There were more than just a few—the dates of these absences establishing a timeline much as she had found with the voyages of the *Velvet*.

This chronology, as in Ontario, opened the door to the possibility— or probability—that Delpro was doing more than shipping fish to Texas. She explored the available documents relating to the facility promoted by Spot On at Rio Barranca. The project had gone ahead, reportedly with great success, and was currently under full operation as *Peces Tropicales*

Transamericanos—or simply PTT to local fishermen who were happy to get top prices for their catch even though it was not enjoyed by Costa Ricans but shipped north to the United States.

As she reviewed the records of PTT, she found, again much as the case with Natural Products, Ltd., the Costa Rican company seemed to import a variety of products from a number of companies around the world—some, at least, recognizable as Delpro affiliates. This, in and of itself, was noteworthy, as these products, cited on customs, tax, another official documents as items such as fertilizer, lime, vegetable starch, seed oils, and vitamin C, had logically little to do with exporting fresh iced fish or even processing quick-frozen fillets which was PTTs second production line.

Delving deeper into PTTs bank records, given the stated level of business, there seemed to be a remarkably low level of capitalization. Fishers were paid in cash for their catch. Most likely, this would require that considerable cash reserves be kept in a local bank. Furthermore, as officially a stand-alone Costa Rican firm, there should be regular influxes of capital from the US into a local bank from the sales of the fresh fish airfreighted to the Texas processor, not to mention receipts from frozen products. No such transactions appeared. Not only was there more financial activity than could easily be explained, including the importation of a wide variety of unusual products, but the local financial institutions, at first glance, were not at all involved in the affairs of PTT. It was most unusual.

As Sue Ann continued to study PTT, one thing that stood out was that, while most of the company's officers were either from Costa Rica or the US, there was one senior board member from Guinea Bissau—a certain Senior Tomas Ferreira. While a Lusophone from West Africa might not be too strange, what really caught Sue Ann's eye was not so much the person nor his home base but rather the fact, as she examined the gentleman's story, that he seemed to make quarterly trips to Costa Rica via Lisbon. This was not only a long haul, but it looked difficult to justify the high cost (carrier records showed Tomas always flew first class) for someone who was only a board member.

Sue Ann pursued Senior Tomas Ferreira through the archives. Though there was not a wealth of information, the man himself remaining largely an unanswered riddle, she was able to ascertain that he was on the board of directors of several other companies scattered about the globe. Among these were some of the suppliers of the products imported by PTT. In trying to piece the puzzle together, of special interest were three international suppliers with joint ventures in the country: Trusted Industrial Products Ltd., Poseidon Consignments, and Western Farm Supply, Inc. Although she was not able to link these firms directly to Delpro as she had been able to do for Natural Products' suppliers, these three companies unquestionably fit the mold of Delpro subsidiaries. Moreover, they were unquestionably coupled to PTT and PTTs obscure activities that exceeded the popularly acknowledged business of fish exports.

Sue Ann confirmed that Senior Ferreira was on the board of two US companies, Simpson Investments and General Industrial and Chemical Products, that were indicated by reliable sources to be tied to Delpro. Additionally, she was able to place Senior Tomas on the board of a company based in Tanzania, Equatorial Management, but was unable to build a solid case for Delpro's direct involvement in this large, diversified pan-African operation.

In the process of following Senior Tomas' trail, Sue Ann did turn over some stones that soldered another link in the growing chain. Though she could not connect Western Farm Supply, Inc. directly with Delpro, after examining documents obtained with great difficulty from their San José offices, she was able to couple this company to two very large and amorphous firms: Ace Foods and Farm Services. Furthermore, her trusted contacts indicated the strong probability that these two veiled intercontinental mega-enterprises had close bonds to Delpro.

Circles within circles and twisted webs. Delpro was everywhere.

Much of this was not surprising given Delpro's known partnership with Spot On. Yet, for every discoverable link in this lengthy chain, Sue Ann was convinced there were a dozen more hidden in the shifting sands.

There was a great deal going on below the surface.

Once more, this conclusion was based on a liberal measure of supposition. But there were definitely enough threads upon which to pull to see how intentionally tangled the PTT activities could be and how interwoven they might be into all variety of nefarious transnational actions. Yet, these were Sue Ann's thoughts, not the formal results of her assignment. She was Charlie's legal assistant, and her mandate was much narrower than the analyses she had undertaken.

She had amassed a profuse quantity of data. She had not only exceeded the demands of the assignment, but she had also exceeded her own expectations. She had managed to acquire a wealth of material.

She made voluminous notes for herself, complete with her references and photocopies. These were the files for her basket—her cache. Then she wound up her work for Charlie, reducing and filtering her material into an adulterated version that contained just enough of the untoward facts to lay a foundation upon which Charlie could build for his assignment with their master Robin McCandless, but also which could, at Sue Ann's desecration, be expanded and magnified to incorporate other troublesome bits of information if this tactic proved to be to her advantage in future matters pertaining to Charlie's tasks for the higher-ups.

For Sue Ann, things were working out.

ⵉ ⵉⵉⵡⵉⵉ

Sue Ann was a professional.

Although her findings could have been construed to highlight a tapestry of criminality, and although all the material leading to this possible conclusion was thoroughly documented in her own files, she prepared very succinct and neutral reports for Charlie. She avoided all aspersions of wrongdoing. She simply and clearly outlined the various other possible actors in the projects that had been implemented in Ontario and Costa Rica along with Charlie's role in these larger operations. There was no drama. There was no innuendo. There were only the barest of provable facts.

Initially, Charlie accepted Sue Ann's work at face value. He saw (in, Sue Ann thought, a little too much of an oversimplification) the two analyses as abstract case studies and not real-life actions with which he had personally had a role. He saw them as models of how a multiplicity of organizations and actors could work in unison where the whole was truly greater than the sum of the parts. He saw them as testaments to the good management of Delpro and, by inference, the good leadership of Robin McCandless.

Trying to follow Robin McCandless' marching orders as closely as possible, Charlie saw Sue Ann's analyses of his own earlier work as the components of a compound lens (like in the Swift microscope from biology class) through which he could now assess other operations, starting with the targets of his recent European trip. His leading takeaway from Sue Ann's efforts was that successful operations required the knitting together of a host of structures that provided for a viable and profitable set of investments while also offering the necessary protection from unwanted scrutiny—protection provided through the intricacies of the knitting.

Robin McCandless was, Charlie understood, interested in the potential negative impacts of meddlers and busybodies, as he called them. Robin McCandless was, Charlie understood, interested in making sure Delpro's corporate ass was covered. And, as he had made clear at the mansion, for what were to Charlie still unfathomable reasons, Robin McCandless was interested in having all this done by an untested "lad" who had, as far as Robin McCandless was concerned, fallen in his lap.

But things were as they were. And there were things to get done.

It was time to move forward and show Mr. Robin McCandless that Charlie Stancik, formerly from the lakebed and now from the lakeshore, was up to the job.

Charlie felt Sue Ann's analyses of his early work provided a good approach to examine specific activities, evaluate where and how unwanted outsiders could be the most worrisome. Accordingly, while he took time to go over Sue Ann's reports in detail, he had her start on applying the same techniques to the activities of EHT as well as Delpro/Spain; he instructed his assistant to deal with the two matters as distinct but being diligent for any threads that might connect the two European operations.

At Sue Ann's suggestion, however, Charlie agreed to a slightly modified approach. Unlike the first two analyses which were looking at past actions, the current pair of assessments was contemporary. Their work could conceivably impact on ongoing operations—for better or worse. Given this potential for influencing actions in progress, it seemed more prudent to move slowly. A calendar was drawn up, not based on the progress of the analyses, but based on what they hoped were safe increments of time to avoid any unforced errs on their side. The last thing they wanted to do was to irritate or otherwise jeopardize people or activities they were intending to assist. So, Charlie and Sue Ann would meet every three days to go over progress—adjusting their priorities as they went to minimize any vulnerabilities. Charlie would, if possible, then meet with Robin at least every fortnight to make sure they were on track when viewed from above.

It would all work out.

ᛗ ᛗ ᛗ ᚠ ᛗ ᛗ ᛗ

And it pretty much did.

Charlie and Sue Ann worked together and then Charlie briefed Robin McCandless and got his feedback—strategically, avoiding sharing any of the specific results from Sue Ann's first two pilot analyses. He informed the master only that they had developed a framework for conducting the reviews he had requested based on previous efforts.

Charlie and Sue Ann were not expecting interconnections among all the projects they assessed. After all, some siloing of operations was a common and even favored practice.

They were surprised—and it surprised them that they could still be surprised by their findings.

As much as the episodes in Ontario and Costa Rica were fully disconnected from the issues regarding Geneva and Granada, some common denominators did slowly emerge.

This was chiefly prompted by Mr. Smith's communiqué. In his hand-carried file, he briefly summarized the extensive and diversified agricultural operations that were a major part of Delpro's Spanish portfolio. He glossed over, but subtly underscored, the importance of labor provided by many refugees found in abundance in the southern portion of the Iberian Peninsula—labor provided, in the context of the present communication, in unexplained ways. He followed with a hasty reference to the fact that these operations not only relied on foreign labor but also imported a variety of primary products from other Delpro operations across the globe. Then, referring back to the alien workers, he noted that a large number of charitable organizations and religious groups was increasingly attempting to assist these migrants.

At times, he signaled, representatives from these groups contacted Delpro seeking information about their immigrant labor force. To be better prepared for providing undistinguishable and sterile replies to these bothersome queriers, Mr. Smith had engaged a local consultant to prepare some case studies of Delpro farms were there would be carefully selected indicative data that hopefully, for all intents and purposes, would be taken by the troublesome scrutinizers as representative of all Delpro actions underway across the country—even if this were, in truth, a complete sham.

It was uncertain if the ruse would work. When they knocked on Mr. Smith's door, the bighearted questioners, as they undoubtedly saw themselves, were hard to ignore. Then, when local journalists touted high and low the sufferings of these poor people seeking refuge in Spain, public passion stirred and anyone in regular contact with these miserable folks was susceptible to an extensive, and in their case, undesirable close examination.

Mr. Smith concluded his correspondence, acknowledging that he, and probably most of Delpro management, was not a fan of a public airing of the company's affairs. These matters were complex. These matters were confidential. These matters were best kept under wraps.

It was not too big a stretch to see some similarities with the issues that had taken Charlie to Geneva and EHT. It was again a kind of yin and yang tale. In this dualism of the dark and the bright, EHTs humanitarianism was the bright side, glistening for all to appreciate. ICDI was the evil twin who, under the cover of democracy, opened the door for such apparently candid charitable actions so that these could equally serve as an entrée to much more disreputable, yet profitable actions. ICDI was the dark and deceptive twin who, for the good of all, needed to be formally disavowed from the rest of the family much as Delpro's inglorious role needed to be invisible.

As with all its interventions, Delpro was at its best in the shadows. Publicity and spotlights were to be avoided. But these could not easily be side-stepped when throngs of people were swarming about—unintentionally or not poking into Delpro or tendrils of the Delpro group. Any event that potentially raised the level of public sentiment was a possible threat—a possible risk of some unknown somebody inadvertently but very openly uncovering matters that Delpro worked very hard to conceal.

On the other side of the coin, Delpro had had successes using third party do-gooders to their advantage. A case in point was the support they were able to engender from the missionaries for their fishery investments in Costa Rica (the irony not lost on Charlie and Sue Ann that potentially Delpro funds were surreptitiously funneled to community shepherds while missing members of their flock may well have been press-ganged into Delpro slave labor camps).

Mr. Smith's correspondences had further speculated that it wasn't the do-gooders themselves that were necessarily the major problem. If properly targeted, they could be an asset. But if left free to follow their whims, the chances were high they could accidentally stumble upon the roots of Delpro which Mr. Robin McCandless and his cohorts had hoped had been buried deeply in the sand (the perhaps persistent probability that Murphy's Law would rear its head, Charlie reflected).

Digging up roots was to be avoided—strenuously avoided.

As Charlie and Sue Ann reviewed this part of the puzzle, they came up with a possibly novel solution. When Charlie took their idea to Robin, somewhat unexpectedly, he was ready, even anxious to go ahead.

It was simple. Delpro would set up its own transnational NGO under the cover of one or another humanitarian themes. Then, if the light shown too brightly on Delpro's operations in one place, this altruistic do-gooder group could quickly appear on the scene, create great fanfare elsewhere, effectively diverting attention by using any of a number of bright shiny objects in their quiver. An effective decoy to be used over and over again.

Robin McCandless thought the idea was excellent—a "perfect runaround" he called it. He even had a name for his new NGO: BALJIN.

The Delpro puppet master noticed the quizzical expression on Charlie's face. "It's Romanian."

"What's what?" Charlie was befuddled.

"The name. The name for our new NGO. It's Romanian. It means kindness. It's perfect. And, it has a second meaning. It is also used to describe an unbaptized dead child—some think the ghosts of these children roam the earth. People will prepare food and place it in the cemetery to calm their spirits. We hope our "kind" NGO will calm any who may wish to take a longer look at our work, huh?"

"Yes," Charlie said, catching up, "Yes, indeed. That's a great name and it will be a great tool to address at least part of our concerns."

Thus, BALJIN was born.

⋀⋀⋀⋁⋀⋀⋀

Naming the organization was, of course, just the first step. BALJIN needed to have a charter, to be registered, to have a director as well as a board of directors. Yet, with the help of Fredericks, Higgins, and Woods, this was all quickly accomplished. Communally, they even quickly developed a new letterhead with the NGOs motto: "kindness—strong helping hands and not hand-outs."

Charlie, once again to his surprise, was named as Director and Sue Ann as Assistant Director for Institutional Affairs. They hired a PR person, a secretary, a receptionist, and a bookkeeper. They rented office space in Antioch, twenty miles northeast of Waukegan—Robin McCandless wanting some physical separation from other Delpro-linked locales but still remaining in the general vicinity of northern lakeshore Illinois.

As Robin McCandless had said, it was perfect.

Although Charlie's title had changed, and his salary grown as a result, the job was basically the same. Nonetheless, he was happily out of the dreary offices of Fredericks, Higgins, and Woods. For the first time he felt as though he had his own space. Things were as good as they could be.

Sue Ann continued to wear two hats. While her salary and office were provided by BALJIN, she continued to present herself when it was to her advantage as a legal aid at the firm of Fredericks, Higgins, and Woods. She continued to regularly visit the offices near Artesian Park to use their library and scour their files. She continued to use the partners' private contact lists to get the jump on sensitive topics. She demonstrated skill at working both sides of the street.

Sue Ann and Charlie worked well together and continued to be the center of BALJIN. The newly-hired staff were given the core assignment of making sure the NGO was visible—making sure there was a compelling track record highlighting multiple interventions, be they ever so contrived. Five million dollars of Delpro funds was even immediately released to support overnight improvised token "kind" projects in numerous countries around the world.

Sue Ann and Charlie had to set up practical methods to achieve the master's goals while being camouflaged by the official public face of the NGO. They had to define how BALJIN would be able to assist Delpro operatives and what Delpro operatives had to do to gain this assistance. These guidelines were then sent out confidentially by Robin McCandless himself while the PR team at BALJIN moved forward with a global publicity campaign that presented the NGO as one of the most noteworthy, if not the most noteworthy, humanitarian organizations in the business.

When BALJIN was listed in the census prepared by the well-respected Global NGO Directory, the door was open for a stellar role for another Delpro entity cloaked in the costume of altruism—the guise painstakingly camouflaging the foundation of avaricious predomination that now seemed to creep into every cranny of Charlie's world.

It was complicated, but it was what it was.

And, least he forget, Charlie's slice of the pie now formed an impressive desert in and of itself.

Still sporadically writing in his oft neglected and now shabby diary (but not to his mother), Charlie noted in his journal: *It seems I've been bouncing about like a Ping-Pong ball, maybe BALJIN will bring a smoother path.*

Another corner had been turned on Charlie's journey to his future.

Book II
The Road Back

MTU NI WATU (a person is people)

—SWAHILI PROVERB

Far from the Lakebed

T HE SPIN WORKED. IN five years BALJIN was an omnipresent NGO that gave the appearance of having been in the field for decades—seemingly well-known for its strong and able helping hands.

Over this period, Charlie continued as Director and continued as forlorn lover awaiting Jo to rouse like Sleeping Beauty. Although she did not wake. Although she did not rise from her terribly long slumber as though from a nap. She did not die. Many in a state of lengthy coma never return to this world. By these standards, Jo was doing well. Her brain activity was steadily, if slowly, increasing. Her muscles, almost magically, did not atrophy as expected.

Patients like Jo were evaluated, Charlie learned, on what was called the "Glasgow Coma Scale," or GCS. There was a maximum grade of fifteen points; people who scored eight and above often recovering. Jo had started with a score of five. She had then gradually but tenaciously improved to have a score of eight but stalled there for an extended period. Recently, there had been a burst of progress, Jo now having a score of ten. So, Charlie continued his pilgrimages to the Lake Center trying not to get overly optimistic—but also not to fall too deeply into despair.

On the work front, a regular, if unpredictable, cadence seeped into the daily routine. The preeminence of addressing problematic matters in Geneva or Granda was replaced with focus on new developing hot spots as Delpro's hidden hand pulled the levers of power across the globe.

Although the targets changed, the tactics remained the same. The initial strategy to divert attention through decoys wielded by BALJIN was deemed a success. If snoopy investigators or curious auditors got too close, a calamity would spontaneously uncoil in the vicinity—a calamity that could be efficiently and very publicly addressed by the expertise manifest by BALJIN. It was a kind of open-air prestidigitation. It was a hoodwink as old as time—distract with the right hand while you pick the pocket with the left.

Overlying all this, personally and professionally, was a mask of unreality—a gauzy shroud that seemed to separate the spirit of the man from the lakebed from the spirit of the prestidigitator. As Charlie hopped from Delpro hot spot to hot spot, or sat in his comfortable Illinois office, it was nearly paradoxical to compare the person from the sage scrub to the person traveling first class to the furthest corners of the world. It was as though one could never have evolved into the other. They could not be from the same stalk. They must truly be mirror images of different beings. It was another example of yin and yang. Possibly, Charlie pondered, the bright portion was still clinging to the lakebed. By default, here on the lakeshore, was he therefore in the darkness?

ΛΛΛ∇ΛΛ

BALJIN was, by its own mandate, a humanitarian aid organization. BALJIN was, by its own vision statement, a group of people helping people. BALJIN was, by its own mission statement, a comforting hand for those suffering.

It was hard to imagine BALJIN as darkness.

Other than in those wee hours of the morning when Charlie let his mind float freely, Charlie truly did not think of BALJIN as darkness. After years at the helm, he was convinced, as was the entire staff, the organization was really making a difference. It was compassionate, even if its specific actions were guided in such a way as to provide aegis to Delpro. It was benevolent, even if its actions were intended to give cover to Delpro. It was caring, even if its intended functions were to distract. It was kind, even if the glow of kindness hid the darkness.

This was the bimodal world of Charlie Stancik.

ΛΛΛ∇ΛΛ

Charlie's duties with BALJIN covered the gamut. There were specific one-off assignments, generally coming from Robin McCandless. There was some real effort invested in humanitarian works to justify their reputation and reinforce the outward view of assisting the needy of the world. A main part of his time, however, was spent in replying to issues raised by Delpro affiliates in line with the procedures he and Sue Ann had outlined. He was often sent to fight fires.

An example, in the same vein as the communiqué from Mr. Smith in Spain, was a communication from Mr. Van Houtte, the head of the Zambian office. He had outlined steps Delpro was taking to acquire savannah land on the banks of the Msandile River. The company was seeking to lease 150,000 acres to grow maize and soybeans. Planning and preparation for the farm itself were going well. However, there were possible concerns in getting the lease approved. This was, indeed, the principal reason for contacting BALJIN: problems with NGOs.

Without going into extraneous detail, Mr. Van Houtte described how eastern Zambia, bordering Mozambique, was being inundated by refuges from the civil war going on in that country. These refugees attracted a corresponding flood of NGOs. In one of his rare editorial comments, Mr. Van Houtte compared this to flies being drawn to offal. In and of itself, the movement of displaced persons did not directly impact on the farm project, and the chaotic transboundary ebbs and flows of people offered other opportunities, but, Mr. Van Houtte noted, he would go into this matter in another communication. But there were potentially significant indirect impacts of this disorder. With the multitude of NGOs, the public offices, the ministries—the same ministries with which Delpro needed to work to get their farm going—were being overrun by the representatives of these supposedly philanthropic organizations. These outside helpers who had parachuted in were seeking approval, assistance, or funding for all manner of things purportedly linked to aiding the fleeing Mozambicans. The problem was that this ever-present population of upright and naive NGO staff made it difficult for Delpro representatives, using a carrot and stick approach, to get quick approval of the lease by their newly minted friends in the relevant government agencies. In short, any attempts to promote or perchance prompt corruption were under close scrutiny due to the mob of do-gooders migrating about the capital.

Not only did all this growing external influence make it difficult to covertly leverage the action required, it also laid the groundwork for expanding unwanted oversight. With large sums of money being allocated to humanitarian efforts, senior ministry managers were, rightfully so, worried about misappropriation. Therefore, there were increasingly strict measures being put in place that adversely affected Delpro's guileful efforts to get going on its new farm. Inducements to expedite approval of the lease were hard to consummate with everyone evidentially looking over everyone else's shoulder.

Quiet, discrete corners were becoming difficult to find.

Charlie was struck by the similarities with the issues first raised by Mr. Smith. These had been among the founding principles of BALJIN, so they should be well prepared to assist their colleagues in Zambia.

Working with Sue Ann and some of Mr. Van Houtte's staff, Charlie first established the premise upon which BALJIN would intervene. They needed to pull attention to an area away from the Msandile Valley in Eastern Province and create enough confusion through this decoy that Mr. Van Houtte would be able to get his lease signed.

Opportunity presented itself. Southern Province Zambia was suffering through the second year of a record-breaking drought. Southern Province Zambia was about 500 miles to the southwest of the Msandile Valley; far enough to create an effective diversion. The capital of Southern Province was Choma.

Charlie dispatched a staff member from the Illinois office to Zambia to join someone from Mr. Van Houtte's office and then go to Choma to rent some simple facilities where BALJIN could set up shop with great fanfare as they came to town to help drought-stricken farmers.

This was one of the rare occasions when Delpro was fully, or maybe almost fully, out of the darkness and into the light. Delpro was cast as one of a handful of important Zambian companies that were partnering with BALJIN and kitting up to cover most of the expenses relating to the aid to Southern Province. It was simply good business. And it was good advertising.

While the logistics were being organized, Charlie and Sue Ann put together a more comprehensive plan to assist 1,000 families—that should catch some attention. They calculated that if they gave each family $300 (about half the price of a bottle of top-quality Chateau Mouton Rothschild Bordeaux, one of Mr. McCandless' favorites, Charlie thought), the equivalent of over 300,000 Kwacha in local currency, this would be a windfall for the families and cost Delpro only $300,000—less than the salaries of the staff who were putting on the theater. They would convene a series of press conferences and interviews with beneficiaries. They would organize a roundtable on drought. They would do all they could to focus the spotlight of the donor and NGO communities on Choma. This would, they trusted, open the corridors, so to speak, of the ministries such that Mr. Van Houtte could find a quiet and discrete corner to do what he needed to do to get his lease quickly approved.

It was a good plan.

ᛰ ᛰ ᛰ ᛯ ᛰ ᛰ ᛰ

Pending Robin McCandless' approval of the details, Charlie prepared to join the team in Choma.

Final arrangements required a visit to McCandless Manor. Robin was generally quite satisfied with the measures being put in place to assist Mr. Van Houtte—a gentleman, he underlined, whom he had visited several times in Lusaka. The entire BALJIN Zambian project was speedily endorsed by the Big Boss. Nonetheless, he had an addendum as regarded Charlie. He wanted the BALJIN Director to extend his travels in the region, going on to Uganda to meet his brother.

"Have I mentioned my brother?" Robin McCandless asked over a superb cup of heady coffee and fresh croissants as the two sat poolside.

"Not directly," Charlie offered, still not sure if he should add a "sir" to his replies.

"Well, I'm not exactly sure what I've already said, but I have a younger brother Horace—not Horace Smith but Horace Barthley. He actually goes by Sir Horace—apparently some off-the-wall Cambodian somebody or other gave him some sort of weird title. But it was enough for him to become forever-on Sir Horace."

Well, there's my "sir," Charlie thought, not disclosing that Julian had already provided a succinct biography of the brothers. "I'm sure being any type of nobleman is fine." Charlie realized it was an odd reply.

His host continued unabated, "We're brothers—same parents—but we were put up for adoption early in our childhood—family issues. Horace went to live with a family in the UK and I came here. Yet, in spite of the ocean that separated us, we managed to remain close—to remain brothers.

"While, as you see me now, I'm in the upper echelons of Delpro, Horace, too, is a key part of the organization—preferring to be more in the bedlam of the action on the ground than, as he sees it, the dreary confines of the office."

Flagging for future thought his boss's reference to being upper echelon and not the boss, Charlie offered a mundane, but more on target, retort, "Well, it's great you and your brother are still together."

"Indeed, it is," Robin said, appearing to trickle away, perhaps thinking of times gone by, "we have always truly complemented each other."

"Anyway, enough babble of family and personalities. We're all about business and in the business of today I want you to meet him. He's apparently enjoying the Source of the Nile—I don't know if it's business or a respite, but it'll certainly be interesting."

"That it will."

"So, when you leave Lusaka after dealing with all the goings-on in Choma, fly to Entebbe. We'll arrange for a car to pick you at the airport and drive you to Jinja where you'll hook up with Horace. Route your return through Nairobi but leave the dates open as you'll have to see first what if anything Horace has in store—whatever, shouldn't miss this opportunity to have you two chat."

"No problem."

"Excellent. I'll have someone drop a letter for Horace off at your office before you leave. Otherwise, I wish you good travels."

Another encounter at Chateau McCandless put to rest.

⋀ ⋀ ⋀ ⋁ ⋀ ⋀

The BALJIN Communications Officer, Laura Foti, Sue Ann, and Charlie traveled together to Zambia. The Southern Province event was large enough to warrant a good showing from BALJIN headquarters and a good chance for the two ladies to see new sights. The trio flew from O'Hare to Heathrow where they connected with a flight to Johannesburg from where there was a short hop to Lusaka. It was a long journey with the fatigue only partially offset by the embellishments of first class.

In Lusaka, Mr. Van Houtte's staff, helped them traverse arrival formalities and shepherded them rapidly to the Intercontinental Hotel where they spent a full thirty-six hours overcoming the jet lag before they plunged into the work at hand—this starting with meetings in Mr. Van Houtte's offices to the south of town, on the road to Chilanga—the same road that would later take them to Choma.

There was no reason to review Delpro activities in the country. This was not their job. Clearly, the objects of their attention had little directly to do with Delpro. They simply needed to launch some shiny objects that captivated the thoughts and deeds of local aid workers and their organizations for sufficient time to open a window in the bureaucracy for Mr. Van Houtte to do the needful. Nevertheless, an opportunity was an opportunity, and this was an opportunity for BALJIN to take center stage in some very well-choreographed ballet. This was an opportunity for BALJIN to be seen as a key player. This was an opportunity for BALJIN to be viewed as impactful. And these added bonuses were worthy in and of themselves.

Thus, the meetings in Lusaka were chiefly dealing with the best ways to widely publicize BALJINs activities in Choma to ensure a significant in-person participation, thereby clearing the overloaded hallways of the capital and opening the path for Mr. Van Houtte.

Laura had come prepared with brochures and posters hyping BALJIN's work worldwide and specifically in Zambia (truthfully, a country where BALJIN had never been before). Mr. Van Houtte arranged for slots for her on local television and radio stations while Sue Ann drafted memos under United Nations letterhead to invite all the leading charitable organizations with country offices in Lusaka to send delegations to Choma.

Throughout, Charlie coordinated and liaised. He made sure his advance guy in Choma, Stu, was ready with all the facilities set up in the provincial capital. He worked with Mr. Van Houtte to seed the audience for the Q & A session following the roundtable. It wouldn't do to have embarrassing questions asked so publicly about BALJIN's Zambian program—or even its global program, for that matter. Concurrently, they prepared briefing notes for the attending journalists, with Laura and Sue Ann's help, that clearly steered any conversation away from awkward subjects. When it was all said and done, this event not only needed to send afloat bright shiny objects that served the function of lessening pressure on approval of Delpro's farm, but it also needed to polish BALJINs good name, leaving it equally bright and shiny.

∧ ∧∧∨∧ ∧

All went to plan.

Accolades were lavishly bestowed upon BALJIN and all the partners contributing to the much-acclaimed events. On the day of the roundtable, the halls of the ministries were almost eerily empty, allowing Mr. Van Houtte all the space and obscurity he needed to get his farm in the Msandile Valley approved at no small cost—but to the eternal gratitude of several senior civil servants whose bank accounts were mightily increased as the roundtable concluded. After an extra day in Choma for photo opportunities with the gratified beneficiaries of Delpro's largess through BALJIN, Charlie flew to Nairobi and on to Entebbe while Mr. Van Houtte, framed by Laura and Sue Ann, held a televised news conference about how happy Delpro had been to work with its partner BALJIN—a respected humanitarian NGO with celebrated activities around the world—to help the suffering farmers of Southern Province.

Charlie made it to Jinja without incident. Sir Horace was staying at the Nile River Resort, about five miles out of Jinja, on the banks of the Victoria Nile, where a room for Charlie had been reserved. The resort was slightly over eighty miles northeast of the airport, the road traversing the capital and largest city, Kampala. As Charlie sat in the passenger seat of the silver Range Rover next to the taciturn driver, he gazed at the fuzzy video of life that played on outside the deeply tinted windows while the vehicle slowly made its way through the crowded byways. It was practically shocking, the differences when compared with the cinematics he had viewed on the drive going to and coming from Choma. As opposed to the semi-arid and arcadian plains of Zambia, here everything was lush, green, and bustling. There seemed to be an abundance of food and people everywhere. The patent dissimilarities touched the cities themselves. In contrast to the widely spread-out and reserved Zambian capital, Kampala appeared concentrated and modish, shouting for attention.

Charlie had no idea if there was a Delpro office in the city. Probably. This was not something that was widely publicized nor listed in the yellow pages (if there were yellow pages in Uganda, Charlie didn't know). From what Charlie had seen, these offices were in plain sight but their presence and certainly their activities only divulged to those with the need to know.

For the case of Kampala, he did not need to know.

When they exited from the city, the commotion slackened, but still greatly exceeded that that Charlie had witnessed in Southern Province. They entered more rural areas, driving through sugar cane plantations and the Mabira Forest before crossing the Nile and turning downstream to the resort.

After Charlie had checked in and tried to find the driver to thank him for the ride—but he had already disappeared—the desk clerk gave him a note. It was from Sir Horace: *Welcome. Have a rest and we'll meet at the bar for tea.*

After Charlie had showered, it was indeed teatime and he headed downstairs to the open-air bar that fit the safari atmosphere of the resort.

There was no uncertainty as to who Sir Horace was when Charlie entered the bar. He was a slightly more compact (a little shorter and wider) version of his big brother, complete with the alabaster hair and the rosette complexion. From a distance, one of the distinctions appeared to be in their manner of dress. Robin was often rather conservative in the cut of his cloth and his color choices. And, when he did opt for more colorful wear, it seemed to be chosen to downplay or blend with his natural coloration. Horace was the evidentially the opposite. He was, at least today, a flashy and florid dresser porting colors that magnified his own tones. Seated at a corner table, he was bedecked in a bright pink shirt with a wide silver-tipped collar topped-off with a crimson ascot; all this over bright white slacks, maroon socks, and red wing tips.

"Sir Horace?" Charlie queried as he approached the table.

"Of course, kid, have a seat."

As he took the captain's chair across from the would-be nobleman, Charlie noted the "lad" had been replaced by "kid"—same habits, different wrapping.

Sipping a pink-colored concoction that blended nicely with his complexion, Sir Horace asked, "What'll have?"

Charlie remembered seeing the movie *My Fair Lady* with his parents years ago. He remembered vaguely some scene that portrayed Cockneys—scenes, or maybe that was the whole film. He couldn't recall. Still, the accent of those few words Sir Horace had uttered reminded him of the script from that film all those years ago.

"A beer's fine," Charlie belatedly responded, "thanks."

With a sweating bottle of *Nile Special* on the table along with a new glass of pink something, Sir Horace looked as if all was in readiness.

"So kid, thanks for coming. My brother said you're an up-n-comer so I says to me-self I should get a glimpse of ya. I'm sure Robin told ya the whole story. We're brothers right enough—it's just that one of us grew up in the US and the other in the UK.

"Now that's all well 'n good 'n the reason for all this happening is water under the bridge. Thing is, we started off together and now we're back together—if not in the same place, at least do'n the same work.

"So, if you's help'n Robin you's already help'n me and maybe we can expand this to where you's help's me even more. Make sense?"

"I guess so . . ."

"Course it does. Easy smeasy. After all, it's not just that Robin and I are one family. We're all one family. We're all Delpro, huh?"

"Of course."

"So, here's the thing. I want you to take a lit'l drive w' me. If you're up for it, we'll leave tomorrow and cross over into Kenya—drivers getting the car ready as we speak. I wanna show you some stuff. Then we'll make it to Kisumu where I'll introduce you to someone—you and he'll have a bit of a chat while I carry on and fly back to Nairobi. Sound good?"

"Fine."

There wasn't much more at that sitting. There was another round of drinks. There was some chitchat about the drought in southern Africa. Then there was an agreement to meet for dinner in the dining room later that evening.

All told, there were few revelations up to the time they finished their English breakfast buffets at the sophisticatedly rustic resort dining room. Sir Horace reveled little of substance. Charlie's main takeaway from the two meals he had shared with the wannabe blueblood was that this gentleman could handily scale his "Cockneyishness" like one tuned a radio. He could completely adopt the vernacular to the point Charlie could scarcely follow, or, on the other end of the scale, he could speak what one would truly call, The Queen's English.

Other than this possible eccentricity (Charlie finding it eccentric because the good gentleman would literally change channels mid-sentence), his boss's brother seemed to be an able conversationalist with a strange dose of charm. He asked Charlie questions about growing up. He asked about living in the Chicago area. He made a short exposé on the challenges facing those living downstream along the mighty Nile. He even spoke with apparent knowledge about the Kenyan football (soccer, Charlie reminded himself) team. The meals were, indeed, passed in a cordial atmosphere with no mention of Delpro, BALJIN, Robin McCandless, nor anything work related.

They departed the banks of the Nile in the same Range Rover with the same driver who had brought Charlie to the resort, allowing him to wonder how Sir Horace had arrived at the river's edge. This question remaining unanswered, they headed east along the A109 but avoided the more northern border crossing at Malaba, turning southeast on the Kisumu-Busia Road to the Busia border station, crossing with no delays. They had an early, light lunch at a restaurant, bizarrely Charlie thought, called the Texas Luau Grill. Unusual name or not, they both found the food to be of excellent quality.

Continuing south to the lake, before teatime they arrived in Port Victoria and at Diya's Lake Resort where Sir Horace had booked rooms on the lakeshore. However, as opposed to rejoining their rooms, after checking in, Sir Horace wanted to take Charlie on a *tournée*, as he called it. Across from the resort was the Port's agricultural marketing office. Pointing out this facility as they slowly seemed to drive in ever-increasing concentric circles, Sir Horace began what gave the appearance of being a prepared talk.

"This is an area with a great deal of farming—all kinds. We're going to drive by fish farms, cereal farms, vegetable farms, and even orchards. Much of this land between Bukoma and Siaya has been reclaimed from the Lake. It is rich. It can make people rich."

Unappreciatedly, Charlie interjected, "I was born on a lakebed. I know a lot about reclaimed land."

"Great, kid." Sir Horace grimaced, cutting his audience short and picking up where he'd left off, "I wanted you to see this area firsthand. Robin and I discussed this. It's important you really grasp the essence of this place, so you'll not only know it, you'll feel it. This is one of many areas scattered around the world where there are unique opportunities—areas where you can get rich.

"This is important to us. This is important to Delpro. This is important to your pocketbook. Places like this are places for Delpro—it's practically preordained. We can grow crops for the locals. We can grow crops for moneyed Europeans or Americans. We can process harvests here; we can export the raw materials and process elsewhere. There are so many openings. These opening, I might add, becoming wider if we grease the hinges with good neighborliness—what they call here *baksheesh* or *mattabisch*. A little generosity to those in need can lead to much greater things.

"But and you may understand this well since you say you're from the lakebed, there are a lot of mixed feelings about reclaiming land. One might go so far as to say there's a lot of opposition to reclaiming any more land. There's a lot of bleeding-heart environmentalists who say draining off the lake water is a horrible thing—it destroys nature. Well, I, we, don't see it this way. But of course, we can't really get involved directly in the discourse. Delpro doesn't act that way. So, we'll count on you to see how you can help. You'll be meeting a friend of ours tomorrow in Kisumu and I hope you'll find a solution. This would make Robin very happy. I'd make me happy too, of course. So, kid, this ain't just a joy ride. There's work to be done."

As the conversation ended, Charlie noted they had miraculously retuned to the resort. After a quick beer at the bar to top off all the heady discussion, they agreed to meet for dinner that evening at eight.

The evening meal and the morning's full English breakfasts were reruns of their predecessors on the banks of the Nile. Once more, Sir Horace was the affable companion guiding the exchanges away from any reference of work or Delpro.

On the two-and-a-half-hour drive to Kisumu, evidently in spite of the driver's stoicism, Sir Horace (hyped up, Charlie thought, on caffeine and sugar from breakfast) regaled his passengers with trivia from a mental scrapbook covering the history of British East Africa. Between the Kisumu airport and golf course, they left the highway and turned south, following Kisumu Bay, to the Lake Sands Hotel—the main part of the city on the other side of the bay.

At check-in, Charlie was surprised to find he was the only one with a reservation. Sir Horace, before scurrying off to the bar, informed his former co-excursionist that he would be flying back to Nairobi on the evening flight. They should expect their friend for a late lunch, after which the prospective patrician would go to the airport.

Charlie went to his room, with a pleasing view of the Port of Kisumu and Laung'ni Beach across the bay, to catch his breath before participating in Sir Horace's finalé. He sat on the room's small veranda, realizing that he was, as a bird flies, less than 120 miles from Jinja along the lake's northern margins. A short distance, but so much happening between here and there—so many villages, so many people, so many lives, so many families.

Charlie's reverie was broken by the phone buzzing—the front desk calling on Sir Horaces's behalf to advise their lodger that he was kindly awaited in the restaurant to join his party.

Charlie entered the much more austere hotel dining room—none of the safari ornamentation of the resorts. The business-like atmosphere reminded him more of a corner diner in Waukegan. And, seated at a table in the shade of the outside deck with nearly the same view as his room's, was Sir Horace with a stout, brown-haired man probably in his mid- to late-thirties. As Charlie drew closer, he noted the clean-shaven man had a sun-tanned, solid frame dominated by a generous and seemingly gregarious smile.

"Good afternoon," Charlie offered.

"Great," Sir Horace retorted without any smile of greeting, "both kids are here. Charlie, this is Peter and vice versa."

The smiling stout man stood, extending his hand, "Peter Volman."

Picking up the firm grip, Charlie replied, "Charlie Stancik."

"So," a still sullen Horace jumped in before things could go, in his view, awry, "now you've met, let's get down to business, I've a damn plane to catch.

"I've briefed young Charlie about the issues here in Kenya and potentially around Lake Victoria and even elsewhere—nothing much more for me to say—you two will see how you think things should go—smart buggers y'are (Charlie noting Sir Horace, for no apparent reason, seemed to have set the dial of his linguistic meter on coarser talk when around Peter).

"I've also talked with young Peter about some unrelated issues in Mozambique—but, though unrelated to the specific subject here on our table on the shores of Lake Vic, not unrelated to our wider work. I won't go into this now—I've got a bloody plane to catch—but Peter, you and Charlie can talk about this and I'll have you catch me up later. Any burning issues—I've a frigg'n plane to catch?"

Passing the baton to Peter, settling into his chair, absorbed in an iced chartreuse drink of some sort of another, Sir Horace seemed to forget about his plane he had to catch. He even seemed to forget about the others with whom he shared the table on the deck overlooking Kisumu Bay.

Before Peter could pick up the proffered baton, Charlie broke in with, to him, an urgent question, "Volman. I don't know if that's a common name or not, but I met a couple named Volman—missionaries in Costa Rica."

Quickly changing gears, Peter replied with an even wider smile, "Yep, that's my grandparents. I come from missionary stock. I was born in Ghana. My parents were missionaries there—my dad following in grandad's shoes."

Before Peter could go any farther, Sir Horace seemed to forcibly tear himself away from concentrating on his drink, draining the glass with a great gulp, standing up, and fixing the two young men with cloudy but stern eyes.

"Enough of the bullshit. You've got god damn work to do. I've got a god damn plane to catch. Don't fuck up!" With that, and no other adieu, he was gone, in the silver Range Rover en route to the airport just a short distance away.

In his wake, Peter smiled again. "He's an acquired taste. I've been in his orbit for quite a while. Small doses often work best. But all that aside, it's amazing you met my grandparents—small world."

"Truly, I was there on an assignment for Sir Horace's big brother, Robin McCandless."

"Heard of him, heard a lot actually thanks to the surly Sir farts-so-high, but don't think I've ever met the man."

"Well, I guess we'll have ample time to chat about personalities and experiences, but right now I guess we'd best do as the old man (Charlie observing it seemed so easy to refer to Horace as an old man while this distinction hardly if ever was used to characterize his big brother) says and see what we think about the questions here at hand in western Kenya. It seems we're 'on the clock'"

With that, the serious discussion began. After more than a few more beers and a light evening meal still, at this belated point somewhat uncomfortably, seated at the same table on the deck, the other side of the bay now lit only by the occasional streetlamp, they managed to develop a strategy in adequate detail to share later with Sir Horace—Peter to do the sharing.

BALJIN would, according to their proposal, open a temporary office here in Kisumu. There would be one staff member assisted by a part-time secretary to make a good show. The staff member would be from outside Kenya—Charlie reminding Peter that an expert was someone fifty miles from home, so an outsider from Kenya, but probably an East African would likely attract a little bit more attention. They agreed that Peter, with his office at Equatorial Management in Dar es Salaam, would look for a Tanzanian to recruit for the Kisumu assignment. They would then mount a subtle campaign on how lake reclamation was good for the economy. They would shine a light on the Green Revolution and the need to, in the country's president's words, grow the agricultural program and produce more food for a growing number of mouths to feed. They were unsure if this embellishment would gain any immediate traction or truly affect any opinions, but it would, at the very least, put in place an established conduit through which to reach out to local leaders and provide incentives for them to, as Peter pointed out, see both sides of the story (unsaid was the understanding that the BALJIN side of the story would likely be more well-paying for the conductors of the communities, not to mention for Delpro and all her obscure family at large).

It was a beginning. It was not a recipe to instantaneously give Sir Horace or Delpro all they wanted. This was a first splash in the pond—and it would be a long slog. Still and all, they were satisfied it was a practical way to begin—a plan that just might succeed.

Before they could congratulate themselves for their proposal, Peter immediately jumped into what he dubbed "The Mozambican Problem" alluded to by Sir Horace. As the man from Dar summarized, Mozambique was a high priority country for Equatorial Management. He wasn't sure of the Delpro context, but obviously, if the old fart was harping about it, it was important to folks up the ladder. Anyway, internal politics aside, as those who paid them were interested, it was up to them to at least look at the situation.

"Maybe . . ." Charlie was about to open a counteroffer with furrowed brow.

Peter realized Charlie would prefer to take one subject at a time—one subject at a sitting. He obviously liked to digest well his subject matter. Charlie was, Peter thought, still on the learning curve—working in a whole new corner of the world. And, irrespective where he was on his on-the-job education (Peter having great respect for hands-on instruction—he himself having relied heavily on this practical approach to get where he was (wherever that was)—and having no real insight into his colleague's background), Peter had quickly decided Charlie was a good and serious guy who thought before he leapt—here quite different from his own impetuous self. His new comrade was someone who liked to get as much information up-front as possible and thoroughly consider the options.

"Here," Peter offered, to intercept his compatriot's possible uneasiness, "they say *fanya kazi kabla ya kucheza*—to paraphrase, what your mother would likely have often reminded you when you were growing up: work before play. But at least, we can have another beer with our last bit of work."

"OK, OK . . ." Charlie relented.

"The old man," Peter mused as additional encouragement, "always says, 'Don't fuck up' upon departure. Like I said, he takes some getting used to. And another of his parting admonitions is, 'Don't shit where you eat.' He's really a lovely guy. But, when you scrape off the vulgarity, he's generally providing some forewarning. He raised the flag over Mozambique so we'd best salute."

With that, Peter disclosed what knew about the subject.

Mozambique was in a state of civil disruption—most would and did call it a war. Nonetheless, Peter reminded his across-the-table confederate, war was good business. In the broadest strokes, the conflict pitted the seated Marxist government headed by the FRELIMO party against the opposition RENAMO party. The clash had sucked in a multitude of countries including all the neighbors as well as much of Europe, the US, and the Soviet Union. Zimbabwe, a landlocked country, was particularly engaged as she fought to keep open the corridor to Beira that was their main artery to the sea. However, much of the struggle was taking place northwest of Beira in Tete Province toward the Zambian border and south to the capital of Maputo—Maputo and Beira separated by 750 miles. The extreme north, centered around the Island of Mozambique which had been the capital of Portuguese East Africa in the 1800s, was on the margins of much of the worst atrocities. This area was also relatively isolated—over 1,400 miles from Maputo. Here there was the deep-water port of Nacala off the Baia de Fernao Veloso and with connections to the Nacala Railway that headed west into Malawi. The extreme north was rich in land and water. The extreme north was accessible by rail and sea while there was also an airport in Nacala. The extreme north was an area of interest to Equatorial Management as a market for fertilizer and other agricultural inputs along with being a supplier of diverse agricultural products that made their way to Europe. This outlying territory's commercial pathways, Peter added, certainly transported more than agricultural supplies and agricultural commodities.

Without opening up the underbelly of the most corrupt dealings reportedly coming out of the extreme north—dealings with which heretofore he had generally been personally disconnected and which only surfaced through occasional conjecture—it sufficed to say, Peter wrapped-up, that Equatorial Management and likely by default Delpro, was very interested in being a major player in whatever was going on in this remote and largely uncontrolled part of the country.

When, Peter added, Sir Horace had briefed them about BALJINs work in Choma, they—Equatorial Management, Peter clarified—immediately thought of the extreme north of Mozambique. While things were largely laissez faire today, the environment was changing rapidly, and one never knew when peace would pop up—bringing with it more regulation and monitoring of the hinterland. This could cut into Equatorial Management's profits. However, if they were linked through a benign presence such as a humanitarian NGO, they would be able to furtively influence decisions and minimize their losses.

Although Charlie's first reaction to Peter's tale was to be leery of getting involved in too much at one time, wary of activities that were too blatantly venal, he could not discount his own history. It wasn't like his work from Blind River all the way through to Choma had been totally virtuous. He had been "in the business" for some time and was still "in the business." Yet, he was able to at least delay any commitment for direct involvement in the extreme north of Mozambique. They were, as they understood Sir Horace's directive, to give precedence to the issues on the table regarding western Kenya. For this, they had their proposal. They had a starting point. It was now only to be on stand-by while Peter pushed this proposal up the system through Sir Horace. Neither knew the degree of their future involvement until the powers that be had spoken.

The nitty-gritty of the next steps for the extreme north of Mozambique would come later. For now, Peter and Charlie were both on the same page. Charlie would add a sentence or two in his trip report that, with colleagues from Equatorial Management, he was assessing opportunities to expand into Mozambique. That should placate any immediate concerns. For now, while Peter was ordering more beer, Charlie was thinking of bed. It had been a long day.

ᛉ ᛉ ᛉ ᚹ ᛉ ᛉ ᛉ

After another impressive full English breakfast, Peter flew back to Dar via Nairobi. Charlie would follow the next day. Heading back to Nairobi in the late afternoon, he had an evening connection for a Kenya Airways flight to Amsterdam, connecting there again for his return to O'Hare.

Before the last leg of a complicated trip, after all the commotion that had accompanied his present assignment up to now, he was relieved to have a few hours to himself in the peace and quiet and obscurity of being a simple tourist on the shores of the world's largest tropical lake.

The churlish driver along with the silver Range Rover had disappeared so, after Peter's departure, Charlie took one of the ever-present city taxis to the city center where he simply wandered aimlessly. People, in a panoply of color, flowed blithely through the heart of this, the county's third largest city and the capital of Nyanza Province. The warm, bordering on hot, air was filled with music that seeped from bars serving fragrant plates of *nyama choma*—grilled meat—mingling with the fusion of dozens of languages—some screamed, some whispered.

Charlie picked the closest bar, sat down, ordered a *White Cap* beer with a plate of *nyama coma*, and tried to absorb the ambiance. It was a long way from Antioch. It was a long way from his lakebed—notwithstanding that he was close to another. It was a long way away from everything and he wished Jo were here to share it with him. Jo would've loved Kisumu.

Quagmire

ACK IN HIS APARTMENT in Abbott Park off Highway 43, with a weekend to recover from his travels, Charlie tried to digest his first major African assignment, or assignments, or adventure. He guessed, from his vantage point in the king-sized bed under a luxurious down comforter (all thanks to Jo—he still thought of it as their bed and their comforter), things had gone OK. The real test, naturally, would be in Robin McCandless' reaction. Still, he felt, all things considered, the trip would be tagged as a success.

The BALJIN-Zambian portion of the assignment had already really succeeded before he had left that southern African country; Delpro had the farm. For the rest, he had avoided any open altercations with that old dotard—but he really wasn't, Charlie knew—Sir Horace. And, given the boss's brother's often offensive, if at times engaging persona, it could have been easy to impetuously react imprudently, which was undoubtedly exactly what the veteran grifter wanted.

Charlie's thoughts took a tangent as he again wondered why he and evidently many others thought of Sir Horace as a dawdling old man when he was, in fact, Robin McCandless' younger brother and virtually no one thought of Robin as burned out or hoary—generally, he was widely respected, if not revered, as someone on the cutting-edge of his field. The real challenge with Robin was defining his field. No one questioned his energy nor his zeal—maybe only his ethics.

Still, as regarded the younger sibling, it was likely all about appearances—both attire and attitude. Sir Horace tended to dress and act dramatically. While this was all assuredly by design, an unavoidable consequence was that people saw and remembered the thespian in the drama and not the true person under the guise. Sir Horace was perhaps a victim of his own success.

Back on the central topic, the results of the time spent in East Africa were also positive—or should be. He and Peter had a plan to try and promote more reclamation along the shores of Lake Victoria. And, as they had noted in preparing their strategy, in the event the public-facing portion of their effort was not well received, having an above-board organization on the ground would provide a vehicle to try and leverage support and influence decisions—even if these latter efforts were done behind closed doors.

Then, as they were able to better assess their tactics in Zambia and Kenya, they would be able to adjust as necessary and come up with a revised version to put in place in the extreme north of Mozambique. Among the sites, this was the most difficult. This was potentially also the most rewarding. From what Charlie had been able to glean from Peter's descriptions, the sheer size and variety of activities that could be planted in and transplanted to this area were phenomenal and, of course, potentially extremely profitable. An effective catalytic role for BALJIN in Mozambique would be a tremendous breakthrough for this group within the wider Delpro organization, despite the fact that these actions could largely go unnoticed by the outside world—indeed, if they did, all the better.

Charlie's mind swung in a great arch and landed upon Peter. Charlie still put a lot of weight on first impressions and his first impressions of Peter were good. He liked him. He was friendly, but in a most sincere way— quite a contrast to most he had met as he moved along his path. He was smart—but not pompous. There was a simplicity about him that, like his goodwill, seemed genuine. Furthermore, possibly because of his upbringing, he appeared to be very much in tune with people and culture—he was sensitive. All in all, he seemed to be a good guy. Charlie really hoped his first impressions were not later dashed by a big shot of reality.

⋀ ⋀ ⋀ ⋁ ⋀ ⋀ ⋀

Charlie started out his new back-from-Africa working week with an extended visit to the Lake Center. While Jo's metrics had moved infinitesimally upward, she was still outwardly gone to the world around her and lost in the world within. Nevertheless, Charlie sat by her side and, minute detail by minute detail, recounted to her his trip to southern and eastern Africa.

Back in the office, Charlie was glad to see Laura and Sue Ann were already hard at work. The three of them had a working lunch in the conference-room to share any relevant experiences about what had transpired in Zambia after Charlie's departure and about the basics of Charlie's travels in Uganda and Kenya as well as a third-party (objective, he hoped) introduction to Peter Volman.

Zambia was on hold pending any follow-up requests from the office in Lusaka. The prime focus now was Kisumu, but here most of the activities pivoted around Peter; Laura was more than able to make sure he had any needed equipment to be able to get a small satellite office up and running on the shores of Lake Victoria.

Charlie and Sue Ann, generally in the role of advance guard, concentrated on Mozambique. They sketched-out a two-step strategy to assist Delpro in its aims of getting a firm foothold in this rich territory. Unlike in Zambia where the intent was to refocus attention—be it ever so fleetingly—more in-line with the thinking for Kenya, the BALJIN planners saw their role in the extreme north of Mozambique as one of breaking ground.

Very much under the umbrella of their global mission, BALJIN could establish an office in Nacala for humanitarian assistance. Specifically, they could target helping internally displaced persons engage in economic activity. In that area, this meant helping people, in one way or other, invest in agriculture—whether it was though a minimum-wage, day-labor job or a modern processing facility. Accordingly, BALJIN could present themselves as a conduit to agri-businesses—enticing international employers to establish operations in the extreme north of Mozambique. They would become the Nacala farmer-centric Chamber of Commerce. In this role, they would prepare the terrain (by prearrangement) for Equatorial Management and at least two other Delpro affiliates to set up shop.

BALJIN would, furthermore, very noticeably offer its services to help design the best formulae for these outside enterprises to establish operations in Nacala. BALJIN would raise funds (or use Delpro's shadowy resources) to build the *Centro de Revitalização da Agricultura* (the Agriculture Revitalization Center)—a kind of one-stop-shop for stimulating farm and farmer-related action. This large center would be an impressive facility certainly supported by the city fathers of Nacala. It would put education, financial support, technical assistance, processing, and marketing all under one roof—one very large roof covering a very large structure built by local entrepreneurs, using supplies from local retailers, on lots purchased at top-dollar from local landowners. The community would have a vested interest.

BALJIN itself would have a small office in the imposing *Centro* from where it would be able to provide direct aid to the neediest while monitoring the overall set of interlocking activities. It was ambitious. It was a good plan.

Charlie made an appointment to see Robin.

∧ ∧∧∨∧∧

Robin was ebullient.

The prospects from the Zambian farm alone were more than a little encouraging. They were in a better position in Kenya while real progress seemed to being made in Mozambique. He knew his brother would share his excitement.

As they went into more detail on the Mozambican venture, the headman was still in high spirits. The proposal was innovative and quite possibly very advantageous on multiple fronts. His only stipulation was that, if and when things moved forward (he'd have to reach out to some folks before he could green light the operation), he wanted Charlie to make sure the architectural plans for the center were drawn up by his architects: Slattery and Long in Highland Park (naturally, Charlie thought, he had his own architectural firm just down the road—what would you expect).

In the meantime, Robin wanted Charlie to make arrangements for a visit to Mozambique in a month's time—by then he should be able to see the bigger picture. He wanted, moreover, for Charlie to arrange a stopover on the return leg in Tunis as there were some people there who might be interested in Mozambique.

Then, before dismissing his sometimes spokesperson, Robin McCandless' aura changed. There was a somber seriousness as he eyed his young employee.

"Charlie, lad, you should know, things may be warming up a bit."

Charlie, off guard, could only offer, "Huh?"

"Well, now's not the time, but you know full well we do a lot of things. We're all over the place with fingers in many, many pies. I guess it's to be expected that off and on we'll get more attention than we'd wish. It's like the Chicago winters—they come and go."

Charlie nodded.

"So, we're getting ready for a chilly time with regard to some of those nosey federal regulators. I don't think it's anything to worry about and I don't want to alarm you."

"Fine."

"Still, do take care. We're not yet completely sure who's prowling round out there and how much they know about who we are and where we are. Hopefully, you're off their radar. We've tried to keep you out of much of the business side of late."

"Good."

"But if you do have some unexpected visitors, just stay cool. Call me. If you can't get me, call Fredericks, Higgins, and Woods."

Maybe Charlie wasn't too worried, but the seeds had been planted—the kernels reinforced by the recurring references to "we," and the complete lack of any idea as to who "we" were.

⋀ ⋀ ⋀ ⋁ ⋀ ⋀ ⋀

There was no more said about regulators nor snooping feds. Robin apparently did his due diligence and then called Charlie to give the go-ahead for the Mozambique operations. With this Charlie finalized his travel arrangements and went to the Lake Center to let Jo know he was leaving for a while.

Once again, he found himself in Jomo Kenyatta International Airport, Nairobi. This time he was to meet Peter in the *Kenya Airways Pride* Business Class Lounge before the two got on a flight to Maputo. The four-hour flight, changing one time zone on the massive continent, was more than comfortable in the business class cabin. Accompanied by endless beverages and a seemingly equally endless array of tempting edibles, Peter and Charlie had both time to reflect on their plans for Kenya as well as time to lay the groundwork for their current assignment in Mozambique.

The Kenyan discussion was brief. Laura and Peter had been making all the arrangements. Peter had identified three possible candidates to run activities on the lakeshore. He expected to have someone sitting in the newly rented Kisumu office in a fortnight.

Equatorial Management's role in both projects needed to be undertaken behind the scenes, Peter recalled. In the Kenyan case, their part was likely to continue more in the background as their involvement was more based on geographic proximity to the activities than on direct engagement as an investor until such a time as more land resources became available, at which point Equatorial Management would likely come out of the shadows and take a proactive position in securing areas to build farms.

In the upcoming Mozambican case, however, the situation was very different. Equatorial Management was already seen as a major actor, but only in the second phase. In the first phase, as far as was publicly acknowledged, everything was being done by BALJIN—Equatorial Management was not even to be officially acknowledged as being present in the extreme north of the country until later—after (emphasis on "after") BALJIN had set up full operations.

This notwithstanding, Peter continued, Equatorial Management already had activities in Maputo and Beira—mostly involving movement through the ports of the two cities. They had small teams working in both areas expediting the inward and outward flow of cargo. One of their best employees was Jorge Braga, a middle-aged *mestiço* with a Portuguese father and a Tsonga mother (reference to the mixed-race couple pulling on Charlie's emotions as he thought of Jo so far away in so many ways) with very good language and organizational skills. Peter had reached out to Jorge and he had made all the preparations for the in-country work on their present assignment.

Given the distance and logistics, once they had finished some housekeeping work in the capital, they would take a chartered Piper Seneca six-seater to Nacala (the mention of a small, chartered plane adding to the pull on Charlie's emotions). Once finished there, the plane would drop the two Americans in Blantyre, Malawi, before returning to Maputo with Jorge. It was all well-arranged, Peter assured his countryman who seemed to have been bequeathed by the shrouded leadership with a special place in this amoebic labyrinth where he, Peter, still somewhat to his own surprise, found himself, and was never completely sure why. For some unknown reason, this recalled one of his father's frequently quoted scriptures (and there were many): Proverbs 23:18, "Surely there is a future, and your hope will not be cut off."

Moving quickly to untangle his thoughts from any Biblical morass, Peter was about to propose another drink when the seatbelt light illuminated, the landing gear loudly ground down, and they touched down at Mavalane International Airport with a bit of a smack. After clearing Mozambican formalities with Jorge's adept assistance, they spent a night at the Maputo Polana Serena Hotel, starting and ending the evening in the bar, finding common ground, among other things, in their appreciation of good beer. As much of the pending work-related discussion had taken place on the flight from Nairobi, most of the evening's dialogue, though at times theatric, was about growing up; one on the lakeshore in Ghana, the other on the lakebed.

Charlie's first impressions were reinforced.

He and Peter got along well.

The next morning there was another full English breakfast (no possible local favorites such as *Bolo de arroz* or *Estaladinhos*). The savory and hefty Anglo-South African fare was sadly losing some of its appeal, especially after a night of rather excessive imbibing. The underappreciated repast passed quickly if somewhat laboriously and was followed by an equally quick check-out and pick-up by Jorge in his Corolla.

Then it was off to the ministries.

What Peter had called "housekeeping" turned out to be registering in good faith BALJIN as an NGO authorized to operate in the country. Jorge had already prepared the foundation and identified the key individuals who, with a modest incentive, would be quite happy to move the dossier forward. Basically, all that was required, with the terrain already well primed by Jorge, was Charlie's signature as director on a multitude of documents, all in Portuguese, none of which he understood, but all of which Jorge assured him were routine.

It was then time to return to the airport, but this time to the private hangars and the over three-hour flight to Nacala.

Charlie shivered as he took his seat in the Piper. Jo's spirit was unquestionably seated beside him.

On arrival, they were picked up in a Mercedes 200-D by a stranger who was obviously part of Jorge's network. The man, the driver, was friendly and helpful. The car was dented and dusty—the windscreen cracked.

They were dropped at the Nacala Plaza Hotel where, after confirming they each had a room, they convened in the bar to rinse their dry throats and go over the program for the next day.

Jorge informed his colleagues that he had been here ten days ago. Based on his reconnaissance, he felt the best thing to do was to rent a house near the church, *Igreja De Cristo De Ontupaia*, southeast of the city center. This was far enough away from the port to avoid any unwanted subliminal links to any of the more unsavory activities that took place in this, and all ports. Moreover, being close to a place of worship would indirectly bolster the humanitarian image of BALJIN. Finally, having an office in a home was very typical for NGOs—Jorge already had identified a very suitable premises only a block from the church.

The next day, they needed to visit this site to make sure they were all in agreement. Jorge had then arranged a meeting at eleven a.m. with the mayor. Jorge had already contributed generously to the mayor's election campaign (as if there were really elections) and could confirm to his colleagues that *Senhor prefeito* was fully supportive of the excellent work that would be done by BALJIN and offered all assistance from his office to expedite the establishment of this renowned NGO in his city. Then, with Mister Mayor's blessing, there was another meeting at three p.m. with city officials to sign more formal documents for opening BALJINs Nacala office. They should have everything buckled-up in time to return to hotel for cocktails. The flight on to Blantyre was the following day.

It was fast. It was hectic. But it all worked.

It took just a little over two hours to fly the nearly 400 miles to Chileka International Airport in Southern Region in the Malawian commercial capital, Blantyre, the centenarian city named after the birthplace of David Livingstone. Here they took a taxi to the Delpro offices situated on the third floor of a venerable brick structure near the city's center. They had not made any concrete plans with the Delpro staff because they were not exactly sure how much time would be required in Mozambique. Nonetheless, Jorge had made bookings at the Mount Soche Hotel, so they were guaranteed beds in which to sleep. The office stop was really just a courtesy visit. They summarily briefed the Delpro office manager, Mr. Singhe. No real details at this moment were necessary and nothing in the foreseeable future was planned for his area. However, if they were ultimately successful, incoming and outgoing Delpro cargo from Malawi would benefit from the channels to be set up through BALJINs activities.

Mr. Singhe was effectively stoic through the concise briefing. However, at the end of their more formal exchanges, the office manager offered, "You're Americans. Somehow, I thought you were here about that other American, Eddie, a surveyor or something, whose been doing things here—sent here from Zambia by the Lusaka office. Never sure if it's good to have total outsiders around too much. But you guys come right from the core of the Organization so I'm happy to see you."

Unsure how to reply and unaware of any work in their portfolios for Malawi that involved any surveyor, American or otherwise, Peter and

Charlie simply informed Mr. Singhe that they would make sure his concerns were brought to the attention of their colleagues in the Organization.

The formalities were over and another Delpro office ticked off the shrouded list of company agencies around the globe.

After another night in another hotel, the pair flew one more time to Jomo Kenyatta where, in the departure area, they shared a few final beers as they watched the cultural pageant of world travelers pass by. Peter then took the short flight to Dar while his American confrère went on, as requested by Robin McCandless, to Tunis, having to fly first to Paris and then connecting to Tunis–Carthage Airport.

It was a really long haul.

Fortunately, it was first class.

ᴧ ᴧ ᴧ ᴠ ᴧ ᴧ ᴧ

Laura had booked him a room at the Sheraton and the hotel had limousine service from the airport—in short order he was sleeping off his voyager's fatigue in a king-size bed on the fourth floor.

The next morning, the Mediterranean fare was a pleasant and welcome change from the full English breakfasts. Well-rested, he tried to absorb the city as the Delpro driver in the late-model BMW adroitly navigated the crowded byways. Delpro's office was located on Rue Amor Jebali in the neighborhood of Cité An-Na Jah. The head, in line with Delpro's policy of having managers work outside their own home areas (some of the American staff, of course, the exception), was a Lebanese, Mr. Ferjal Shaheen.

On arrival, Charlie was shuffled immediately into the manager's unobtrusive corner office. Mr. Ferjal Shaheen rose and extended his hand as Charlie approached his mahogany desk overflowing with papers of all sizes and colors.

"Welcome, and as they often say here, 'Peace be upon you.'"

"Thank you, Mr. Shaheen," Charlie replied with a smile and a firm handshake.

"Please," the office manager offered, "call me Ferjal—this is just a friendly visit. We're all friends. After all, Ferjal in my country means someone prosperous or rich and I guess that's why we're both here."

Charlie wasn't completely clear about why he was where he was, so he smiled and let the local Delpro Rep continue.

"I got a call from Robin—Mr. McCandless—the other day. He said you were heading up an NGO that was working with the Company on a number of fronts including agriculture. He wanted me to show you—show off, actually, I guess—what's happening hereabouts.

"As you've clearly seen, since you flew in via Paris, Tunisia is at Europe's doorstep—just a small body of water separating us—separating us here from very lucrative and often under-supplied markets.

"Here we've got lots of land, we've got lots of sunshine. We've got pretty good communications and infrastructure. We're kind of short on water, but new technologies that are leaping ahead are assisting in addressing this constraint. We're also short on labor, but we're finding ways to get more people involved.

"When you put it all together, we've got a good setup. We've got a good setup to provide Europe with what they need and what they want.

"And we mustn't forget our country here is a pretty easy place to get things done. In many ways we've fewer regulations and fewer taxes. We've fewer, or can arrange to have fewer, people controlling our every step. In short, it's a good place to do business—a good place to farm."

"Sounds wonderful," Peter lamely observed.

"Well, I don't know if it's wonderful—it is what it is—but it is pretty good. Mr. McCandless thought it might be helpful for you to see things firsthand—in the flesh so to speak. So, I've arranged for you to go on a tournée tomorrow.

"You'll be able to see for yourself how well this country has done. In recent years, agriculture production has really jumped ahead. A great deal of effort has been directed to better water management with an increasing number of farms irrigated. We produce and export olives and olive oil, citrus and other fruits, vegetables, cereals, and also beef. And, even with all this food going outside, we're self-sufficient in most of our foodstuffs. I guess it is wonderful.

"While most farms are not mechanized with less than 125 acres, Delpro is among the small but growing number of investors getting on the ground with state-of-the-art large modern farms—honestly, agribusinesses, we're doing processing too. We're able to bring in more machinery and add good quality fertilizer and better seeds along with all kinds of other things to get higher yields and use less manual labor. Still, with the crops commonly grown, labor is a continuing challenge. It can be hard to get all the hands needed, but we manage. You'll be seeing it all tomorrow."

This all rolled out as scheduled. Charlie, with the same driver and BMW, spent the entire day from sunrise pickup to sunset drop-off visiting farms, processing and marketing facilities, and ag suppliers. It lived up to the images Ferjal had painted. The integrated supply chains could well be models for sites where larger agricultural enterprises were being considered—especially big-ticket projects overseen by Delpro.

Back in his room at the Sheraton, he had to admit he was bushed.

The next day he had a wrap-up with Ferjal and then had some most welcome free time until his evening Air France flight to JFK, connecting on to O'Hare.

The wrap-up was basically wrapped-up before it started. Ferjal was following orders from headquarters. Some young American was in the vicinity and the bosses wanted him to see some sites—even though these sites were those of company operations and not those of old Carthage. The sites had now been seen and, from Ferjal's seat, well explained. There was nothing more to do than to wish the visitor peace, prosperity, and *bonne voyage.*

This was all accomplished in roughly twenty minutes over cups of very strong coffee.

There was now free time.

Charlie arranged for the driver to pick him up at nine p.m. for the airport, organized a late check-out from his room, had a light lunch at the hotel, then set out to see something more than a Delpro farm.

He ambled about, understanding only a tiny portion of what he was seeing. But seeing enough to know how much history and knowledge was buried beneath the surface.

He ended up in the *Les Berges du Lac* neighborhood, as the name indicated, on the shore of the Lake of Tunis, a natural lagoon upon whose eastern shores had been located the center of ancient Carthaginian civilization so long ago (so long, in fact, that Charlie could not really believe that ages ago something so rich and accomplished had really ever existed on this very lakeshore so far from the lakeshore where he now resided—it must be, or seemed as though it should be, a hallucination).

Still feeling the pull of the past, he entered the Barista Brwawa for a respite and a cup of strong coffee to begin building the stamina needed for the nighttime Transatlantic Crossing. While Tunis sported a veritable farrago of ethnicities and physiognomies, Charlie's waiter looked much more like someone he would have expected to see in Nacala than Tunis.

Ever curious, and often blunt in a rather subdued way, Charlie asked his attendant if he were Tunisian. This obviously took the man aback, not only for its candidness, but also due to the fact that such cardinal but imprudent questions were most frequently left unasked—taboo. With an unflappable veneer, the man replied, "*Pardon, Monsieur?*"

"Sorry, do you speak English?"

"*Juste un peu*—only a little."

"Excuse me. I know it's probably too frank, but I was just curious. You see, I've just come from Mozambique and you reminded me of people I'd met there."

This simple openness from this obvious American—the pure Americanisms of his nonchalant questions—had an unfamiliar effect on the man who waited the Barista's tables. The waiter, who was far too accustomed to just the opposite approach to his presence as an outsider in a country of insiders, almost relaxed.

"It's OK," the man offered blandly in quite acceptable English, "normally such discussion is not part of our discourse with patrons. But it is nice to see someone like yourself at least looking at the servants as people and not objects. So, in that vein, you are right. I am not from here. I am a *Burkinabé*—from Burkina Faso."

"That is interesting. How did you end up here?"

"That, sir, is a subject for another place and time. May I take your order please."

With that, Charlie ordered coffee and *brik*—a thin fried pastry, in this case filled with fish and vegetables—quite similar to sambusas or samosas found in other countries. As he slowly consumed the tangy food and drink—each pungent in its own way—he watched a few small feluccas glide across the lake's glossy surface much as they had in the time of the Carthaginians. This reminded him of the water striders. How far he had come.

⋏⋏⋏⋎⋏⋏

Charlie left the barista with several hours to spare, planning on taking an equally slow pace back to the hotel as he had when, earlier that afternoon, he drifted onto the lakeshore. Crossing the street, he spied his waiter alone, on a bench, having a cigarette. Charlie approached, "Thanks. The coffee and pastry were excellent. Hope everything works out well for you."

"OK, appreciate your kindness. I've a ten-minute break. Time for a cigarette." He took the pack from his shirt pocket, offering Charlie a smoke.

"No thanks, but thanks for offering." Without being asked, Charlie plopped down on the bench, "still curious, is now a better time?"

With that, Djibril, as he introduced himself, recounted his story much as one might unload in a confessional. It was a story, he added, that was stirred by his customer's reference to Mozambicans—Djibril too had known Mozambicans.

He had been raised in Sourou, a rural agricultural area with irrigated rice paddies, 160 miles to the northwest of the capital Ouagadougou and thirty miles east of Mali border. Times were hard. There were few jobs—especially in the hinterland. There were few jobs for someone with a primary school education. There were few jobs for someone whose family owned no land or livestock. Times were hard.

The Eldorado for the unemployed and the unemployable of Sourou was France—the old colonial power where anyone could find some sort of paying job. Where anyone could manage to buy jeans and sneakers and watch TV. When a group from northern Togo came through Sourou on their way out, fleeing what seemed to be perpetual political turmoil in their country, Djibril and three others from his village joined them for a pilgrimage north. They crossed into Mali, following the RN19 ever northward. They moved by any means available; foot, hitchhiking, even camelback, and the occasional paid public transport if they could manage the fare (sometimes the coins used to pay for a broken-down bus seat garnered by street-corner begging the previous day). In Algeria they moved slowly along the N6, N1, and N3 until they reached the Tunisian border and the P3 that took them to Tunis. Along the way, one of the Togolese died, another seemingly wandered off, while two of the *Burkinabés* decided to turn back home. Yet, these losses to their group were more than compensated for by the addition of two Malians and three Nigerians. After a journey of more than 2,500 miles, when they illicitly crossed the border into Tunisia in the dark of night, they were an exhausted group of nine disheveled, undernourished, and ill-equipped young men knowing not where to go nor what to do.

On the streets of Tunis, survival was all about adaptation (a point with which Charlie could well relate). Survival was also all about avoiding recognition. It was not the more the merrier. It was the more, the more visible. Each went his own way, looking for his own shadows. Djibril never saw any of his brother pilgrims again.

He did go to a mosque for Friday prayers. Outside the mosque he a found a young man like himself recruiting workers to go and help grow fruits and vegetables in Spain. He was told there was a labor shortage. He was told wages were high. He was told this new employer would arrange for all the travel and formalities for him to be able to go and work and get rich in Spain. He was even offered 350 Tunisian Dinars, approximately 100 Euros, as an incentive.

It appeared to be the answer to his dreams—to the desires that had motived him as he had suffered step by step on the long and painful road to riches.

He followed the young man and soon he was one of a small group that was staying in a house in the suburbs, the young man now their contact with the world. After about three weeks, when their numbers had reached twenty-five, the young man came in one evening with some other young men. They shepherded the group into a truck and, after about two hours, the would-be workers found themselves in the port. They were moved into a container—assured by their escorts that all would be fine—this was normal practice. In truth, in spite of several days of hell, locked in an oven with little water and no toilet facilities, when the container was opened, they did find themselves in Spain—they did find themselves at farms needing workers. What they did not find was any sort of payment nor any sort of employment—it was slavery.

Always under the watchful eyes of armed guards, they worked in fields, they worked in canneries, they worked in all manner of jobs that prepared delicious foods for European consumers. They were now among several hundred coerced workers—slaves—providing labor where labor was hard to find.

It was there that Djibril had met the Mozambicans. There were three of them who had had nearly the same experience as he. But theirs had been even more horrible. They had been loaded into containers in Beira and shipped to Rabat from where they had been moved into Spain. They considered it a miracle they had survived.

But survived to do what—to become what?

Slaves.

One of the Mozambicans had devised a way to escape. His name, Djibril remembered clearly, was Jordao. He had been fleeing the war, trying to cross into Zambia, trying to find a better, safer life when he had been caught in a net very similar to the one in which Djibril himself had been ensnared in front of the Mosque. Jordao had been offered a pathway out of the carnage that was taking place in his home and he had found only enslavement. But he was determined to get out. And, he had generously shared his plans with Djibril. The plans worked. When Jordao had successfully fled, Djibril waited for the furor to die down then he tried the same thing—crawling up onto the chassis of a truck being loaded with produce for high-priced markets in northern Europe and cramming himself into a pocket-sized space between the bed and the frame. He had made it through the tightly guarded gates and down the road several miles before he rolled off the truck as it slowed at an intersection. He had managed to make his way to Mallorca where he got a no-questions-asked job gardening at a tourist resort, paid only in board and room.

But it was better than being a slave.

Djibril had stayed at the resort a long time, making contacts, seeking opportunities. When the opportunity arose, it was unexpected. He managed to stowaway on a cruise ship that had stopped at Palma and was heading to Sardinia. From there, he managed to convince some soft-hearted fisherman, for whom he had worked for free for two weeks, to transport him to Tunis.

He was back where it had started. He had made a full circle, but he was much the wiser for the wear.

He now had a job at the barista where being a good and very cheap waiter was more important that assuring this person had all his papers in order. He was where he was. He was still unsure of where he should be. Would he return to Burkina or stay in Tunis? He didn't know.

"That's an incredible story," Charlie offered, feeling these words were completely inadequate to cover the harrowing tale. "You have certainly suffered and sacrificed to be where you are today."

"C'est la vie," Djibril replied in conclusion, a wry half-smile seeping in through the corners of his mouth.

Each went their own way, Charlie wondering if indeed life was simply about fighting against the odds just to get back to where you started.

ᴧ ᴧ ᴧ ᴠ ᴧ ᴧ ᴧ

That night, Charlie flew back home—back to Illinois.

As he flew from New York to Chicago, he thought that he was covering a distance in an airplane in a matter of hours that was one-third the distance Djibril had completed from Sourou to Tunis over the course of many weeks.

Getting back and getting going were now a routine. There was the debriefing with Jo; here a heavy focus on Djibril's tale. There was the debriefing with Robin, results met with guarded optimism. There was the debriefing and planning for next steps with Laura and Sue Ann.

Soon Charlie was fully immersed in BALJIN's global program that now was actually a real thing and not just a PR fabrication—some of the real things being Delpro derivatives and others honest-to-gosh people-helping-people issues. To his great satisfaction, BALJIN was truly interfacing with vulnerable people. BALJIN was assisting underprivileged communities. BALJIN was, of course, also doing Delpro's bidding.

The office in Kisumu was up and running. The campaign to encourage new reclamation projects was well underway. The NGO was able to make a strong, if totally ill-founded, case that all the attention on protecting lakeshore areas and conserving wetlands was simply a political ploy to keep land and jobs out of the hands of the lakeside citizenry—environmental extremists literally (in BALJINs spin) taking shillings out of the pockets of lacustrine families. It was a delicate line to walk but so far, they had managed not to get crosswise with local authorities.

BALJIN was becoming a shrewd if at times unassuming actor.

The office in Nacala was gearing up. If all went to plan, this would be one of the major foci in the African Region. This site offered significant opportunities to Delpro and her subsidiaries to the point that Charlie was unsure how much they would be able to do in the surrounding districts where folks were suffering so from war and chaos. Still, he was certain they would be able to do something to aid the misfortunate Mozambicans.

They had kept a presence in Zambia with the centerpiece remaining the office in Choma. This became an epicenter more to balance Delpro's pursuits in other parts of the country than to directly aid the poor and the needy. Nonetheless, they continued working with farmers in Southern Province, seeing tangible positive results in the adoption of coping strategies for the persistent drought.

There was more—much more. They had environmental-related assignments in Costa Rica and Ecuador (complete reversals of their stance in Kenya—a turnabout that so far seemed to stay off the outside world's radar—BALJIN was nothing if not flexible). They were engaged in education and adult literacy in Bangladesh and East Timor. They were key players in health programs in Haiti and Egypt. There were rural infrastructure and general agricultural development projects in Columbia, Indonesia, and Azerbaijan. They had humanitarian operations in Ethiopia, Sudan, Niger, and Yemen. They were preparing substantial proposals for Guatemala and Guinea Bissau while laying groundwork in a number of countries including Rwanda and Nigeria.

It was a lot.

Charlie was busy. Charlie was engrossed. Charlie accepted his present circumstances as, if not the endpoint of his search, at least an important lay-by. In moments when he could not control his mind totally, he continued to think of Jo—these thoughts now joined by images of Djibril's tale that seeped into his deepest reflections.

Through it all, the days clicked by, transformed into years.

ᛟ ᛟ ᛟ ᛦ ᛟ ᛟ ᛟ

The Mozambique Project took center stage. The *Centro de Revitalização da Agricultura* began to take shape, molded from the new office in a house near the church, *Igreja De Cristo De Ontupaia,* as recommended by Jorge. Jorge himself spent a lot of time in Nacala during the early part of the initiative until they were able to hire a local office manager cum BALJIN Rep, Lázaro Arruda.

Jorge vouched for Lázaro. He had very little experience in community development or humanitarian aid—really very little direct experience in any area where BALJIN was working. But his technical skills, as Jorge highlighted, were really of little importance. Lázaro was a local boy. He knew everyone. He had a good head on his shoulders and was, critically, the epitome of discretion. It was rumored that he had been involved in smuggling across the northern borders, but apparently the case had never been proven.

With Robin's benediction, Lázaro was anointed BALJINs *Diretor do Centro.*

Then, following Robin's orders, the job of designing of the facilities was passed to Slattery and Long while Lázaro put together an office team and began the groundwork of building good community relations—sometimes buying a beer for an important community member, other times providing more tangible (or bankable) incentives for influential leaders.

Word came back from Slattery and Long, the terse wording implying this was coming with Robin McCandless' aegis, that the architects had determined the new center would require two structures—not everything under one roof as initially planned. BALJIN had already setup temporary operations in the office transformed from the home near *Igreja De Cristo De Ontupaia.* Therefore, as now advocated by Jorge and apparently supported by Lázaro, they would keep and improve these facilities as their main base. This was a simple job of remodeling and upgrading; partitioning some rooms into compact offices, expanding the electrical and telephone systems, installing air conditioning, along with catering for staff and client parking. It was all basic stuff.

However, they still needed a second building—a warehouse-like structure that could have areas for training, demonstration, and storage. At one point, confusing Charlie, the architects called this a "holding unit." They wanted to build this structure from scratch on a lot somewhere between the railway yard and the port. Lázaro had to find the place. To guide the site selection, Slattery and Long were busy with blueprints that would provide the general requirements in terms of space and utility services.

These blueprints came to Charlie for forwarding through BALJIN channels to Lázaro. Charlie noticed that they were sketches and just that, very rough sketches giving the overall dimensions of the building to be built as well as its requirements in terms of electrical and water supplies. There were no specifics.

While this information was adequate for Lázaro to find a lot that had these prerequisites, it provided no details for Charlie to be able to look at functionality, staffing, operating costs, or any other feature that he required to be able to comprehensively plan the Mozambican Project.

Charlie made an appointment with Slattery and Long. He met with the chief architect, Rob Nelson, Messrs. Slattery and Long, the founders, now leaving most of the real work to a younger generation.

Charlie and Rob were in the office's conference room. When Charlie let his colleague know he needed to see the detailed plans, Rob excused himself, returning about five minutes later with several rolls of blueprints.

"Sorry to keep you waiting. I had to get approval from up the ladder to remove the blueprints from the company safe—they're locked-up when not in use."

"Is that usual?" Charlie wondered out loud.

"Not always, but in important cases."

"So, this is especially important?"

"So it seems."

"Well," Charlie said, trying to be pragmatic, "from my seat, all our offices are important, and this is just one of many—but one of many that I do really need to see to be able to make the necessary preparations. And you can imagine, these offices are expensive. The bosses don't like surprises when we haven't made the necessary allocations to be able to pay the light bill."

"Understood," Rob offered as he unrolled the blueprints on the large glass-topped table.

Charlie was surprised with what he saw and what was explained.

The building's footprint was over 40,000 square feet and it had three levels—one below ground requiring considerable excavation. The main floor had, in addition to warehouse space, expansive multi-purpose suites, meeting rooms, and a lunchroom as well as toilet amenities including full showers. Half the basement and half the second floor were principally large open areas for storage of bulk materials. This made sense as much of the work was foreseen as focusing on agricultural development—BALJIN importing large quantities of fertilizer, seed, and other inputs for local farmers while, more truthfully under the Equatorial Management logo, considerable quantities of agricultural products would be exported by rail or sea—this too being held, presumably, in this facility.

The other part of the upper floor was designed for more secure storage for possibly more valuable items as well as a communications hub and some offices. It was the other portion of the basement that was the most worrisome. This had several rows of six-by-eight rooms that could only be called cells. It looked like a bird's-eye view of part of a prison. And, Rob confirmed, that was reportedly exactly what it was.

Rob had no real explanation of why it was what it was. This was what they were asked to design and what they had designed. This was partially the reason the facility had such high-water requirements as each cell had its own tap.

Rob had nothing more to offer including his inability to give Charlie copies of the blueprints since these were deemed to still be under restricted circulation.

Back in his own office, Charlie attempted to reach out to Robin McCandless, but the great man was unavailable.

⋀ ⋀⋀⋁⋀⋀⋀

Would reaching out to the master help?

Would answers—real answers—be forthcoming?

The tangle of threads woven into the Mozambican Project was abstruse. A tapestry of questionable if permissible business practices or a tapestry of malfeasance and intrigue, it didn't matter. Charlie doubted he would know the whole story if Robin even deigned to expose any part of the intricate narrative.

Mozambique was but one slice of the job and Charlie was under pressure on several fronts. Sudan was an increasing priority. This dangerous terrain offered the possibilities of major profits. Agriculture and food supplies were a main concern. BALJIN now had a much-envied track record in these areas. It was up to Charlie to cast the net and reap the harvest (or set the trap, he thought).

Preliminary discussions had once again underscored the advantages of joining hands—at least from Delpro's perspective—with Equatorial Management. BALJIN could intervene on the short-term assistance and the medium-term policy adjustments. Equatorial Management could then jump in as a partner to implement these new policies; and, of course, could supply the materials necessary for this implementation.

Charlie and Peter agreed to once more meet in Nairobi to strategize before going on to Juba. They agreed to meet at the Thorn Tree Café at the New Stanley Hotel in downtown. The acacia tree out front was used as a message bulletin board for wayfarers and a suitable rendezvous for the two young men. They would spend the night at the hotel that had hosted Ava Gardner and Grace Kelly before flying on to Sudan.

Over *Tusker* beers, after a few pithy salutations, the pair swooped into the topics of the day as fresh beers were ordered.

"Sudan's a mess," Peter began, "there's a long history and multiple problems everywhere and now even more serious rumblings coming from a part of the country called Darfur."

"I haven't followed too closely," Charlie said, providing an anemic interjection.

"Of course," Peter continued, almost as though Charlie had said nothing, "we've seen disruptions and problems everywhere—Mozambique is at war, Zambia is awash with refugees and other ills, even here in Kenya—supposedly stable and prosperous—there's a lot sizzling under the surface. But all these complications—even the terrible things in parts of Mozambique—are spotty and we can pick and choose our site to be able to hopefully stay out of much of the fray.

"Sudan is different. It's a wide-open stage. There are no private corners for us to maneuver. There are even more actors than usual. We have to be careful."

"Yeah," Charlie offered, "that seems pretty clear."

"Yeah, and I mean real careful. This is the same strategy we've used often—you guys get set up on the ground and open some doors and we come in to follow through."

"Yep."

"Well, we anticipate in Sudan there will be a need to produce a lot of food. We figure you guys will get a running start as there's already a lot of attention to all the suffering and starvation. You'll be able to help channel food to the starving and push the leadership to back more sustainable food production—this will, we assume, we anticipate, include commercial or industrial farming requiring a lot of agricultural equipment.

"Equatorial Management is preparing the terrain for us to be seen as, among other things, acknowledged suppliers of farm machinery."

"Good."

"Maybe. I'm worried we're getting too far out into risky territory. But we're all too far into the soup to do anything but just plod on forward."

With that rather somber note, and more unknowns than knowns, Peter and Charlie decided to go to the restaurant rightly named the Carnivore for a meat-filled dinner.

They also decided, though they did not say so, that they were pretty good friends.

The next day Peter and Charlie flew to Juba. Upon arrival, they showed no indications they knew each other. They even stayed in different hotels.

⋀ ⋀ ⋀ ⋁ ⋀ ⋀ ⋀

While Peter and Charlie were familiarizing themselves individually with the realms of the national and international caregivers assembled to assist the unfortunate of Sudan, the United Nations was completing a major report reviewing two decades of humanitarian assistance—two decades of, according to the authors, NGO fraud and collusion between staff and outside service providers—public and private.

The UN organized a conference to name and shame the most flagrant of the unscrupulous offenders, as they called them. At the same time, they announced a more comprehensive investigation since only the most blatant and criminal operations were identified in the first phase of this widespread effort to uncover wrongdoing in the foreign aid arena. Over the course of the coming year, they explained, they expected to add a considerable number of bad operators to the list of the shamed.

Once identified, it would be difficult if not impossible for organizations to continue. They would be black-balled—become pariahs. Host countries would refuse them access and donors would refuse them funds. It was a death knell.

ᴧ ᴧ ᴧ ᗐ ᴧ ᴧ ᴧ

Bridges and foundations were built according to plan in Juba—BALJIN and Equatorial Management had both set stakes in the hard and fissured Sudanese ground. Peter and Charlie flew back to their respective bases without sharing another beer.

Back on the shores of Lake Michigan, after a visit to the Lake Center, Charlie briefed Robin McCandless. The principal overseer followed the events in Sudan with great interest, topping off Charlie's recounting with a re-emphasis of the great potential for profits offered by this, in his words, destitute country.

Given his boss's upbeat nature at the thought of great profits, Charlie considered he had an infrequent opportunity to effectually input into the wider collection of issues looming on the horizon, "Just to quickly change the subject a bit, sir."

Robin McCandless looked a somewhat askance but said nothing.

Taking this as the go-ahead, Charlie continued, "About Mozambique."

Only a slight nod from the host.

"About the plans—Slattery and Long's work—I was wondering about what I guess are cells?"

"That's for another day," Robin McCandless replied in almost hushed tones.

It was time for Charlie to go.

ᴧ ᴧ ᴧ ᗐ ᴧ ᴧ ᴧ

As Charlie was driving away from the mansion, the manor's lord got a call on a private line. It was his younger brother.

Over a scratchy line, Sir Horace nearly yelled at his brother, "It's this Sudan thing. There's an added wrinkle. Equatorial Management want us to add to the mix one of the tactics we've previously employed with varying degrees of success—but never anywhere as difficult as Sudan. You know, things are a nightmare there. Lots to gain and lots to lose."

"Yeah?"

"Yeah. I know we've done this before, but it's really risky in Sudan. They're planning on going all-in supplying farm machinery and ag processing equipment."

"So?"

"This is big time. We'll certainly be able to provide the Sears Catalogue of farm supplies—tractors, combines, caterpillars, pickups . . . you name it . . . we'll get it."

"Great. So, what's the problem?"

"Well, as always, the devil's in the detail. We'll get it, but according to present plans, we'll get it used. It'll be good stuff mind you. Not junk. And we'll have it overhauled by our mechanics—painted, lubed, and ready to go. But used."

"Hmmm."

"Yeah: 'humm.' This can be a tough sell anywhere. But in Sudan people are really looking at everything. It's like we're all under the magnifying glass. It's a massive humanitarian crisis seen around the world, much more so than most of the places we go, and everyone wants immediate results, but they also want to do this without a lot of the typical shenanigans."

"OK."

"So, think about it. We've—I've—gotta get a boatload of painted-up, used farm machinery and other stuff through customs under the eyes of inspectors who are not going to be easy to convince to look the other way."

"You're worried."

"Yeah."

"Is it bad?"

"This isn't going to be easy. If it blows up in our faces, we'll lose a lot."

"Are we protected?"

"We're protected—we're protected personally. But we're potentially exposed financially. We've got to front all the money for all the machinery—new or used."

"And the profits?"

"In principle, huge."

"Go ahead."

The line went dead.

Robin thought his little brother worried too much. It was what it was. It was that simple.

Deeper in the Swamp

S ILAS AND MIKE, OR Brother Mike as he was known by most, didn't know Charlie, but they were affected by his assignments.

Silas and Mike didn't know each other. They were separated by nearly 3,000 miles, as a bird flies.

Silas and Mike, although unknown to each other, shared a common moral code. For them, profits were not the ultimate determining factor. For them, principles were important. They wanted to do the right thing. They wanted to help their neighbor and their brother.

Silas and Mike were both, through no fault nor desire of their own, caught in a web of Delpro or its agents.

ᛗ ᛗ ᛗ ᚥ ᛗ ᛗ

Silas Otuaro was in Peter's address book.

He had never met Charlie.

However, Charlie had heard of Silas.

Charlie was preparing a proposal for submission to WHO in Nigeria for assisting residents of high-density ghettos with cholera prevention— providing education on improved household and family sanitation.

Charlie wanted to get a foothold in Nigeria.

Silas lived in Lagos.

Silas was a medical doctor; wiry and slight, with a large polished bald head sitting on a sinewy toffee-colored frame. Silas was the head of a clinic in the Idi-Araba section of the city—near the teaching hospital. For more than three decades he had lived across from the church on Ilajai Road in Akoka, a neighborhood on Lagos Lagoon. His wife had passed a few years ago, their three children now living in the UK and the US.

Silas was a Yoruba, born in Sagamu, forty miles northeast of Lagos. His father had been a mid-level civil servant in the colonial government. He had gone to medical school at the University of Edinburgh—the Scottish weather making him long for the sticky heat of Lagos.

When Silas had returned from his studies, he had started as an intern at the teaching hospital and then moved into private practice. He had taken a break from serving his patients during the Biafran War when he had volunteered to work with the wounded from both sides, temporarily moving to a field hospital in Igboland near Obiaruku, along the River Ethiope.

The war, a breakaway effort by the Igbo People, led to hundreds of thousands of casualties among the warring parties and the civilian population which suffered not only devastation due to the conflict itself, but also due to an accompanying famine, leading the international community to raise a cry of genocide and starvation.

In many ways the Biafran War set the stage for brutal and disastrous clashes that appeared across the continent in the years following the end of the colonial period and in the latter phases of the Cold War.

The Biafran War certainly set the stage for Silas—it was as though he had viewed firsthand a theater he never wanted to see again. In his personal life, he did all he could to sooth the waves of ethnic and religious discontent that trickled, at times flooded, through the country. On the medical front, he not only opened a special part of his clinic for the most needy (and the least able to pay), he also devoted his resources to improving the general public health conditions of the megalopolis.

Silas did all he could to make things better.

𖤣𖤣𖤣𖤣𖤣

Silas' clinic had been involved in the healthcare arena for years in the most impoverished slums of the mega-city that was Lagos—a city with a population greater than that of many countries. Much of the material Charlie was using in his proposal came from Silas' work.

This was a fact Silas never fully knew, and one he likely would not have appreciated if he had known.

This was something that Peter learned at a later date. He was proud of his good friend—his mentor—Silas for all his excellent efforts and valuable precedents he had established. He was less sure that BALJIN, and by default Delpro, would honor the principles of this selfless health worker in their own work.

ʌ ʌ ʌ ∨ ʌ ʌ

Still, Peter was not with Charlie when he was moving about, office to office, in the Nigerian Federal Capital of Abuja to garner support for his proposal and the million-dollar budget to which it was attached.

Once again Charlie found himself at a Sheraton. Once again, as so often, he found himself in the early evening hours hanging off the hotel's bar, wondering what he really should be doing. But unlike many similar evenings, when he looked about over the froth of his freshly pulled pint, tonight he saw coming his way one Sir Horace Barthley, gleaming in a pale green double-breasted, brass-buttoned jacket that offset a cobalt tie under the collar of a navy-striped shirt, all above khaki slacks and polished saddle shoes.

"Hey kid, what brings you to Naija?"

"Well, Sir Horace," Charlie said, trying to present a camaraderie he was not sure he felt, "how good to see you—I was just wondering what I could do to spice-up the evening and, *voilà*, here you are."

"You know me, kid, the god damn proverbial dirty penny that turns up anywhere and everywhere—but what brings you all the way here?"

"BALJIN is preparing—I guess I should say, I am preparing—a proposal for WHO for public health education and I need to make an extended tour of the ministries to get the needed contacts and support. All very boring nuts-n-bolts stuff."

"Well, keeps you from fucking up I guess."

"Maybe."

"Hope so."

"And your good self. Robin had made no reference of me seeing you here. What brings you to one of Africa's newest capitals?"

"I'm here kinda on my own business, but you've planted an interesting seed."

"Yeah?"

"Aye, son. It's really outside your wheelhouse, but I've got some stuff going on down in Rivers State—lots of bloody petrol—lots of bloody money. Sadly, the governor doesn't want to play ball. Run into these real bastards from time to time."

"I guess."

"Yes. Well, I can't figure him out. I tried sweetening the pot and he just got more adamant. What a fucker. But he doesn't know Horace Barthley."

"I imagine not."

"Damn straight! But he'll get to know me—you can bet you last fuck'n kobo on that."

"I'm sure."

"Fucking A. I'm get'n ready to show that asshole."

"Really?"

"Damn straight 'really,' son. These bush folks don't know Sir Horace."

"Suppose not."

"I've got contacts."

"That's good."

"Yes. I've got god damn good contacts."

"Excellent."

"Probably so. I know frigg'n guys and I know guys who know guys."

"Great."

"You bet great! Before this poor bastard knows what hit him, he's gonna find hisself outside the Governor's Manson sitting on the curb wondering who just cut off his balls."

"That's pretty severe."

"That's what it takes."

"OK."

"You bet. That sod is out and be damn sure, the new guy will play ball with me, or he'll lose his cobblers too."

"Hope it's worth it."

"Ham and cheesy, and then some—this is the land of fok'n black gold—there's sacks of coin involved and no Cozzers around, so I'm told."

"So, moving on from your castration project (Charlie realizing the Cockney meter was in overdrive), what's this you said about planting a seed?"

"Uh-huh. Sidestepping Barney Rubble, what do ya think your chances are for this tea leaf project you're work'n on?"

"Pretty good I'd say. Unlike your good self, I've not met any unreasonable personages. I've found people very willing to, as they say, 'make market.'"

"Well good on ya."

"Yeah. I'd give it better than an even chance. 'Course, here you never know until the last minute."

"Damn right."

"Still, I've got the key folks in the ministry on board—wasn't cheap, but they're there," he indicated his pocket.

"So, lad, let me give you a flip'n hypothetical and cut the Pony and Trap."

"OK."

"If you get this god damn ship afloat, let me know. I'm sure there are some parts of the bloody work on the ground that require medicaments and I've got shelves full—the best facsimiles from India—just waiting for a home. Won't fuck'n cure much but they'll help refill your pocket."

"I'll let you know."

"Of course." Sir Horace finished his drink, announced he had another appointment and, with a rapid step, left the bar.

⋀ ⋀⋀ⱽ ⋀⋀

BALJIN was awarded the WHO project. As was their practice, BALJIN set up a project office—in Lagos, not Abuja. Charlie contacted Sir Horace.

When the project was operational, the Lagos *Daily Nation* published an extended article on page four outlining the project and the NGO responsible for its implementation. Silas read the piece with interest, noticing the project's strategic similarities to his personal approach to public health.

Silas was invited to the project's inaugural workshop as a guest speaker. Thereafter he was put on a project mailing list for a quarterly newsletter. WHO asked Silas to be part of a review committee that periodically examined public health activities in Lagos State.

⋀ ⋀⋀ⱽ ⋀⋀

Brother Mike lived in southern Rwanda.

Brother Mike, or Michel van Leuven as he had been baptized in Ghent, near the Leie River, was a member of the Brothers of Piety. He had spent his adult life in the monastery on a hill overlooking the fishpond where he would shelter when life's pressures built as he tried to do God's Work and be worthy of God's Love in the Land of a Thousand Hills.

Brother Mike in particular, and the Brothers of Piety in general, were active in the broader development agenda for the Southern Province where they resided. Brother Mike frequently represented the Abbot for meetings of the Provincial Planning Commission. Through this Commission, he became aware of BALJIN when the NGOs Director attended a regular meeting to pitch a proposal for a famine resilience program that his group was elaborating for potential UNDP support.

Brother Mike met Charlie for a cocktail after the meeting. Although the monk was in Peter's address book, too, he had no idea Charlie knew Peter.

Not surprisingly, however, Peter knew Charlie was going to Rwanda albeit he had no clue Charlie might stumble across the good brother whom he himself had encountered in Bujumbura several years back—the brother had been busy buying fish from Lake Tanganyika for his community.

Peter and Charlie had discussed their plans—more correctly, Equatorial Management and Delpro's plans—for the near-future in this small but strategic country. As they had done numerous times before, BALJIN would be the plow clearing the road for Delpro or one of her adjuncts.

Naturally—they hoped naturally—everyone was in favor of minimizing the impacts of famine, but the real ambition here was to open official commercial channels supplying agricultural products—fertilizer, improved seed, and the like. Once the pipeline was in place, they would, following on some existing insider tips and solid reconnaissance, set up parallel covert inbound pathways to supply arms to a government filled with paranoia and fears of ethnic reprisal. The outbound functions of these pathways would be to surreptitiously move out wolframite—a very, very valuable mineral found in this area called the Great Lakes Region.

There was always business to be done.

⋀ ⋀ ⋀ ⋁ ⋀ ⋀ ⋀

At the after-meeting reception, as random small groups coalesced around tables brimming with frosty bottles of *Primus* beer, Brother Mike and Charlie found they both liked beer and liked chatting about work. Between portions of grilled kebabs (*brochettes*) and *frites*, Brother Mike opened the portal, "This your first planned intervention in Rwanda?"

"I guess it's the first that's got this far. We've outlined some earlier thoughts, but this is the first time someone, me in particular, has come to actually take the next steps and try to get the thing off the ground."

"We've a lot of projects."

"That's what I gather. Say your English is really excellent."

It was unclear if Charlie was trying to divert the subject, but the good brother stayed the course. "Many Belgians speak several languages—including English. And many of us at the Abby have seen many projects come and go—many leaving less in place than when they came."

"There's a lot to do."

"Of course. But that's not the crux of the matter. You have to understand who you're helping, and you have to be honest. Do you?"

"Do I?"

"Do you understand the people you're here to help, and do you plan to be honest in this help?"

"Naturally."

"Well, my son, I must confess it's not all that natural—it's not all that common. But I hope you're being honest now with me."

"Of course."

⋀⋀⋀∀⋀⋀

Several months later, UNDP funded the BALJIN proposal as part of the National Development Scheme. BALJIN was assigned work in Southern Province and therefore some of the oversight for their efforts was provided by the Provincial Planning Commission.

BALJIN set up an office in Gitarama. There were quarterly meetings with the Planning Commission to evaluate progress, these attended by BALJINs local representative. There was also a larger annual meeting in Kigali for all the partners in the national program. Charlie attended this meeting.

In a rerun, over pints of chilled *Primus*, Charlie had a chat with Brother Mike. This time it was Charlie who took the first step and said, "Brother Michael, good to see you—hope all is well at the Abby."

"My friend Charlie." Brother Mike smiled. "Good to see you back here."

"Happy to be back. How do you find our work so far?"

"Honestly, while I'm glad you asked, I can't answer. Everything is months behind schedule. We understand this is not your fault. There are underlying programmatic issues and logistic concerns that have led to, what UNDP calls, unavoidable delays. But so far it is not 'so good'; it is 'no good.'"

"That's why I'm here. I hope we can get all these things sorted out and get back on schedule."

"We all hope so."

∧ ∧∧∨∧ ∧

The delays, while not all that uncommon, were not only bothering Brother Mike. Robin McCandless was howling, and this had Peter at Charlie's heels. It was slower than normal—much slower. But eventually, outside the purview of the Planning Commission, with the tacit approval of several high-level dignitaries, BALJIN was able to facilitate the adoption of several agricultural policies that supported production systems far more sophisticated than the peasant farming practiced across much of the hinterland. They managed to convince the key decision-makers that hybrid seed and inorganic fertilizer were the keys to food security. This logically led to the need for large imports of these items and the amazing appearance on the scene of Equatorial Management ready, willing, and able with boatloads of seed and fertilizer at Mombassa only awaiting final approval for trucking into the country.

Soon the Equatorial Management trucks were routinely flowing between the Kenyan coast and the Great Lakes. Almost as soon, with the addition of some pressure from senior military officers, the seed and fertilizer were accompanied by quantities of unregistered arms for homeland security. Then, known only to a select few, the trucks returned to the coast with a few crates of wolframite rattling about their otherwise empty beds.

The cycle was complete.

∧ ∧∧∨∧ ∧

Equatorial Management was shoe-horned into operations in Sudan through BALJIN, although the connections were never publicly aired. Soon the company was engaged in multiple actions, supplying overpriced goods and services while putting down roots to inveigle themselves into other areas where suffering presented opportunities.

Funds flowed in to feed the famished. Among other aims, these were used to start cereal-growing projects where Equatorial Management was able to make serious headway. However, these projects were dwarfed by a series of impressive oil seed ventures where Equatorial Management controlled the entire value chain, making hefty profits at each step.

A big part of the oil seed activities involved the sale and installation of a number of seed presses and bottling factories. Peter was responsible for facilitating the arrival and set up of the equipment—only learning much later that it had all come from Ukraine. The Soviet-Union-era machinery with thick coats of shiny paint (all covered with Sir Horace's fingerprints) was supplied across a swath of the countryside where large tracts of oil seeds were being planted.

Initially, everything went well. Villages once again had ample supplies of good quality local cooking oil. Then the equipment began to fail. People were angry. Local folks wanted local justice. They wanted vengeance. And Peter was in the center ring.

He was arrested by the authorities. As a US citizen, he reached out to the nearest consulate. But he was informed that, according to their information, he was traveling under fraudulent papers. The consulate legal attaché visited him in jail. But this was only to decide if the US government wanted to add charges to those already lodged against him by the government of Sudan.

Peter was brought before the bench for the high crimes of larceny, extortion, and fraud—the US Consulate charitably declined to press for any additional charges. The witnesses for the prosecution described how this unknown white man had appeared and convinced them to invest in tasks that were doomed to failure—tasks that only lined his pockets with ill-gotten gold and worsened the conditions of poor people already horribly scarred by famine.

Peter was sentenced to fifteen years in Borh Prison, 125 miles north of Juba along the White Nile.

⋀⋀⋀⋁⋀⋀⋀

When Charlie heard about Peter's imprisonment, he was stunned. Charlie was taken aback with a wallop—in a way that had not affected him since Jo's terrible accident.

When Sir Horace found out about Peter's imprisonment, he was irate. He was angry at the unfortunate turn of events. While he liked the young man, he felt no remorse. Peter was just one of his many tools.

Still, the hoary patrician reflected, it was too bad the Sudanese activities had taken a hit. They had been very promising and would be difficult to resuscitate. Maybe that damn Peter deserved to be in jail—he'd spoiled a very profitable portfolio of ventures.

Peter's real innocence in the matter—he having had no role in choosing the equipment to provide for the oil press project—was not even a thought that entered Sir Horace's head. Someone had fucked up. Things had turned to shit. It was time to move on.

He assumed the once up-and-coming Peter would never see the outside of Borh Prison. And so much the better. While he had been frugal in how much he had divulged to his hireling, the kid was sharp. Maybe worse, the kid had a lot of connections. He was likely able to interpret much more from the scant information shared with him. He gleaned a little and extrapolated a lot. That had made him a valuable tool. It also made him a potential threat if he were ever to walk freely again. But there was little chance of that.

So, Sir Horace had to start to backfill. He called his big brother with an update. He began looking for new people to move into new places. Peter was not irreplaceable. There was always business to be done.

Λ Λ Λ V Λ Λ Λ

While Peter was suffering on the banks of the White Nile, seeds he had helped Charlie plant at the source of the Nile in Rwanda and in Naija had germinated. They were, in fact, in full bloom. And the blooms were rapidly withering.

Overzealous (and underpaid) inspectors in Rwanda had uncovered shipments of wolframite while their counterparts in Nigeria had done the same for shipments of pirated and ineffectual medications from India. Not knowing the full scope of these operations, but understanding they were catalyzed by United Nations' funding, in their respective countries, through the local UNDP offices, Brother Mike and Silas launched official complaints against BALJIN and its partners. The Belgo-Rwandan friar and the Nigerian physician proved to be key witnesses in cases that reviewed BALJINs activities—cases that ultimately resulted in the cancellation of BALJIN projects in the two countries and the closure of the NGOs offices.

It was ruinous. While Delpro was not explicitly cited in these formal complaints, the repercussions reached into Delpro's core. From some corners there were whispers (so far only whispers) linking Delpro to objectionable if not illicit activities.

The situation became even more damning when a global UN conference on human trafficking cited several operations in the Iberian Peninsula where Interpol had recently intervened and where it was rumored international cartels were involved in a medley of illicit affairs. Many transnational businesses reportedly had been highlighted as possible culprits in a confidential annex to the conference's main report. The threads to Delpro had not been uncovered, but Robin McCandless could feel the pressure.

Then, as if to add insult to injury, the UN produced an updated register of blacklisted NGOs accused of all manner of disreputable actions. High on the chart was BALJIN.

BALJIN and its staff were persona no grata everywhere except Antioch.

Robin McCandless got a FAX from Horace Barthley, "Everything's gone pear-shaped!"

Robin decided something had to be done.

ʌ ʌʌⱲʌʌʌ

Robin's actions were multi-pronged.

For decades he had been operating in plain sight. He and Delpro and BALJIN and a myriad of other entities had done their business in public—in the open—in view of everyone. From the onset, some had counseled Robin that this was audacious—that this was dangerous. Nevertheless, it worked. From his lakeside estate Robin had pulled strings that led across the globe. Still, he was not the master puppeteer. He, too, had his own strings and his own overlords. As the situation deteriorated, at least in the eyes of many, his own strings were pulled, and a change was required.

Very discretely, he put his chateau on the market.

He canceled long-standing contracts and other formal pacts with a large population of Illinois-based firms that had been part of his hub. He kept the contacts open but set aside any legal or semi-permanent affiliations.

He closed BALJIN. It simply was no more—dust to dust.

Charlie was frustrated. Charlie was down, practically bitter. He blamed himself. He blamed others. He blamed the gods.

He understood all too well the need to make BALJIN disappear. Yet, while his mind accepted the decision, his gut revolted. There should be another option. There wasn't.

He still felt a deep personal bond to the work, good and bad, that had emanated from BALJIN. Frankly, he realized this had principally been a smoke screen for a profusion of flagrant, often deceitful actions. Nevertheless, there had been some positive outcomes—some people in need had truly been helped (or at least he tried to convince himself of this hoped-for conclusion).

He also still felt a strong bond to the staff, especially Sue Ann and Laura. They had been tremendous assets. Fortunately, with a dose of creative writing and some help from some friends (more indebted associates than real friends, he reckoned), he had been able to find them excellent positions at other NGOs—the ladies being able to distance themselves satisfactorily from the real and imagined sins of BALJIN.

And now BALJIN was gone.

Most of the other entities with which Robin McCandless had surrounded himself were self-sustaining. They had other minor clients and other areas of focus. For them, it was now a question of refocusing with a stronger emphasis on these other areas and other customers—their main sugar-daddy was gone (and they had all done well—very well—under Robin's wing).

He opened an office in Kansas City—the Kansas, Kansas City—in the northwest suburbs. Here he offered positions to the chief lawyers, accountants, and others who had been critical to all his efforts over the years. He offered these positions with such a generous salary that it was difficult if not impossible for people to decline—refusal was highly discouraged.

This arrangement was in part to provide the needed support staff for his future operations without having them physically close as had been the previous situation. This was also a strategy to keep these essential people with long memories and annotated personal files close to him— keep your friends close and your enemies closer. These were not *sensu stricto* enemies, but, in some permutations of his future, he realized they could conceivably be threats.

Charlie was an exception.

Robin had grown to appreciate the young man. He actually, he imagined, had some sort of bizarre paternal affection for the lad.

He offered Charlie a position as his personal assistant. This was a big deal.

Charlie realized the potential of the offer—all the more relevant since he had just lost his job as head of BALJIN. But it inevitably meant leaving Illinois. Certainly, a move was part of Robin's plans and if he moved, what about Jo?

Fortunately, he guessed, he was able to have this candid discussion with his former and possibly future boss. A solution was found. Since Jo was doing well and still making tiny steps forward, it would be best to keep her at the Lake Center where she was comfortable and where the physicians and other caregivers knew her situation well. Still not disclosing where he planned to move his operations, Robin proposed to Charlie that Delpro would pick up any and all health-related expenses for Jo that were not covered by insurance as well as pay his air fare and hotel expenses for a quarterly visit to his beloved.

This, combined with a more than handsome salary that was a significant increase over his already more-than-generous BALJIN compensation sealed the deal. Charlie was Mr. Robin McCandless' personal assistant.

⋏⋏⋏⋎⋏⋏

It took several months to put all the pieces in place. But once the new structures and arrangements were functioning, Robin announced to Charlie that he would be relocating to Candy Point, Virginia, on the banks of the Potomac where the river entered Chesapeake Bay.

The overlord stressed, his cheeks nearly radiating a crimson mantle, this was not common knowledge. This was not a location known to anyone else. Robin McCandless and Delpro were shifting from overt to covert—they were now under deep cover. Charlie had to understand and respect this condition. He, as well, would be residing near Candy Point but no one was to know. The days of high visibility and a public persona were over.

Robin had opened a post office box in Charlie's name in Heathsville, the county seat of Northumberland County, just about ten miles from Candy Point. He had also rented for Charlie, as an official physical address for all concerned, a small house on St. Stephens Lane, across from the Episcopal Church. To the outside world, this was Charlie's new home. Robin had gone so far as to register a community assistance group on the census of the Northumberland Social Services Department—this group was located at Charlie's address on St. Stephens Lane. The paper trail Robin had seeded showed that Charlie had left BALJIN for a substantial yet altruistic post of assisting the rural poor of the Commonwealth of Virginia.

Robin relocated to Chesapeake Bay with remarkable speed. One day he was seated poolside at Crab Tree Lane and the next he was not. All enquiries were referred to an office in Kansas City.

While Robin had vanished to Candy Point, there was obviously a big job preparing his estate for sale. This had not only been Robin Mc-Candless' luxurious home, it had been his office. Some of his selected personal possessions were quietly shipped to Virginia while everything else was given to local charities. But dealing with his home office was another matter—a sensitive matter to say the very least.

This job fell to Charlie.

Robin had given Charlie access to all his private files—electronic and hardcopy. He had had two personal safes on the premises. He had emptied both, taking special items with him when he left, handing the rest over to Charlie to join the great volume of Delpro-related documentation that had to be sorted—some sent east, some shredded and burnt, and a small subset sent to Kansas City.

Robin had given Charlie a handwritten list of all the items he needed to move securely and discretely to Candy Point—the moving was part of Charlie's job—personally hiring a rental van and being THE person who assured the transfer of this material from one mansion to another. There was a much shorter list for Kansas City—this to be attended to by private courier. The material to be destroyed was to be destroyed by Charlie himself.

There was a lot of stuff. It should have taken Charlie a good two weeks to catalogue and cull, putting each item in one of the three categories. In fact, it took him twice as long. It took a lot longer because he privately scanned or otherwise copied all the documents, regardless of the pile in which they ended up.

Charlie felt he needed some protection. He was not really sure of the true import of all these documents. After all, Robin McCandless had taken a fair number of files with him. And he was not really sure if he was in any jeopardy. Although his work had ended in disaster, everyone linked to Delpro including Robin McCandless had always treated him well.

Nonetheless, Charlie was all too aware of what had happened to Peter. Charlie liked Peter. He respected Peter and he knew Peter was careful and methodical. If Peter could get in trouble, anyone could. What's more, it was not the getting into trouble, it was the getting out. It seemed that those who could possibly help Peter out were willing to sit on the sidelines and watch him be imprisoned in Sudan—possibly for the rest of his life.

While Peter had been given a fifteen-year sentence, Charlie had heard rumors. And, where there's smoke.

Once safely tucked away in some obscure site, apparently it was not uncommon for embarrassing people to simply disappear. Charlie was not sure how egregious the highest echelons felt Peter's errs to be. The outcome could be awful.

To add to the poignancy, Charlie knew from his beer-laced chats with his friend that Peter also had a very serious partner—a partner whose relationship Peter himself compared to Charlie's relationship with Jo. Pete's significant other was Evelynn. Charlie had never met Evelynn, but Peter had discussed her in such glowing terms that he felt as though he had. In his mind, he did equate Evelynn with Jo. At first, he had been happy his friend was not going through what he was going through with Jo. But when Peter ended up in prison, this meant that Peter and Evelynn were going through some sort of the same hell that tainted every minute of every day of Charlie's life since that damnable day at Campbell Airport.

They deserved better.

He deserved better.

While his own problems were not directly job-related, Peter's were. And if the job could do that to Peter, it could do it to Charlie. He needed a backup plan. He needed leverage. He hoped—he trusted—that copies of all these critical documents would give him what he needed.

ᚼ ᚼᚼᚼᚼᚼ

In many ways, everything looked as it always had.

Indeed, Robin McCandless and Delpro had been operating openly—but only openly to those who even knew they existed. By far, the majority of organizations and institutions who paralleled Delpro's areas of activity never even knew this veiled company existed, let alone that it potentially was a competitor. In full sight of all, Delpro had stood upright in the shadows.

Delpro and Robin McCandless had now closed the blinds. But no longer seeing what one never clearly saw really made little difference. Delpro continued to do what Delpro had always done—and making windfall profits in so doing.

Even Robin McCandless' lifestyle had not demonstrably changed. He had never been a very public person and he was still shrouded in privacy.

The true change was psychological. Being unseen and unnoticed was different than being noticed but unseen. Delpro's hand was now noticed, be it fleetingly (they hoped), as a power that potentially pulled many levers in many places.

Much of this noticing, furthermore, was being done by the wrong sort of people. This recognition was not a plus even if the seekers seemed to be chasing illusive specters more than bona fide transactions.

The veil had to hold. After all, no one could really describe Delpro. No one really knew who was at its helm nor where it was located. This had been the case and it was still the case.

Nonetheless, people were looking. People from all over were looking into things they should not—things that jeopardized Delpro's hidden world.

It was not the physical move from Illinois to Virginia. It was not changing from living behind an open gate to behind a reinforced stone wall. It was not shedding all the support entities that had been instrumental to getting Delpro and McCandless where they were. It was simply knowing that others knew—others were coming.

This was the underlying stress. This was the new reality that made working for Delpro and Robin McCandless at Candy Point different.

On the outside, it was all the same. Inside, it was all different.

Onlookers

OBSERVERS LIKE SILAS AND Brother Mike had raised warnings about the Delpro network without even knowing the existence of this transnational amoeba. They had seen the misadventures ensuing from the seemingly compassionate deeds—people helping people—of a reputed big-hearted aid organization: BALJIN. For them, misdeeds on the ground, in the community, had been enough to sound the alarm.

For other lookers-on, their concerns grew more slowly out of a process of deduction.

꘠꘠꘠꘠꘠꘠

Hal Schleider and Rodney Mills lived in the greater D.C. area. Hal Schleider and Rodney Mills were a couple.

Hal Schleider and Rodney Mills worked in the same nondescript office building among a row of 1950's brick apartments along Blue Plains Drive, not far from the Potomac Job Corps Center. The stodgy exterior belied a modern and bustling interior with a swanky reception with an equally fashionable receptionist behind the high oak table. These were the head offices of the Division of Enforcement of the Security and Exchange Commission in Washington, D.C.

Hal had been among the founders of this branch, coming to the SEC as a veteran of both Vietnam and the CIA. He was a hands-on type of guy. His younger counterpart and companion, a Harvard-trained lawyer, came to the job from an academic environment—having possibly a more juristic view of the division's efforts to halt, or at least minimize, wrong-doing of some of the country's most formidable malefactors.

The division took long and deep looks into a wide variety of nation-al and international enterprises—most compliant and respectful of laws and regulations. A minority abused the system and deceived both share-holders and regulators. An even smaller subset of the felonious group were real villains, respecting nothing and no one beyond absolute power.

The villains were the most clever. It frequently took years to really pick up a spore—even then, with far too many dead-ends.

For some time, Delpro had been a prominent item on the division's radar.

ꟼꟼꟼꟽꟼꟼꟼ

Hal had flagged Delpro as a subject of interest several years earlier. At that time, by pure chance (those things that never should happen, but do), he had, practically by a fluke, discovered his nephew, Eddie, had worked for Delpro in Spain and southern Africa. Eddie, a surveyor, had initially seen his assignments as relatively straightforward mapping tasks. How-ever, as his work progressed and punctured several of the veneers put in place by Delpro, on both continents he began to have concerns about the company's true activities. Eddie uncovered fragments and shreds that seemed harmless in isolation, but when inserted as pieces of one larger intercontinental puzzle, began to portray actions that were highly cor-rupt—misappropriation of land, falsification of agricultural products, and more, including kidnapping people and forcing them into slavery. It was a potentially damning scenario—and, Hal knew, revealed only a small soupçon of Delpro's operations.

Sadly, in Zambia, Eddie's wife Samantha had been killed in an auto-mobile accident that Hal strongly felt was in fact a murderous act to drive Eddie away in despair. And, it had worked. Eddie returned a widower to his native Pacific Northwest where, to his shock, he, in spite of himself, encountered other acts of corruption and falsification that were ulti-mately tied to Delpro. It was as though Eddie could not lose the demon on his back.

Finally, after the death of Hal's big sister, Eddie's mother, an uncle-nephew dyad was formed in the hopes of addressing the ills that en-meshed Eddie's life, especially avenging Samantha's death. They revisited many of the sites where Eddie had earlier scoured pieces of the puzzle; this time to dig deeper and to get other members of the SEC crew on the scent. Through these combined efforts, the Delpro case actually went before a grand jury and indictments were handed down against five top Delpro officers. To build the case, Eddie would need to testify.

Sadly, again, midway through these processes, Hal suffered a fatal heart attack. A heart attack that was not a heart attack. Thanks to Rodney's dogged pursuit of the facts, they were able to demand a particularly detailed postmortem that showed that Hal had, in fact, been poisoned.

Hal's unfortunate departure disrupted the SEC crew's plans for moving ahead with prosecution. Nonetheless, even in death, Hal had, through his notes discovered posthumously, left a number of trails to follow. One led to General Industrial and Chemical Products.

This investigation took great effort. It was like trying to follow a single leaf in an autumn windstorm. After looking through heaps of domestic and international data, they could only conclude General Industrial and Chemical Products was a shell corporation. There seemed to be a snarl of subsidiary enterprises scattered around the globe. Many initially looked like relatively small companies targeting localized markets. There were, however, some large and, in their own right, perplexing operations. Two that stood out were Ace Foods and Farm Services. Simple names for multimillion-dollar undertakings with on-the-ground presences on at least three continents.

Ace Foods was highly diversified but seemed to concentrate on fruit and vegetable products grown on large farms in Africa, Asia, and Latin America to supply European and North American markets. Perhaps logically, Farm Services addressed the other end of, in many cases, the same value chain—providing fertilizers, agrochemicals, and machinery to some of the same farms as well as a broader swath of clientele.

Ace Foods had farms in Ghana, Mozambique, Tanzania, and Sénégal; produce from farms in these countries processed in Spain for sale in the European Union. This led them to Evergreen Ocean Transport, a company accused of smuggling container-loads of illegal aliens and illegal produce into Europe—also the company that transported Ace Food's fruit and vegetables from Ghana, Mozambique, Tanzania, and Sénégal to Spain. Evergreen was owned by Delpro.

Through Evergreen and Farm Services, they found Ace operations in Ghana had connections with businessmen in Guinea Bissau who shipped cocaine from Bissau labeled as Farm Services' fertilizer or inserted into hollowed-out pineapples for delivery to Spain.

Ultimately an intricate three-dimensional pyramid took form with Delpro at the apex. Delpro was indeed networked with Ace Foods and Farm Services as well as their parent General Industrial and Chemical Products. This became a very big piece in the overall Delpro puzzle.

⁘⁘⁘⁘⁘⁘

Before Hal's untimely departure, he had identified two brothers as key players in the Delpro drama: Robin McCandless and Horace Barthley. They were full brothers. While Romanian by birth, each had been adopted by a different family—one in the US and another in the UK. Robin, the older US-raised sibling, seemed to be one of the main people in Delpro. The younger Horace remained more of a riddle—not to say Robin was not a puzzlement. The UK-raised Horace, now using the sobriquet "Sir Horace," seemed to appear and then disappear all across the globe.

Robin, for all his clandestine impropriety, seemed to stay pretty close to home. He had first surfaced in Illinois, having a superb home on the shores of Lake Michigan. He had then moved east, possibly to be closer to the seats of power. Ultimately, through a labyrinthine investigation, they discovered he had a lovely manor on Chesapeake Bay, at Candy Point, that was more than an equal to his previous palatial residence outside Chicago.

⁘⁘⁘⁘⁘⁘

As Rodney continued to try to piece together the puzzle, one of the critical questions was the local command and control for all the nefarious activities that were being overseen at the highest levels by Delpro and being implemented by a variety of international firms.

Yet, like they say—all politics are local. The ability to finally do what was being done required considerable on-the-ground support. Local actors worked in concert and were part of broad and effective communications networks. How was it all orchestrated?

One of the leads for identifying the functioning conduits came by chance (as so many) through the efforts of an American working in Geneva for the Ecumenical Humanitarian Trust—EHT.

Paula Patterson was a cultural anthropologist who had started her international work through the Peace Corps and continued via a variety of assignments and employers. She had worked an extended period with EHT, moving up in the organization, becoming a close advisor to the Director General.

González Philip Albardi, the EHT DG, had been, as per the EHT mandate, working to help the vulnerable. The trust had been established in 1946 with private funds coming from the estates of several venerable Italian families and with the original imperative to help those who had lost everything in the war. The present-day fortunes of these original benefactors, still active in several modern economies, maintained EHT in good standing.

Through initially innocent background research, Paula discovered close links between EHT and the International Center for Democratic Ideals. ICDIs professed mandate was to promote democratization. The Center reputedly developed tools and policies addressing and mitigating social and economic disorders as ways of helping the common man. Unlike EHT, ICDI worked on a cost-sharing basis—their grants requiring matching funds from host governments. The hope was that the combination of external and internal support would allow the core actions to continue through time. However, Paula's contacts verified that ICDI support had often been redirected to the political leadership—the tools for the common man were actually bribes for local elite. These same contacts also verified that conservative political groups across Western Europe and North America were in fact the major ICDI donors. Reportedly, the real intent was to support right-wing governments with whom the donors of ICDI would subsequently enter into very favorable trade relationships.

Paula further documented that much of EHTs current operating capital came from ICDI—apparently the old Italian families could no longer carry the load. ICDI, with all its shady network of conservative political interests, was indeed the major supporter of EHT. And their relationship was more than that of donor and recipient. Overlaying maps of countries where ICDI's pro-democracy interventions had resulted in very lucrative trade agreements with ICDI donors, compared to priority countries where EHT claimed to be making a difference, demonstrated the two maps were identical. EHT was indeed a conduit for ICDI.

Rodney's team discovered that ICDI was also, though it was deeply hidden, a subset of Delpro activities. In effect, ICDI belonged to Delpro—it was one of their outreach arms.

Paula had lost her job over her discoveries. She had returned to the States and Rodney had visited her at her office at the Center for Equitable Social Policies on Haycock Road, just off the I-66, in Falls Church. While Paula had detailed and voluminous knowledge of EHT, her understanding of the functioning of ICDI was practically non-existent. She had uncovered the secret relationship between the two organizations—the unsavory and probably illegal arrangements. However, she had naturally only viewed the problem through the EHT lens.

This was of little help to Rodney although it did corroborate a number of facts he already knew. From his vantage point, the major actor through the Delpro lens was ICDI, not EHT. Still, this organization had revealed very little under Paula's examination. Rodney needed new sources.

ᛘ ᛘ ᛘ ᛦ ᛘ ᛘ

The answer to Rodney's search, as was so typical, came through unusual channels. Although Paula's information had been useful if not groundbreaking, through his interactions with her, Rodney came to know that, while at EHT, she had had an internee from Tanzania—Evelynn.

Rodney also had many agents digging into Delpro-related subjects across the world. One of the best was Joe Thompson, who worked mostly in eastern and central Africa. Joe had coincidentally met Evelynn. These were the type of interactions that caught Rodney's attention—unusual actors whose roles were probably more than accidental.

Joe informed his boss that Evelynn's boyfriend was Peter—Peter Volman. He worked for a company based in Dar es Salaam called Equatorial Management. This firm was involved in shady affairs all across the continent and was closely tied to Sir Horace Barthley.

The pegs were lining up. Evelynn and Peter. Paula and Joe. Sir Horace.

Then things changed demonstrably for Peter. As Joe explained to Rodney, Peter had been arrested in Sudan for selling faulty or improperly labeled agricultural equipment. The Sudanese had shown no pity. Peter had been imprisoned in Borh Prison on the White Nile.

Joe was able to visit Peter in prison and to confirm he was panicking. He was close to breaking. He had never imagined such horrible events could befall him. He was ready to do whatever he could to end the nightmare and return to some sort of normal life.

ᴧᴧᴧᴡᴧᴧ

The Delpro investigation was now growing by the day. There were increasing leads, there was an expanding number of locales. It was becoming a worldwide morass. It was becoming an investigation that justified its own individual standing to attract dedicated staff and funding.

Rodney had previously worked on some similar large operations, most focusing on organized crime issues. One of the biggest targeted a Ukrainian-born Russian considered to be the boss of bosses of the Russian mafia syndicate, the Solntsevskaya Bratva crime group. Rodney recalled the word "bratva" could be translated as meaning "lads" in English. Thus, he baptized the Delpro investigators as the bratva—the lads. Soon it became simply BTF—the Bratva Task Force.

Separate BTF groups probed every available aspect of Robin's and Horace's lives. Other staff explored sites and businesses across the globe. It was a major undertaking.

The truth was deeply hidden. Progress was slow. One of the most promising leads remained Peter. Rodney made sure that Joe was closely watching their target as well as he could from outside the prison walls. Rodney even wrote some personal notes for Joe to give to the young inmate on those occasions when he arranged for face-to-face visits.

As the BTF crew sifted through Peter's life, they came across his relationship with Charlie Stancik—the two not infrequently having been at the same place at the same time. Through Charlie, they came to BALJIN.

Charlie and BALJIN were much less challenging to unwrap—at least during what Rodney called, "The BALJIN years." The NGO was now history and offered no new discoveries, but perhaps was a door into past disclosures. As an acknowledged—some would say well-known—international humanitarian NGO, there were ample records about its interventions, staff, and ancillary activities. As the director, Charlie's role, or at least his public role, was equally visible.

With the closure of BALJIN, however, things had changed. Charlie had left a mosaic of contacts and relationships in the Chicago area and was now reportedly living in Heathsville—not far from the BTF offices and, probably not surprisingly, not far from Robin McCandless' new domicile at Candy Point. Still, they could uncover no recent interactions between Charlie and Robin.

Rodney was convinced Charlie was an important resource, but it was going to take time to get the necessary bigger picture. In the interim,

Peter seemed the best target. He was, after all, in prison. He was going nowhere, and he wanted to go anywhere.

Rodney made sure Joe was on top of the Peter situation.

∧ ∧ ∧ ∨ ∧ ∧

Rodney needed the bigger picture for Charlie, but he realized all too well he needed the bigger picture for everything. Robin McCandless was tucked away, trying to be invisible at Candy Point. Horace Barthley was truly nowhere to be seen. And, Rodney knew, Delpro was doing all manner of things in all manner of places—none of them good for the law-abiding citizens of the world, even if they were very profitable for the czars of Delpro.

For the moment the most promising lead remained Peter. He knew all about Equatorial Management and likely a raft of other information. He reportedly knew the infamous Sir Horace well. He was the key Rodney needed to open the door.

Then things changed.

While Rodney had his doubts that Robin McCandless was THE overlord at the absolute pinnacle of Delpro, McCandless had finally, in spite of multiple delaying measures, been summoned to appear before a grand jury on a wide variety of federal changes, with additional state charges pending. Rodney and his crew were confident their evidence, now compelling, would lead to an arraignment.

Robin McCandless, apparently, was also sure he was in trouble. He tried to flee the country by boat, leaving from Candy Point evidentially to meet a seaworthy craft somewhere in Chesapeake Bay. However, his speedboat had just left the dock and crossed the Virginia-Maryland state line when the craft exploded.

BTF had immediately seen this as a ploy to vanish—Robin McCandless probably not even onboard the demolished vessel. However, when they reviewed the images from the surveillance cameras they had surreptitiously placed all around the McCandless Estate, there was incontrovertible proof that Robin had indeed boarded the boat. Moreover, when the Coast Guard came in response to the explosion, they were able to recover three badly burned bodies. It was difficult, but the coroner had ultimately been able to identify Robin McCandless through dental records.

Rodney and his superiors as well as key staff from DOJ had pains-takingly reviewed all the available information, in the end declaring Mc-Candless dead (probably at the hands of his colleagues).

This was a setback. The main actor had been removed from the stage. Nevertheless, BTF felt they still had a case against Delpro. They decided to even further widen their investigation to collect the neces-sary additional evidence to be able to seek new indictments against other members, still to be identified, of Delpro's management.

ᐱ ᐱ ᐱ ᐁ ᐱ ᐱ

Charlie had been at the dock to help Mr. McCandless with his luggage and to give him some last-minute correspondences. He had not been privy to McCandless' legal jeopardy. As far as he knew, everything was fine and his employer was simply going off on a business trip, taking the boat as he had been concerned that he was under surveillance, as he said, "By the damn feds."

Charlie had helped his boss get settled on the thirty-five-foot Sports Coupe craft; waiting for the mate to serve the ship's master a glass of wine while the captain prepared to push off. Once all was in readiness, there had been a final handshake, and that was that. Charlie stood on the dock as the boat slipped into the darkness, leaving only a foamy wake and the echo of the throaty gurgle of the accelerating 700 horsepower twin Volvo engines.

Then the sky was alight, there was a roar.

The boat was gone.

Breaking Camp

C HARLIE WAS AT A loss.
He had felt the swoosh as the energy from the explosion flowed over the dock. He had smelt the fumes. He had tasted the heat.

The boat was gone.

Robin McCandless was gone.

He was at a loss.

He sought explanations. He sought ideas of what to do.

From those first trips across the lake on the *Velvet*, Charlie had at least subconsciously acknowledged he was part of a criminal organization. While denial had dominated, he rationalized his participation under the flag of "no one gets hurt." This argument to his better angles had lost ground as he fell deeper and deeper into the Delpro maze. It pretty much disappeared when he realized they (the "they" including himself) were preparing to build cells in a warehouse in Mozambique.

Still, he valiantly tried to play down the criminality, thinking—trying to convince himself—that they were really providing needed services and helping many along the way. This whitewashing, too, pretty much washed away of late and he had, in spite of himself, accepted the reality of his situation when he had decided to make copies of Robin's files.

Yet, all this notwithstanding, he had never thought of Delpro, of Robin McCandless, of himself as assassins and cutthroats. They were crooks, right enough. But it was white-collar crime, wasn't it?

As the ashes settled on the foam of Chesapeake Bay, it appeared to be clear that it wasn't. This matter was much more tainted and much more dangerous than he had ever realized.

Charlie no longer had a clear idea of his role in all this. He was no longer sure what he did—what he had done. Was he at risk of going to jail? Was he at risk of being killed like Robin?

As far as Robin was concerned, Charlie had no doubts. This was no boating accident. The craft was in excellent shape and impeccably maintained. Such a massive explosion could only be one thing: murder.

Was his own name on someone's list?

Were the others, those encapsulated in the oft-mentioned "we" of Robin McCandless' discourse—were they after him?

He had done many rotten, probably scandalous, things.

Now, he had (though no one should know, he reminded himself) a large pile of potentially incriminating files.

He was at a loss. What should he do?

$$\wedge \wedge \wedge \vee \wedge \wedge$$

In a white haze of uncertainty and dread, Charlie recalled the Romanian proverb he had heard Sir Horace echo: *A well-turned lie pays better than the truth.* Like much of the fiery old man's tart gibber, this had generally passed unnoticed—unabsorbed. Yet, it was true. Charlie had been tied to well-turned lies for years—lies he had broadcast for Robin and others in leadership—lies he had told himself about his work and his windfall payoffs.

From the beginning, from that day he left the lakebed, he had been following not only his dreams but also his edacity—his rapacious appetite to not only see more and to do more, but to have more. Now charred flotsam on the polished surface of Chesapeake Bay changed everything.

$$\wedge \wedge \wedge \vee \wedge \wedge$$

Charlie needed to leave Candy Point. He needed to leave Heathsville. And he did.

He went back to familiar terrain. He went to Chicago.

He did not go to Antioch or Abbot Park. He went back further. He went back to West Haddon Avenue—the location of the apartment Mihaela had arranged for him all those years ago, now feeling like a lifetime ago.

While his whole life had changed and been turned upside down, the neighborhood around St. Volodymyr Ukrainian Orthodox Cathedral seemed untouched by the outside world. It was as it had been. It was his refuge.

Luckily finding an apartment to let, Charlie, basically back to his old cardboard suitcase and a few newer bags along with his heap of files, returned to the desired sanctuary of the past.

⋀ ⋀ ⋀ ⋁ ⋀ ⋀ ⋀

Robin had warned Charlie about, the feds. Early on in their relationship, in a joking way, he had advised his young employee that all their actions would, at one time or another, be under a government microscope. After that, Robin McCandless had periodically complained, sometimes vociferously, sometimes more placidly, about harassment by the government. He would generally write it off for Charlie's sake as the manifestation of the jealously of underpaid civil servants. Yet, with growing severity, he was acutely aware of ongoing surveillance.

It was troublesome at the very least. It was not a nuisance. It had become a real threat.

As the feds apparently became bolder, Robin became more informed about what they were doing and what they were planning. He had even learned the name of his chief nemesis, Rodney Mills.

Robin McCandless had cautioned Charlie to avoid Rodney Mills at all costs (apparently Robin respected Mills as this alert was made in a way Robin reserved for referring to those he appreciated—generally colleagues and not government agents).

While Charlie was seeking a route out of any possible limelight, Rodney was seeking to shine as much light as he could on Delpro—all parts and hidden corners of Delpro.

Most members of the BTF remained unconvinced that Robin McCandless had truly perished in the explosion. Yes, his corpse had been identified through dental records. But . . . There were always many buts.

BTF forged ahead. Joe continued to stay close to Peter to see how he could best be used. Rodney himself briefed Eddie about testifying before a new grand jury that was still to be constituted—another case now without Robin McCandless at the spearhead. A pair of BTF investigators had been sent to locate and interrogate Sue Ann Hoffman who had been identified as a key actor in BALJIN. Rodney's first impressions (which were more times than not spot-on) were that Sue Ann had undoubt-edly broken the law but there was no real justification for pursuing her legally. Nonetheless, she likely had insight into BALJINs activities that could possibly be traced back to Delpro. She was someone to whom to pay attention.

Every day, some new dirty shard of Delpro's work surfaced in the BTF offices. Progress was slow but all were motivated by the sheer impact this company—or, more likely, these companies—had on people around the world.

⋀ ⋀⋀∀⋀⋀

Charlie was not a rich man. He was comfortable. By comparison to the young Charlie who had wandered aimlessly around the Pilsen neigh-borhood of Chicago, today's Charlie was, however, a member of the landed gentry.

He had been well paid in his various assignments and jobs that re-lated to the wider Delpro umbrella. Furthermore, through his contacts in these companies, he had been privy to all manner of financial advice that, when filtered and studied, had led him to significant profits.

Charlie was well-to-do.

And, so far as he knew, Jo's expenses were still being paid automati-cally through arrangements made by Robin. There had been a kind of trust established that could pay these expenses for the remainder of her life if need be (Charlie, of course, hoped this would not be the case).

In any event, living in an apartment on West Haddon Avenue put no stress on Charlie's finances. It did put abnormal stress on his psyche and his spirit.

He was totally unsure if he was under observation—a person of interest, as some said. Given recent misfortunes, it seemed highly likely.

He tried not to be paranoid. Yet, he stopped visiting the Lake Center. Definitely, he felt, if he were under surveillance, most probably, so was Jo.

His schedule had always been erratic. He had come and gone almost spontaneously. People were used to his being out of touch. To many, he was nearly a phantom. Now he needed to be a better phantom.

He had the wherewithal to dodge and remain unseen. This was his immediate goal.

⋀ ⋀⋀∀⋀⋀

Rodney, on the other hand, wanted to be seen. He wanted to stir the pot—he wanted it to boil—to boil over. He wanted to scrape the scabs off all that was Delpro.

At the moment he had a growing number of leads to follow while still keeping close watch on Peter and, he himself, reviewing for the umpteenth time the documentation compiled by his dear departed Hal.

A new grand jury was soon to be empaneled and Rodney had to make sure all was in readiness including Eddie's testimony. There was no shortage of criminal law to present to the jury nor any shortage of background information—hard evidence, in Rodney's eyes. Yet, one never knew the outcome. All too often there are unwelcome surprises.

ᛀᛀᛀᚥᛀᛀᛀ

By chance, Charlie's efforts in some ways again mirrored Rodney's. Charlie definitely wanted to avoid any and all unwelcome surprises.

He avoided all his old contacts—he wasn't sure if, beyond Jo, he really had any old friends.

He adopted a sedentary life centered around his apartment on West Haddon Avenue. He had arrived using a cane—affecting a limp. While few people asked, and probably no one cared, he offered a story that he had been in a serous automobile accident in Florida—rammed off the road by some redneck jackass in a massive 4X4—and had come back to a safe and sane Midwest to recuperate.

No one seemed to recognize him nor remember that he had once before been a lodger in the shadow of St. Volodymyr's.

About a twenty-minute walk (longer if one hobbled) due north of the church was the Bucktown-Wicker Park Branch of the Chicago Public Library. Charlie still had a dogeared copy of Mihaela's reading list. His major extramural activity, beyond hunting and gathering food, was going to the library to find books to complete the task given to him by his dear friend so many years ago.

This, of course, brought back a surge of memories—some delicious to revisit, others bitter. It was easy to let his imagination roam, wondering what would have happened if Mihaela had not been taken away so early in their relationship. Would she have taken her final vows? Would she and he still be friends if she had? Would she have fled the order and become one with Charlie in those ways which undoubtedly both had imagined but neither had acted upon? It was always, "What if?"

If Mihaela were still in his life, would Robin have entered? He thought of Mihaela. He thought of their watching the water striders in the canal. He thought of the insects' shape. It reminded him of Robin's boat at Candy Point—dark, marquise-formed, and practically menacing. He saw again the flames—smelling again the acrid smoke.

Robin had been many things.

He had, unquestionably, been a criminal. He had been arrogant. He had been ostentatious. He had often been rude and ruthless. He certainly had the capacity to be cruel and malicious. Yet, for some unknown reason, he had accepted a know-nothing kid from a lakebed and pushed him up the ladder—even if this ladder was within a completely corrupt cluster of felonious organizations.

Robin was gone.

What would Mihaela have thought of Robin?

He imagined the two would not have liked each other very much.

ᐱ ᐱ ᐱ ᐯ ᐱ ᐱ

One day, at the library, while looking over the magazine rack, Charlie came across a quotation from Norman Vincent Peale—"One of the greatest moments in anybody's developing experience is when he no longer tries to hide from himself but determines to get acquainted with himself as he really is."

He recalled Mihaela had been a big fan of Norman Vincent Peale (he generally avoiding spiritual, religious, or inspirational writings—give him a good espionage novel any day). His indifference to emotive passages notwithstanding, the words of Norman Vincent Peale, undeniably of interest to Mihaela, struck a solid chord.

He had to face reality.

Then, almost mystically, as though Mihaela's hand had flipped the page, the next page of the unheard-of magazine whose pages he was absently skimming, provided another possibly forbidding quotation—this time from the Bible, Deuteronomy 1:6–8—"You have stayed at this mountain long enough. It is time to break camp and move on."

Charlie was not one for the otherworldly. Nonetheless, here in a library of the sort so loved by Mihaela, there seemed to be messages aimed at his soul—messages from his lost soulmate.

Was this his lost friend trying to reach out to him in order that he too not become lost? He wondered.

⅍ ⅍⅍Ⅴ⅍⅍⅍

Almost as though theirs were binary lives, Rodney, too, wondered. He wondered how he would present his evidence in a convincing way. But more critically, he wondered exactly whom they would name under the indictments being requested from the new grand jury.

They had names, lots of names from the myriad of companies, firms, and groups that had been intertwined with Robin McCandless, and, by default, Delpro. Some of these individuals were influential leaders, some were industry captains, some were financiers. But in the global frame, they were all minor actors. They were the B team.

The B team would be pursued. There would be some form of legal action, at least against those chiefs that headed the subsidiary operations. Still, this was more a question of doing what had to be done—showing the broader public there was a need for people, all people, to do the right thing and not ignore the law.

These people would be named, indicted, tried, defended by high-price-tag lawyers, convicted, and then given token sentences. It would serve a purpose. But it would not serve THE purpose.

Rodney needed to look up not down. He needed those at the highest level. While there were conflicting opinions as to whether or not the corpse floating in the Chesapeake had been Robin McCandless, there were no conflicting opinions on one point: Robin McCandless had never been the *Capo dei capi* (as popularized by films of Mafia families)—the boss of bosses. Delpro had never been the sole capstone. Robin McCandless and Delpro were undoubtedly high up in the hierarchy—but they were not the whole show—not by a long shot. There were more powerful individuals and more expansive organizations still hiding in the clouds.

Rodney needed some way to get a hook into these specters of world ascendancy—these manipulators of the planet's resources and markets. Those whose creed was "power at any cost."

He could see their shadows. But there was no face, no address, no footprint. He wondered if they would ever be brought to book.

⅍ ⅍⅍Ⅴ⅍⅍⅍

While Rodney speculated as to the best tactics to lure the real bosses of bosses from their lairs, he had to deal with the present. He needed to have witnesses, people considered as ordinary folk, to come before the grand jury when it was up and running to explain the breadth and depth of Delpro under Robin McCandless' hand. Rodney could then hopefully build on this foundation to extract indictments on the people whose names he badly needed—and he needed them yesterday.

But he had birds in hand. Eddie would be able to explain a great deal about Delpro, having been enmeshed in its activities on three continents. He might even mention their probable role in his first wife's death though there was really no hard and fast proof, albeit there was ample supposition. Eddie would need some coaching, but he would be an important witness to lay the initial groundwork.

Rodney also had Peter—he just wasn't sure exactly how he "had" Peter. He pushed Joe to find a solution, they needed Peter available to the grand jury.

Robin McCandless' death (or reported death, who knew?) had had a significant impact on scheduling court actions. Empaneling a new grand jury was taking longer than expected. Rodney had to devote considerable effort to simply convincing the decision-makers to take this next step. However, he could use this hiatus to his advantage by finding a way to get Peter to where he needed him.

Ultimately, Joe came up with a very elaborate and very expensive plan to extricate Peter from prison and get him to a safe haven. Rodney never knew all the details, but he certainly knew the price tag—it was impressive. One way or another, Joe was able to grease the wheels and get Peter out of jail. He was also able to get him reunited with Evelynn and get the two across the continent to Cape Verde where he had them under the watchful eyes of colleagues and available to Rodney where and when required.

In the process of preparing for Peter's liberation, Joe had been making arrangements across a wide swath of the region—laying out not only the escape itself, but the long road to a sanctuary on an island in the Atlantic. As he was traveling between two of the pivot points for his intricate plan, he was in the departure lounge of Jo'burg airport awaiting a flight up to Dar. Like many voyagers, waiting for Joe was best done in a bar with a cold beer in his hand.

He was just finishing his drink and preparing to go to the gate when a man walking down the causeway caught his attention. The first attention grabber was the clothing—a broad-brimmed hat with a faux leopard band topping a pale salmon-colored safari suit and orange cravat that looked like it had just come off the hangar from one of the airport's touristy duty-free shops. Then the man was talking very loudly in what Joe recognized as a Cockney accent. Finally, addressing a less vividly clothed colleague, the singular salmon-colored man announced much too loudly, "They're all fucking up!"

While he had never met the gentleman, Joe had studied him thoroughly to get ready for his initial questioning of Peter in Borh Prison. There was no question in his mind, the salmon-colored man was Sir Horace Barthley.

There was honestly nothing to be done. Joe did contact Rodney as soon as he landed in Dar to inform him of the sighting. But it was just another data point, not a revelation.

ΛΛΛΨΛΛΛ

Rodney was glad to have a sighting of Horace Barthley, the younger brother taking up a more important position in the BTF offensive with Robin McCandless, in whatever way, off the field.

Seeing the old man in Africa was no surprise, although he could and did surface literally anywhere. Nonetheless, much of this aging hooligan's focus, as highlighted by Peter, seemed to be in this part of the world.

Sir Horace had never been seen as key a player as his big brother. However, thought Rodney, this assumption was purely based on the fact that, for much of his career, Robin undertook his illegitimate actions in the full light of day. In a quiet—almost muted—yet completely visible way, Robin McCandless had openly directed his employees and his firms to engage in all manner of illegality—the profits pouring into his, and undoubtedly others' coffers.

This in-your-face business model had likely, Rodney understood, overshadowed others who were equally culpable. It was highly possible the younger brother was even more of an evildoer—just one who rarely came out of the darkness. BTF needed to spotlight the flamboyant Cockney as a high-level person of interest.

Rodney was able to assign a significant subset of the BTF crew to what became known as the "Horace Hunters."

He had been spied several times at Jo'burg airport, so the searchers started there, trying to find some sort of connecting air links that could lead to some form of base in southern Africa. They found it. Horace Barthley was regularity booked on Air Namibia, shuttling between Jo'burg and Windhoek.

They concentrated on Namibia.

They could find no land nor business owner named Horace Barthley. However, as Rodney's agents began methodically showing Sir Horace's photo around the capital, a number of people linked the man in the snapshot with Shilli Shigwedha, a well-known owner of a 20,000-acre cattle ranch, Southwest African Beef Company, near Mururani, south of the Mangetti National Park, 375 miles north of Windhoek.

Rodney, at least temporarily, quickly refocused on Southwest African Beef Company. With an impressive financial network at his disposal, he was able to tie this Namibian company to a European parent, Bayerische Fleisch, Ltd. (Bavarian Meat, Ltd.). He could then connect this German firm with a very large, but often not recognized transnational, Matadero Global (Global Abattoir), headquartered in Argentina. It was like those Russian nesting dolls, the *matryoshka*—layers on layers, pealing the onion.

Of special interest, after a lot of skillful digging, was the discovery that the head of Matadero Global was Heinrich Fuchs, described in meat-marketing circles as *"Der Feinschmecker"* (The Gourmet).

Numbers of Nazis had fled to Argentina after the second world war. Fuchs, whose *non de guerre* had been "The Fox" after the English translation of his surname, had not been a central actor in the war. In fact, he had seen very little of any battlefield. He had been a *Standartenführer* in the Waffen-SS—a colonel—who was an economist as opposed to a military strategist. He had been assigned to work with Wilhelm Karl Keppler, one of Hitler's more prominent supporters and economic advisors.

While the Fox, rumored to be an extremely adroit and shrewd financial analyst, had become the Gourmet after the war and relocated to the *República Argentina*, he apparently remained cunning and furtive like his namesake. After some very sketchy post-war reports from Argentina, Heinrich Fuchs had disappeared for decades. It was only due to a chance reporting of an automobile accident in Kenya fifteen years ago that he, still surprisingly (or arrogantly, Rodney couldn't be sure) using his birth names, had officially been flagged by the intelligence community as living in Malindi, a coastal tourist town with a relatively large German population.

Rodney knew it was a lot to digest—a coarse thread that started in Africa, touched two other continents and then doubled back, nearly to its starting point. Moreover, it was all based on second- and third-hand information. Horace Barthley and Shilli Shigwedha could and should be considered as solid subjects; the rest had to be verified and ground-truthed. And, he had the resources to do just that.

ᛉ ᛉ ᛉ ᚥ ᛉ ᛉ ᛉ

However, in the absence of Robin McCandless as the centerpiece of—now the hole in—the complete Delpro investigation, everything had stalled. It had been a difficult reality with which to grapple. Rodney and the entire BTF crew felt as though they had whiplash. Their work had been progressing—gaining momentum. Then a screeching halt.

They needed to cope. They needed to look elsewhere. They needed firm leads.

Fortunately, information generated by scraping the Sir Horace scab led to some hopefully excellent trails to follow.

The Horace Hunters set about defining as fully as possible the old gent's relationship with Shilli Shigwedha and the Southwest African Beef Company. Another team opened a full-press examination into Heinrich Fuchs as well as his present links to *Matadero Global*. A third team looked into the bonds between *Matadero Global* and Delpro.

There were many moving pieces.

There were also very strict and highly confidential reporting protocols.

Rodney, correctly or not, felt he was like a clownfish living among beautiful, and poisonous, anemones. He remembered from freshman biology these two dissimilar organisms were obligatory symbionts—each dependent on the other. The corollary, his human interdependency, was not only in regard to the relationship between the overall BTF crew and their skipper, Rodney, it was also in relation to the bonds between the BTF and its objectives. To justify its operations, the crew had to achieve its aims—it had to defeat Delpro. To do this, Rodney understood, required many forms of symbiosis—some more palatable than others.

While many in SEC outside BTF had heard of the clownfish metaphor, it was rumored no small number preferred comparing Rodney to a pilot fish guiding and bolstering the shark that was or had become the BTF crew.

Rodney knew of the shark. He hoped it was true. Yet he was unsure. Whether through finesse or pure power, Delpro had to be defeated. But this was just the start—the proverbial tip of the iceberg (as much as he hated clichés). Delpro was a part—he did not know how big a part—of a larger and sordid whole. Delpro was a start but it was not, by far, the only concern.

The clown fish could attract others into dangerous territory. The shark could simply and forcefully pull others into danger. With one tactic or the other, Rodney knew he needed to make a crack in the wall. He needed to have someone from the adversarial camp, knowingly or not, enter into dangerous territory where he or she could be trapped, pressure applied, and hopefully turned as not only a reliable source, but also a reliable witness.

Rodney needed a target.

Given what he knew, he focused on Heinrich Fuchs.

The man was despicable. The man was old. The man knew a lot.

Working hard to convict Heinrich would likely make the old man shut down—possibly stoically accepting his fate as part of the greater good as he saw it. And, even if successful, this fate would be but a few years in prison given the man's age.

Yet, if the old man could be turned—by force or by finesse—he could undoubtedly open many doors.

It was unlikely the old man would deal with Rodney simply because it was the right thing to do. There would have to be an offer on the table—an offer that could shift the values in Heinrich's life from those revolving around power, wealth, and anonymity to liberty and comfort.

Rodney felt confident that, if he really dug into Heinrich's life, he could make the old man's daily routine miserable and, in all likelihood, find some issues—trivial or major—that could put him in jail for his remaining days.

With that leverage, Heinrich could be offered the choice: give evidence against others and remain a free man with a modest government stipend or go to jail.

It was an unpleasant scenario for Rodney. He in no way wanted to vindicate the old criminal—guilty of so much. But, practically speaking, he needed to do the distasteful for the larger benefits of reaching their aims—for the opportunity to put a stop to Delpro and hopefully bring-in Sir Horace in the process.

Rodney needed to penetrate deeply into Heinrich's life.

ᚼ ᚼ ᚼ ᚥ ᚼ ᚼ ᚼ

There was a history.

Wilhelm Karl Keppler was born in Heidelberg in 1882. He was an engineer, a businessman, and a member of *Nationalsozialistische Deutsche Arbeiterpartei*, the National Socialist German Workers' Party. He was a Nazi.

Keppler was seen as a link to legitimacy and financial support for the party's foremost leaders, Adolf Hitler, Hermann Goering, and Heinrich Himmler. He was named *Kommissar für Wirtschaftsfragen* (Reich Commissioner for Economic Affairs), from which post he established the *Freundeskreis der Wirtschaft* (Circle of Friends of the Economy), a network with industry to ensure the Third Reich could attain the economic and military development required to achieve the Führer's goals.

However, as might have been said today, Keppler was not the sharpest knife in the drawer. And the Führer wanted only the brightest and most talented at his side. But to openly get rid of Keppler was to possibly weaken critical links with industry. Hitler could not take this chance. Keppler needed to be strengthened. The task fell to Himmler.

The *Reichsführer* of the SS concluded Keppler needed a very skillful and intelligent assistant to guide him in his efforts to ramp-up the country's economy. Himmler looked to his own SS, finding in his hometown of Munich a young SS Colonel with impeccable credentials. He had found his exceptionally capable (and devoted) economist. He had found Heinrich Fuchs.

Keppler's fate was probably sealed due to his own shortcomings. Even with the able assistance of Heinrich Fuchs, he proved time and again he was really not up to the job. He was ultimately very discretely moved aside (literally, moved to the embassy in Vienna as Reich Commissioner) and replaced by Hjalmar Schacht; president of the *Reichsbank* and a critical actor in the setting up of IG Farben (*Interessengemeinschaft Farbenindustrie*), at one time one of the largest companies in Europe.

Fortunately for Heinrich Fuchs, he was not tied to Keppler's coat tails. He had effectively demonstrated his remarkable agility as an accomplished and innovative economist. He remained a part of the inner circle—Keppler's circle—never seeing a battlefield except when en route to high-level economic meetings.

Fuchs, known as the Fox, lived up to this antonym's nature—he was very sly. He was also able to fully rationalize his activities. True, he was an SS colonel. But he was not a combat soldier. He was not really a Nazi. He was an economist. He was an intellectual. He knew there were atrocities—terrible atrocities. But he chose not to see. He chose not to look.

He was an economist. His goal was to make the economy better for his people (and, of course, for himself).

While he was never on the battlefield, he was regularly in the halls of commerce. There were deals to be made; deals on behalf of the *Reichstag* that, coincidentally, also lined his own bank accounts. He was an unquestionable asset to the *Agentur für Wirtschaftsfragen* (Agency for Economic Affairs) as it built the country's war-chest. Simultaneously, he significantly built his own assets.

When the outcome of the war became clear, he took his briefcase (beautifully tanned leather, a gift from the Führer himself) with the documentation for all his Swiss bank accounts, donned his Homburg, and, using his SS credentials, boarded one of the rare trains still running to Zurich. He had no real family nor friends. He did have plentiful deposits in Swiss Francs. He could go anywhere. He could do anything.

However, ever the pragmatist, he knew there would be those seeking out Nazis after the war. While he was convinced he was not, and had never been a Nazi, he knew painfully that others would inevitably throw him in that bucket. He was at risk.

Although he could go anywhere, prudently he sought a destination where his earlier affiliations could be turned to advantage while minimizing the risk of any unfortunate discovery by the growing number of anti-Nazi bounty-hunters. He (along with many of his kindred) went to Argentina.

In post-war Europe nothing was as easy as it should have been. Fuchs maintained two sets of identities—both using his real name. In one set of IDs, he was a Swiss economics professor from a Catholic high school in St. Gallen. In another secreted set, he was still Heinrich Fuchs of the SS.

After ensuring his fortune was secure, using the first set of papers, he traveled from Switzerland to Spain. The official version for anyone asking was that he was on a pilgrimage, the *Camino de Santiago*—The Way of St. James—ending at the shrine of the Saint at the cathedral of Santiago de Compostela in Galicia. This fact was corroborated by a letter from the Bishop of The Roman Catholic Diocese of Saint Gallen.

What Heinrich sold to inquirers as a sacred pilgrimage, others would have called an escape through the ratlines, as the pathways of flight used by ex-Nazis came to be called.

It was widely reported that President Perón had a standing invitation to any and all from the German homeland. From Spain, Heinrich was able to use his secreted second set of IDs to get in contact with the *Organisation der ehemaligen SS-Angehörigen* (ODESSA—Organization of Former SS Members). Through ODESSA, he was able to establish a new life in the medium-sized subtropical Argentinian city of Comodoro Rivadavia, with a teaching position at the *Universidad Nacional de la Patagonia San Juan Bosco*. There, he was also easily able to blend into the multicultural environment which, in 1903, had received an injection of several hundred Afrikaner families after the unsuccessful (for them) end of the Second Boer War.

There was a smattering of public material describing Heinrich's early days in Comodoro Rivadavia—pictures in the university's yearbook, a few short newspaper clippings, and one fuzzy photo taken at Rada Tilly beach south of town. It wasn't much. Then there was nothing.

Heinrich Fuchs, the Fox, the economist, slipped into oblivion.

For years there was nothing. Then a new Heinrich Fuchs popped up for fleeting moments. This Heinrich Fuchs was nicknamed "the Gourmet." This Heinrich Fuchs was affiliated with the well-known and highly esteemed Buenos Aires restaurant, Churrasquería Argentina. This Heinrich Fuchs, the Gourmet, would appear in a brief say-nothing article or ad and then disappear.

These ephemeral crumbs left along the way became all the less frequent. They also shifted from highlighting a steakhouse operator to the rare spotlight on a major actor in the global meat market—the manager of *Matadero Global*.

The scarce trade journal article or news blurb would only mention his name and his highly regarded efforts to supply customers with excellent cuts of meat; no specifics, no contacts.

Then Heinrich Fuchs, the Gourmet, slipped into oblivion.

There was only a blank slate. Nothing until that odd by-chance event on the B8 motorway north of Mombassa, Kenya. Near Kilifi, a late-model Mercedes had a bad accident with a *matatu*—the taxi driver apparently inebriated. The driver of the Mercedes, a certain Mr. Heinrich Fuchs with a postal box in Malindi, was unscathed while three of the taxi passengers were seriously injured and one was pronounced deceased at the site of the accident.

The Mombassa *Standard* had a short article on the accident, naturally concentrating on the dead and disabled with only scant mention of the driver of the other vehicle, an expatriate, who was reportedly exonerated of any charges.

From that point on, it was as though Heinrich Fuchs did not exist. Rodney closed the file.

He needed to contact Joe Thompson.

⋀ ⋀ ⋀ ⋁ ⋀ ⋀ ⋀

While Joe Thompson prepared to go to the Kenyan coast and search for an elusive ex-Nazi, Rodney had to redirect his energies to other pressing matters. Even without Robin McCandless and without solid leads on Sir Horace, the case against Delpro was still ongoing. The team was preparing a case for moving forward to indict unknown party or parties who functioned in the same role as Robin McCandless. They were confident that Delpro did not stop even if McCandless was dead. Moreover, the continued functioning of this complex organ would require someone doing the same things, pulling the same threads, as Robin McCandless had for years. To keep up the momentum, they needed to indict Delpro.

Part of this process was the testimony of Eddie and Peter. The former was easy. Eddie and Rodney already had a good relationship thanks to Hal. Eddie was already totally committed to testifying and doing all he could to topple Delpro. He had seen, he had experienced all too personally the evilness of this entity—this group of unseen puppeteers doing anything and everything for personal gain.

Rodney needed to work with Eddie to frame his statements and make sure he incorporated all the necessary elements that would support indictments. But this was straightforward. Once the grand jury was impaneled, Eddie would be ready to go.

Peter was a different story. Joe had Peter and Evelynn safely "in storage," as Joe called it—safely situated and looked after in Cape Verde. But, since fleeing prison, Peter had received only bits and pieces of information concerning the potential legal actions planned to be undertaken against Delpro, and probably against his former employer Equatorial Management. He had to be fully briefed, his story vetted, and his testimony thoroughly outlined. To add to the complexities, as more of the couple's story emerged, it was highly possible that they would also want Evelynn to testify about her work at EHT. Rodney's team had learned that Evelynn had been an intern of sorts with one of his other possible pivitol corroborators, Paula Patterson—Evelynn's, like Paula's, work quite possibly linked through very circuitous ties to Delpro. Evelyn, now holed up with Peter on the wind-swept islands in the Atlantic, would require nearly the same level of preparation as her partner.

In all the hopefully influential witness statements, Rodney knew the challenge was to guide the testimony such that it comprehensively detailed past and present acts without conjecture about motives nor future expectations.

It was time to begin the preparations. Eddie, on the West Coast, could receive an initial briefing over the phone and then come to D.C. for a more all-inclusive rehearsal prior to testifying. For the folks in Cape Verde, however, Rodney deemed it best to send a team to work closely with these important witnesses *in situ*. Paula was kept on hold.

There was a lot of work to be done.

⩗ ⩗ ⩗ ⩗ ⩗ ⩗

At the same time as Rodney lined-up his witnesses, Joe landed at Moi International Airport, rented a car, and drove across Mombassa Island, skirting Fort Jesus, and heading north on the B8 to Malindi. He hoped to find a world-class villain in an area that, although now a tourist attraction, had been a center for the ivory, rhino horn, and slave trade from the arrival of Vasco da Game in 1498 (memorialized by the still present Vasco da Gamma Pillar that sits at the end of the little thumb of land that thrusts into the Indian Ocean) until its incorporation into the Sultanate of Zanzibar in the nineteenth century.

Once in Malindi, Joe took a room at Lawfords and, with the out-of-focus snapshot from Rada Tilly beach in hand, went to the Palm Garden.

Palm Garden was THE rendezvous point for Malindi.

Lawfords and a handful of other beachside resorts had rather prudish regulations regarding entry onto their premises by what they saw as undesirable persons. These measures were certainly seen as unwelcome by many of the tourists who considered part and parcel of their vacation being the chance to interact with these same ostensibly undesirables. After all, many male and female tourists came looking for intimate—albeit short-term—male or female companionship—even if frowned upon by their lodger.

Where there's a will, as the story goes, there's a Palm Garden. Here tourists freely intermingled with boys and girls of their choice, making arrangements to bring the selected special person back to their room by one means or another.

Palm Garden was the place to make inquiries.

It took Joe the better part of two days, plying a covey of hard-working girls and boys with free *Tusker* or *White Cap*, before he landed on someone who thought an old German man with a Mercedes living at a beachfront villa at Casuarina Point might resemble the blurry photograph from Argentina.

The house at Casuarina Point, across the street from the marine park, looked very tropical—high-pitched thatched roof, wide encircling veranda, with hardwood siding. It was not outstanding but had a subtle elegance.

Joe went down the frangipani-lined walkway and up to the sculpted mahogany door where his knocks were meet by a middle-aged black woman with a brilliant red head-tie that matched her moumou-style flowing dress. Affecting his best South African accent, Joe spouted some nonsensical phrases about the home's electrical service. Rudely repeating the same gibberish with increasingly garbled and loud speech, the effect was as Joe had hoped. The woman called to a man ensconced deeper in the house whom she called her husband.

A heavyset but still rather athletic-looking gentleman with close-cropped white hair and amazingly erect posture for someone who should probably be at least in his mid-eighties appeared behind the colorfully appareled woman.

"Yes," he said with a strange assonant tonality that Joe imagined was a result of native German being married to Spanish and English with perhaps a dash of Kiswahili for a true polyglot.

"Sir," again Joe said, with the South African inflection, "my apologies. I used the subterfuge of senseless twaddle in the hopes of being able to talk with you. Could we speak?"

Somewhat to Joe's surprise, the gentleman stood aside to welcome his still unknown and uninvited guest into his home. He and his wife led Joe down a short hallway to a large high-ceilinged, wood-paneled great room with one wall adorned with the heads of three antelope of different species offsetting a beautiful if disheartening leopard skin.

With the men seated in leather armchairs, the wife left briefly, returning with three pints of beer.

"I suppose, for a South African (this spoken with slight incredulousness) it's always a good time for a beer," the woman said, offering the pints.

With a smile, Joe accepted the frothy glass as did the man he assumed was Heinrich Fuchs. Then, after a much-appreciated gulp, Joe decided he should candidly go straight to the point and not play games when likely all knew the true origin of the visit.

"Sir, may I call you Heinrich?"

The octogenarian showed no bewilderment. He made no attempt to be deceptive. Matter-of-factly he announced, "Heinrich is fine."

While his host sipped his beer and his wife looked on nervously, Joe set out his spiel which he had practically memorized.

"Sir, I mean you no harm. I represent a group that is eager to talk with you about your post-war business affairs. We are in no way interested in meddling in your past nor in pursuing any possible leads regarding the war. We are solely focused on your business relationships."

There was no reaction from the former SS officer.

"I would hope you would agree to meet with one of my colleagues for a few hours to review your business history. If that could be possible, we would assure you it would be done with complete discretion—anonymousness assured. We would then also be happy to offer our services ensure that this anonymity was maintained."

There was only the slightest nod of the close-cropped head. There was the sound of a deep exhalation coming from his wife's seat.

Finishing his beer, agreeing to return in one week's time, and thanking the couple for their hospitality, Joe left for his hotel to call Rodney. He felt Rodney should get to Malindi as soon as possible, understanding that he himself had to keep Heinrich Fuchs under close surveillance until Rodney arrived in case to old Nazi had a change of heart.

⋀ ⋀ ⋀ ⋁ ⋀ ⋀ ⋀

Rodney was grateful for the, as usual, good results provided by Joe Thompson. He left for Casuarina Point as quickly as possible, flying from D.C. to Frankfurt, connecting there for a flight to Moi International Airport where he was met by Joe for the two-and-a-half-hour drive north to Malindi. Joe had hired a second person to keep an eye on Heinrich Fuchs when he had other obligations like meeting his boss in Mombassa. Thus, with some sense of certainty their quarry was still on-hand, Rodney was able to have a restful night at Lawfords before undertaking the ten-minute drive to the elegant house across the street from the marine park.

As before, Heinrich Fuchs and his wife, later identified as Samira, a native of Mombassa, met their unsought visitors in their great room—this time offering aromatic Kenyan coffee. This began a series of two days of interviews (some would call it interrogation)—Heinrich and Rodney moving to a private corner of the veranda for the storytelling.

Rodney started by candidly spelling out the case. Heinrich was in trouble. They—the SEC—had ample evidence showing a multitude of ill deeds. Heinrich could be extradited to the US—the process was straightforward. He, as well as possibly his wife, could be tried in Kenya as some of his indictable crimes were of an international nature. He, or they, could even be taken to court in both countries—not to mention other conceivable ills if the Israelis were brought into the picture. It was a mess—a mess for Heinrich Fuchs.

But, Rodney continued candidly, any trial of Heinrich would tie up resources and ultimately put an old man, and possibly his wife, in prison—in prison where the old man would likely die not too long after incarceration. It seemed, Rodney concluded, an inefficient path to follow (an unavoidable conclusion that galled Rodney, highlighting his role as the clown fish and the need to make distasteful compromises—the symbiosis ever-present).

Rodney, confirming that, in spite of the inefficiencies, he was ready and willing to follow this painful pathway, offered an alternative. If, as an old man who, in whatever context, was no longer one of the most engaged actors, Heinrich was willing to voluntarily and honestly submit to detailed interviews by SEC staff including but not limited to Rodney, the SEC would provide him with legal documents exonerating him from any criminal or civil liability and agreeing to pay him a modest stipend for the rest of his life.

The choice was Heinrich's.

With visible discomfort, Heinrich Fuchs chose to be a *collaborateur* (as he dubbed it), resentfully signing the non-disclosure and witness agreements Rodney had prepared in anticipation of a positive outcome.

The deal was done.

The work followed—hours and hours of questioning.

By his third night in Malindi, Rodney had two legal pads filled with notes and felt he was getting into diminishing returned. There was still a tremendous amount of information to be mined, but he would leave it to others to do the probing for the multitude of minutiae that could be provided by Heinrich Fuchs; the Fox turned Gourmet turned informer.

The crux of the matter from Rodney's respective was the opening of the door on the wider operation—the over-and-above Delpro operation. Heinrich Fuchs confirmed he, in a role very similar to Robin

McCandless', was responsible for coordinating the activities of *Matadero Global*. In the global organogram, *Matadero Global* was responsible for animal husbandry including the marketing of all meat and fisheries products. Delpro was a mirror image for the rest of agriculture. The two had overlapping areas including food processing facilities, the unions of staff of these facilities, agricultural research, pharmaceuticals (animal and plant health products—real and faux), and others. A critical area of overlap was that of human trafficking to find cost-effective labor supplies to fill the needs of the wider agriculture sector.

Heinrich referred to these thematic or specialized branches as the arms of an octopus. In addition to Delpro and *Matadero Global* the other arms embraced banking and finance, medicine and pharmaceuticals, construction and housing, industry, transport, and, of course, a catch-all tentacle for the staples of prostitution, arms, and drugs.

Even at his level, Heinrich Fuchs was not completely clear about the structure, functions, and staffing of the superstructure—the body of the devilfish that was the global nerve center. He would have regular contacts with individuals from upper echelons, but often with different people with seemingly different areas of interest. He would submit an annual report to a bank in Zurich but the bank itself seemed to be only a minor player—really a cutout.

There were rumors the heart of the super organization was in Ukraine, but he was not sure. What he did know, or thought he knew (one was never sure), was that the overarching organization was simply referred to as *Domov*, a word for "home" in slavic tongues, sounding much like domo. The overlord of this structure was called the *Maliar*, the mortician.

In general, the octopus' appendages, the subunits, operated with great independence and nearly full autonomy as long as operations followed those principles prescribed by the overseer (or overseers). Moreover, as demonstrated by the cases of Delpro and *Matadero Global*, the subunits were generally hermetically sealed from one another except in specific areas where there were common goals or a need for collaboration.

This was and wasn't what Rodney needed to hear. He now had as close to corroboration as he could hope for the fact that Delpro was not an end unto itself but a part of a much larger and more menacing organization. Sadly, but wisely from their part, the solid compartmentalization of this overall organization made it nearly impossible for one individual to have the whole picture. There were glimpses. There was innuendo.

There were even scattered verifiable facts. But things were murky at best—murky, but clear enough to move ahead.

Rodney arranged for a three-person team to come from D.C. to continue extracting all that could be obtained from Herr Heinrich Fuchs. He instructed Joe Thompson to hand over to this team then continue the search for the slippery Sir Horace.

Rodney then returned to D.C.

ᐱ ᐱ ᐱ ᐁ ᐱ ᐱ ᐱ

Rodney had a full slate back in his office.

There were unconfirmed sightings of Sir Horace in North America—still unsubstantiated reports from both Canada and the US.

Perhaps more worrisome were new and substantiated reports that different parts of the Delpro network were closing—vanishing. From small satellite firms like Spot On to country offices across the world, Delpro was downsizing—maybe evaporating. Whole pieces of Delpro were either shrinking perceptively or totally gone.

The word was out. Someone was pulling the strings. Delpro was either transforming or dissolving. This was certainly, at least in part, due to the events surrounding Robin McCandless' supposed death. Yet, it could also be a quick and decisive response to recent interactions with Heinrich Fuchs. It was time to change gears—stop thinking about Delpro and concentrate on Domov. It was time to break camp and move up a notch.

The Lakebed

I N THE WORDS OF William Shakespeare, "What's past is prologue." Growing up, Charlie (having been forced to read *The Tempest* in high school literature class) was sure that this meant that the way things were done in the past would be the way things are done in the present and the way they would be done in the future. It was like the old saw folks loved so much, *if it ain't broke, don't fix it.* No one felt the way things were on the lakebed was broke—there was nothing to fix.

This had been at the heart of Charlie's youthful puzzler. While the way things were was fine for many, and he felt he had had a good childhood wrapped in the quilt of tradition carefully crafted by preceding generations, he did not want to see the future, his future, immutably chained to the past. While it may not be broken, he felt it could be fixed to be better. He had had to find a way to overcome the adamant adherence to the way things had always been in favor of the way things could be.

He hadn't been running from anything—he had been running to something—to his ambition, his goal. He now wondered if this aspiration had been a mirage—a shimmering bright spot at the end of a high desert highway that one never reached.

His pilgrimage had been very costly in many ways.

After escaping the lakebed, Charlie didn't think, had probably subconsciously trained himself not to think, much about home and growing up. Back at the beginning of what had now become his odyssey, Charlie had seen that the only option for him to have the life he wanted, the life he needed, was to cut ties with his home and family. In his mind, this was not a permanent separation; it was a necessary short-termed exercise to overcome what he saw as the factors that held him back. He loved his family. He loved his home. He loved the land where he had been born. He would come back. But to survive he needed to leave—fully understanding that this was the only way to come back.

But, of course, it had been more difficult—more circuitous—than he had ever imagined. He hadn't wanted to reach out to his family until he had succeeded in having some semblance of a stable and a good life. He knew his family would be worried—very worried. He had vanished. Still, he hoped—or wished—they would understand. They should know him—he was their son and their grandson. They had surely witnessed his inability to easily slip into the slot that had been meticulously prepared for him on the lakebed. They had surely seen how he was always trying to look to a different and brighter—a more modern—future. They would, he was sure (he hoped) understand why he had left and know he would contact them when the time was right.

However, it was never the right time.

In spite of Mihaela's encouragement and prodding, he had never been able to find the right time.

Soon he was overcome by a combination of denial and guilt. He could physically feel it as a cramp in the pit of his stomach. He lied to himself, saying he wasn't doing anything wrong—the time wasn't right. They would understand.

Then, knowing he was lying to himself, he became guilty about doing nothing—saying nothing.

This guilt was added to by the guilt of knowing, even if not totally accepting, that he was involved in criminal acts. He had run away not to find a better, more honorable lifestyle (one about which he could be proud to write home), but to become a criminal.

The guilt weighted heavily—especially in those dark hours when its burden could rival that of the weight he felt trying to come to grips with Jo's (as he convinced himself) slow recovery.

And, the weeks of silence to his family turned into months into years. Then he was unable to say anything. What could he say after years of saying nothing?

If he thought about it, he felt ill. He was not angry with his family. They were blameless. He loved them. And, he had tortured them.

His behavior filled him with regret. It filled him with pain. He forced himself not to think about it. He forced it—the home of his birth—into a cubbyhole in his mind. He carefully wrapped it and placed it in storage.

Then, having locked the door, his own early life faded. His own growing up became like something he had read in a book—one of Mihaela's books. It was no longer his story. Life on the lakebed was a novel—someone else's story.

ᛉ ᛉ ᛉ ᛦ ᛉ ᛉ ᛉ

In truth, Charlie's story of growing up on the lakebed was not unique nor special. It was just a story of a kid becoming a young adult.

He had been born in a typical wood-frame two-story home on Railroad Avenue, on the other side of Third Street. He was the second son born to Felix and Celestina, called Celeste by all, Stancik. His older brother, Lionel, was five years his senior.

Felix and Celeste had been born in Broken Bow, Nebraska where Felix's father, Barnaby, called Barney by all, had been a young blacksmith cum farrier following in the footsteps of his father. Well past their prime of life, when their son Felix had already married his high school sweetheart Celeste, Barney and his wife Astrid decided it was time for a change.

This shocking transformation and decision to pull up roots was apparently, to many, precipitated by Barney's friendship with some fellow Bohemians coming from Minnesota and members of the group *Západní Ceská Bratrská Jednota*—both a Czech language newspaper and a Czech community assistance organization. As Barney's connections to this group strengthened, friends, neighbors, and customers found the normally jovial and generally contented blacksmith to be a changed man as though, pushed by unseen forces, he had to do all he could to see more and do more before his time on this planet expired. He established ties with the Czech Colonization Club and with little forewarning sold his home and business and, assembling his son and daughter-in-law, with Astrid, moved west. He moved to the lakebed.

Here, he built a home, a mirror image of his home in Broken Bow. Here, he built a forge and became the local blacksmith cum farrier as he had been in Broken Bow. Then, when the business began to grow, he helped his son build a home only a block away from his own. This was the home where Charlie had been born.

As Barney found the work of the forge more and more challenging, Felix took over the business with his father more of an armchair advisor than a real sculptor of iron and steel. All the while, people were coming to the lakebed. The town was growing. Farms were growing, especially with the newfound interest in cultivating horseradish. There was a lot of business for a blacksmith cum farrier.

In true family tradition, Felix thought Lionel would follow him to manage the forge. The boy, already helping out in his spare time, was strong of back and agile of mind. Felix had great expectations.

Charlie's path, through his father's eyes, was less clear. Felix saw his younger son as someone possibly too smart for his own good. He and Celeste were both proud and a bit taken aback by their junior son's apparently superior mental capacity. He was quick. But maybe he was too quick. He grasped things almost instantaneously—but then was equally quick at losing interest. In the end, he was a mediocre student not because he was mediocre but because he could not keep his interest in his schoolwork.

Charlie loved his big brother. He would follow him to the forge to help clean up as soon as he was big enough to handle a broom. He would help Lionel with his chores—principally keeping up the yards of his grandparents' and parents' homes. But the highlight of all was going to the Lava Beds with Lionel.

The Lava Beds was a national monument about half-an-hour south of town.

The Lava Beds was great. Going there was going to a different world—leaving the day-to-day rut of the town and the farms and entering into a special space. This was a space with massive herds of deer and flocks of waterfowl. This was a space with ancient petroglyphs and more contemporary signs Indigenous peoples' struggles (as well as being near the Tule Lake Isolation Center where Japanese Americans were forcibly segregated during the Second World War). This was a space of lava flows and obsidian mountains. Most specially, this was a space for caves. There were magical caves with ice stalactites and stalagmites—pillars of ice that reflected the colors of the rainbow—floors of ice that seemed to be channels to the center of the Earth.

The Lava Beds National Monument was great.

Charlie and Lionel would go to the Lava Beds as often as possible, coming back, feeling refreshed—feeling anointed. Although Charlie never told anyone, when he came home after an outing to the Lava

Beds, he felt the same way his grandmother said she felt after she had had communion.

Still, the Lava Beds was the exception, not the rule.

The rule was the monotonous routine of the lakebed.

ᛗ ᛗ ᛗ ᚥ ᛗ ᛗ ᛗ

It was this routine, definitely not the Lava Beds, that Charlie had sought to change. It was this monotony that had pushed Charlie away years ago—that had made him break connections with home and family. Now he was again breaking connections, or at least trying to do so—this time connections with his own recent past. And, up until now, his guilt and his embarrassment had made him resist his automatic reaction to run home—home to the lakebed—to go back to the womb. But, in the calmness of an hour before sunrise, he realized there could be no better time than now to go back to the lakebed and to see what of his past he could find. Yes, he unquestionably could, and probably should, be criticized (condemned, he thought) for running off and never even letting his family know he was alive and (basically) well. Yet, what was done was done. He had the real possibility of some very unpleasant trials ahead of him. This was a good time to start making amends and facing a new reality.

As he thought about it, it sounded overly dramatic—almost a martyrdom. After all, who doesn't screw up. He'd screwed up, maybe big time. Nonetheless, he'd also done what he'd set out to do; he'd found a remedy for boredom. He had, he smiled to himself, succeeded so well that it might be a welcome relief to try and find some of that childhood monotony.

Thomas Wolfe's novel *You Can't Go Home Again* had been on Mihaela's reading list—a tome to which she had personally attached great affection. Maybe it was true. Maybe he couldn't go home. But he'd try.

He remembered when he had been in third grade his grandparents had gone back to visit Broken Bow. They'd taken the train—the *Shasta Daylight*. They'd returned to the lakebed dispirited. Nothing had gone as they had imagined. Nothing was the same. None of their old friends were there. No one remembered them. They certainly had not been able to go home.

Charlie decided he'd take the train, too—Amtrack. He hoped, at the end of it all, he'd be less dispirited than his grandparents. But he tried not to imagine any outcome.

He disembarked in Klamath Falls; the 1,800-mile journey had taken over sixty hours. He rented a car and headed south to the lakebed. As he entered his birthplace, everything was the same and everything was different. On the surface, the small town had changed little. As he drove about, he noticed the Sage Diner, Downtown Garage, and the gas station all seemed untouched by time. The grade school resembled the place where he had started his formal education, although there had been some well-deserved remodeling and expansion. The two hamburger joints he remembered were now specializing in pizza and tacos, respectively. The building that had been his father's and grandfather's forge was still there, but now a derelict shell of rusty iron and galvanized roofing sheets on a castoff weed-filled lot. His parents' and grandparents' homes were also there, pretty much as he had left them, only a little the worse for wear.

He started at his own home—or what had been his own home—knocking at the door now in need of paint (something his father would not have tolerated). An elderly lady answered the door—a stranger. When he enquired of Felix and Celeste Stancik, the lady looked puzzled and curtly replied she had no idea who these people were.

"Sorry to bother you," Charlie said, "but these people are my parents. They built this house."

"Don't know'm," the rude lady replied.

"Perhaps it was from them that you bought the house?"

"Bought! Ha! I'm renting. Been here sixteen months. The rent's too high and the stove doesn't work. What more do you want to know?"

That was that.

Charlie had a similar experience at his grandparent's house.

He decided to try City Hall, which, at least from the outside, looked exactly as he had left it.

The clerk told Charlie she was a relative newcomer to the community but was friendly and helpful. While she could not provide all the details, she could say that the two houses in question were owned by a Klamath real estate agency and had been rentals for some time. Her only advice was to check with the attorney who was listed with the city as the contact for the rentals, J. Banks Esq. at the corner of Main and Sixth Street. The clerk let Charlie use her phone and he made an appointment, Mr. Banks Esq. himself answering the phone, in one hour's time.

With some time to spare, Charlie left City Hall, noting that the City Library, much as it always had been, was across the street just as the library had been across from his apartment on the corner of Country and Clayton Street—the library where he had met Jo.

There was sharp pang as he thought of his dear Jo.

Avoiding the library and all its reflected memories, he walked a block north to the T Canal; he strolled along its bank, somehow enjoying its musty odor as the cocoa-colored waters swirled onward to thirsty fields. Stopping to poke a dry cattail at a brazen bullfrog, he noticed the water striders skimming across the water's surface.

How free. How elegant. How conniving. The water striders of the lakebed, the water striders of the Chicago River. They had become his totem.

Then he found himself seated across an old school desk (or so it seemed) from Jacob Banks Esquire, member of the bar, and attorney for the lakebed. His office was a small, very small, converted home—it was a one-man-show.

Mr. Banks was past middle age and also a little beyond slovenly. Nevertheless, he had a warm smile, a firm handshake, and a pleasant demeanor. He welcomed Charlie into his disheveled and, at first glance, disorganized office with a bit too much flourish; seating his guest in an uncomfortable straight-backed chair opposite his scared teacher's desk.

"My apologies," the barrister said, "things are a bit here-and-there—not the busiest place in the world as I am sure you can imagine. But, enough about stuff, what brings you here?"

"Well." Charlie swallowed. "I was born here."

No reaction from the good attorney.

"My name is Charlie Stancik, son of Felix and Celeste Stancik, brother to Lionel Stancik. Grandson of Barney and Astrid Stancik. I don't know if you know any of my kin?"

Jacob's continence softened as he replied, "Indeed I do. I am so happy to meet you—to see you."

Charlie was at a loss for words.

"Let me get you some tea and I'll explain."

Moving from the face-to-face arrangement across the well-used desk, Charlie's newest host escorted him to a small dinette tucked away in a corner. He then disappeared for a few minutes, returning with a pot of tea and two delicate cups on a tray accented with a small pitcher of milk and sugar bowl—it looked as though sitting down for tea was a regular part of Mr. Banks' routine.

Over a surprisingly delicious cup of tea, the attorney recounted to Charlie the story he had been wont to tell for years.

He, Jacob C. Banks Esquire, had once been a top-line lawyer in the Bay Area. There had been some unfortunate events which he need not go into, but these had made a move an appropriate tactic if he wanted to be able to avoid major problems. Thus, from the upper crust of San Francisco County to the dusty stretches of the lakebed, he had transitioned from a three-piece suit wearer driving a Mercedes to a golf shirt wearer driving a Toyota. But such was life.

He had arrived in town roughly a year after Charlie had left the scene. This, he underscored to his guest, was a polite way of saying, "vanished." Charlie's mother had come to see him as she frantically sought solutions when the family had apparently failed with all alternative avenues. She recounted that, once they had discovered Charlie had left home with no notice, they had reported his absence to the local police along with the county sheriff. When her son had been unaccounted for for seventy-two hours, she had expanded her plea in panic to the state police. Yet, after a month, there was no news—no trace. After three months, the police said they would keep the case open but had to label it as a runaway, assigning to it a low level of threat due to foul play. It was then, exhausted and feeling completely beaten by the system, that Celeste Stancik had come to see Jacob Banks.

Jacob admitted he was able to do little other than provide a sympathetic ear for Charlie's parents as well as a more formal vehicle for them to continue to write letters to police and politicians seeking urgent help to be reunited with their lost son. Without belaboring the sad details, it obviously led to naught. The Stanciks of the lakebed never heard anything more of their son.

The disappearance of one son did, however, have a great impact on the other. While it was widely believed he was next in line to take over the family forge and already a long way down this path, with Charlie's departure, Lionel became the center of the family. Everyone, Lionel included, was now determined that the remaining son would really become something—he would show the world that the Stanciks could properly raise a boy. He would not just become a blacksmith cum farrier. He would become important. And he did.

The entire family, with support from a sympathetic community, poured all they could into Lionel. He graduated cum lauda from the state university. He went on to medical school at Johns Hopkins with a full scholarship. He specialized in neurology and now was a world-renowned surgeon at that same institution.

When Lionel left to go east, the family basically fell apart. Barney and Astrid passed within a year; only a month separating their funerals. Felix developed a severe heart condition and died two years after his parents. Celeste pushed through it all with shear will power, becoming a matron of the community and only passing two years ago.

As part of her engagement in the community, Celeste had become very active in a youth support group that assisted children from farming families and farm laborers in passing their GED for high school equivalency. As the last of her family still remaining in the lakebed, she bequeathed all she had to this group. She even assured the houses would become rentals with the proceeds going back to her favored charity.

Still and all, and this was important Jacob highlighted for Charlie, she did leave a letter for her youngest son with him. She had never forgotten her little boy and, before finishing her earthly affairs, she had prepared a package for her boy in the hopes that one day he would truly come home. She had never given up hope.

Jacob C. Banks Esquire again briefly disappeared, returning with a brown-paper-wrapped package about, Charlie thought, a quarter the size of a shoebox (this reference drove Charlie's memories further back to his mother's two pairs of good shoes that she kept in the original shoeboxes for safekeeping—always wishing her closest could have been filled with boxes of lovely shoes).

"Your mother confided this with me." The lawyer concluded, "As her health was waning, she, to her total heartbreak, realized she would never see you again. While she had never given up, at the end she had to admit she did not even know if you were alive—truly believing you could not have lived all these years without reaching out to her. Still, all speculation and hope aside, she did want to leave something in the possibility, as she so prayed, that you would one day return to your roots—her words, not mine.

"In addition to this small package, she asked me to ask you to do two things: visit your family's graves in the cemetery near the canal and then go to the church and, if not in your name, in theirs', offer prayer for their souls as the prodigal son who sadly returned too late—again, her words, not mine."

Charlie thanked Mr. Banks for all his kindnesses and for his support to his family. Accepting the small package, he shook the firm hands of the kind and rumpled man, the one-time San Francisco bigwig now stuck on the lakebed, and returned to his car for the short drive to the cemetery.

Crossing the canal as he entered the graveyard, he immediately saw two water striders scooting away—it was as though they had been waiting for him. But now, he cautioned himself, he was letting his thoughts carry him far too far away.

Although those interred in the community's small burial ground covered lakebed residents over decades since the waters had receded, their numbers were small and their stories were long. It was not difficult to find four Stancik graves, lined up side-by-side in death as they had been in life.

Charlie felt an honest sadness—a true loss. He felt a familiar lump in his throat and ache in his stomach. He bowed his head and tried to pray, tried to cry. Neither the words nor the tears came. He could only stand there in silence—the low whisper of the wind across the sage only accompanied by the soft shush as the canal waters moved on. Even the town offered no contribution to the sounds of his personal funeral.

After what seemed like too little time to compensate for all he had done and not done, he rejoined his car for the fifteen-minute drive to the church to complete his mother's requests (demands).

His hometown had no Catholic Church. While his family considered themselves as Orthodox, they accommodated their new life by adopting the "western" Catholic faith—parents and grandparents being devout followers of Christ. St. Augustine's in the neighboring town on the west side of the lakebed was the closest Catholic Church.

Charlie entered the empty sanctuary, his shoes, echoing off the hard floor, the only sound. He genuflected, remembering the moves from his childhood, and knelt in the front pew. For a second time, there were no words nor tears. There was only a profound sadness.

When his knees ached and his head throbbed because he could not think of the right things to think, he retraced his steps, stopping at what his mother used to call the "devotional area" to light four candles for his departed family—family, some would say, who were looking down on him, but family that he considered now part of his history to be respected, even (in his own way) revered, but, as had apparently always been the case, not driving forces in his life.

After the quick trip back to Klamath Falls, he turned in his rental and got a room at a hotel on the east end of Main Street. The next day, he would take a taxi to the train station for his long run back to Chicago. He had done what Jo would have called "the needful thing."

In his mousy room, after a tasteless sandwich in the hotel cafeteria, he turned his attention to more uncommon things—he turned his attention to his mother's package. As with everything she had ever done, it had clearly been the object of meticulous effort. The everyday brown wrapping paper was carefully trimmed and folded to make each corner just right. These corners were taped with ordinary tape, but with not one wrinkle nor overlap—just the right amount of tape used in just the right way. Simple things that so reflected his mother's ways.

Charlie undid the wrapping, refolding the brown paper along the deep creases as he removed a small box that, according to the label, had originally held a Red Cross canvas ice pack (for his father's aching muscles, he imagined). Inside the box were three items, two of which he immediately recognized. One of the familiar items was an olive-wood cross reportedly from the Holy Land that Mother's cousin had given her years and years ago. There was also, what he had so often seen as a child, his father's signet ring that his father had been given by his own father. And there was a handwritten letter on flax paper with a small iris in the corner, the sort of stationary his mother used only for her most important correspondences—again, carefully, painstakingly, folded so the corners all lined up perfectly.

Charlie set the cross and ring aside and settled back in his chair to read his mother's words.

> *Our Dearest Son: I do not know if you will ever read these words—*
> *I pray you will. I pray that one day you will come home. I cannot*
> *express the misery and anguish your disappearance has caused*
> *all the family. We have horribly suffered. We are heartbroken. But*
> *I do not want to dwell on the negative. I do not want to make*
> *this into a mother scolding her son. I do not want to blame you.*
> *But I cannot understand you. I cannot understand why you have*
> *done what you have done and why you have stayed away for all*
> *these years. In my heart I know you are alive. In my heart I know*
> *this was not an abduction of my child. You did, as you always do,*
> *what you felt you needed to do. I know, and I believe we all knew,*
> *that you were never truly happy at home. You were a good boy. I*
> *believe, and I know your father believed, that you always loved*

us. But it was never enough. Your grandmother says you were unhappy in the shadow of your big brother whom we all assumed would go on in your grandfather's and father's footsteps and manage the forge. Your grandmother says this pushed you away as it made you feel you had no place. I know this is not so. Yes, you worked with us all at the forge just as you worked in the yard. But this was never what you wanted. You were always looking at the distant hills. So, you see, I do understand why you felt you needed to explore—to go out on your own—to do more—to see more—to be more. I do understand and I would have understood if you had told me. But to vanish. My boy, this was a hard thing to accept. I have to believe that you really wanted to let us know you were all right. I have to believe that you had your own reasons that you felt justified the total silence you maintained over the years. I have to believe you thought you were doing the right thing. I have to believe because I love you. But it was so hard. I only hope you found that for which you were so devotedly seeking—that which replaced your family and your home. I say this not to reprimand you—the time to reprimand is long gone. I say this simply as a mother who is now at the end of her life and who will go on to the next world never again holding her boy—hugging her boy—laughing with her boy—crying with her boy. It distresses me, of course. But I have learned, we all had to learn, to live with the unavoidable reality. So, my son, our son, as you read this, and I pray you do one day read this, know we all love you. We all thought of you each and every day. We all prayed for you. We all hoped we would see you again. But even in your absence, we all wished only the best for you in whatever it is that has so captured your attention as to keep you away from us for all these years. So, if you are sad, if you are agonizing now about what you may feel you have done, please stop. We all grew to accept the reality. It is done. We cannot go back. We shouldn't weep in the present nor be distraught in the future. Know only that we have never stopped loving you. Go with God our dear Charlie, Mother.

Now there were tears. There were still no words, but there were loads of tears. His eyes so blurred that he nearly missed the PS at the end of the letter. His mother had added: *I hope you will agree with me Charlie that it would be a good thing to reach out to your brother. Lionel's address is 96 Lichfield Circle, Baltimore, Maryland. He misses you!*

ᛘ ᛘᛘᚥᛘᛘᛘ

Back on the eastbound train, Charlie let his mind float above the hypnotic clack-clack-clack of the cars as they kept a steady pace toward the rising sun. He was wearing his grandfather's and father's signet ring, which fit perfectly (he wondered if it really fit perfectly or if his mother had had it resized, as he did not imagine his hands to be as big as the powerful hands of the two blacksmiths). Absently, he twisted the ring about his finger as he thought of home and family—past and present (avoiding the future).

Back on West Haddon Avenue, Charlie felt adrift. The need to, the obligation to go home had always been there. Indeed, it had been an albatross around his neck, but it had also been an aspiration. It had always been something he knew he needed to do but that he had always managed not to do. Now he had done it. The intention had become a reality. In its place, there was nothing.

There was an empty apartment.

There was an empty life.

ⱭⱭⱭⱯⱭⱭⱭ

The days and weeks clicked by. There was no sign of the feds—no unpleasant letters or phone calls from the assiduous Rodney Mills.

Not only was there no apparent immediate jeopardy from the authorities, there was no apparent anything. He had even managed to complete Mihaela's reading list—all the while, avoiding the Lake Center.

Having gone home and got away, he ultimately concluded he had no life. His adopted (forced, he felt) circumvention of anything and everything that represented the life he truly wanted to lead was becoming a burden worse than the threat of possible incarceration.

His current situation was no longer tolerable.

After all, if he hadn't gotten away, if he had been swooped-up after Robin's passing, he could negotiate. He had bargaining power—he had copies of Robin's files. He had years of first-hand experience. He could and should be a valuable asset to someone like Rodney Mills.

ⱭⱭⱭⱯⱭⱭⱭ

Charlie decided to reverse his tactics.

He no longer limited his life to a corridor between his apartment on West Haddon Avenue and the Bucktown-Wicker Park Branch of the Chicago Public Library. He began visiting Jo on a weekly basis—spending hours telling her of all that had transpired since his last visits. He even, unsure of the consequences of deploying what he considered a talisman but knowing his mother had felt it to be a cherished item of great vitality (and knowing his mother would agree with his actions), placed the olive-wood cross from the lakebed on Jo's bedside table.

Beyond the Center, Charlie moved in ever-increasing circles. He went to restaurants. He went to the park. He traveled into the city center. He tried to retool to a more normal and rewarding life.

As he had known, consciously or subconsciously, one day it happened. There was a knock at his apartment door and, upon opening, he found the fit figure of a well-attired gentleman who handed him his business card. It was Rodney Mills.

Deluge

R ODNEY NOW FELT HE was inundated with what he considered as good, solid evidence. He had witnesses to many parts of what was materializing as the complex Delpro hydra. Without even opening the door that led to Charlie, with his recent successes in turning Heinrich, combined with the testimonies of Eddie and Peter, all overlaying the mountain of documentation amassed by his entire team, there was no shortage of corroboration for the multitude of crimes in which the transnational had been, and probably still was, engaged.

The case to the grand jury was already well prepared and strong.

Rodney felt he was in a good place to do what he needed to do, to wipe-out Delpro.

This was his opening to Charlie.

"Charlie Stancik," Rodney said softly as he extended his hand, crossing his prey's threshold, "we finally meet."

For his part, Charlie was not surprised, but nonetheless, somehow stunned, uttered, "Uh-huh."

"I've been looking forward to seeing you," the fed, using Robin's classification, continued. "I would have come sooner, but I've really been flooded—overwhelmed—chasing bad guys being hard work, and all that."

Ignoring Rodney's possibly weak attempts at lowering the temperature between stalker and quarry, Charlie nearly subconsciously latched upon the word "flood." For unknown reasons, one of Mihaela's oft-used verses when talking about Romanian politics flew into his mind.

Mihaela would refer to the flood, the *potop,* and then cite the Old Testament Prophet Amos, 5:24: *Justice must flow like torrents of water, righteous actions like an ever-flowing stream.*

"Well?"

Charlie was brought back to the here-and-now. "Come in, I guess. Can I get you a drink?"

With that began a new relationship, though fragile, that was ultimately welcomed by both parties. A relationship that effectively swept away even the tiniest crumbs of Charlie's slice of the pie.

ⱯⱯⱯⱯⱯⱯ

Before Rodney's knock at the door, Charlie too had been flooded—flooded with thoughts and emotions. He had been consumed by the emptiness of feeling at the precipice. He had jumped a freight and headed east. He had never looked back until he had gone back. Now both the life he had found at the railhead and the life he had left on the lakebed were history. The love of his life was considered a vegetable by most. His family, except a brother he truly did not even know, were gone. He was at the cliff's edge. Should he jump?

He tried to digest his life. Objectively, in spite of all, he had been lucky. He had, in fact, been luckier than many. Indeed, he, a boy from the backcountry with a modest education and no real skills, had been able to become, by the standards used by most, a success. He had money. In the grand scheme of things, he definitely was not rich, but he had more than enough money and unquestionably more wealth than the majority of souls he encountered as he trekked along the sidewalks from West Haddon Avenue to the Bucktown-Wicker Park Library.

Yet, money or no money, he was, he knew, not a success.

First, he had to accept he was, or at least had been, a criminal. He felt surprisingly little guilt over this fact (certainly nothing like the guilt he had felt about not going home nor contacting his family). He continued to rationalize that he had been a "good" crook. Nonetheless, this did not wash away the fact that he had been and quite possible still was someone who made a living from crime.

Second, he was alone. He had fled a life and a home where he had been surrounded by family and friends. He had ultimately found a bleak apartment in a bleak neighborhood in an impersonal teaming midwestern city. Still, as he mentally danced between yin and yang, the road that had led to this gloomy apartment had taken him to wonderful places, shown him marvelous people—all things that would have never happened if he had stayed on the lakebed.

Finally, he had nowhere and everywhere to go. Success, he felt, should be like a spotlight that illuminates your way forward—that lights up your life's pathway. But for him, there was no floodlight.

Nevertheless, while in many ways feeling lost, in other ways he felt he had some version of the total freedom that was sought by so many. He had it and he didn't know what to do with it. He should have been able to turn the page, shift the gears, or employ whatever cliché fit his mood, and go on to, hopefully, bigger and better things. He had money. He was young and healthy. He had, he now knew, a good head on his shoulders (although he had always resisted his mother's assurances of this fact). He should be able to fly to new heights if he could just figure out how to takeoff.

To say he was frustrated was an understatement. Was he confused? He didn't know. If he could have talked to Mihaela or Jo—that would have helped. If his parents were still around, would that have helped, too? He wasn't sure—they had been on different wave lengths and probably would have remained so even if they had all continued to live together under the same roof.

The know-it-all person in the white lab coat on his television said people like him, people feeling stress and uncertainty, should seek professional help—preferably at his clinic located somewhere accessible to people from everywhere.

Charlie wasn't going to go to this or any other clinic.

He would work it out.

But for the time being, he felt engulfed by the waters of uneasiness.

Then Rodney knocked on the door and at the very least his now appreciated freedom came into question

⋀ ⋀ ⋀ ⋁ ⋀ ⋀

It had been a big decision for Rodney, whether or not to knock on that door. For some time, Charlie, like many others including Sir Horace, had been under close observation. Charlie had been a target for months and was not going anywhere without Rodney knowing his movements if not his thoughts.

While Rodney now knew of Domov—now knew he needed to expand his view from the already far-reaching Delpro into the massive Domov—he also knew he had to do all possible to wrap up the Delpro case. And, he had to do this relatively quickly after the reported death of Robin McCandless to use that momentum to push the case through the grand jury. He could then refocus on the bigger picture and the larger threat.

In some ways, as he now had solid evidence, it was time that was against him. He was comfortable that the documentation and witnesses he had accumulated would be more than enough to get the indictments. But what of getting a conviction? Who should be indicted? Who could be convicted?

For the immediate, Rodney decided he would make his case against Delpro as a US corporation—attempting to obtain an indictment against the company. With what he had in-hand; he felt his chances of success were good.

But they would then go to trial.

Here things were a little less solid. His witnesses often had second-hand information and information about irregularities outside the US. Nearly none of Heinrich's attestations dealt specifically with US concerns. Sir Horace, though there were some unsubstantiated sightings of him in North America, was apparently confining his efforts to areas outside the US. Rodney needed stronger evidence of crimes committed in the US.

He needed the names of particular individuals to fill in under the Delpro indictment. He needed defendants. He needed specific information linking to specific litigants. He needed more than he had. He needed information from Charlie. And, Charlie needed, or felt he needed atonement.

ᴀ ᴀ ᴀᴠ ᴀ ᴀ ᴀ

It wasn't a perfect fit. But there were some reasons for each working with the other. There were some common benefits.

Rodney needed to bring closure to Delpro. This was not really about career development. Rodney had already built his career—and built it in an impressive and outstanding way. This was about doing his job. In this sense, it was about duty. But it was more. It was also about retribution. Hal, the love of Rodney's life, had been taken from him by Delpro. This demanded a reprisal.

Charlie also needed closure. This was not closure of a duty-bound task or even a morally inspired task. This was closure of a chapter of his life.

Charlie would have been, he understood, more than willing to continue with the status quo—to continue as Robin McCandless' adjutant.

The position had been exhilarating. It had frequently been compelling. Moreover, it had been profitable.

Now, this was not an option.

The sphere of Delpro had dissolved or significantly weakened.

With the closing of this portal, there was the growing possibility that the total freedom that Charlie considered as one of his unique assets could be lost. He could go to jail. The man who had knocked on his door could send him to jail.

So, Charlie needed to bring a negotiated closure to this episode whereby he could maintain his freedom and ideally even bring some sort of peace to the spirits of his family whom he considered to be in disarray and quite possibly distraught due to his own befuddling lifestyle.

Each viewing circumstances through their own lenses, Charlie and Rodney seemed to intuitively sense that they had more to gain by working productively, if not really amicably, together. Still, this was not a fifty-fifty split. Charlie was undoubtedly on the more tenuous side of the equation. While Rodney could have some possible professional and personal setbacks if he did not succeed, Charlie could end up in jail—end up in jail for a long time.

So, after a beer and some rather harmless chatter, after that first impromptu encounter, Charlie and Rodney met regularly. Rodney's aims were clear from the onset. Charlie's role in these events was less clear. He was vulnerable. There was ample proof of his involvement with Delpro. He did not even attempt to deny his actions and relationships. Rather, he attempted to gauge the emerging relationship to decide how and when to drop the fact that he had copies of Robin's papers. This was his main, maybe only bargaining chip. But it was, he was sure, a biggie.

After all, Charlie, the kid from the lakebed, the homeless guy on the park bench, had, under the aegis of one Robin McCandless, developed some special skills. As the Delpro sojourner with the boss's blessings, he had developed a talent for reading other people—adversaries as well as allies. He had also honed remarkable negotiating skills—having helped Delpro expand their already overflowing bank accounts. Charlie had, in short, become a cunning and adept arbitrator.

He hoped he was on a par with Rodney.

As he understood more and more about Rodney's plans when the agent described all the legal processes underway—partly to intimidate his target and partly to demonstrate the opportunities, as had befallen Heinrich, for collaboration—Charlie realized he had items that were indeed very valuable, possibly essential to the fed. Still, Charlie kept his own council for weeks. He would recount fragments of his activities in Ontario or Costa Rica—in Mozambique or on Crab Tree Lane. He would offer bits of the jigsaw without, he hoped, revealing the larger picture.

Rodney was well aware of Charlie's tactics. He had been doing this for a long time. Charlie was, in his humble opinion, unequivocally not the toughest nor most scheming bad guy whom he'd gone up against. Quite to the contrary, Charlie was, from all initial indications, a good guy in a bad job. Charlie was also smart and someone who had been successfully organizing and compromising with many clients over a number of years. He was a worthy rival.

Charlie hoped his boyish bonhomie would adequately camouflage his shrewd and calculating maneuvers.

Rodney hoped his stern and nearly admonishing bearing would rapidly convince Charlie that the best choice, really his only choice, was to get on board and move ahead.

As each continued to take measure of the other and as the weeks passed, Charlie noticed a renewed restlessness in his interrogator. As much as Rodney tried to ignore it, rationalizing that engaging with witnesses had its own unavoidable rhythm, time was against him. He needed to be better prepared to go to trial. He instinctively felt Charlie had what he needed. He understood it would take time. But time was now running out.

The day arrived when there was no more time to be coy. Rodney had to be brash. During the latest in their seemingly never-ending series of meetings, this one at a local coffeehouse in effort to keep their encounters informal and less menacing, Rodney had to push.

"OK. You know, of course, that I'm a busy guy. I remember when we first met, I told you I was flooded. Well, the flood waters are rising, and I simply cannot devote all this time to chatting with you, as pleasant as it might be."

No reaction from Charlie.

"I have my bosses," Rodney continued, "and they want results—they tell me the time is past. So, we've got to get down to the real granular details if this thing is going to move forward and you're not going to find the whole weight of the United States Government on your head."

"OK," Charlie said, realizing the bluster was part of the game but that it was highly probable that Rodney was truly now under some pressure as this probing had been going on for a very long time when seen from the timeline of juries and trials.

"So," Rodney said, stiffening, "this is possibly the last hand to deal, what's your bid?"

Charlie figured the time had indeed arrived. "I've got items I am sure you will find helpful—invaluable. I have Robin McCandless' files—copies of his files, I should say, to be correct."

More than a little curious, Rodney countered, "And . . ."

"And." Charlie half smiled. "I want basically the same deal you described you gave that old German. I'll share my files with you. I'll sign affidavits. I'll even testify. But I will not go to jail. I will not be punished. You will help me get started in a new life and we'll go our separate ways once you've achieved your goal."

"That's it?"

Ignoring the sarcasm in Rodney's voice, Charlie retorted, "Oh yeah, thanks for reminding me, I want you to move me, at your expense of course, into a nice new home you'll purchase or somehow get for me somewhere out West—you government guys have your ways, I know."

"That's it?"

"Yeah, I guess."

"I'll have to get back to you on that."

The meeting was over.

∧ ∧ ∧ ∨ ∧ ∧ ∧

At least temporarily leaving Charlie to his established routine and his unfolding machinations for the ongoing investigation, Rodney briefly escaped from Chicago but did not check out of the government-paid long-term studio he had been renting during what had been dubbed by some as "The Charlie Affair." He went back to his more welcoming and familiar apartment in D.C. where he could comfortably and persuasively pull back and take a good hard look at the situation from thirty-thousand feet.

At home, over a glass of good Merlot accompanied by a soft rendition of Brahms Symphony No. 2, he took stock of his opponent—reviewing pages of notes from endless hours of questioning. Charlie was one of those folksy individuals with a warm personality and a pleasing smile who was immediately accepted by even the most distant stranger. Hal would have said that he would have been a good used car salesman.

But hand-in-hand with the affability and charm was a very agile mind and a strong dose of common sense. In spite of, or possibly because of the fact that he had not gone too far in his studies, he easily and rapidly applied practical and doable solutions to perplexing problems. He was a pragmatist and a realist. He was truly an able opponent.

And he was damn hard to characterize. Since he had, as Rodney had learned through their long series of one-on-one sessions, fled home after high school, there was no real consistent tract to follow. Until he had started working with Spot On there was really no official record—and even then, it was erratic and, overall, insignificant.

Charlie had dodged in and out of the shadows for years.

While Robin McCandless had been a person of interest for a long time, surely throughout his operations from Crab Tree Lane, he had been but one of many. He only truly surfaced as a very major actor after he had moved to Candy Point—a move that he had evidently thought had enhanced his obscurity but, being in Washington D.C.'s backyard, had really triggered more warnings and led to his prominence on the SEC team's list of top malefactors.

It was at this time, when Charlie would make routine visits to the McCandless Estate that was under microscopic twenty-four-seven surveillance, that the young man from Spot On evolved into an important person of interest in his own right. Charlie was then acknowledged as a key character in a very complex and elusive drama.

Rodney understood more than most that, notwithstanding his perceived importance, the price Charlie was trying to extract for his full cooperation was high—not unheard of, but high. It required a full analysis of the options as well as approval from above.

From whomever, by whatever means, Rodney badly needed more explicit and verifiable information about Robin McCandless' actions—Robin McCandless' part in driving Delpro forward. He needed authenticated data to build his case.

The chief alternative appeared to be to go more forcefully after Sir Horace. Rodney had never been able to verify reports that the venerable Cockney had actually been in North America, let alone that he had been in the US. Since first following the old scoundrel back to Namibia, Rodney had had him under observation. His movements seemed to have tapered off in recent periods and he was, as far as Rodney's team could tell, principally traveling about Africa with the occasional sortie to Asia or Europe. Yet, his itinerary aside, there was no real new information that could build a strong case against the old man here in the US.

Given the costs and the returns, Rodney decided to pull his team off Sir Horace—basically letting the aging conniver keep doing what he was

doing, as what he was doing was not really providing Rodney with anything that he needed. Rodney informed Interpol and the South African
authorities and brought his team home.

This made Charlie the only figurine in the centerpiece.

ᛗᛗᛗᚥᛗᛗᛗ

Charlie understood Rodney's dilemma. He himself had a difficult time
explaining Robin McCandless' exact role in all the things in which he,
Charlie, had been personally engaged. A big block of his time had been
covered by the screen of Fredericks, Higgins, and Woods. Another block
had been occupied by BALJIN with its own arcane shields. So often there
had been intermediaries between the action at field level and the command and control likely, but unproven, coming from Robin McCandless
via a multitude of circuitous and buried channels.

Charlie thought of Rodney and thought, once again sponsored by
Mihaela, of Janus, the God of Doors with two faces—one looking to the
past and the other to the future. Charlie shared with Rodney (and Janus)
the need to look into the past to be able to see the future. However, Rodney, from Charlie's impressions over hours and hours of discourse, also
had two other faces, each covering different personalities.

Rodney was often the stoic, methodical agent; the fed who always
got his man and was unsympathetic to the lawbreaker—a man seeing
the world in black and white. Yet, in those infrequent moments when his
other face shone through, Rodney proved himself to be a considerate and
emphatic man with a nearly hidden polish and eloquence.

Charlie understood, Rodney was not his friend (he knew this all
too well since he recognized he had few if any real friends over and beyond Jo). Rodney, in stark terms, was his antagonist. Still, like everyone,
Rodney was a complicated human being. From this perspective, Charlie
had an advantage. Thanks to Robin McCandless, Charlie had dealt with
hundreds of complicated human beings from around the world—he had
developed a skillset that could tactfully and productively interact with
this amalgam of humanity. These same skills could help leverage his position with Rodney. Nonetheless, Charlie accepted the truth that Rodney
was a talented and intelligent opponent.

Rodney was an adversary and an adversary on a mission. It was, in
fact, this aspect of this mission that gave Charlie the greatest hope that
he just might be able to come out of this whole sordid affair in relatively

good shape. Rodney needed to squelch Delpro. He needed to crush the organization—wanting to pound it to sand in honor of his dear Hal. It was this mission before everything. It was this mission that took precedence over putting Charlie in jail.

If Charlie could help Rodney unravel the precise roles of Robin McCandless and, in the process, come up with the names of others to add to the list of indictees, then Charlie felt he could win—he could remain free.

ᴧ ᴧ ᴧ ᴠ ᴧ ᴧ ᴧ

There was a confluence of sorts.

As Charlie rehashed in his mind the various misdeeds he had orchestrated, concentrating on those exploits that had engaged most directly Mr. Robin McCandless, Rodney was also focusing on the same Mr. Robin McCandless. Charlie reviewed the copied files. Rodney discussed Charlie with his higher-ups.

Most of the files Charlie had copied were relevant to distinct Delpro activities. One, which Charlie had nearly discarded, contained documents Charlie considered to be of a personal nature—records of medications, arrangements for payments of utilities, automobile papers, and more—all records relating to Robin's private life or his home or his cars while living at Crab Tree Lane.

As Charlie thumbed through scraps that framed his former boss' life, he was still unsure if he should keep these in the pile of critical papers to use to negotiate with the feds or relegate these more private records to a stack of less important archived items. Then, by chance, his eyes fell on a six-by-nine manilla envelope emblazoned with the address: *J.O. McTavish, DDM, 347 Sylvan Road, Lake Bluff, Illinois 60044.* Opening the envelope, Charlie noted a perfunctory letter from the dentist congratulating his patient on a good checkup and informing him, as requested, a set of X-rays and exam notes were included as Dr. McTavish understood his long-time client and friend would be moving east and needed records to pass on to a new dentist. Folded in the letter was a photocopy of a set of tables evidently giving great detail of Robin McCandless' teeth. There was also a card holding eight shiny X-rays, darkly reflecting back at Charlie like the eyes of a cat (the eyes of many cats, he imagined).

Charlie was confused.

Charlie's documents were copies, how did he end up with a set of X-rays?

He could simply conclude that, given the volume of the files and the hectic period at the time of Robin's move (including his hurried and unauthorized copying), he had inadvertently replaced the copy of this file with the other originals and mistakenly kept the master copies of Robin McCandless' personal papers. He could only imagine the difficulty he would have been in if Robin had not perished in the boat accident (or whatever it was). His duplicity would have inevitably been uncovered and he would have had a difficult time explaining his actions to his boss—and, to what end?

Be that as it may, he now possessed Robin McCandless' dental X-rays.

An idea hit him—a tactic to push the balance power in his negotiations a little more to his side of the scale.

He called Rodney.

"Say, as a token a good faith, I wanted to let you know, I've been organizing Mr. McCandless' files and discovered that, quite by chance, I find I have a copy of his original dental X-rays. Are these of any interest to you?"

Rodney immediately saw the possible value of this find. He needed those X-rays, realizing that he would subsequently be indebted to Charlie—not a position he envied. But the potential gain was worth the price. There had been considerable doubt if the purported head of Delpro had truly lost his life on that boat on the Chesapeake. He could now have a second set of X-rays to add to those obtained from the Virginia dentist who, as Robin McCandless' professed caregiver, had provided the X-rays that had ultimately been used to identify the body. He could double check. He could even possibly put to rest all the questions circling around Robin McCandless' death.

ʌ ʌ ʌ ∨ ʌ ʌ ʌ

The appearance of the X-rays on the landscape made it all the more indisputable that Rodney would need to negotiate with Charlie. At the end of the day, it was most likely Rodney would have to agree to Charlie's demands in order to get his full support and have access to the crucial documentation, including the X-rays.

Rodney believed this was a concession well worth making. But it was not a step he could take by himself. Actions such as these needed the blessings from the very top.

Therefore, after broaching this dilemma with his immediate superiors, Rodney arranged a string of meetings with central senior decision-makers and analysts to review the full situation through a wide-angle lens. This had an overview of both Delpro and Domov at its core.

Personal feelings or local politics aside, there needed to be, and there was a consensus that the agency's aim was the complete dissolution of both Delpro and Domov—along with any other related felonious bands they could ensnare. Nevertheless, it was the bird-in-the-hand adage. Delpro was the bird in the hand. While the BTF team was making inroads into the newly uncovered Domov, they had amassed volumes of material on Delpro. They had prepared numerous draft charging documents, laying out Delpro's illegalities across the globe, and specifically in the US. They had been ready to charge Robin McCandless before his purported death. However, with his removal from the scene, they were left only with the option of bringing their case against an impersonal company with no other codefendants identified. It was far from ideal.

Undeniably, Domov was the real trophy. Its collapse would be the preeminent distinction for the agency and have meaningful impact on the never-ending battle against worldwide crime. The downfall of Domov was, Rodney assured all, a possibility. Yet, it had to be built upon a successful attack on Delpro.

Naturally, Rodney emphasized to his superiors and their superiors, even if they were able to take meaningful action against Delpro, the real issues would not be resolved. Domov was not only like an octopus, it was a starfish. If the Delpro arm was excised, another arm would grow in its place. Somewhere, somehow Domov would reconstitute Delpro—different name, different people, same criminality.

Domov was pervasive. Domov was aggressive. Domov was dangerous.

Sadly, at this juncture, they were a long way away from having a consequential case built against Domov. It was coming. But they were far from where they needed to be to be able to take any action.

At this point in time, Delpro was the key and Charlie was the key to Delpro.

𝕸 𝕸 𝕸 𝖁 𝕸 𝕸

After much debate and fidgeting, the agency gave Rodney the green light. Among other factors, Charlie would be formally and officially pardoned for all infractions and crimes (pulling strings, this exoneration to cover federal, state, and local levels of law enforcement) and assisted to resettle and re-establish. This gift would, however, only be delivered at the end of legal proceedings when the crew would be able to go to trial, regardless of how long it took. Furthermore, a small team would accompany Rodney back to Chicago where they would secure some office space and pour over Charlie's files, word by word.

Once they had determined if both sets of X-rays were identical and that Robin McCandless was indeed probably gone, they would scour Charlie's files for the names of those who would be listed on the updated grand-jury documents as defendants. If the review of dental records did not result in a match, they would conclude Robin McCandless was still alive, the boat accident an elaborate hoax, and they would cite him as the principal defendant as they had originally planned, but adding the names gleaned from Charlie's files as codefendants.

It was a lot. Rodney returned to Chicago to find Charlie waiting—both feeling the pull of the floodwaters.

Rising Waters

THE *MAKLAKS* UNDERSTOOD THE waters. The waters rose and fell. The waters rose and fell as there were seasons of plenty and seasons of hunger—as there were periods of conflict and periods of contentment. The lives of the *Maklaks* were intertwined with the waters. By virtue of their interrelationship with the shifting waters, the *Maklaks* had adopted of culture of pragmatism often verging on fatalism. It was what it was.

What it was for the *Maklaks* was a teeming wetland homeland that provided the bounty of the lakes and marshes for their meals, homes, and clothing. It even provided riches such as obsidian from which they could craft stunning arrowheads of a superior quality to trade with other tribes for those few items the wetlands did not offer.

The *Maklaks* were one with their elements—feeling as fluid as the waters that nourished their lands. Then chaos hit. Outsiders came. What was was no longer. Many died. Many were sent to a faraway place called Oklahoma—Indian Territory. The *Maklaks* were driven from what was to become the lakebed, never to return.

Born on the lakebed, a refugee from the lakebed, Charlie felt as though he too had been, and possibly still was intertwined with the water—not the water of his home, but with water as an essence for life. His life's path seemed to follow the indiscriminate channels etched by the waters. He had slipped over the surface of the Great Lakes, he had crossed the great oceans, and his job had ended in a seething pyre among the waves of Chesapeake Bay. His talisman along the way had been the water strider, the Jesus bug.

He clearly visualized the water striders following him from the drainage canals back home to the margins of Chicago. He began to feel that he too had been like the water strider as, on behalf of Mr. Robin McCandless and Delpro, he had manipulated people with fear, even if subtly, in a way similar to the way the insects used fear to intimidate a mate. Now, with the end of Robin McCandless and Delpro, he needed to fine-tune these tactics to leverage the decisions of government—the decision that affected his future and his freedom. He needed to influence the other side, even if through the fear of their own failure, such that his adversaries were forced to comply with his wishes—forced to guarantee his freedom.

This was Charlie's sole focus.

It was what it was. And it was time for a change—a change abated by Messrs. Rodney Mills et al.

                              ⋀⋀⋀⋁⋀⋀

Rodney knew nothing about the *Maklaks* but he understood all too well Charlie's focus. Why not? At some level, every criminal was the same. Every criminal wanted to commit the crime and, if they couldn't get away physically, at least get away mentally unscathed. Of course, they all wanted, if apprehended, to remain free. Charlie was, in many respects, no exception.

Yet, at the same time, Rodney, unusually, had a strong dose of empathy for young Charlie. He clearly was not a hardened criminal. In truth, his personal profits from the illicit deeds he had coopted and coordinated had only come from his regular salary. He was, from one vantage point at least, just another salaried white-collar worker—working hard and making good bucks. While his salary, from the records Rodney's team had uncovered, had increased through time, this was commensurate with his experience. He seemed in no way to have benefitted directly from any of the ill-gotten gains derived from the actions he catalyzed on behalf of Robin McCandless and Delpro. He was a kid who'd run to the city and fallen in with the wrong crowd.

This, in Rodney's view, in no way exonerated him. He was, as his own recent negotiations had confirmed, guilty. He had knowingly committed crimes. He had (possibly unknowingly) injured people. He had supported and promoted criminality.

Nonetheless, while all true and provable, Rodney continued to believe Charlie's cooperation was worth the price of his freedom.

ᛗ ᛗ ᛗ ᛦ ᛗ ᛗ ᛗ

When the results from the comparison of the X-rays came back, Rodney was all the more convinced. The two sets of X-rays did not match.

There was ample reason to think the X-rays from Illinois were truly from Robin McCandless. Dr. J. O. McTavish was still practicing. The BTF team had visited McTavish's offices, spoken to his staff, and meticulously studied his files. It seemed clear Robin McCandless had been his patient for years—the files documenting two crowns and one root canal—all three procedures mysteriously lacking from the X-rays from the Virginia dentist who seemed to have vanished from the Mid-Atlantic area after the accident.

It was premature to declare Robin McCandless alive. But it was well past time to block any official declaration of his death and to formally classify him as missing.

This change in status was also adequate for Rodney's crew to revert to the original set of charging documents where Mr. Robin McCandless was the prime defendant. However, they still needed codefendants to cover their bases in the case that they actually did come up with a *corpus delicti* of good ol' Robin McCandless.

ᛗ ᛗ ᛗ ᛦ ᛗ ᛗ ᛗ

The X-ray review had yielded another heretofore unknown tidbit. Dr. McTavish filed his patients' records based on billing address. While it apparently had not shown up on the file that Charlie had inadvertently kept, when going over the files in Lake Bluff a Ms. Cynthia Owens appeared as another of Dr. McTavish's patients who was billed at the same address on Crab Tree Lane. The dentist vaguely remembered Ms. Owens as a youngish (compared to McCandless) woman with a pleasant personality who had come in twice at Robin McCandless' request to have her teeth cleaned by McTavish's hygienist.

Circling back to Charlie, the young man had no knowledge of a Ms. Owens and from the dentist's record's it looked as though she had been at Crab Tree Lane before Charlie had appeared on the scene.

Rodney then mustered all his forces and took a deep dive into anyone named Cynthia Owens who had been in the Chicago area at the time of the dental appointments. After much digging, they found a Ms. Owens who had flown from O'Hare to Paris/de Gaulle, reportedly on a one-way ticket. Rodney then reached out to Interpol who, after but a slight delay to get their facts right, confirmed that from the date of the arrival of the flight from O'Hare up to the present Ms. Owens was listed as living near Saint-Fargeau in the 20th Arrondissement of Paris. There were no details about her profession, employment, or social status, nor sources of income. She was a name and a place with no past nor, strangely, present.

⋀ ⋀ ⋀ ⋁ ⋀ ⋀ ⋀

The appearance of the heretofore unknown Ms. Cynthia Owens in the mix underscored the need to take a microscopic examination of Robin McCandless' complex life. And, when finished, do it again to make sure.

In Chicago, Rodney and his team easily found temporary office space and set about pouring through Charlie's files once Rodney had confirmed, sealed with a handshake, that the young rapscallion would be pardoned for all ill-doing and helped to resettle—of course, all this contingent on Charlie's testimony and complete cooperation.

It was evident that a major watershed in McCandless' history had been the move from Crab Tree Lane to Candy Point—Charlie's documentation only covered the period up to this move. Therefore, Rodney set up a second team in D.C. to filter every grain of sand from the McCandless story once he took up residence at Candy Point.

The fulcrum for this cross-country move was also a critical juncture. What had McCandless done with his operations scattered about the Great Lakes region when he had shifted to the Eastern Seaboard?

Charlie had no files for this transition period but could personally attest to Robin McCandless' consolidation of his operations from the Chicago area to Kansas City for those activities he did not simply close for good. In the northwest suburbs of Kansas City, Charlie informed Rodney, McCandless had assembled the chief lawyers, accountants, and others who had been critical to all his efforts over the years. McCandless had, Charlie added, really coerced these people to move further inland by offering them such generous salaries they could not refuse.

With this news, leaving Charlie to be the key reference for those exploring the McCandless files, Rodney went to Kansas City. It had not been difficult for his colleagues in D.C. to uncover the specific firm in Kansas City as they were tied into all the critical databases of the country. It turned out the catch-all Robin McCandless had established was named Inter-Act—either a very unimaginative name or a name cloaked with great hidden meaning (time would tell, Rodney thought). The head of this firm, according to the records Rodney's team accessed, was one Mr. Don Drumpfsh—basically a person unknown to anyone with no note-worthy recorded professional nor family background (at least, none that had made its way into the federal data sets). There were but a few years of tax payments on file as well as a mortgage for a home in Kansas City. Both the income cited in the taxes and the home cited in the mortgage were common middle-class assets ringing no alarm bells.

As Rodney pulled into the expansive Inter-Act parking lot in front of the expansive single-level brick structure (remembering that his staff had said this had once been a very large regional office of a major nation-wide insurance company that had subsequently further decentralized and Robin McCandless had picked up the lease for pennies on the dollar), it was clear things were happening. There were scores of vehicles in the car park—many late-model sedans with healthy sticker prices. Deliveries were being made. The grounds were being well maintained—even the windows washed.

At the well-appointed reception he was guided to Mr. Drumpfsh's office, having made an appointment well before departing Chicago. The man himself seemed to fit the name. Just a smidgin over six feet, he was a bit shorter than Rodney. He was also many pounds heavier and gave the impression that it had been a long time since he had broken a sweat with any physical exertion. His head was topped by a bizarre coif of yellow hair that seemed to sit upon an unsmiling and puffy orange face. He was, indeed, quite a caricature.

To add to the nearly comic appearance, the manager's office was done in red and gold tones that seemed to reflect off his orange complex-ion. All in all, it was an unusual experience bordering on the whimsical.

It was an unusual and peculiar experience that got more unusual but in the usual way.

When Rodney tried to initiate a serious discussion with the colorful Mr. Drumpfsh, it became evident this was practically impossible. The man was totally full of himself (Rodney quickly coming to this more gentlemanly conclusion than the obvious statement that he was full of shit). The nearly cartoonish office manager went on what appeared to be an animated and rehearsed tirade about how, in spite of never-seen-before opposition and challenges, Inter-Act was doing great and wonderful things under his superb guidance without even once stating a hard fact about the company's accomplishments.

To Rodney's highly honed senses, it quickly became obvious that Mr. Drumpfsh was nothing but an empty bag controlled by others; but an empty bag who was convinced he was doing fantastic things. It was going to be necessary to take a very hard look at Inter-Act, but the doorway for this was not through Mr. Drumpfsh.

According to protocol, Rodney requested some basic documents from Inter-Act befitting a visit by an SEC agent, accepting Mr. Drumpfsh's probably dishonest promise that this material would be forwarded to his D.C. office forthwith. Back in the car, he contacted this office, not to advise them of the coming parcel from Inter-Act but to pull off a small contingent of the larger BTF team to refocus and exclusively target Inter-Act as a chief subject of their investigation.

While Rodney had hoped he would be able, through time, to progressively concentrate his team's effort, he was encountering exactly the opposite. Every step into the Delpro morass opened new topics and posed new questions. Their work was expanding rapidly.

ʌ ʌʌʌ ʌ ʌ

In fact, it was snowballing. Back in Chicago, the group working with Charlie announced they had some names. Dissecting the files, they already had a long list of names of individuals linked to various Delpro activities in various ways. What stood out immediately were, cutting across numerous actions, the names of mid- and high-level civil servants at the Pentagon and the Departments of State, Commerce, and Agriculture. The most glaring included an Adjunct Second Deputy for Advanced Capabilities at the Department of Defense, Lieutenant Colonel Fritz Murphy, a Deputy Secretary for Business Affairs at the Department of State, Dr. Christine Miller, an Assistant Secretary for International Trade at the Department of Commerce, Ms. Florence Gardner, and an Assistant

Secretary in Foreign Trade at the Department of Agriculture, Dr. Lance Newcastle. The name of an advisor at the White House also appeared frequently in Robin McCandless' files. As with the other four, Dr. Howard Dunford was prominently described as a Delpro asset—an active Delpro ally attributed with a variety of questionable dealings on McCandless' behalf. And, for all the named parties, the files included precise details as to what was called "salary support" that was paid by direct deposit into the assets' accounts—these sums formidable even considering the ample pay scales for senior staff.

While the Chicago BTF team developed files on the dozens of public servants spotlighted through the piles of Robin McCandless' documents, they concentrated on the top five, building strong fact-based cases against each for not only blatantly breaking their oath of office but for outright criminality.

Initially the team did not reach out to nor surveil these targets. They were concerned at the possibility of having critical defendants cut and run. To add to the difficulties, for all the government employees, the notations in the files stopped roughly a month before Robin McCandless' departure from Crab Tree Lane.

Looking at the full set of documentation, this noticeable reduction in record-keeping prior to leaving Illinois was evident from all angles of analysis. Mr. Robin McCandless either had another set of his most recent files that were not among those left in Charlie's charge or he had begun keeping less voluminous documents, possibly feeling he was under closer observation by the feds he so wished to avoid.

Whatever the explanation and no matter how thin the latest files, there was more than adequate material to build powerful arguments against the top five civil servants who were now seen as being the co-defendants they needed and the individuals to be cited next to Robin McCandless in the grand jury case.

A big pothole in their road to the grand jury came when, with the now completed individual files, the team tried to locate the current whereabouts of the top five.

They could not be found.

There can often be quick changes in large federal bureaucracies and there had never been any guarantees that today these individuals would still occupy the posts described in the files. Given their substantial boost in income through their affiliations with Delpro, there easily could have been incentives to leave public service as soon as they could remove whatever hooks Delpro had implanted in them at the onset. Nonetheless, even with the considerable resources of the agency, the five functionaries were, like Ms. Cynthia Owens, missing, although this latter had been seen in France.

Thus, it was time for pragmatism.

BTF prepared a full set of grand jury documents charging Robin McCandless, Cynthia Owens, Fritz Murphy, Christine Miller, Florence Gardner, Lance Newcastle, and Howard Dunford—all in absentia. They were confident they had solid lawsuits and should move ahead with the legal processes while they tried to locate the subjects of their litigation.

It wasn't ideal. But it was well worth the effort.

ᗰ ᗰ ᗰ ᗱ ᗰ ᗰ ᗰ

It was a juggling act. There were satellite investigations into Inter-Act, Cynthia Owens' French activities, and Robin McCandless' business affairs while at Candy Point. Simultaneously, the main thrust of BTF was, under the guidance of the federal prosecutors and other relevant Department of Justice staff, to present a solid case to the grand jury while, at the same time, tracking down the top five missing people of interest—or targets, it still wasn't completely clear (not to mention Robin McCandless himself whose condition and whereabouts remained unknown).

The petition brought before the grand jury was detailed and tightly crafted.

Eddie Hall, Peter Volman, and Charlie Stancik offered well-prepared and thorough testimonies. Peter's contributions were more to set the global stage, to highlight the truly enormous and diversified nature of Delpro's actions worldwide. Eddie was able to complement the international aspects of the transnational's misdoings as well as present domestic misdeeds. Charlie was the keynote. He could even build further on the international scope and reach of the omnipresent Delpro. And, more critically, he could and did provide the minutest facts linking operations overseas to those inside the United States.

The BTF team was then able to provide equally explicit explanations of the roles of Fritz Murphy, Christine Miller, Florence Gardner, Lance Newcastle, and Howard Dunford based on the material contained in Charlie's copies of the McCandless Files—Charlie himself apparently not knowing personally nor by reputation any of these individuals. Cynthia Owens remained an enigma. However, there were adequate threads to pull to include her in the charging documents as long as they could subsequently muster more evidence for the trial.

The specific domestic acts were damning and varied. They included collusion with the armed forces in awarding contracts for their mess facilities. There were similar conspiracies with federal agencies regarding the sales of counterfeit inputs in everything from pharmaceuticals to fertilizers. There was the widespread supplying of common produce with forged organic certification. There were the fraudulent sales of public lands. There was the marketing of bogus materials and supplies. There was extortion of voters during elections at all levels. There was the intentional recycling, relabeling, and mislabeling of expired food and health products—many going into public programs for schools and hospitals. There was the suppression and intimidation of labor unions and the nonadherence to legal hiring and safety practices. There was bribery and theft. There was human trafficking. And there was more. There was a lot.

Rodney was very satisfied with the top-notch presentations made by everyone on his team. Rodney was impressed by the zeal with which the US Attorneys pursued the cases. Rodney was more than pleased that it had all paid off. All seven individuals were indicted.

⩗ ⩗ ⩗ � ⩗ ⩗ ⩗

With the indictments, the formal court cases moved fully over to the Department of Justice and the US Attorneys. The BTF crew shifted into a critical-support role—tasked with completely outlining the cases, filling in any holes, and compiling files and files of evidentiary documentation.

Rodney reshuffled his team after the indictments to better prepare for the lengthy trial where Delpro would undoubtedly be represented by some the country's highest-paid lawyers.

Teams were weighted by the critical nature of their subjects and the volume of work involved. The largest team was assigned the difficult job of unraveling Robin McCandless' activities while at Candy Point—this was the biggest hole in their story. Another significant team was given the duty of digging into the roots of Inter-Act while avoiding Don Drumpfsh (or ignoring him as irrelevant). Yet another team was tasked with trying to locate Robin McCandless, Fritz Murphy, Christine Miller, Florence Gardner, Lance Newcastle, and Howard Dunford. Finally, a small group was dispatched, with the full cooperation of the French and Interpol, to try and undo the puzzle of Cynthia Owens. Throughout all, Eddie Hall, Peter Volman, and Charlie Stancik were told to be on standby.

It was a lot. But it was what they did best.

∧ ∧∧∨∧∧∧

The team's files were filling up. Subpoenas were served. A trove of data was mined at Inter-Act which illuminated McCandless' activities when at Candy Point. This was basically more of the same, however.

The phenomena, as Rodney mulled to himself, of Robin McCandless and Delpro was that so much had been done defiantly in the open and openly. Definitely, there were layers upon layers. There were very deeply hidden actions and operations. Nevertheless, the overall landscape had been clear for all to see.

It was emerging that there had been a relatively recent effort to paint a picture of Delpro as an offshore organization—possibly to limit scrutiny and subsequent liability within the US. Nevertheless, as the agents dug and dug deeper, it was clear that everything was intertwined. While the branches of the tree, by whatever name, may have arched to foreign versus domestic targets, the roots always returned to Robin McCandless. And, Rodney now understood, these same roots were even more deep-seated, going down all the way to Domov.

When Rodney discussed this with Charlie, his principal resource referred to an old Hawaiian song about the Princess Pupule—Charlie recalling how his initial conduit into McCandless and Delpro, Julian Badescu, had first employed this reference about the beginnings of the now dishonored Delpro. There had always been tangled messes, intentionally convoluted to twist the words and deeds that most often were uttered and undertaken in plain sight.

It was all a jumbled cluster like some sort of modern art placed in the city center. Everyone stared at it for a while. No one really knew why it was there. Soon all looked, but no one saw it. Then, when the eyes were open again, there was a lot to see.

The contracts and contractors, the payments and shifting of funds, the acquisitions and sales, the legal finagling and pursuance, all the day-to-day functions and even the planning were plainly accessible through the records of the staff at Inter-Act. Delpro was alfresco. Its invisibility was achieved because it was little-known, because no one looked, because no one cared.

This fact notwithstanding, the core actors were nowhere to be seen. So far, Robin McCandless' status had been impossible to confirm. Similarly, there were a variety of stories overlaying the status of Fritz Murphy, Christine Miller, Florence Gardner, Lance Newcastle, and Howard Dunford. Two were said to be on holidays. One was said to be attending a retreat. Another was said to be on sabbatical. A fifth had simply vanished.

There was more success for Cynthia Owens. While there were few if any records in France, BTF agents, with local support, were able to determine that the American travelled frequently to Istanbul. Refocusing on Turkey, the team, with a new set of local partners, was able to locate the probable object of her attention. She was registered as the CEO and only employee of a local NGO called *Özgürlük* (Freedom) located in the *Kücükköy* district of the city. The organization was situated in a three-story home cum office with upper two floors, according to local accounts, converted into some sort of dormitory. After additional prying, there emerged a picture where *Özgürlük* targeted Syrian refugees, professing to be able to relocate them to European cities where they could get good jobs. It came out, though, that most ended up as effective slaves in big agri-business facilities scattered across the rim of the Mediterranean. Cynthia Owens was a slaver.

◬ ◬ ◬ ▽ ◬ ◬

Overall, the impact of the indictments and the continued pressure as preparations for trials accelerated was that Delpro seemed to shrink like a violet in the hot midday sun. From one day to the next, offices around the world closed—disappeared. It was as though they had never existed. There were no discernible footprints. Activities, operations, projects undertaken under the Delpro flag had either dissolved or had miraculously been recast under a different non-Delpro management scheme.

All enquiries ended the same, "Delpro, what's that? Never heard of it."

Most of this vanishing act was witnessed overseas—Delpro had, in fact, been reshaping, repainting, and restructuring their domestic actions for some time. The only significant remnant was Inter-Act and the BTF team was already well imbedded in this group, including its tentacles that reached from shore to shore.

Charlie and Rodney spent hours foraging across maps of the globe, looking at satellite imagery, reading trade and development journals, and in any other way rummaging about to try and find some crumbs Delpro might have forgotten to sweep into their dustbin. There were few morsels to ferret out. Nonetheless, even the tiniest bit was pursued. Using local contacts or sending out agents from D.C., in one way or another, every lead was followed. Few added to their body of data. They were unquestionably in diminishing returns.

In spite of the changing scenery and the growing frustration at gaps in their data, the US Attorneys decided to go ahead and schedule the cases on an overloaded court calendar. They had concluded the best tactics were to file individual cases. Thus, there was a panoply of cases charging corporate Delpro as well as Robin McCandless and his six named coconspirators (knowing this was just a sliver of the full scope of the matter).

After aggravating delays and postponements, one by one, judges gaveled the cases closed with all defendants exceptionally found guilty in absentia—this very unusual court action based on the accepted severity and urgency of the cases. At this stage, this was an expensive, time-consuming formality since no bad guys were in the dock to get justice. In many ways it was very disconcerting to Rodney. This was not how he did things. This was not how he had imagined things happening. This was not the outcome he so badly wanted. This was not the justice for Hal he sought.

But Rodney realized this was a necessary step in a long and complex process. Delpro and its named associates may have retreated—they may even have been convicted in court. Still, Rodney knew, the decision-makers, the powerbrokers, the real top-tier folks were still doing what they had always been doing—manipulating the world's economy for their benefit (maybe a rather grandiose statement, but apropos and true—very true—Rodney thought).

With the revelations of Heinrich Fuchs and the discoveries about Domov, it was clear that the actions taken to date by the BTF team were nothing more than removing a carbuncle from the posterior of a giant worldwide powerhouse. It may well be a first move, but it was a pittance in terms of what was needed to be done to be able to do what was necessary to combat the enemy in a meaningful and durable way. It had been the first volley.

It was necessary to move on.

It was time to broaden the search. It was time to go wide and to go deep. It was time to do all possible to uncover the hydra that was a real global infestation.

It was also time to help Charlie get the freedom he so avidly pursued.

ᛗᛗᛗᚥᛗᛗ

Charlie did not want to go back to the lakebed. There were many considerations, lots of reasons—but the overriding issue was that he had spent his life trying to get away. Why go back now?

Nevertheless, he still felt the pull, the pull of the waters. In some weird sort of debate with himself, he decided he needed to keep this connection even if he had abandoned the lakebed. His solution was to follow the great river that drained the basin—follow it to the sea.

With the help of Rodney's team, and with the caveat that he would be available as needed to revisit all the issues of Robin McCandless and Delpro, he was able to procure a scenic plot upon which to build comfortable home west of the Redwood Highway, on the south side of the river, on Saugep Creek, just a few miles from where the river joined the sea.

He had staked a claim. He would have a home.

ᛗᛗᛗᚥᛗᛗ

A home, however, especially a home enveloped by the redwoods, had not always been part of Charlie's immediate and changing plans. He had remained in the shadow of St. Volodymyr's during the hectic and endless hours and days and weeks when Rodney's team had poured over and over the McCandless files. He had been interrogated, investigated, and interviewed. He had been turned inside-out. He had teased apart the Delpro and McCandless tapestries thread by thread with Rodney.

They had entered the labyrinth but felt they were being led on a mighty chase outside their control by the still unseen Minotaur.

It was enervating. It was frustrating. It was eye-opening.

Despite Charlie's apparent closeness to the seemingly all-powerful Robin McCandless, as the blinds were opened, he had to accept he had been completely unaware of many of the actions—now the crimes—his boss had overseen through Delpro. He now had to admit he had been ignorant—naively ignorant—of many of the goings-on. He had been oblivious to the many high-level accomplices entangled in the swamp, the unimagined tainted sums involved, and the unbelievable power being applied to influence decisions around the world. In the end, Charlie was overwhelmed by that of which he had been a part.

Yet, it was strange.

On the one hand, Rodney and his colleagues did not treat Charlie as a criminal. He was seen as a critical resource and almost as someone for whom to feel sorry given the way he had, from some perspectives at least, been manipulated. Many of the team members, some would say looking through rose-colored spectacles, for all intents and purposes saw Charlie as a kid in over his head in an intricate and treacherous international puzzle.

Charlie, knowing full well he was no longer a kid but accepting he well might have been in over his head, realized his work had been much more scandalous than he had understood—even after uncovering such scurrilous acts as building cells in an agriculture development center to feed a network of slave labor traffickers that crept into concealed corners across the globe. There was a lot he had not known but a lot he had known. And he had continued to go along. He had continued to add to Delpro's wealth and power. Yet, now sitting with Rodney's investigators and telling his story, he felt no remorse. It was what it was. At the time, it had been good for him and to him. It was now over. It was finished. All he wanted to do was to turn the page and move to a new phase of his life where, like those on the lakebed from whom he had fled, he could serenely sit on his porch and watch life go by.

In some curious way, as he looked back to his activities in one way or another linked to Robin McCandless, it was as though he was seeing the life of another—reading a novel or watching a movie. This was not really his tale. This was the tale of another Charlie Stancik. While he felt there should be, there was no guilt. There were no regrets. There was only wonder.

D-2

I T WAS TIME TO reconfigure.
Rodney needed to regroup.

The team needed a makeover.

To maintain momentum, a reshaping was required.

To ensure the patronage of those on high, they had to undertake a renewal that offered promise—a revivification.

For the moment at least, Delpro was an antecedent. The center of attention was Domov. One of Rodney's bright young agents proposed they close the BTF in favor of what he dubbed the "Delta-Beta Force"— arguing this needed the "D" for Delta in the eponym since both Delpro and Domov started with a "D." Moreover, this was the second front for the wider attack, hence the terminology of "beta."

Rodney appreciated the convoluted reasoning but thought that Delta-Beta Force was a little too close to Navy SEAL Ops for comfort so, accepting the rational, opted to brand the new team the "D-2."

D-2 it was.

⋀ ⋀ ⋀ ⋁ ⋀ ⋀ ⋀

In practice, D-2 was scarcely a transformation of BTF. It was a fresh paint job (like those freshly painted old agricultural implements that had entrapped Peter, Rodney reflected). It was the same people effectively doing the same jobs in the same places. It wasn't truly a redesign; it was more a renaming to ensure the old new thing continued to receive the necessary political and budgetary support.

Initially, the major building blocks remained the files used for the Delpro cases. Rodney now had his crew pouring over the same material for what seemed to be the hundredth time, but with this iteration putting on a new set of glasses—looking through the Domov lens. Looking for any ancillary information that may have been previously sidetracked as not being germane directly to the Delpro case but that could be a lead to far-reaching clues about organizations linked to yet outside Delpro such as an encircling aura from some reported super entity like Domov.

Most of the core information came from Charlie's files along with that vacuumed up at Inter-Act. In both instances, Charlie was still an indispensable resource. While trying to bore down some roots into the hard-packed soils along Saugep Creek, Charlie was reachable nearly anytime by his cell (an amazing offshoot of his pager of many years ago, Charlie observed) and, if things got crazy, he was about two-and-a-half hours from Rogue Valley International Airport from where he could catch a flight east with minimal delays.

Still and all, while Charlie could fill in many blanks that arose regarding Robin McCandless' activities, and to a lesser extent Delpro, he had no understanding of Domov. At least, he did not know that he knew anything.

This stage of the investigation turned out to be more of a chess game. And Rodney was very good at chess.

Heinrich Fuchs' circle had been more animal husbandry and Robin McCandless' more crop agriculture. Where did the two overlap? Where did they have common needs and share common problems?

Both needed land, labor, water, and energy. Both were challenged with marketing, distribution, and logistics, as well as dealing with regulations they likely considered overly burdensome. It was set theory with pivotal areas being the consonant areas where both camps shared necessities. It made sense (although this observation was no reason to think it was true, Rodney acknowledged to himself) that common solutions to these common priorities could be dealt with most expeditiously at a higher level in the hierarchy—whether or not this next step up the ladder was Domov or another intermediary consortium.

Rodney zeroed in on two topics: labor and transport. They already had voluminous data on the sourcing and use of illegal (slave) labor by Delpro-related firms as well as on the means of transport employed, not only for these laborers but also for products to markets around the world. The D-2 teams revisited the files, looking laboriously over and over again at the recounting of the use of, really the kidnapping of, refugees for, among others, European farms. These data were interwoven with others covering the transport of a wide variety of products grown in tropical countries (under uncontrolled conditions) to Western European and North American markets.

It looked highly likely that Cynthia Owens had a prominent place in this mosaic. But she remained a riddle. Neither Rodney's own agents nor Interpol and French teams could uncover anything meaningful about her activities in France while she seemed to be underground in Turkey. Rodney's contacts in Istanbul could only conjecture that she was being protected by the very highest levels of power—these allies citing the Quran *(Surah At-Tauba, 51)*, "Never will we be struck except by what Allah has decreed for us; He is our protector."

Rodney concentrated on the shipping lines. He had maps prepared for the movement of Delpro products (human and otherwise) up both coasts of Africa, into the Arabian Gulf including the Persian Gulf and the Red Sea, across the Mediterranean, along with the Black Sea, and even into the North Sea. Clearly, this web circled the orb, but he needed to bite off what he could chew.

He needed to produce results. Both his bosses and his staff needed some tangible outcomes.

He needed to function at two levels: the global and the local—the macro and the micro.

He needed to show D-2 was having an impact.

Rodney began to, keeping to some sort of personalized set theory, draw out the interrelationships—his unique mixture of a logical analysis and a crap shoot. Geographically, he mused, what could be the interconnections? *Matadero Global* had been centered in a Spanish-speaking area but had seeped into all corners of the globe. Delpro was English-based although active also in Spanish-speaking and other regions. What would an intersection look like? Rodney speculated, really only on a hunch, "Maybe Lusophone?"

With that framework in mind, what do plants and animals have in common—where would Delpro and *Matadero Global* overlap? Plants are part of animal feeds and pharmaceutics. Both food sources need to be delivered one way or another to the consumer.

Lusophone feeds and medicaments?

Brazil was a major soybean producer. Soy was an important ingredient in animal feeds. Angola was supporting a major country-wide program to expand cassava production. Cassava was an important ingredient in many medications.

Exploring the many ports of Brazil, Rodney and his group zoomed in on Porto de Victória. This was reportedly the least developed port with a low volume of containerized shipments—a good spot for people wanting to ship bulk agricultural products with a minimum of inspection and red tape. Looking at soy shipments, one company stood out: *Alimento Atlântico*. *Alimento Atlântico*—Atlantic Foodstuffs—also shipped cassava products out of the port of Luanda. Even more interesting, out of the same port *Alimento Atlântico* shipped considerable quantities of slaughtered Botswana beef. Botswana did supply beef to the EU. But the closest port by far was Durban—a quarter of the haul timewise when compared to Luanda. Why would exporters choose a longer and much more costly routing?

Completing the picture, *Alimento Atlântico* seemed to principally use the Portuguese Port of Faro, located in the extreme south of the country and less than five hours due west of Granada where, among many other places, Delpro had had known offices.

Alimento Atlântico appeared to be a good next step for D-2. It would not displace the existing channels of investigation, but it would add an entirely new optic to the broad-based inspection of Domov even though the very existence of this structure was still to be fully validated.

In many ways, Rodney understood all too well, Domov remained a phantasm.

D-2 had a big job.

ᴧ ᴧᴧᴠᴧᴧ ᴧ

While Rodney was reshaping his work to encompass *Alimento Atlântico*, Charlie, when not on call for the D-2 team, was trying to see how best he could reshape his life on the banks of Saugep Creek.

This was not the wilderness, but it was not the lakebed either. And it certainly was not the shoreline cities of Lake Michigan. He was about twenty-five miles south of Crescent City and nearly three times that distance north of Eureka. The diversions and the services of the city were, therefore, not that far off. For more immediate and routine needs, he was only five minutes from the little community of Klamath. So, while he felt he was in a whole new world on the margins of the Trees of Mystery, he really was not, in many ways, that far away from the life he had led in the Prairie State just months ago (although it seemed like years ago).

The feds, as Robin had sneeringly labeled them all, had been very good to Charlie. Indeed, he too had been of considerable, some would say great help to them. But they had reciprocated.

He had been able to keep all his assets. It was deemed that these were in truth compensation for his time and effort even if this time and effort had been devoted to the illicit aims of his employer. While he had kept his identity, he had been relocated to Saugep Creek at government expense and provided with a no-interest loan (also at government expense—not the free ride for which he had hoped, but pretty good just the same) to be able to set up a home and reestablish a new life (including buying a new Iconic Silver Super Duty F-250 4X4–quite a change from his bright red BMW).

Way back when, before his life had shattered into a bazillion pieces (or so it seemed), he and Jo had talked about their dream home. They would continue their careers. They would work and save and when their life calmed, when their children were grown and out of college, when they had sewn all their wild oats, they would build their dream house to be their comfort zone as they prepared for old age. Charlie had even gone to an architect to draw up blueprints for this little bit of nirvana. Sadly, Jo had had her accident before she ever saw them. But Charlie had kept them and now he was going to build THEIR home.

With the help of a none-too-cheap contractor from Crescent City, he built their home on the banks of Saugep Creek where the cool evening breeze whispered through the big windows carrying the murmur of the creek and the trill of crickets. Under the shake roof there was an ultra-modern kitchen and a massive shower in the master bedroom for the two tenants to shower as one. There was the big stone fireplace they both wanted. There were equally big plate-glass windows overlooking the valley. There was the two-car garage and the ample workshop. There was everything.

He was surrounded by Redwood Parks—national and state. He had trekking opportunities that put his hiking in small city parks to shame. The possibilities were nearly endless. But he needed something.

He got a dog.

Charlie, as so often happened, simply stumbled into the whole dog thing. He was getting gas in Klamath when the owner's female golden retriever came around the corner followed by a gaggle of puppies. As the family came over to sniff the newcomer's leg, the owner asked, "Need a puppy?"

That was that.

Ralph joined the household, named in honor of Charlie's Freshman PE teacher (whom Charlie could not remember if he liked or not, but it was the first reference that popped into his mind for naming his new best friend).

Charlie and Ralph set up a home as they explored the redwoods together.

⋀⋀⋀⋁⋀⋀

All the while, Rodney explored Portuguese connections to Domov. This was becoming an increasingly important and tangible lead as the shrinking Delpro continued to dwindle on the world stage. Offices either melted away, no one able to remember they had ever existed, or they completely retooled into something else (in one case, an agricultural consulting firm, in another a nutrition center). Just like that, although the archival data and information remained, it was nearly impossible to validate *in situ* any purported misdeeds. It became more and more like a historian trying to make a case without a reasonable doubt why the Romans invaded Gaul—Delpro was rapidly (and intentionally, Rodney reminded himself) fading into history.

The presence of Angola and Botswana in the latest scenario under study made Rodney think back to Sir Horace. Rodney had effectively cut the old man loose as being more of a diversion when stalking his older brother. Now perhaps it was time to revisit the clever Cockney gentleman.

Rodney reassigned agents to Namibia—Sir Horace again under close watch.

Results were slow in coming. But they arrived eventually.

First, they discovered that the Namibian Southwest African Beef Company had a Botswana subsidiary; New Twsana Cattle Company in Tshootsha, seventy miles southwest of the well-known cattle area of Ghanzi and 425 miles west of the capital Gaborone. This link was important. Due to stringent EU control measures, most beef imports to Western Europe from southern Africa came from Botswana. From all indications, beef from Southwest African Beef Company was surreptitiously inserted into the New Twsana Cattle Company's export stream and then these illegally merged consignments inexplicably routed via Luanda. Moreover, these exports were apparently exclusively shipped via *Alimento Atlântico*.

There was the first hook snaring good ol' Sir Horace into the mix that was becoming Domov.

Then, the D-2 team got a real break.

Contrary to his normal routine of staying pretty close to home in southern Africa, Sir Horace took a trip to Bucharest. The D-2 team initially thought the old guy was just making a trip to his homeland—kind of a last pilgrimage before his time was up.

What they discovered was quite different. Sir Horace met his big brother Robin McCandless. McCandless was alive and seemingly well and probably living in Romania. He had come full circle and was back at his origins. The "how's" were unknown. The "what's" were clear. Robin McCandless was still potentially a prime actor.

A new and enlarged D-2 team was assigned to Romania.

While the initial Horace overseers (the reconstituted Horace Hunters) awaited the arrival of their colleagues just assigned to the case, they continued to monitor the two brothers.

The pair left Bucharest, Robin driving, going east via the *Autostrada Soarelui* (the Motorway of the Sun) for three hours to Vama Veche. This small town near the Bulgarian Border on the Black Sea was an increasingly popular tourist destination. The south of town, called the Turquoise Peninsula, through recent gentrification had become a high-end residential area suitable for a home in line with Mr. Robin McCandless' fine tastes (additionally, providing a bolthole, not across the Chesapeake or Lake Michigan, but just a skip and a jump to cross the border into Bulgaria).

As Rodney's crew watched the two brothers do what any brothers would probably do at a reunion after what was probably years of separation, it was unclear if the watchdogs' labor would pay-off. It could well be simply a family reunion.

Then the team was rewarded yet again.

Robin and Horace received a visit by none other than Ms. Cynthia Owens.

Robin McCandless' new Crab Tree Lane or Candy Point, namely Turquoise Peninsula, was only sixty miles south of the coastal city of Constanta from where one could catch a ninety-minute flight on Turkish Air to Istanbul. Or, as Cynthia had done, a ninety-minute flight to

Constanta from where one could easily rent a car for the short hop to the Turquoise Peninsula.

As the details filtered into Rodney's office, the first thoughts were for extradition of the now guilty in absentia Robin McCandless. However, a quick check revealed that the extradition treaty between Romania and the US was still a work in process. This could be a future possibility, therefore, but not a present plan of action.

They needed a different tactic.

They wanted to attack. They had the necessary instruments to attack.

An attack would be good for morale. An attack would be good for their politics (which were enmeshed in everything). An attack would be good for the soul.

Sadly, however, under present circumstances, an attack was neither a sound idea nor a legal maneuver.

Nevertheless, they had their targets.

⋀ ⋀ ⋀ ⋁ ⋀ ⋀ ⋀

A target was an aspiration, not a done deal. Rodney was painfully aware of this fateful maxim. It was once again time to send teams around the globe to shadow people in the shadows. The revived Horace Hunters would be back in full force as would be their mirror image following the resurrected Robin McCandless.

Cynthia Owens was more problematic. She was, in the first instance, not really in the shadows. She did much, if not all, of her ignominious deeds in the full light of day through her counterfeit NGO in Istanbul, *Özgürlük*. Then, monitoring her in the open in Turkey was far from straightforward. Turkish security forces were renowned (both for their efficiency and their brutality) and she seemed to be under their wing.

Rodney decided to focus attention on activities in Romania. Horace's squad would follow him if and when he went back to southern Africa. But the concentration of effort would be on the reawakened Robin McCandless and his return to his roots in the country famed as the home of Vlad Dracula III (*Draculea*), *Vlad the Impaler,* the *Voivode* (warlord) of Walachia in the 1450s.

This in some ways possibly closed the loop, roughly corresponding with Heinrich Fuchs' recounting of some sort of superstructure, a nucleus, based in Ukraine. At least, Rodney hoped more than believed, they might be in the right part of the world.

Still, however one looked at the work ahead, it was a slog.

Weeks oozed into months, and the brothers unabashedly enjoyed the Black Sea beaches apparently as much as they enjoyed each other. Cynthia came and went after a few days. There were no other curious visitors—a few tradesmen along with some part-time household staff, but basically the brothers kept to themselves.

Turquoise Peninsula, as all Robin's nests, was well chosen. The villa was at the south end of a short string of equally luxurious homes, all siting in open ground in what, not too long ago, had been a grain field. The elegant chateau was, furthermore, only about a hundred yards from the open sandy beaches for which this area was so well known. In short, surveillance had to be done from a distance relying more on technology than sharp human eyes.

Yet, through eyes or machines, the same events were always seen—effectively nothing—certainly nothing to write back to D.C. about. The siblings seemed to putter about the property, making regular visits to the beach, and irregular visits to the shops of the small town in McCandless' Glacier White S-Class Mercedes sedan.

Then, after far too long, the brothers did receive an unusual visit via taxi from a middle-aged man in a sober suit and tie (reading the surveillance report, according to the description, Rodney had thought if this had been in D.C., it would appear that Robin and Horace were being visited by some sort of religious missionary—like the Volmans). This man stood out. This man also catalyzed much-awaited movement.

The man, whom they later identified as Mr. Radutu Botezatu, reportedly an established Romanian businessman with investments all around the country as well as outside, spent the night. The next day, at an early hour for the two sleep-in brothers, the trio got in the Mercedes and drove to Bucharest. They drove straight to the *Cetatean Banca Comert Transilvania*, the CBCT—the Citizen's Commercial Bank of Transylvania—not far from *Piata Iosif Save* and close to the city center of this metropole of approximately two million inhabitants whose origins corresponded to the time of Vlad Dracula III.

Rodney's overseers were, of course, unable to ascertain what transpired in the bank. The agents were able to follow their prey into the lobby, but unable to follow them as they took a private elevator to an upper floor.

At teatime, the brothers came out, got in their car, driving to the Epoque Hotel. The hotel was just a ten-minute walk from the bank if one went through the *Gradinile Cismigiu*—the thirty-six-acre English-style garden-park dating back to the 1840s.

Over the next three days, Robin and Horace migrated between the Epoque and the CBCT before driving back to Turquoise Peninsula on the fourth day. Never once did they take the time to amble through the beautiful park to or from the bank, always preferring the plush leather seats of the Mercedes and a drive that was three times as long as the walk (even with valet parking at both ends).

Given the time invested away from the seclusion of their beachfront manor, and the increased risk of discovery by a random urban passer-by, Rodney could only conclude that the CBCT was a critical piece in the game that now occupied the once-dead Robin McCandless (and, of course, his younger brother). He mobilized a group of banking and finance experts to burrow deeply into CBCT affairs.

As always, this was time consuming, encountering many barriers—some temporary, others more permanent. This was painstaking—deciphering thousands of transactions in dozens of languages. This was laborious, leafing through thousands and thousands of pages of commonplace banking activities to unearth those cloaked extralegal transactions that sucked CBCT into the sphere of Delpro, Domov, or whatever organization and whatever devious acts had attracted the venal personages of Robin McCandless and Horace Barthley. The siblings shared not only incarnadine complexions and Romanian roots, but also innate talents for conscienceless behavior.

ᛗ ᛗ ᛗ ᚥ ᛗ ᛗ ᛗ

While the inglorious brothers enjoyed a lackadaisical life back at the seashore, their surveillance was open-aired and monotonous—like watching a pot boil. Rodney was able, therefore, to shift considerable effort to track and study Mr. Radutu Botezatu—the new man on the scene whose given name Rodney learned from his guys in the field meant "happy man." Rodney hoped that Mr. Botezatu's happiness would prompt him to make some mistakes that would allow D-2 to pick up some much needed and heretofore unknown leads. They needed to till new ground.

And till they did. Mr. Radutu Botezatu, as a person and as a businessman, was examined by D-2 researchers in excruciating detail on both sides of the Atlantic. He had been born fifty-three years ago near the Ukrainian border in the middle-sized town of Radauti in Suceava

Judet (county) in the historical region of Bukovina. Much like Charlie, it seemed, from his early teens until the age of forty, there was no visible trace of Radutu Botezatu. When he did reappear, he was reportedly a much-sought-after member of the upper crust with businesses across the country—economic if not hereditary nobility. While his financial portfolios were thick and diverse, he appeared to have a particular penchant for investments in tourism and the retail trade—in regard to this latter, he owned numerous outlets that sold sports and hunting paraphernalia as well as hardware and building supplies.

Mr. Botezatu's interests comprised a number of hotels and tourist destinations including remote mountain-side chateaus. One such palatial structure in the Fagaras Mountains, smack dab in the middle of the country, stood out. In addition to attracting celebrity visitors from around the world, after considerable searching in the cracks and crevices, it was discovered that this thirteenth-century estate was the site of a very secretive and exclusive meeting that seemed to take place on Easter weekend each year.

The existence of these meetings, as intended, had almost escaped notice. While the estate was waitlisted for rooms for would-be notable guests throughout the spring and summer months, inexplicably it was closed for repairs every Easter weekend. A casual enquiry of the management revealed the official explanation for these closures was that annual maintenance was done in early spring. However, D-2 agents could find no plumbers, painters, nor carpenters who worked at the chateau over Easter. Quite to the contrary, local craftsmen indicated the Easter holidays were universally respected and few if any would schedule major jobs during these sacred days.

The obvious question, what did happen at the chateau every Easter?

It had been exceedingly difficult to scrape away the many layers of camouflage and subterfuge to highlight the scantest features of the Easter meetings. Finally, after struggling for every bit of intelligence they could garner, D-2 analysts were able to conclude with some level of confidence not only that there were regular Easter meetings but that the participation in these meetings was always the same—at least the core participants, in addition to Radutu Botezatu, were the same. This core included Liu Li from Singapore, Raymond Girard from Canada, Janco Momberg from South Africa, Bohadan Kushnir from Ukraine, and Sebastian Carvalho from Brazil. This core included some of the most powerful people in the world.

These were not people who were published in *Forbes'* lists nor who appeared on page two of the *Financial Times* or *Le Monde*. These were people known to but a few—people shrouded in nearly impenetrable obscurity—people who paid fortunes to remain unknown and invisible.

During the time that Rodney's team developed biographies for the sextet, it was impressive to see the scope of their global reach in all segments of the economy—banking, real estate, construction and manufacturing, agriculture and food, research and technology, transport and communications, medicine, and even education. They covered it all—and this was just in regard to their legitimate endeavors (probably only a fraction of the total envelope, Rodney imagined). As the profiles of this group of global controllers filled in, it became indisputable that these six individuals held immense power and oversaw immense wealth—power and wealth obviously joined at the hip.

Given the incontestable clout of those attending the Easter meetings, it was evident to Rodney that Robin McCandless and unquestionably Horace Barthley had never been that high up in the hierarchy. Robin, and to a lesser degree Horace, had been central to many operations yet when taking the widest-angle picture, the brothers had been several echelons below the seats of absolute authority in the worldwide organization—whatever it was called and wherever it was located.

Moreover, today the aging Romanian siblings were probably more like pensioners—retirees kept around as references (more storytellers, Rodney thought) of times gone by. Robin and Horace were most likely on a downward slide. And, critically, the sextuplet forming the nuclei of the sub-rosa Easter meetings were, from all indications, on an upward trajectory.

With more urgency and an expanded scope, D-2 combed thoroughly through the lives of those who spent Easter in the Fagaras Mountains.

᠕ ᠕᠕ V ᠕᠕ ᠕

While Rodney coordinated an updated sharpening and triangulation of his team's efforts, Charlie and Ralph explored the ancient forests and their own seashore. The calls from Rodney or others at the SEC became increasingly rare, much to Charlie's satisfaction.

Had Charlie been able to see things from Rodney's seat, he would realize his satisfaction was well warranted. Along with Eddie Hall, Paula Patterson, and Peter Volman, he had played his part. He had made his contributions. Rodney knew, if the others didn't, that the overall investigation would not have reached the highly developed state where it was today without the inputs from these disparate individuals. Yet, like Robin and Horace, they were now more references for past events as opposed to resources for upcoming action.

If Charlie had known this, it would have been fine by him.

ʎʎʎʌʎʎ

At the moment, before zooming again out to a global scale, Rodney wanted to uncover as much as he could about the goings-on in Romania, about Radutu Botezatu and his ties to the going-out-to-pasture brothers now lounging in Vama Veche.

Delpro was rapidly receding in the rearview mirror. While Robin McCandless and Horace Barthley may have survived in some fashion or other the recent dismantling and re-ordering of their firms, Delpro as an international entity was gone.

If (and, Rodney had no idea, he admitted to himself, if this was a "Big If" or a "Small If") Heinrich Fuchs' description had been correct and there truly was an overarching organization referred to as Domov with an overlord called the *Maliar*, Rodney felt it was unlikely that Radutu Botezatu was the rumored *Maliar*. These doubts extended to the other five routine participants in the Easter meetings.

All six individuals were definitely persons of interest. They were all rich and powerful. They all did all they could to operate in the shadows, engaging in a litany of legal and probably illegal operations. They all merited microscopic examinations in regard to their roles in international criminal involvement. Nonetheless, as veiled as these individuals were, as masked as they were able to keep their actions, they were still on the radar of a number of law-enforcement organizations over and beyond the SEC's D-2. The top level of their hierarchy, the *Maliar* or whomever, would be much more deeply entombed—beyond the ken of all.

Among the barely visible, Radutu Botezatu emerged as particularly perplexing. It was not only the hole in his history covering more than a score of decisive years. In the decade-and-a-half that he had been in the public eye, he had demonstrated a valuable mixture of business and diplomatic acumen. He had even been appointed as a special advisor to the Vatican's *Council for the Economy*. His strong and charming personality appeared to naturally percolate to those around him, including through the binoculars of a surveillance team.

However, Radutu Botezatu, as the other members of the Easter Sextet, seemed to be mysteriously disconnected from any tangible action on the ground. While he was by far the most obtrusive of the group, they all, as D-2 researchers exposed, had highly diversified investment portfolios and highly influential, if discrete, frequently muted, positions ranging from the CEOs of some of their companies to sitting on the boards of directors of numerous prominent for-profit and not-for-profit organizations. In the aggregate, undoubtedly by design, they formed a financial and quasi-political network that encircled the globe. Yet there was no cause and effect. When criminal acts surfaced, without exception, there were never any interconnections to any one of the sextet.

Rodney had his crew again go back to the Delpro files (innumerable repetitions plus one) where they had voluminous data on grassroots misconduct accompanied by plenty of case studies and individual lawsuits for examples of past and present illegality. In revisiting these heaps of information, they focused on any foreshadowing of upstream linkages. The primary investigations themselves had focused on Delpro, Robin McCandless, and their transgressions. It was now clear that the strings were being pulled from an even higher level that had not been presumed during the original enquiries.

Although these upper levels had not surfaced in the first runs of these data, maybe that was simply because they were not looking for higher pathways. The team needed to reprocess these files with an objective of identifying any connections to Domov or any other higher-level structures.

With all this, Rodney was rapidly overshooting his resources. He had neither the staff nor the budget to keep large teams in the field to follow important persons of interest while, at the same time, he needed equally large teams to dig through vast stores of data that was still being harvested from the most isolated corners of the planet.

This required a reset. D-2 was a construct of BTF. D-2 now needed to be reimagined in light of recent disclosures. This demanded an entirely new combination of strategies and processes. There were old familiar targets and new persons of interest overlain with potentially completely heretofore unrecognized management structures. It was time to reconstruct D-2.

ᛘ ᛘ ᛘ ᛟ ᛘ ᛘ ᛘ

The modified and remodeled D-2 Rodney forged reflected a reduced effective in the field with an emphasis on expanded and intensified office-based research on multiple fronts (trading the high maintenance costs of field teams for the high support requirements of researchers). This included the now possibly passé activities of Robin McCandless, Horace Barthley, and Heinrich Fuchs, the on-going interventions of Cynthia Owens, the dubious pursuits of the Easter weekend powerhouses, as well as recently highlighted firms like New Twsana Cattle Company and *Alimento Atlântico*. Field surveillance now centered on Radutu Botezatu.

At the same time as the large recast crews of researchers plowed through everything from the popular press to previously totally unknown information sources, an experienced team of agents reformatted their coverage of Radutu Botezatu. Overall, it was a lot of drudgery with few immediate rewards.

For the office-based researchers, one of the easiest questions to pursue was why did Botswana beef get trucked all the way to Angola for export to the EU? While it seemed probable that avoiding the more-strictly-controlled Port of Durban in favor of the more laissez faire Port of Luanda was a good choice for those not wanting their consignments too closely scrutinized, this, in and of itself, was not an answer.

The researchers concentrated on the supply side. What, beyond beef, was coming from *Alimento Atlântico* and out of the Port of Faro?

With the help of Interpol, D-2 analysts documented a wave of bogus medications that was ending up on the shelves of pharmacies across the Costa de Sol and into the Côte d'Azur. These were packaged as expensive, specialty pharmaceuticals for everything from arthritis to cancer. Unfortunately, in spite of exorbitant price tags, laboratory analyses showed they all were basically compressed cassava flour with an organic binder from the *Landolphia owariensis* plant that was native to the Congo and produced a type of natural latex. Although the leaves and bark of this plant had long been used in traditional medicine and were attributed with a variety of healing properties, its use in the counterfeit tablets in no way imparted on the commercially sold imitation products any form of legitimacy. Its use, however, combined with an identification of the exact strain of cassava used to make the flour, did point to the Kongo Central Province of the Democratic Republic of the Congo as the probable origin of the raw ingredients.

The researchers were then able to more theorize than definitively conclude that the material had been fabricated in or around the city of

Mbanza-Ngungue (once a resort town called Thysstad during the Belgian Period) where there was the needed infrastructure to operate a factory capable of producing the large quantity of product being found in Mediterranean markets. Equally important, Mbanza-Ngungue was four hours north, over the border, of Mbanza-Kongo in Angola where Aeroporto Pedro Moisés Artur offered connections to Luanda.

It was highly likely, if the hypothesis held, that the fake medications were concealed in the beef shipments—fake medications and who knew what else. Yet, even if true, how did this bring D-2 any closer to any better understanding of Domov or whatever? This smuggling of contraband was unfortunately commonplace, in the current investigation, traceable all the way back to Charlie's initial boat trips on Lake Michigan and undoubtedly much, much further back.

At the very least, this did provide more information on *Alimento Atlântico*, validating the decision to maintain them as a group of interest. Having a strong basis to look even more closely, the researchers explored the other part of the route—the Europe to Brazil portion.

Using an approach similar to the one employed in Faro, they scratched away at Porto de Victória. Here, with the assistance of UN agencies, they examined which items of contraband would be the most profitable. As the region had local supplies of drugs, existing villainous syndicates, and areas where prostitution was an accepted vocation, some of the most frequently globally pirated goods and services did not appear to apply here. Nonetheless, the UN did underscore the extremely dynamic and lucrative market for arms at locales with recent and ongoing political unrest—chief among these, frictions between Ecuador and Peru along with the Paraguayan People's Army. UN Peacekeepers provided even more details. Based on weapons recovered by UN Blue Berets from a variety of battlefields across the region, preferred arms for insurrectionists were the Czech-manufactured *Ceska Zbrojovka 88G* assault rifle, the *Zbrojovka ZBII Falcon X* anti-material rifle, and the *Ceska Zbrojovka 99W* automatic pistol. Moreover, the UN experts were able to backtrack the local origins of these arms to Porto de Victória.

With the assistance of other more clandestine US operations and operatives, sluggishly but steadily D-2 researchers exposed more about the movement of these arms. Ultimately, they were indeed able to link their arrival in Brazil with *Alimento Atlântico*. While not surprising, this added significantly more information about the transport routes and cargo of this company.

As the investigation became more and more precise, researchers were able to tie the Czech arms shipments to specific dates and on specific *Alimento Atlântico* vessels originating from the Port of Faro. Then, as they had done with the pharmaceuticals, they worked backwards. From factories in Czechia, with great difficulty and superb intelligence, they were able to identify a frequently used route for shipments south to Constanta.

From southern Romania, the path was nearly impossible to follow. But thanks to some good luck and excellent contacts, with enough time the D-2 researchers were able to tease out a specific thread that led from Constanta, by freighter, out of the Black Sea and across the Mediterranean to Málaga, Spain. The cargo was then transshipped by trucks to Huelva, Spain, and its sheltered port that was home to numerous small craft that would carry the arms to their final European designation of Faro.

It was an amazing piece of detective work that potentially caught up a number of the current group of persons of interest, even maybe snaring Robin McCandless. Rodney was ecstatic.

The persevering D-2 researchers added to Rodney's elation. Matter-of-factly they unearthed more elements of the arms movements out of Czechia. Of particular note was the Romanian portion of the trip. From previously sealed records, the analysts were able to document that the arms traversed Romania as shipments of hunting supplies imported and exported by *Articole Sportive Moderne* (Modern Sporting Goods), one of Radutu Botezatu's companies.

They were then able to isolate *Articole Sportive Moderne* shipments out of Constanta, finding a wide web including large consignments to Libya and Western Sahara via Morocco—hotspots easily accessible through Mediterranean shipping lanes.

These were all singular pieces of a byzantine cryptogram that was taking shape as D-2 widened the window that had formerly been looking solely at Delpro and Robin McCandless. These were, Rodney understood all too well, singular pieces that still could not be sewn together into a unified tapestry. There were certainly ways and means to do the stitching, but it was more than a little complicated—requiring a commitment of not only staff and finances, but also political will. This was critical. Rodney had learned the hard way that many of the bad actors who spent so much time and effort contriving these twisted labyrinths counted on the fact that political will would dry up well before there were any real threats to their continued flagrant operations—before there were any tangible consequences.

Rodney grasped from too many less-than-successful campaigns
how fickle the political leadership could be. He needed to do the nearly
impossible. He needed to be able to hold their attention over the additional months and likely years required to thoroughly probe and prod
the global goings-on that would hopefully lead to a solid case against
Domov or whatever transnational body was calling the shots on so much
integrated criminality. Criminality that was devastating to many and en-
riching to a select few.

⋀ ⋀ ⋀ ⋁ ⋀ ⋀ ⋀

As Rodney tried intently to devise an internal plan that would allow him
to attack his external enemies, Charlie and Ralph got accustomed to a
new home with all its fancy accoutrements and its beautiful view. Charlie
and Ralph got accustomed to and found favorite haunts in the nearby
mountains and beaches. Charlie and Ralph found an easy cadence to
their lives. It wasn't just sitting on the porch, but it was fine.

Charlie had not been contacted by D.C. for months and that was just
the way he liked it.

⋀ ⋀ ⋀ ⋁ ⋀ ⋀ ⋀

Rodney was indeed toiling tenaciously to find a formula for D-2's continued operations that could be effective in bringing the wrongdoers to
justice (or, at the very least, shutting them down) while doing so in a way
that garnered the support of the political elite. As everything of late, it
was a formidable task.

One of the crucial challenges that had been dogging Rodney persis-
tently over many months was the job itself. D-2 was an informal entity
within the SEC. The SEC had exceptionally picked up the Delpro file
years ago under Hal's watch (Hal having considerable influence in a decision to formally engage in an area many considered outside their remit)
and under the SECs mandate to protect US investors.

Long ago they had blown through the original guidelines for their
work. It was difficult but possible, stretching all the rules that stretched,
to justify SEC involvement when Delpro was plainly undertaking a mixed
bag of domestic activities that were ultimately detrimental to US investors—not to say criminal.

Now, with staff everywhere from the hinterland of the Amazon to the Fagaras Mountains, it was becoming practically impossible to rationalize the SECs continued engagement. They had far exceeded their core directives and their allowable budgets. It was no longer sustainable.

There had been meaningful results and more in the pipeline. But these, as noteworthy as they were, could not change the equation. Word came down from the very top that another approach, another methodology was required.

No discussion, no debate; now was the moment for a major correction. The SEC needed to disconnect itself from activities that had gone on far too long far too far from its principal edicts.

Even though Rodney's crew had always collaborated closely with other agencies—foreign and domestic—this was not enough. D-2 still hung its hat in the SEC closet, and this had to change.

The higher-ups were clear and emphatic: this could NOT continue.

Rodney grappled with the problem. There seemed no other option. They would simply have to close the books and shut the door. D-2 would cease to exist.

To Rodney, this was a drastic and really unacceptable measure. The criminals were there. They, his team, knew many and there were many more. These ill-doers were adversely affecting US investors as well as everyone else. They needed to be brought to count.

While no one supported the bad guys and all were uncomfortably aware of the consequences of leaving international criminals a free hand to do all manner of misdeeds, many directly touching Americans, there appeared to be no recourse.

If he were honest with himself, Rodney realized that the SEC had truly not been the best fit. They had simply done what they could with the resources at hand in spite of the potential bureaucratic and technical mismatch.

Rodney remembered his chemistry lab back at college that had been overseen by a graduate student named Hubert. One day, when outlining the day's experiment, out of the blue Hubert announced, "If you guys think you're really smart, become a criminal. If you can be a criminal and not get caught, then you're really smart."

It looked like Rodney's adversaries were really smart—not to mention lucky.

Then, as Rodney had experienced more than once before, the gods smiled.

Some of the senators to whom Rodney had reached out had finally overcome inertia and pushed for a remedy to this problem that, as per Rodney's portrayal, jeopardized their constituents' livelihoods. With politics able to go where logic could not, the complete (former) D-2 dossier was transferred from the SEC to the Office of International Affairs in the Department of Justice.

It was the right tool for the right job.

Even though this meant that he would be transferring his work to others, Rodney appreciated that, given the scope of events they had uncovered over the years, this was the correct decision.

When the paperwork came through, there was another big surprise. The upper echelon of the D-2 team including Rodney, his assistants, and the senior analysts, would be detached to the Department of Justice for the duration of the investigation. Furthermore, Rodney would be the Activity Coordinator.

He was still there, at the head of what had been D-2—still chasing the silhouettes of Robin McCandless, Cynthia Owens, Radutu Botezatu, the *Maliar*, and all those from the ashes of Delpro and lurking in the shadows of Domov. He was still there, in the swamp, in the thick of it. Maybe this time he'd be able to bring closure for his dear Hal. Maybe this time the good guys would win.

As Rodney prepared for a new address, a new office, a new boss, and an old challenge, one of the key senators who had pushed for the shift to DOJ got a call with no caller ID. "Jake," the husky voice, almost a whisper, intoned, "you've gone too far, my friend—really too far. There will be consequences."

Outro

CECILY McCORMICK HAD NOT visited her daughter at the Lake Center for some time. The visits weighed heavily on her, and she found she used any excuse to avoid them. Her daughter was not getting better, in her eyes, in spite of what the doctors were saying. She left in tears after each visit—heartbroken.

Weeks had gone by—probably months Cecily acknowledged. She needed to go and see Jo.

Entering the center, as usual, she checked in at the front desk. To her shock, when she precisely stated she was there to visit her daughter Jo McCormick, the receptionist replied, "Who?"

This had never happened before. Cecily demanded to see the doctors. She demanded to see the head nurse. She demanded to see the director. She demanded to see anyone who could take her to her daughter—and right this minute.

After much too long a wait in a much too uncomfortable waiting room chair, the director, Dr. Laurey (Cecily had met him only once before but remembered him due to his polkadot bowtie) appeared, he too remembering Cecily.

"Missus McCormick, how nice to see you," he said with a bit of a tone of consternation.

Standing, Cecily McCormick tried to calmly reply, "Dr. Laurey, thank you for seeing me. I'm here to see Jo. I always come here to see Jo. But when I checked at the reception, they seemed to say Jo wasn't here! What's happened?"

"Missus McCormick, I thought you knew?"

"Knew what?" Cecily almost screeched, eyes bulging, thinking her dear Jo may have passed and no one told her.

"I'm sorry. I thought you had been told. I was sure you would have known. Please take a seat and calm down, it's OK."

Cecily forced herself to be even more erect, standing rigidly before the director, trying to ignore the balloon that was bursting in her chest.

"Don't placate me! Where's my daughter?"

"Missus McCormick, again I apologize. Your daughter was released last week."

Cecily crumpled into the chair.

"It was what some would call a miracle," the director continued, visibly flustered, "she had been doing better, then one day she just got out of bed and her doctors said she was fine—not able to explain really why."

Hyperventilating, Cecily asked, "Well where is she?"

"Why," Dr. Laurey replied with even more consternation, "she was picked up by her partner, Charlie."

ᴧ ᴧ ᴧ ᴡ ᴧ ᴧ ᴧ

If anyone had been watching, they would have seen Jo and Charlie, snuggled tightly together against the cold south wind, walking along Patrick's Point not far from Lagoon State Park.

Jo and Ralph got along just fine.

ᴧ ᴧ ᴧ ᴡ ᴧ ᴧ ᴧ

In December of that year, Lionel Stancik received a call from his long-lost little brother offering New Year's greetings.

Afterword

CHARLIE STANCIK, OUR PROTAGONIST, along with Eddie Hall (*The Agate Hunter*), Paula Patterson (*Waiting—almost there*), and Peter Volman (*Son of Paul*), represent quintessential elements of our society. They were born into relatively typical families of their day and grew up in more-or-less commonplace small communities. As young people, they were caught in the push and pull of finding themselves. Their families in particular, and society in general, perhaps foresaw them as assuming a normal role for a normal person—falling into step with whatever individual mold others had cast. Actively or passively, each fought against taking this preordained pathway. Each sought their own avenues and byways—often encountering difficult challenges seemingly out of their control—enduring varying levels of turpitude and angst. None of them were water striders, effortlessly gliding across life's surface. Although often victims of their own individual foibles and vicissitudes, at the end of the day, they all wanted the same two things: to do something they felt was meaningful and to do the right thing. They were not so much seeking to build a legacy as to simply look back and say, "I've had a life well-lived."

www.ingramcontent.com/pod-product-compliance
Lightning Source LLC
Chambersburg PA
CBHW051140030726
47504CB00004B/966